Caroline couldn't wait to show Austin the evidence she'd found.

She found him at his desk, having obviously just returned from somewhere. He still wore his brown leather bomber jacket over faded jeans that flouted the police department's dress code. His aviator-style sunglasses were shoved on top of his head; his hair was tousled, and his face was slightly windburned.

He must think he looks pretty sharp like that, she thought, not sure whether she wanted to smile or frown. Nah, on second thought, he didn't just *think* he looked good. He *did* look good. The fact was, he probably had women trailing behind him everywhere he went.

She was supremely annoyed to discover she found Austin Lomax attractive. Of course, any human being with two X chromosomes would find him attractive. The trouble was, he *knew* it....

Dear Reader,

This month marks the advent of something very special in Intimate Moments. We call it "Intimate Moments Extra," and books bearing this flash will be coming your way on an occasional basis in the future. These are books we think are a bit different from our usual, a bit longer or grittier perhaps. And our lead-off "extra" title is one terrific read. It's called *Into Thin Air*, and it's written by Karen Leabo, making her debut in the line. It's a tough look at a tough subject, but it's also a top-notch romance. Read it and you'll see what I mean.

The rest of the month's books are also terrific. We're bringing you Doreen Owens Malek's newest, *Marriage in Name Only*, as well as Laurey Bright's *A Perfect Marriage*, a very realistic look at how a marriage can go wrong before finally going very, very right. Then there's Kylie Brant's *An Irresistible Man*, a sequel to her first-ever book, *McLain's Law*, as well as Barbara Faith's sensuous and suspenseful *Moonlight Lady*. Finally, welcome Kay David to the line with *Desperate*. Some of you may have seen her earlier titles, written elsewhere as Cay David.

Six wonderful authors and six wonderful books. I hope you enjoy them all.

Yours,

Leslie Wainger
Senior Editor and Editorial Coordinator

Please address questions and book requests to:
Silhouette Reader Service
U.S.: 3010 Walden Ave., P.O. Box 1325, Buffalo, NY 14269
Canadian: P.O. Box 609, Fort Erie, Ont. L2A 5X3

KAREN LEABO
INTO THIN AIR

Silhouette®
INTIMATE™MOMENTS®
Published by Silhouette Books
America's Publisher of Contemporary Romance

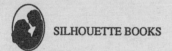 SILHOUETTE BOOKS

ISBN 0-373-07619-3

INTO THIN AIR

KAREN LEABO

credits her fourth-grade teacher with initially sparking her interest in creative writing. She was determined at an early age to have her work published. When she was in the eighth grade she wrote a children's book and convinced her school yearbook publisher to put it in print.

Karen was born and raised in Dallas. She has worked as a magazine art director, a free-lance writer and a textbook editor, but now she keeps herself busy full-time writing about romance.

For Carla Cassidy,
who knows how to motivate me.

Prologue

The screams lasted long into the night.

Terri Zamasko curled her knees up against her grossly swollen abdomen and stuck a thumb into her mouth, something she hadn't done since she was five. But she wasn't just scared now; the fear was about to swallow her up. For the first time since she'd been brought into the home five, or maybe six, months ago, she'd lost hope that someone would find her, would rescue her.

She had also stopped believing anything Odell said. If the old witch really cared about anyone but herself, she wouldn't have let that girl—whoever she was—keep on screaming.

Marcy. Yeah, that's who it sounded like. Marcy was the blond girl with the chubby face who cried a lot. She lived in the room directly below Terri's. Marcy was the only one who had been here longer than Terri herself, and she was as big as a house. Yeah, the screamer had to be Marcy.

The ruckus had started right after dinner. Terri didn't know what time it was now, but she could tell from the passage of the moon outside her tiny, barred window that it must be late.

She wondered if she would scream like that when her time came.

How much longer did she have—a month, maybe two? Odell was some kind of nurse or something, and she did cursory physical examinations of the girls every so often, but she never answered any questions. Terri had come here in July, that much she knew, and it was getting close to Christmas. So she had two more months at the most. She had only that much more time to figure a way out of here. But she'd been racking her brain ever since she got here, and she'd exhausted every possibility, or at least the obvious ones.

Even before her body had become big and unwieldy, she hadn't possessed the strength to overcome Odell. Terri had tried more than once to tackle the mountain of a woman, hoping to wrest the shotgun out of her grasp. It was like running at a brick wall. She had earned herself bruised knuckles, several painful slaps and uncounted days in the "dungeon" for her trouble.

Even if she could overpower Odell and clear the chain-link fence topped with barbed wire, Terri had little chance of making it to freedom. Odell had two dogs, a bloodhound and a vicious German shepherd, with the deceptively gentle names of Phoebe and Bella. One could track a mosquito through the woods, and the other could bite. They served their mistress well.

Obviously Terri couldn't outsmart Odell by herself. But there were only two on Odell's team—herself and that creep, Henry— while there were ten or twelve girls at the home at any given time. If they could coordinate their efforts, they could take Odell by surprise and overpower her.

Terri's thoughts had followed this path before, and always to the same depressing conclusion. To coordinate, the girls needed to plan, and planning was an impossible task when even the simplest communication was forbidden. Odell kept the girls separated most of the time, and when any of them were in the same room, they weren't allowed to talk to one another.

Occasionally a few whispered sentences were possible in the exercise yard. Terri had tried to summon some support for her idea to conspire against Odell, but the other girls always shied away from Terri. No one wanted to risk Odell's wrath by associating with a known troublemaker. They believed Odell when she told them that if they just behaved until after their babies were born, they would be released.

At one time Terri had clung to that belief, too. It was the only thing that had kept her sane. She didn't believe anymore. Three girls had already had their babies and were gone. If they'd been released, why hadn't they brought the police down on Odell's head? Anyway, Terri'd been watching out the window when Henry had put Jennifer's body—dead?—into the back of Odell's Suburban and driven away.

Marcy's screams reached a crescendo, then degenerated into a series of pitiful moans and sobs, followed by a sudden, frightening silence.

Chapter 1

Carolyn Triece sat at her corner desk, nursing a cold cup of tea and reviewing her cases—and she had a pile of them. The holidays, with their incipient anxiety and depression, always brought with them an onslaught of disappearances. This year was no different.

One case, at least, Caro could mark closed. She'd found Helen Shepherd in a women's shelter, sporting a black eye and a missing tooth. The woman had begged Caro not to tell her husband where she was. Two days earlier, the same idiot husband had stood before Caro straight-faced and told her he couldn't imagine why his wife would leave him. He'd been positive Helen had been kidnapped.

It would give Caro great pleasure to inform Mr. Shepherd that his wife was safe and sound, and that she never wanted to see him again. Caro could only hope that Helen would go through with her plans to divorce the SOB and take him to the cleaners. He deserved worse.

Caro looked at the long list of phone calls to be made and sighed. Sometimes she felt like the receiver was growing out of her ear. Figuring she might as well get started, she reached for the phone, then halted. She felt someone looking at her.

"Yo, Caro." It was Tony, who occupied the desk in front of hers. After working four years together in Missing Persons, she and Corporal Tony Villaverde had developed a finely tuned sensitivity to each other. As he strode across the room toward her, the worry lines in his forehead said a lot. He didn't have good news.

"What's happened?" she asked as he slapped a stack of folders onto his desk, directly in front of hers.

He turned to face her, lacing his fingers through his thick salt-and-pepper hair. "The body they found by the dam at Cedar Creek?"

"Yeah?"

"She's been positively identified—she's your Marcy Phelps."

As Caro absorbed the blow, her gaze wandered to the bulletin board on the wall next to her desk, decorated with the photographs from every unsolved case that had crossed her desk. There weren't too many; most cases solved themselves in a matter of days.

Not the Marcy Phelps case. Marcy, blond and chubby-cheeked, smiled back at her, showing a mouth full of braces.

"Cause of death?"

"Preliminary guess is that the fall broke her neck."

Oh, God. "Any idea when?"

"The ME says the body's no more than a week old."

"A week!" Caro's mind reeled. Marcy Phelps had been missing for more than six months, and yet she'd been dead only a week. Where had she been? Was she just another runaway who'd succumbed to the evils of life on the street, or was there more to the story?

"There's one other weird thing," Tony said. "Apparently the girl gave birth only days, maybe hours, before she died."

Caro's stomach turned. She'd already had to get Marcy's dental records from her parents for purposes of identifying the body. Their reaction hadn't been pleasant. Now it would be up to her to tell them their fifteen-year-old daughter had been pregnant, too.

"I suppose CAPERS wants the file," she said.

"You got it. Whether Marcy jumped or someone helped her along, there's a baby somewhere. Austin Lomax is taking over the case."

Caro grimaced. Although she'd never met Marcy, she felt as if she knew the girl, and giving up her case wouldn't be easy. It galled Caro to think that some stranger would be the one to solve the mystery surrounding Marcy's disappearance and death, if it could be solved. And Lomax, of all people. He'd been working with homicides for, what, two weeks? His specialty was missing cars.

"You don't like Lomax?" Tony, as always, read her body language.

She shrugged, feigning indifference. "Don't even know him. It just strikes me as odd that they'd give a tricky case like this to a greenhorn."

"He's been working in Homicide for a couple of months now, partnering with Frank Feldman," Tony said as he propped his lean hips against the back of his chair and stuffed a piece of purple bubblegum into his mouth. He chewed gum almost constantly since he'd quit smoking almost a year ago. "Besides, after seven years in Auto Theft he's not that green."

"Cars aren't the same as people."

Tony narrowed his eyes shrewdly. "I think maybe you'd be pissed no matter who took over the case."

Caro straightened her spine. "What's that supposed to mean?"

"I mean that maybe you're getting tired of teenage runaways and deserting husbands, and you wish you could investigate Marcy's death."

Caro reared up, almost out of her chair. "That's a crock. I'm perfectly happy doing what I'm doing."

"Yeah, okay. Then why are you coming at me like a snapping turtle with PMS?"

She didn't dignify his accusation with an answer. Instead she reached for the phone and swiveled her chair so that she faced the wall.

"Chicken," Tony said under his breath. "You won't even argue with me."

"Buzz off, Villaverde." She angrily jabbed at the telephone keypad.

Okay, maybe she was feeling overpossessive about Marcy Phelps, but that didn't mean she wanted to actually investigate the murder. She'd already given the case everything she had, and it hadn't been enough. The girl had been somewhere near Dallas, right under their noses, for the past six months, and yet Caro hadn't turned up a single, solid lead during the entire course of her investigation.

She had to let it go. For all his inexperience, Lomax was reputed to be sharp, if a tad self-absorbed. He would go over every inch of ground Caro had covered, and more. Maybe a fresh, enthusiastic mind would spot something she had missed.

The phone on the other end of the line rang ten times before she hung up. Better not to waste any time, she decided. She pawed through her file drawer until she found the pitifully thin Marcy Phelps file. Caro had three-day-old cases with fatter folders than this one. The folks in CAPERS would think she hadn't lifted a finger.

No, of course that wasn't true. Until four years ago, she'd worked in CAPERS—the Crimes Against Persons division—in the Sex Crimes Unit. Most of the investigators over there knew her, and she would like to think they respected her work. They would know she'd tried. But had she tried hard enough?

"I'm heading downstairs, anyway, so I'll take that over for you," Tony offered, totally unaffected by her attempted brush-off. That was one nice thing about Tony; it was impossible to hurt his feelings. "Lomax'll want to talk to you, of course, after he reads the file." There was a pause. "Uh, looks like you have a new case."

"I do?" She saw him then, the man lurking near the doorway, an uneasy expression on his face.

"I heard Sergeant Quayar giving him your name as I came in," Tony said before taking the Phelps file and sauntering away.

Caro knew the newcomer was trouble before he'd even opened his mouth. He had that haunted look around the eyes, the one that said he'd already been through hell. He was dressed in a conservative suit, but the tie was slightly askew, like he hadn't quite cared to get it right. He clutched a foam cup as if the coffee inside it was the only thing keeping him from diving over the edge.

Someone he loved had abandoned him, and he was looking for a way—any way—to explain it. It always amazed Caro that some people would rather discover their loved one was the victim of some heinous crime than face the fact that the person had simply walked away.

The man cast a glance around the busy, impersonal room with those tragic eyes, which eventually settled on her desk, her nameplate. She met his gaze squarely. Although she wanted to give the man a smile of encouragement, she couldn't do it, not when she knew the odds were against his finding out something to his liking.

Throwing his shoulders back, he strode purposefully toward her. "Are you Corporal Triece?"

She stood and extended her hand, well accustomed by now to the look of incredulity that went with the question. At five foot two and a hundred and five pounds, with long, curly brown hair that she wore in a single braid, she looked more like a high school cheerleader than a police detective. She had long ago given up on being defensive about her looks. "Yes, I'm Carolyn Triece. And you're..."

"Russell Arkin." He gave her hand a perfunctory shake. His hands were ice cold.

"Have a seat, Mr. Arkin," Caro said crisply as she reclaimed her own chair, pushing thoughts of Marcy Phelps to one side for the moment. "Are you here to report a missing person?" As if she had to ask.

He nodded. When he didn't jump into his story, she busied herself with opening her notebook and laboriously printing his name at the top of the first blank sheet, giving him time to collect his thoughts.

"My daughter," he finally said.

Caro winced. Whether they were runaways or nabbed by non-custodial parents, missing children were the hardest. "I'm sorry," she said automatically. "Her name?"

"Amanda. Amanda Lee Arkin."

"Age?"

"Eighteen."

That surprised Caro. Russell Arkin didn't look old enough to have an eighteen-year-old child. She'd pegged him at about her own age, which was thirty-three. "Mr. Arkin, you do realize that your daughter is no longer a minor. If she left of her own accord, there's—"

"She didn't."

He sounded so positive. But then, they all did. Parents had a hard time facing a child's voluntary desertion.

"All right, let's start at the beginning," Caro said, all business. "When did you last see her?"

"Yesterday—that would be Wednesday, December 21." He watched to see that Caro recorded the date, which she did. "She left the house for a doctor's appointment at around eight-thirty," he continued, "just as I was leaving for work, and she just...never came home."

"Did she make it to the appointment?"

"No. She was supposed to meet with a psychologist, Virginia Dreyfus, at the..." His words trailed off. "Anyway, I talked with Dr. Dreyfus first thing this morning. Amanda never showed."

"Why was she seeing a psychologist?"

"Is—is that important?"

"Her emotional state is very important."

He pursed his lips and looked at the ceiling, then down at his hands. "Dr. Dreyfus works at a family-planning clinic over on Harry Hines—I think it's called the Women's Services Clinic, or something equally euphemistic. Amanda was...is pregnant, and she was supposedly receiving counseling about her options." His words had a certain bitter twist to them.

"You don't sound as if you approve."

He emptied the coffee cup in one gulp, then began systematically shredding the foam. "That clinic is nothing but an abortion mill, pure and simple. I can't imagine that Dr. Dreyfus would do anything except sell Amanda on the clinic's services.''

"You definitely don't approve." A picture was forming in Caro's mind, and not a pretty one. "Did you and your daughter disagree over this issue?''

He flashed her a look of pure hostility. The silence between them was punctuated only by the sound of his busy fingers shredding the cup.

"Mr. Arkin, I'm not asking out of morbid curiosity. I need to know as much as possible about Amanda's state of mind at the time of her disappearance. Anything you can tell me about what was going on in her life would be helpful.''

"If I tell you we disagreed about abortion, you're going to automatically assume that Amanda and I had a fight and that she disappeared of her own accord.'' He slammed his hand on the desk. "But, damn it, that's not what happened!''

Caro felt for him, she really did, but she wasn't in the mood to be second-guessed. Her job would be a hell of a lot easier if people would just answer her questions. "I don't intend to jump to any conclusions or dismiss any possibilities at this point. Now, did you and Amanda disagree on the issue of abortion?''

He gritted his teeth, but he answered this time. "We discussed it. She was seriously considering it. I advised her not to. But I made it clear that whatever she decided, I would support her. Amanda and I have always had a very close relationship.''

Yeah, right. Caro had heard that one before. "What was her mood like yesterday morning?''

He shrugged. "Nothing out of the ordinary. We were both on our way out the door, and she said she was going to look for a Christmas tree after her appointment at the clinic. She'd been giving me a hard time because, with her away at school, I hadn't done any decorating. But that was always her department. She gets such a kick out of it.'' He looked around the room at the pitiful excuse for holiday decorations Caro and her co-workers had managed— an anemic-looking tree in the corner, only half decorated, and some lopsided paper snowflakes on the windows, courtesy of Tony's seven-year-old twins. "She used to make snowflakes like those.''

"So, Christmas was generally a good time for Amanda?''

As Russell Arkin began to open up a bit, a portrait of his daughter emerged. Amanda had been a straight A student at a private Catholic high school—a state spelling-bee champion, no less—and had just completed her first semester at University of North Texas in nearby Denton.

"How were her grades in college?" Caro asked.

Arkin smiled wistfully. "She's no Rhodes Scholar, but she did all right. She didn't flunk anything, at least. I figure once the newness of college life wears off, she'll settle down and study. She wants to be an electrical engineer. She's really into building stuff— radios, televisions, you name it. Had her ham radio license when she was sixteen."

"Ham radio? Who does she talk to?"

"People all over the world. I already checked with some of her regular contacts. They'll be listening for any word from her."

"Good thinking." Caro made a few notes. "In our day, only boys were into electronics."

The man actually smiled, if only for a moment. "Yeah, well, times have changed."

According to her father, Amanda was ambitious, goal-oriented and popular with her friends. She worked a part-time job to help pay for college. It didn't sound as if her father had put any undue pressure on her. "What about boyfriends?" Caro asked casually, but that was the million-dollar question. She wanted to know who had fathered Amanda's baby.

"There's only one that I know of, Scott Humphrey. They've been dating for two years. And before you even ask, yes, Scott is the baby's father. He and Amanda came to me and told me together."

"Have you talked to Scott since Amanda disappeared?"

Arkin nodded. "He's been helping me look for her, and he's at least as frantic as I am. Between us we've contacted everyone we can think of who's even a slight acquaintance. No one's heard from her."

The baby's father would be Caro's first and best lead, she decided. She took down Scott's address and phone number, as well as those of several of Amanda's close friends. Arkin had come prepared.

"Oh, but you won't find Scott at home," Arkin added.

"No?"

"He went skiing with his parents for Christmas."

Alarm bells went off in Caro's head. If this kid was so concerned about his girlfriend, why would he jaunt off to Vail or wherever?

"He had to go," Arkin said as if he'd read Caro's mind. "His parents...well, you'd have to know the Humphreys to understand."

This explanation didn't completely satisfy Caro, but she let it ride for now. "What kind of car was Amanda driving?" she asked.

"A new Chevy Cavalier convertible. Red. It was her high school graduation present."

Nice car, Caro thought. Better than what she drove. "License number?"

"Personalized plates. They say IMA HAM." He spelled it out. "She's serious about this radio stuff."

"That'll make it a little easier. A car like that is pretty hard to miss."

"What do you do, put it on a computer or something?"

She shook her head. "Right now, all I can do is ask around at various places Amanda might go. If we don't get any leads in the next two or three days, we can start to suspect foul play and I can enter her car in the national NCIC computer. But chances are she'll show up before then." Caro tried to sound reassuring.

Arkin's hands stilled, and he pinned her with a penetrating stare. "You're not listening. Whether Amanda is the victim of an accident, illness or foul play, she didn't disappear because she wanted to."

Although Caro disagreed, she didn't argue. She wasn't easily intimidated, but something about Russell Arkin—his intensity, perhaps—made her think twice before crossing him.

She changed the line of questioning, asking about Amanda's mother. Russ had been divorced from his wife for years, and neither he nor Amanda had kept in contact with the woman. Caro made a mental note to check that out. Then she asked more of the usual questions, asking about Amanda's routines, where she liked to eat, her sleeping habits, taste in clothes, food and music. The other investigators in Missing Persons sometimes teased her about her thoroughness, but she had learned not to overlook even the smallest detail. She had once located an elderly man, an Alzheimers victim, because the son had mentioned that his father was a nut for Mexican food. Caro had canvassed every Taco Bell within a five-mile radius of the old man's home, and eventually she turned up an employee who remembered him. The man had been found in a nearby park.

"Does Amanda have money? Credit cards?" Caro asked.

"She has a checking account, but she's constantly overdrawn. She has an Exxon card for gas, and a department store card—Sears or Penney's, can't remember which."

"Could she have borrowed one of your cards?"

Judging from the way his eyebrows flew up and his nostrils flared, she'd paid his daughter a gross insult. "Amanda doesn't steal."

"It wouldn't hurt to check. She might have borrowed a card, intending to tell you," Caro countered.

As he flipped through the contents of his wallet, his expression turned sheepish.

"Well?"

"I lent her my MasterCard to pay at the clinic. I'd forgotten."

Caro made a note of all the cards in Amanda's possession, extracting a promise from Mr. Arkin that he would call later with the numbers.

Next, she took a detailed physical description of Amanda Arkin, right down to the number of freckles on her nose and the scar on her right knee. Her father had also come prepared with a stack of photographs, copies of Amanda's graduation picture. Caro took a moment to study the young woman's face. She was uncommonly attractive, with thick russet hair, sparkling blue eyes and a friendly smile. Caro hoped Amanda had sense enough to use that MasterCard. She hated to think of such a pretty young girl on the streets. The regulars would eat her for breakfast.

"What else will you do?" Arkin asked, looking hopeful for the first time since he'd sat down.

"Besides looking for the car, I'll also question the people at that clinic, if I can get a subpoena so they'll release her information. I'll ask if anyone saw her in the parking lot or the reception area, just in case she got that far. I'll also visit Christmas tree lots between your house and the clinic, since you said she was planning to buy a tree. And I'll talk to her friends, particularly Scott Humphrey. I know you already did that, but they might tell me things they wouldn't mention to her father."

Arkin nodded his understanding.

"I'll talk to the credit card companies and get them to flag the account numbers. If anyone makes any charges, we'll know about it," Caro added.

Again he nodded. "I'm having some fliers printed up," he said. "I'm offering a ten-thousand-dollar reward to anyone who helps me find Amanda."

Caro was slightly uncomfortable with that tactic, and she told him so. "Media attention can sometimes be helpful, but at this early state it's not really warranted. Ninety-nine percent of the cases that cross my desk solve themselves within a day or two."

"Now, you listen to me, lady!" Arkin came out of his chair, showing a burst of emotion that he'd previously kept carefully leashed. He leaned across her desk until he was nose to nose with her. "Six years ago my wife left me. She left for the grocery store and she just never came home. But do you know, I never looked for her? I never called the police, because I'm not some nut-case alarmist. I just waited patiently for the divorce papers to arrive. I knew, even though she'd never said as much, that she didn't want to live with me anymore.

"This is different. I know my daughter, and she would no more leave home without telling me than she would fly to the moon."

Caro didn't back down an inch. "She's pregnant, Mr. Arkin. We get at least one or two pregnant teenagers through here every week. They have tough decisions to make, and usually they need some time to themselves."

"In other words, you don't intend to take this case seriously."

"I didn't say that. I'll do everything I can think of to find your daughter. But I'll bet you dollars to doughnuts she's missing because she wants to be."

When he spoke again, his voice was deadly soft. "I hope you're right, Corporal Triece. I really do. Because if you give this case short shrift and they find my kid in a ditch somewhere, you're going to have to live with that." He spun around and stalked out of the room, skirting the closely arranged desks, bumping a chair with his hip. No one paid him the slightest attention. They had seen it all before.

Tony, recently returned from his trip downstairs to CAPERS, straddled the chair in front of Caro's desk, fiercely chewing his gum. "What was that all about?"

Caro swallowed the lump in her throat. There was no reason for Arkin's words to sting like they had. Maybe it was the combination of finding Marcy Phelps in such a horrible way and now facing a similar case that had gotten to Caro. Wordlessly she handed Tony one of Amanda's pictures.

Tony gave a low whistle. "I guess Daddy's not too happy about his little pride and joy taking off."

"He's not too pleased about the fact that his little pride and joy is pregnant, either."

"Lot of that going around. Like the Phelps girl. At least now we know why she ran away in the first place."

"I tried to tell Mr. Arkin that a pregnant teenager has every reason to split, but..."

"Naturally he didn't believe you."

"I'm not sure *I* believe me. For one thing, Amanda Arkin is over eighteen. She didn't have to run away. She could just leave, and no one could stop her."

"So maybe she did, and she just didn't announce the fact."

"Yeah, maybe. But that doesn't sound like the girl Arkin described to me. According to him, she's never been any trouble.

Good grades, no drugs, never been arrested, never even had a speeding ticket."

"But she did get pregnant."

"True. And apparently she lifted Daddy's MasterCard, although he maintains he lent it to her. I think I better find out what her friends have to say about this supposed close relationship between father and daughter."

When Amanda came to, her head was spinning and her stomach roiling. She was lying on a narrow cot in a tiny room. A small, barred window let in the only light, the thin winter sun of an overcast day. The green walls were blank, the tile floor bare. The only furnishings were the cot, a cheap nightstand, a chair and a metal bar with some unidentifiable articles of clothing hanging from it.

Amanda retched, but there was nothing in her stomach. She'd had morning sickness earlier, she remembered. Then memories of the rest of her morning—or was it yesterday morning?—came flooding back, and a wave of panic washed over her.

Oh, God, I've been kidnapped.

The last thing she recalled, she'd been sitting in her car in the clinic's parking lot, killing time until her appointment with the shrink. She could have sat in the waiting room, like she'd done the time before, but she hated that place. It had been filled with women, some young, some not so young, most of them poor. Some had been there to get birth control or prenatal medical care, but most were like her, facing an unplanned pregnancy and confused as hell. The mood of depression, desperation and hopelessness had been so pervasive that it had almost smothered Amanda.

As the time for her appointment had rolled around, Amanda continued to sit in the car. She would open the door, then close it again, unable to make herself walk across the parking lot to the front door.

She couldn't do it. She couldn't go back into that horrible place.

As suddenly as the sun burst from behind a cloud, Amanda reached a decision she'd been grappling with for two weeks. She would have the baby. Maybe she would keep it, maybe she would give it up for adoption, but she wouldn't get an abortion. She would go through with the pregnancy and birth with or without Scott's support.

With the decision made, a weight seemed to lift from her shoulders. Smiling for the first time in weeks, she had reached for the ignition, intent on stopping at the nearest Christmas tree lot and buying the biggest Scotch pine she could find. Before she could turn the key, however, someone knocked on her passenger window.

A stout older woman waved to her through the glass, a pleading look on her face. Amanda started the car so she could run the electric window down a few inches. The heater blasted to life. "Yes?"

"I'm sorry to bother you," the woman said in a croaky voice, "but I seem to be lost. I'm trying to find the St. Jude's Shelter. Do you know where that is?"

Amanda's heart immediately went out to the woman. It was cold outside, and she wore only a thin coat and no scarf or gloves. "I'm sorry. I don't know where the shelter is," Amanda said.

"I have a map, but…well, I'm afraid I can't read so good. Could you look at the map?"

"Sure." Amanda unlocked the passenger door. Having just decided to allow the life inside her to continue living, she felt unusually charitable. It was Christmastime, when people should help each other. "Why don't you sit in here where it's warm. If I can figure out your map, I'll drive you to the shelter."

The look of gratitude on the woman's face had warmed Amanda's heart. The woman opened the door and climbed in with her worn shopping bag—probably all she had in the world. She reached into the bag and extracted a much-creased piece of paper, then held it out tentatively toward Amanda.

Amanda started to reach for the map. But before she could, a cloth was shoved into her face by a surprisingly strong hand and a noxious odor invaded her nose and lungs. For a moment she was so shocked she couldn't fight it. When she finally did go into action, bucking and screaming and flailing her attacker with her fists, her struggle was brief. Lethargy overcame her and darkness engulfed her.

Next thing she knew, she was here in this depressing little room—no, *cell,* she corrected herself. She took a quick inventory of her body, finding nothing amiss except a nasty scrape on her elbow. She vaguely remembered banging it against something as she'd struggled, maybe the steering wheel. But then she saw what looked like a needle mark on her arm.

Why would anyone kidnap her? She tried to think logically as she sat up slowly, her head still spinning. Her father was comfortable but by no means wealthy, so no one had reason to believe a fat ransom would be forthcoming. She had no enemies that she knew of. She'd been estranged from her mother for several years, but if Trina had wanted to see her, she wouldn't have had to resort to anything this elaborate.

When Amanda could stand without falling over, she made her way to the door. It was locked from the outside, which didn't surprise her, and the bars on the single window were secure.

What the hell kind of place was this?

Panic welled up inside her again. "Hey!" she called out suddenly. "Hey, let me out of here!" She beat her fist against the door. "Let me out, damn it!" She hadn't been screaming for very long when she heard footsteps and the scrape of a deadbolt. She stepped back, balling her hands into fists, prepared for anything.

The door opened, and the "homeless" woman stepped in. She didn't look the slightest bit confused or pitiful now. In fact, she wore a decidedly smug smile. "Well, I see you're finally awake."

"What is going on?" Amanda demanded, although her voice wasn't as strong as she would have liked. The question came out sounding rather desperate.

"You're at the Good Shepherd Maternity Home, my dear Amanda. You'll stay here until you have your baby."

"I most certainly will not. What are you, some kind of rabid pro-lifer who snatches women at abortion clinics?"

The woman's lack of emotion sent a chill down Amanda's spine. "Not at all. It was pure coincidence that I caught up with you at the clinic."

"You've been following me?" Amanda screeched. For some reason, that idea was even more frightening than the fact that she'd been kidnapped. "This is preposterous. You're nuts! You're—you're—" She gasped for breath and the wits to express her utter horror. "When my father finds out about this, he'll have your ass in jail so fast you won't know what hit you!"

"My dear, you don't think I would go to this much trouble on my own authority, do you? Your father is the one who made all the arrangements."

Chapter 2

Austin Lomax read the autopsy report for the third time, not quite sure how he felt about it. Marcy Phelps wasn't the victim of murder or suicide. She'd died from loss of blood, the result of severe hemorrhaging after childbirth. The ME was quite firm about this; unusually cold weather had preserved the body well. The contusions and broken neck Marcy had suffered falling from the dam had occurred after death.

Austin pulled off his tortoiseshell glasses and rubbed his eyes. Technically this wasn't a homicide. But somebody out there was sure as hell guilty of something. First off, the girl should have been taken to a hospital if she was having a difficult birth. Failing that, her death should have been reported. And where the hell was her baby?

Whoever had dumped Marcy's body off the dam knew the whole story, and Austin was determined to find out who that someone was.

"Austin Lomax?"

He looked up and into the face of a heart-stirringly beautiful young woman. She wore little if any makeup, and her retro clothing made her look like a tiny and fragile Annie Hall. The only clue to her age was the hardness around her huge hazel eyes; she probably wasn't as young as she looked.

"I'm Carolyn Triece. You wanted to see me?"

Austin hoped he hid his surprise. "So you're the illustrious Caro. Have a seat." He stole the chair from the empty desk next to his and motioned her into it.

She seemed to have no reaction to his use of the term illustrious. "Is that the ME's report?" she asked.

"Yeah. Have a look. I think you'll be surprised."

As Caro Triece studied the autopsy report, Austin finished off a sticky bun and surreptitiously watched her. He'd been working at this station for almost six weeks, but their paths hadn't crossed before. Still, he'd heard a lot about her. Her days in the Sex Crimes Unit had earned her a reputation—subtle as a butterfly when she wanted to be, or tough as an army boot to the gut. She could do the bad-cop-good-cop routine all by herself. People used to fight over who got to listen first to the tapes of her interrogations. The way she questioned a suspect was a thing of beauty, they said.

He had a hard time believing this delicate little creature could be army-boot tough.

If she was so hot, why was she wasting her time in Missing Persons? he wondered. Her transfer had perplexed a lot of people she'd worked with, but she'd never offered an explanation.

"So Marcy Phelps wasn't murdered, but she might as well have been," Caro said when she finished reading the report.

"The way I see it, whoever delivered Marcy's baby panicked when Marcy died. They dragged the body to the dam and pitched it, hoping to make her death look like suicide."

"And the baby?" she asked, her clipped tones reminding him of a teacher who expects to get a wrong answer.

"An evidence team is combing the area for signs of another body, but I don't think they'll find it. According to the ME, Marcy was full term or close to it when she delivered. Someone out there has her baby."

"Which means others might have seen it or heard it. The sudden appearance of a motherless newborn is kind of hard to explain. Are you bringing in the media?"

He felt even more like he needed to pass some sort of test with Caro, and he was glad he had the right answer handy. "I've already got the Public Information office working on it. They don't think we'll have much trouble getting the coverage we need. There are a host of little towns around Cedar Creek—Trinidad, Seven Points, Gun Barrel City—"

"Egad, sounds like something out of a bad Louis L'Amour novel."

"All of 'em have little weekly papers just dying to print up any scrap we'll toss 'em about the Phelps case. I guess they don't see much action out there."

"I'd gladly give them some of ours." Caro glanced at her watch. "Let's go over the case. I haven't got much time, but then, there's not that much to go over."

"I couldn't help but notice it was a pretty slim file you handed over." Austin hadn't intended the comment as a criticism, not consciously, but Caro bristled like a porcupine.

She folded her arms across her breasts in a classically defensive posture. "There just weren't any leads. I've seen people vanish into thin air before, but this one takes the cake. Of course," she added, "now that we know Marcy was pregnant before she disappeared, that might shed a new light on things."

Austin leaned back in his chair, propped his feet on his desk and flipped open the file. Now that he had Caro on the defensive, he intended to press his advantage. It was his turn to ask questions. "Let's start with the parents. He's an electrician and she's a teacher, but what're they really like?"

Caro pursed her lips as she thought for a moment. "Nice, mild-mannered, middle-class folks. They've been in denial from the beginning, of course. Even after Marcy had been missing a couple of months, they still maintained it was all some kind of mistake, that their darling baby had just forgotten to tell them where she'd gone. When I told them she was dead, they insisted it had to be a mistake. They insisted on seeing her body...." Caro shook her head. "Have you questioned them?"

"They're coming in later this afternoon."

"Don't be too hard on them," Caro cautioned.

"I'll be hard on them if it serves my purpose." He hadn't meant to snap at her, and he was on the verge of offering an apology, but she appeared so totally unfazed by his sharp words that he let it pass. "It says here that they told you Marcy didn't date, that she wasn't interested in boys yet and they weren't much interested in her."

Caro unfolded her arms and relaxed a bit as she became engrossed in the details of the case. "I believed them at the time. Her room was a little girl's room, with lots of ruffles and stuffed animals. She still read young-adult romances and kids' magazines, and she wore her hair in pigtails. I don't think she even wore makeup."

"Doesn't sound like the type to have an illicit affair behind her parents' backs."

"Unless her parents so repressed her that she couldn't even grow up in front of them. But from what her friends said, she really was somewhat immature. She was interested in boys, but still in that giggly, long-distance sort of way. She was a high school freshman and had yet to go on her first official date. Although..." Caro frowned. "Maybe she was raped."

"That could be the answer," Austin said, wishing he'd thought of it first.

"Yet another horrifying possibility those poor parents may have to face. I can see it, though. Maybe Marcy was too ashamed to tell anyone, and when she turned up pregnant she was afraid no one would believe her."

"Enough to make anyone want to run away," Austin said. "If she did have a secret like that, who do you think she'd tell?"

Caro thought for a moment. "There was a teacher she idolized, a Mrs...."

Austin referred to the notes. "Blaylock?"

"Yeah, that's it, Melanie Blaylock. I talked to her. The notes should be in there somewhere. Other than to say Marcy had seemed a little more withdrawn lately, she couldn't shed any light on the matter."

"What about her sisters? Would she have told them?"

"Mmm, doubtful. The younger one, Debby, is real bright, but she's only ten. I doubt Marcy would have confided in her. And the older one was away at college. I didn't like her, by the way. What was her name?"

"Mindy. Why didn't you like her?"

Caro rolled her eyes. "She was very superior in the way only college freshmen can be. Although she'd seen Marcy exactly once since Christmas, she claimed to be an expert on her little sister's personality—knew everything about her. She was firmly convinced that Marcy had been kidnapped, and she kept smarting off that the police weren't doing nearly enough."

"Ah, so she cast aspersions on your abilities as an investigator. No wonder she pissed you off."

"It wasn't anything personal," Caro huffed.

Austin hid a smile as he made a note beside Mindy Phelps's name. He would enjoy questioning her. She might smart off to Caro, who despite her reputation didn't appear very intimidating to him, but Mindy might feel differently when approached by a six-foot-two man with a badge and an attitude. Yeah, he knew just how to play that one.

As for Caro...he wasn't sure how to play her. She had a strange effect on him, and it wasn't just sexual awareness—although that was part of it. Maybe it was the fact that, for the first time in years, his mere identity as a police detective wasn't enough to impress a woman.

Did he really want to impress Caro? That was ridiculous, he told himself. Anyway, the Phelps case was his now, and she would be returning upstairs. They wouldn't have much call to see each other. It was probably better that way.

Virginia Dreyfus hated her job. She hated her office, with its cheap furnishings and dusty imitation silk ferns. She hated her boss, Dr. Holier-Than-Thou Thurman Wayrick, who was amassing a fortune off other people's misery.

She didn't even like her clients. Stupid, ignorant women. Most of them didn't have the sense to get in out of the rain—or to use a condom. She faced them day after day, week after week, one after another, one face blending into the next. She was so tired of smiling and reassuring and trying to shore up their self-esteem, when all the while she wanted to shake them until their pea-sized brains rattled inside their skulls.

Most of all she hated being told what to do by people who thought they were better than she was—like the snotty detective who was now seated in her office, waving her subpoena and passing judgment as she asked her pseudo-polite questions.

The telephone message Virginia had received that morning from Corporal Carolyn Triece had given her a case of the jitters. Immediately she'd thought the police had somehow connected her with that Phelps girl, whose body had been identified yesterday. Virginia had delayed returning the call, arguing with herself as to how much of the truth she wanted to reveal. She didn't mind lying, but only if she was sure she wouldn't get caught.

Then the impatient Triece woman had shown up in person.

Thank God the detective's questions were about something else entirely. Amanda Arkin had disappeared. The fact that the police had connected Amanda to the clinic was unfortunate, inconvenient, but not a disaster.

"I want to cooperate as fully as possible," Virginia said carefully as she flicked the dust off the silk plant that sat on her desk. "But I feel obligated to protect Amanda's privacy. It goes against everything inside me to violate her confidentiality."

"This subpoena supersedes Amanda's right to privacy," Triece said with an impatient sigh. "Anyway, her privacy won't do her much good if she's dead. Now, there are only two things specifically spelled out in this document that I need from you. One is Amanda's state of mind. If in your expert opinion she's suicidal, I need to know. I told that girl's father that I thought she'd run off simply because she needed some time alone to think. Do you believe I'm right? If not, tell me now. If Amanda is deeply disturbed, I'll upgrade this case to critical."

Virginia had a good idea where Amanda was. Odell and her propaganda had apparently found a receptive target in the confused, pregnant girl, who was probably now safely tucked away in the Good Shepherd Maternity Home. But of course, Virginia couldn't tell Triece.

"Amanda's father said she was handling her situation very calmly, very rationally," Triece offered when Virginia remained silent. "Was he right?"

Virginia assumed a deliberately patronizing manner. "I'm sure that's what he would like to believe. Amanda isn't suicidal, nor deeply disturbed, but she's far from calm and rational. She's facing a very tough decision. Her strict Catholic upbringing taught her that abortion is a sin, and yet she feels that to have a baby now would ruin her life. This inner conflict has produced a great deal of anxiety. In my opinion, your theory that she left home to think things through—away from her well-meaning father—is quite consistent with her mental state. I would be very surprised if she doesn't turn up or call in the next day or two."

Corporal Triece visibly relaxed, probably relieved to discover that her own instincts were on the mark.

Virginia felt only a twinge of guilt that she hadn't told Triece the whole truth. In her "expert opinion," she thought Amanda Arkin was one of the most rational, intelligent young women to have come through this office. She wouldn't have even given Amanda's name to Odell, because Amanda didn't fit the profile Odell had requested, but Virginia really needed some extra cash.

It surprised the hell out of her that Amanda had fallen for Odell's line of bull, but that must be what had happened. Now all Virginia wanted was to give the detective what she was looking for and send her on her way.

"How was Amanda's relationship with her father?" Triece asked.

"I don't believe that information was spelled out in the subpoena," Virginia said.

Triece snorted impatiently. "If you have any concern for Amanda at all, you'll help me find her."

"And have her sue the pants off me for violating her privacy? No, thanks." She struggled to soften her stance. "Look, I hope you find Amanda, I really do. And if there were anything else remarkable about her case, I would tell you. But there isn't, and I don't see the benefit in hashing over bits and pieces of confidential counseling sessions."

Triece gave another frustrated sigh. "Just one more thing, and this one *is* spelled out in the subpoena. I need the names of any friends or acquaintances she mentioned. Maybe you can tell me if she talked excessively about any of them."

Virginia pursed her lips, then grudgingly read off several names from her shorthand notes—Amanda's college roommate, her best friend from high school and, of course, Scott. "Amanda didn't talk excessively about anyone except a boy named Scott, no last name—"

"Scott Humphrey, the baby's father," Triece supplied. "It was no secret. Everybody who knew she was pregnant knew who the father was."

"I can't recall that she spoke of anyone else," Virginia said coolly.

Triece responded with a voice like ice. "If your memory improves, please call me. Amanda's father is frantic." She dropped a business card onto Virginia's desk as she stood and put away her notepad and pen. Then she added, almost as an afterthought, "He's offering a ten-thousand-dollar reward."

"Indeed."

Virginia remained impassive until Triece had left. Then she let out a long, low whistle. Ten thousand bucks. Damn. It was almost enough to make her blow the whistle on Odell. But that amount of money would hardly last long if Virginia were unemployed, and she had no doubts that, if she turned Odell in, the vindictive old woman would return the favor.

Unfortunately, Virginia's employment opportunities were limited. Not many institutions wanted a psychologist who'd been fired with cause from her last position, much less her last two.

She'd been lucky to find this job after the incident at Sun Meadows. Thank God Dr. Wayrick was none too picky about her qualifications or her background. And there was certainly no danger that she would repeat her last mistake—romantic involvement with a client—at this place. Dr. Wayrick paid her slave wages, less than half of what she'd made at the swanky rehab clinic. Could anyone blame her for snapping up the deal Odell had offered her?

Virginia didn't like Odell. She was a pompous, self-effacing pro-life crusader who would stoop to anything to prevent an abortion. But she had money, and she paid Virginia fifty dollars per name and address of any girl considering terminating her pregnancy. When Odell succeeded in luring one of those girls to the Good Shepherd Maternity Home, Virginia received a kickback of a thousand bucks—in cash, tax-free. So far she had made over two thousand dollars. It wasn't a fortune, but it helped pay the bills.

The scheme had seemed a fairly innocent way of earning a few bucks and undercutting Wayrick's profits. Of course it was a breach of ethics to divulge her clients' names to anyone, but only a small breach. What was the harm in submitting those mixed-up girls to a bit of well-meaning pro-life propaganda?

But perhaps there were ramifications Virginia hadn't considered—like what had happened to the Phelps girl. Virginia tended to forget her clients' names as quickly as she learned them, but for some reason she remembered Marcy Phelps, a chubby blonde who'd looked as if she ought to be still playing with dolls, not making babies. Since Marcy had been frightened at the prospect of undergoing an abortion, she'd been an ideal candidate for Odell.

Now she was dead.

Virginia couldn't help wondering . . . if Marcy had had the abortion, would she still be alive? Had pregnancy and birth ruined her life so thoroughly that she'd jumped to her death? The radio newscaster hadn't specified suicide, but that's what Virginia theorized.

The news of Marcy's death had shaken Virginia up more than it should have. Lately, she'd started toying with the idea of telling Odell their deal was off. Virginia might not be particularly fond of her clients, but she didn't wish them dead.

The visit from that Triece woman had cemented Virginia's decision to disassociate herself from Odell.

She had been supplying Odell with names for more than eight months now with never a ripple of trouble. Now, suddenly, two girls had come back to haunt Virginia within a twenty-four-hour period.

She had about fifteen minutes before her next appointment. She closed and locked her office door, then sat down, took a deep breath and picked up the phone. Apparently Odell didn't live in Dallas, but she had a local answering service. Virginia dialed the number from memory.

Later that afternoon, Odell returned the call. "What is it, Virginia?" she demanded without preamble.

"My, you're cheerful today."

"Oh, I'm sorry. These girls can bleed the good will right out of a body, sometimes. Do you have another name for me? The home's pretty near full, but I can always make room for one more in the name of the Lord."

"No more names. I'm done with that."

A surprised silence followed Virginia's declaration. "I don't understand. Surely you don't think you're being underpaid for your service."

"It's not the money. It's my nerves. A police detective is nosing around the clinic. I thought I was going to dissolve in a pool of sweat before she finished with me."

"Police . . ." Odell scarcely breathed the word. "What did they want?"

"The Arkin girl. She's missing."

"Amanda Arkin?"

"She's with you, isn't she?" Virginia demanded, surprisingly anxious to know whether the girl was safe.

"Heavens, no. She wouldn't give me the time of day. I believe she's quite determined to compound her sin by murdering her baby. Why did the police come to you?"

Virginia tamped down her disappointment. She'd already started mentally spending that thousand dollars. "The last anyone saw of Amanda, she was on her way to an appointment with me, and her father knew about it. She sure picked a lousy time to go haywire and split. You're just lucky I didn't mention your name. I was sure Amanda was at the home."

Odell gasped. "Are you crazy? Don't even think of telling anyone about our arrangement. You'll get your license yanked for sure."

"Damn it, Odell, I wouldn't really do that. I'm not stupid."

"Then just what did you tell them?"

"I said that Amanda was a very troubled girl, and that I wasn't surprised she'd run off. That's not exactly the truth—"

"Good, that's good," Odell said in soothing tones, apparently uninterested in the truth. "Maybe I got to her after all. I'm glad to hear she hasn't gone through with the abortion, at any rate. Now, what's this about you not giving me any more names?" She spoke as if she were scolding a puppy.

"I won't. I mean it, Odell. I don't like lying to the police. And then there was the Phelps girl. I assume you know about that case."

Odell clicked her tongue. "Yes, I sure do. It near broke my heart when I read about it in this morning's paper. She was a lost soul, that one. Never did fit in here, although I tried hard to help her. She only stayed with me a couple of months, and then she ran off."

"Ran off? And the police couldn't find her?"

"Apparently not."

Virginia vaguely remembered hearing something about the girl being missing for a while. She hadn't paid very close attention, though.

"I count Marcy as one of my failures," Odell went on, "although I did accomplish my primary goal. By the time she left here, she was too far along to have an abortion."

Bully for you, Virginia wanted to say. Poor Marcy. She probably would have had a better life if she'd never heard of Odell. Now she didn't have a life at all. And the poor baby. What had become of it?

"Won't you reconsider, about the names?" Odell asked in her most wheedling voice. "Don't think of yourself, think of the babies you're saving."

"No. Our association is finished."

Odell sucked in a sharp breath. "I could ruin you, you know. If I went to your boss—"

"You wouldn't dare!"

"Don't be too sure. I've got nothing to lose. I've done nothing illegal or immoral. You, on the other hand..." Her words trailed off, and she let her silence speak for her.

"I'll have to think about it," Virginia finally said, galled that she was being blackmailed by the likes of Odell, whose last name she didn't even know.

"That's all I'm asking."

Virginia hung up and blotted her damp forehead with a tissue. Christ, she'd never thought her lucrative little side business would get so complicated.

"Has that Arkin girl shown up yet?" Tony asked as he swiveled his chair to face Caro's desk, again stuffing bubblegum into his mouth. Green-apple flavored, this time.

"Not yet. I talked to the psychologist she was seeing, Virginia Dreyfus. She said Amanda was very mixed up. She wanted an abortion, but she'd been raised Catholic."

"That's a problem, all right," Tony commented dryly. "What else did the shrink say?"

"Precious little. She wasn't the least bit surprised to hear Amanda had disappeared, though. She said Amanda probably needed to get away from her father's pressure tactics and make the decision on her own."

"I thought Arkin told you he was being very supportive, no matter what Amanda decided."

Caro sighed. "Yeah. I guess I can't hold that against him. His idea of supportive might be very different from Amanda's, though. He's remembering what he wants to remember. What I do hold against him is those damn fliers he put up, offering the ten-thousand-dollar reward. Suddenly Amanda's being spotted at every Burger King and bowling alley from Plano to Oak Cliff. But given the slim progress I've made so far, I've had to follow every damn one of those leads."

"You don't have anything else solid?"

Caro shook her head dismally. "I've checked all of her favorite hangouts, right down to the library and her church. No one's seen her or the car. Her friends seem surprised over her disappearance, and none of them has any idea where she would go. There's been no activity in her checking account, which isn't surprising. Her balance is under ten dollars. Nothing on the credit cards, either, but it's early yet. The Denton police are cooperating, looking for leads up where she went to school. So far, nothing."

"What about the boyfriend?"

Caro gave an unladylike snort. "Oh, yes, Scott. He's so concerned, he went off on a skiing vacation with his family."

"So you haven't talked to him?"

"Can't find him. But according to his friends he's due back home on Tuesday. Want to come with me when I question him?" Caro usually worked on her own, as did all of the Missing Persons investigators, but there were times she enjoyed having Tony and his black, intimidating glares with her.

"My pleasure," Tony said with an evil smile.

Chloe Krill bottle-fed her sleepy newborn as she read the Metropolitan section, spread out over the kitchen table. The article about poor Marcy Phelps fascinated her, and she read it over and over. She couldn't shake the feeling that she'd heard the name before. Maybe she'd read something about the girl when she'd first disappeared.

Normally, Chloe didn't share her husband's morbid curiosity about crime news. Don was on the city council, so she supposed he had a legitimate need to stay up on that kind of thing. But she was usually much too busy with her charity work and running her household to pay attention to the news. Sometimes she scanned the society pages, to see if she or one of her friends were pictured, and the food section for new recipes, but that was about it.

Her habits had changed, however, since Justin's arrival a week ago. Now she was homebound. She hadn't realized, until she undertook the care of her newly adopted son, how addicted she was to her freedom to come and go as she pleased. Why, before Justin, she could, on a whim, hop in her car to visit friends, have lunch at the country club or indulge in an afternoon shopping spree.

It wasn't that Chloe was bored. Justin kept her plenty busy, so busy that she was already thinking about hiring a nanny for him. But she craved contact with the outside world. Thus, her new-found interest in the newspaper.

Although there were a terrifying number of heinous crimes detailed in the paper, the Marcy Phelps case held a special fascination for Chloe. Perhaps it was because Marcy had died in childbirth.

Chloe could relate to that. She had been pregnant three times. The first two pregnancies had ended in miscarriage; the third child had been stillborn, and his birth had nearly killed her. Thank God she'd had the very best in medical care, or she, too, might have ended up like poor Marcy.

How very lucky she was, Chloe thought as she gazed down lovingly at her new son. His tiny rosebud mouth was lax now as he slept. She set the bottle down and gently blotted a drop of formula from his chin.

After losing three babies, Chloe had all but given up on being a mother. Her doctor had cautioned her not to risk another pregnancy. She was thirty-five, and Don, forty-five; adoption agencies considered them too old to qualify for a healthy white baby. Even those agencies that would put the Krills on a waiting list had said it would be years before they could adopt.

A chance comment Don had made to their attorney, Travis Beaman, about their frustration had spurred Travis to help. He had made several discreet inquiries among his associates and clients, and one of them had come up with a pregnant teenage daughter who desperately wanted to give up her baby to wealthy, caring parents like the Krills.

The arrangements hadn't been made cheaply, but was anything cheap these days? Chloe would have been willing to pay anything, *anything,* for a baby of her own. She'd hardly blinked as Don had written out the check for forty-eight thousand dollars and change, which covered legal and medical fees. And she hadn't asked too many questions, even though she'd suspected that her own husband knew more than she did about the circumstances surrounding Justin's birth. Don had cautioned her, once, not to rock the boat, and she'd kept her mouth closed.

Chloe stood slowly so as not to disturb the sleeping baby, intent on closing the newspaper and taking Justin to his crib for his afternoon nap. But some odd compulsion made her pause and read over the article about Marcy Phelps yet again.

The body had been found on Wednesday, and the medical examiner said she'd been dead for about a week. That meant she'd given birth on or about December 13—which was exactly Justin's birthdate.

This realization really bothered Chloe. Here was Justin, safe, warm and loved, while out there somewhere, Marcy Phelps's baby, born on the same day, was in God-knew-who's hands, possibly cold, hungry, in danger.

Chloe's eyes moistened with tears. Why would anyone hide the birth of an unwanted child when there were thousands of parents, just like her and Don, who would welcome a baby with open arms? Someone would give that Phelps girl's baby a happy home, if only the child could be found. This was so senseless.

Marcy Phelps. Marcy. Miss Phelps. Is that where she'd heard the name? Whispered between her husband and her lawyer? Or murmured on one of the many occasions when Don talked in his sleep?

She studied the picture of Marcy Phelps—smiling, happy, just a baby herself. Then she looked down at Justin's chubby cheeks and blond peach fuzz. Her gaze darted back and forth between the black-and-white photo and her own sleeping child.

Suddenly she realized she was looking for a resemblance.

A sick feeling began in the pit of her stomach, working its way slowly toward her throat.

Chapter 3

Terri Zamasko watched the new girl carefully, always on the lookout for an ally. Odell had called the girl Amanda. She seemed older than most of the others here, even older than Terri herself, and hopefully that meant she wasn't as naive as the others, either. Honestly, Terri couldn't believe how easily the old lady led these morons toward the slaughter like a bunch of sheep.

Odell sat at the head of the long, rough-plank dinner table. Amanda sat to her immediate left, sullenly chewing on her roast beef and new potatoes. She sported a fresh bruise under her left eye, marring an otherwise flawless face. Terri wondered what other bruises were on Amanda's body.

The routine was the same for every new girl, as far as Terri could figure. She was brought in unconscious and locked in her room. When she woke up she screamed and hollered or cried for hours, but eventually she would quiet down, exhausted, hungry. If she promised to behave, she was allowed to enter into a more normal routine, which included group meals, outdoor exercise, work details and occasionally some television.

If the girl refused to cooperate, she was kept isolated. If she was rude or insolent to Odell, she might even get a slap or two. The really unmanageable girls were treated to a stint in the dungeon—the dank, filthy cellar. It didn't take any girl long in that place to see the light.

The slaps weren't that bad. Hell, Terri's old man had occasionally roughed her up worse than Odell did. It was the food given to her when she was in isolation that finally did Terri in. While subsisting on cold, unappetizing leftovers—and little enough of them—she kept smelling beef stew, corn on the cob and mouthwatering baked goods. After two days, she had finally decided that her chances of getting out of this hellhole would be better if she were allowed out of isolation.

Most of the girls reached this conclusion after only a few hours. Terri had held the record, until Amanda. Amanda had remained locked in her room for almost three days.

That fact was encouraging to Terri. The other factor that played into her hands was that Amanda had taken over Marcy's old room, right under Terri's. The floors and walls of this big old farmhouse were thickly insulated, so Terri hadn't been able to understand what all was said between Amanda and Odell. But she heard every time Amanda pitched a screaming fit, which had been often. And if the girl was as smart as she looked, Terri would be able to communicate with her.

Terri listened with half an ear to Odell, who was at this moment preaching from the Bible. Today was Christmas Eve, and that gave the old woman lots of material to brainwash with. Sooner or later she would ask Terri a question, and if Terri didn't know the answer, she wouldn't get her dessert. Normally that didn't matter, but she'd smelled cherry pie, her favorite, coming from the kitchen.

Odell, however, wasn't of a mind to pick on Terri tonight. Her sights were set on the new girl. She stopped mid-sentence and laid down her Bible. "Amanda, you aren't eating your green beans."

"I don't like green beans," she mumbled, her eyes downcast.

"That's unfortunate, because you have to eat them. You want the best nutrition for your baby, right?"

This time Amanda looked up, her blue eyes staring daggers into Odell's body. "I won't eat green beans," she said, clearly enunciating every word. "They make me throw up."

Terri could almost see the steam rising off Odell's face, which was turning an unbecoming shade of red. Slowly she came out of her chair and then she struck like a snake, grabbing Amanda's arm and jerking her off the end of the bench.

"You dare criticize the bounty the good Lord has provided for you? You have a roof over your head and a decent meal in front of you. God has seen fit to save you from committing mortal sin. You have no right to be ungrateful. Now, you will apologize to me and to the other girls for disturbing this wonderful meal, and you'll eat every green bean on that plate."

"Like hell."

The other girls kept their eyes downcast and continued eating, but Terri stared in wide-eyed admiration. She'd hardly ever seen anyone talk back to the old witch like that. She could tell Odell was itching to slap Amanda, but she seldom did that in front of witnesses. She probably didn't want to engender any sympathy from the other girls.

Instead she turned to her helper, the hulking Henry, who was as loyal as Odell's dogs but certainly not as smart. He wasn't retarded, exactly, but there seemed to be something definitely wrong with him, the way he talked to himself and made those weird faces. "Henry, take Amanda to her room, please. Apparently she needs a few more lessons in humility."

Henry, who was seated at the other end of the table shoveling down his food, now stood and impassively moved around to take Amanda by the arm. When she resisted, he just pulled a little harder until she was forced to follow him or be dragged. His moon face registered little expression except a slight upturn at the corners of his mouth. Terri suspected he enjoyed exercising his brawn.

Odell sat back down with a self-satisfied smile. "Now, where were we? Ah, yes, the Three Wise Men. Terri, can you tell me what gifts the Magi brought to the Christ child?"

For once Terri knew the answer. But she realized she would be blowing a golden opportunity if she gave the correct response. With a small pang of remorse for that cherry pie, she answered, "Oh, I think they brought some sheep, so Mary could make a wool blanket to keep him warm." At Odell's outraged expression, Terri added, "Well, damn it, I know you said something about sheep."

"Young lady, have we not talked about the use of profanity?"

Odell wasn't mad enough, Terri decided. "Yeah, you've talked my goddamn ear off about it!"

That did it. For the second time that night, Odell's complexion approached purple. "Henry!" she bellowed.

Henry shuffled into the dining room, having just returned from his first mission. "Yes, ma'am?"

"Take Terri to her room, also. And the next girl who shows such disrespect will get worse."

Henry clamped his beefy hand around Terri's arm. She made a show of resentment, but only until she was out of Odell's sight. This was exactly what she'd wanted. If she were to have any chance of establishing communication with Amanda, she would have to do it when everyone was busy somewhere else.

Henry more or less threw Terri into her room and slammed the door. She listened to the scrape of the deadbolt and the sound of

Henry's scuffing footsteps retreating down the hall. Then all was quiet.

Terri turned on the light and put her ear to the floor. Nothing.

Quickly she sat on the bed and pulled off one of her shoes, an ugly oxford Odell had provided when Terri's running shoes, which she'd been wearing when she was kidnapped, had fallen apart. The shoe was utterly unfashionable, but it did possess one redeeming quality: a hard heel with a sharp corner. Terri had often fantasized about using the shoe as a weapon; this was the next best thing.

In one corner of her room, which was next to the bathroom, a set of water pipes protruded, covered with pink insulation. Terri carefully removed the insulation, so that she could put it back when she was done with her experiment. Presumably the pipes extended into Amanda's room as well.

Terri gave one of the pipes a sharp whack with her shoe. It gave a resounding, satisfying clang. Worried that she might alert someone other than Amanda, she put a little less oomph into the next strike, finding a volume that pleased her.

Now, how would Amanda distinguish Terri's clangs from the normal protests of the old pipes? The only thing she could think of was "shave and a haircut, two bits." Surely anyone would recognize that. She clanged out the first five beats, then waited.

Nothing.

She did it again. "C'mon, Amanda," she murmured, "wake up and smell the coffee."

Still nothing.

She tried a third, fourth and fifth time. She was about to give up, concluding that Amanda either couldn't hear her or was ignoring her like the other girls, when she heard a tentative clunk, clunk.

Hallelujah! Communication at last. She had no idea where to proceed from here, but she did know that somehow, she and Amanda would learn how to talk through this tenuous link they had found.

It was Christmas Day, the happiest day of the year if you had family and friends with whom you could eat turkey and dressing, rip open packages, sing carols and watch football. But for Caro it was a depressing day. The weather, chilly and overcast, matched her mood, and the cold she'd picked up didn't help matters.

She had decided to work straight through Christmas, afraid that if she abandoned her vigil over the phone, even for a day, she would miss the break she was looking for in the Arkin case. Not that she would miss much at home. She didn't have a tree. She might have sat alone in front of the fireplace, nursing a cup of eggnog, opening the presents her parents had sent from Florida, and letting her cat play with the ribbons. It wasn't a pretty picture, and though she was due a holiday, she preferred keeping herself busy.

But her vigilance wasn't paying off. Although she had dutifully followed several more leads, courtesy of Russ Arkin's infernal fliers, all had been dead ends. Signs were pointing to foul play; if something didn't break today, she would have to concede defeat and turn the case over to CAPERS.

She popped another cold pill, washed it down with hot tea, then blew her nose and tossed the tissue into her overflowing trash can. She had a new batch of cases to work on. One was another runaway—a boy, this time. He'd split twice before, and both times Caro had found him bunking with his older brother in San Antonio. She had no reason to believe this time would be different.

In a matter of minutes she had the boy on the line and had convinced him that if he didn't return home, the police would drag him back, as they had the two previous times. She also reminded him that in another four months he would be seventeen—an adult in Texas—and he could go wherever he damn well pleased. She strongly advised him to bide his time. She didn't want his file to cross her desk again.

She was about to call the parents and let them know their darling was safe when a shadow fell across her desk. She looked up to find Russell Arkin standing there, looking a little worse for wear. He was in casual clothes today, a sweatshirt and gray double-knit slacks. His hair was barely combed, if at all, and he obviously hadn't shaved.

The shadow of beard on his slightly puffy face looked singularly out of place on a man whom Caro guessed was usually well groomed. His pale blue eyes were filled with accusation.

"Mr. Arkin," she said, rising slowly and offering him her hand.

He declined to take it. "Why aren't you out looking for my daughter?"

"I have been," she said just a shade too defensively. She'd been knocking herself out over this case. She didn't need to be second-guessed by some guy who thought he knew more about investigation techniques than she did, simply because he was male. "Those fliers you put up have generated dozens of phone calls, most of them from crackpots wanting to cash in on the ten thousand. Unfortunately, all those bogus leads have been wasting valuable time."

Her words had the desired effect. The fire of accusation receded from Russell Arkin's eyes. He searched for a chair, found one several feet away, pulled it close to Caro's desk and made himself at home in it.

Caro hoped he wasn't planning to take root there.

"Why don't you tell me what progress you have made?" he asked.

Caro expelled a long breath through pursed lips, trying to decide how much she owed him. She felt sorry for the man, she really did. He was obviously worried to the point of exhaustion about his daughter. But that didn't mean he was privy to the details of her investigation.

As if there were any details.

All at once, she decided that if she acted like a know-it-all and withheld information from Arkin, it would only be because she was insecure about her lack of progress. And anyway, it was in her best interest to cultivate Arkin's cooperation. He might yet prove helpful.

"How long has it been since you ate something?" she asked.

He blinked owlishly at her, obviously taken aback by the question.

She stood abruptly. "The barbecue place across the street is open on Christmas," she said. "It's not turkey and dressing, but it's good. I'll give you an update while we eat lunch." She put her beeper on her belt, grabbed the quilted jacket off the back of her chair and headed for the exit, giving him no choice but to follow.

Harwood Street was empty of traffic. The only people moving around were a wino, staggering down the sidewalk with his paper bag clutched to his chest, and the parking lot attendant, who paced outside his booth, stamping off the cold. The restaurant, however, was teeming with business, mostly the unfortunate city employees from the old Police and Courts Building across the street who had to work on Christmas.

"This is the only place I know of where you can get a snout sandwich," Caro commented as she and Arkin waited at the counter.

Arkin made a face. "Does it have nostrils?"

"Uh-huh. Smells good, too."

He tried, and failed, to hide a small smile.

Good, Caro thought. He must not be in too bad a shape if he could find humor in her crummy jokes. She ordered them both a large combo sandwich, fries and iced tea, then paid for it all before he could even come up with his wallet. She expected that under normal circumstances he wouldn't stand for that. There was just enough of the macho male in him to want to pay for a lady's lunch, even when their respective gender roles had nothing to do with this outing. But his overriding anxiety about his daughter had seemingly numbed him to the point that he just didn't care about anything else.

As soon as they were seated, Caro jumped into her explanations. "The fact of the matter, Mr. Arkin, is that at this point I'm simply waiting for a break. The department has issued a local BOLO—Be on the Lookout—for Amanda. That means every Dallas patrol officer has access to descriptions of both her and the car. The car is usually our best lead in a case like this.

"I've talked to all of Amanda's friends, including several from her dormitory at North Texas, her high school friends, your neighbors and the people at the family planning clinic. Of those who knew she was pregnant, most agree with you—that she was handling the problem well, and that you weren't putting a lot of pressure on her."

Arkin's french fry halted midway to his mouth. "Most? Who said differently?"

Caro couldn't legally reveal what Virginia Dreyfus had said. The subpoena had given Caro authority to see the information, not spread it around. "I can't answer that," Caro said smoothly. "All I can tell you is that I still feel it's a strong possibility Amanda disappeared of her own accord."

She could actually see Arkin's whole body stiffen with anger. "I hope to hell you're right. But in my gut I know you're dead wrong."

Caro didn't appreciate his choice of words. She abruptly changed the subject. "The only person I haven't been able to question is Scott Humphrey. His family's skiing vacation seems rather too convenient, don't you think? I thought you said he was distraught over Amanda's disappearance."

"He was. He is. But...well, his parents don't know about Amanda being pregnant. He figured if he tried to opt out of the family vacation, his folks would want to know why and then everything would hit the fan."

"And what a shame that would be. Would Scotty have his allowance taken away? Maybe that fancy car he drives?" Although Caro hadn't been able to talk to Scott directly, Amanda's friends had plenty to say about him. He was in premed at North Texas, training to be a doctor like his old man. And he had money and social connections out the wazoo.

"You can joke if you want, but I frankly don't blame the kid. The Humphreys aren't easy people. Sure, they provide Scott with a lot of material things, but they put tremendous pressure on him as well. I can't even predict how they would react if they found out Scott had fathered a child, but it wouldn't be pleasant.''

This shed a new light on things. All along, Caro had been operating on the premise that Amanda wanted an abortion, and her father, as well as her Catholic background, was pressuring her in the other direction. But what if Amanda wanted to have the child and her boyfriend had pressured her to terminate the pregnancy?

"What did Scott want Amanda to do?" she asked Arkin.

"He said the decision was hers to make."

"But what did he want? He must have had an opinion."

Arkin remained silent a long time before answering. "He never said as much, but I think he was hoping she would have the abortion. But Scott's a good kid. Even after all that's happened, I hope he and Amanda stay together. He's the kind of boy I always hoped she would marry. And I can't imagine, in my wildest dreams, that he would lean on her or argue with her about this pregnancy. Above all, he wanted what was best for Amanda. And I think if she'd wanted to marry him and have the baby, he would have done it and made the best of it."

Or was that just more wishful thinking on Daddy's part? Caro wondered. Then another thought occurred to her. "Could Amanda have gone with the Humphreys to Colorado?"

"Not a chance in hell," Arkin said with absolute certainty. "Scott's parents made life miserable for Amanda whenever she was around them. They wouldn't have tolerated her on their family trip, and she certainly wouldn't have willingly submitted herself to their put-downs. Besides, if she'd wanted to go to Colorado, I wouldn't have objected and she knows that. She would have told me she was going."

Another scenario occurred to Caro, although she didn't voice it aloud. Suppose Scott had opted out of the vacation by faking illness or something like that? Coughing and sneezing, he would have urged his parents to go on to Colorado and enjoy themselves. The moment the coast was clear, he could have rendezvoused with Amanda, and the two of them might be, even now, honeymooning in Vegas.

Or, paralyzed with fear over the prospect of seeing his career plans derailed because of this unplanned pregnancy, he'd done away with Amanda. Given his own disappearance, Scott's involvement seemed more likely with every passing hour. Caro wished she had the manpower and the clout to call all the airlines and track down the Humphreys.

She was glad to see Arkin doing justice to his sandwich. He finished the last bite, then took several gulps of sweetened tea.

"You want another?" she asked.

"No, thanks. My stomach isn't sure what to do with the first one. I guess I haven't really eaten in a couple of days."

"I didn't figure you had."

"Corporal Triece . . . do I have to call you that? It seems so formal."

"My first name is Carolyn, Caro for short." Normally she didn't invite that kind of intimacy. With her diminutive stature and little-girl face, she had enough trouble maintaining an authoritative image. But he was right; titles and last names seemed silly when they were sitting here in Dave's Dive sharing a Christmas dinner of barbecue sandwiches.

He nodded. "I'm Russ. I was about to ask you—"

Whatever his burning question, Caro's beeper interrupted it. She silenced it with a jab of her finger and glanced toward the pay phone, over which an elderly woman in a pseudo leopard-skin coat had firm control. She'd been standing there talking for at least fifteen minutes.

Arkin—Russ, Caro reminded herself—watched her anxiously. "Do you think it could be something about Amanda?"

"I have six other cases besides your daughter's," she reminded him. But in her gut, she knew her sergeant wouldn't beep her during her lunch break unless something major had come down.

Her own sandwich was only half finished. With regret she left it behind, shrugging into her jacket as she headed for the door. Russ was right behind her.

"I'll contact you if I learn anything new with Amanda's case," she said as she shouldered the door open, meeting a blast of cold air.

He didn't take the hint, and instead followed her like a bird dog on the scent. Damn it, if this was about Amanda, she didn't want her father to hear unpleasant news just blurted out. She would much prefer to synthesize any information, filter it, dose it out to him in amounts he could manage. But he insisted on following her up to the third floor.

Sergeant Nona Quayar, Caro's immediate supervisor, was waiting for her. "Corporal Greene in Auto Theft has some information for you," she said, her gaze darting from Caro to Arkin and back. The crease of worry between Nona's eyebrows told Caro more than words could have.

Her call to Dirk Greene only confirmed her suspicions. "Whatcha got for me?" she asked him in a deceptively casual voice.

"The Arkin girl's car has been found. Couple of fourteen-year-olds were joyriding just outside of Taryton and smashed it into a telephone pole. Authorities there ran a registration on it, traced it to the girl's father and tried to notify him. But when they got some weird message on his answering machine, they decided to check here to see if the car had recently been reported stolen. I remembered seeing the memo on it."

"Where did the boys find the car?"

"They say they found it abandoned down by the river with the keys in it."

Caro paused to blow her nose and collect her thoughts. It was essential that everything get handled just right. "Any sign of Amanda?" she asked automatically. Her words caused Arkin's complexion to visibly pale, but she couldn't take time out to worry about his sensibilities. She'd told him to leave, after all.

"One of the boys isn't very cooperative, but the other says they saw who abandoned the car. There was no clothing found in the car, no obvious bloodstains or other signs of struggle."

"Where's the car now?" she asked.

"At the Taryton police's impound lot."

"I'll have it towed here," she said, thinking out loud. "I want it gone over with a microscope, and the evidence guys can do a better job here than there. I also want to question those kids." Her mind raced. To question the joyriders meant a trip to Taryton.

Well, a nice long drive would get her out of the office, anyway. She took down all the pertinent information from Greene and thanked him for his alert response. As she hung up, she saw Quayar scowling at her from across the room.

Caro already knew what her supervisor would say: Turn the case over to CAPERS. Amanda had been missing for four days. With the car recovered and no sign of its owner, there was sufficient evidence to indicate foul play.

Caro made a beeline for Nona's desk. "I'd like to keep the Arkin case for one more day," she said without preamble. "If I transfer it to CAPERS now, the afternoon will be wasted while the new lead detective plays catch-up, and there's a lot to be done."

Nona's scowl deepened.

"There's no hard evidence of foul play, no blood or clothing or signs of struggle in the car."

"What's going on with your other cases?" the sergeant asked.

Caro was about to answer when Tony strolled into the room. Both women stared at him. "What are you doing here?" Quayar demanded.

"A little too much family togetherness," he said with a shrug. "Is there a problem?"

Tony was Caro's salvation. "Tony, ol' buddy, ol' pal, how'd ya like to take over a couple of my cases so I can make a trip to Taryton? I got a break on the Arkin case."

"Sure, no problem."

Nona nodded grudgingly. "You have till noon tomorrow," she said to Caro. "Just be sure you don't screw nothin' up, or CAPERS will be all over both our butts."

"Yes, ma'am," Caro replied, adding the ma'am at the last moment. She noticed then that Arkin was still hanging around, listening to the police officers with an attentive ear and a pasty face. "Cheer up," she said as she returned to her desk, intending to gather together her active cases so she could brief Tony. "This is the break we've been looking for. We've got a big hunk of physical evidence in the form of Amanda's car, and a couple of witnesses to boot."

She didn't add that finding Amanda's car minus Amanda was actually a very bad sign, but she didn't have to. Judging from the look of dread on Arkin's face, he knew all too well.

Chapter 4

Taryton was like many other small east Texas towns, a farming community past its prime with a crumbling, seedy-looking downtown, a long-abandoned train station, and a water tower bearing a faded Home of the Fightin' Taryton Tigers painted on the side. Caro had grown up in just such a town, where her father had been a deputy sheriff and her mother a police dispatcher. She had learned to love law enforcement at their knees, and there had never been any question as to what career she would choose.

Her decision to work on the police force of a big city had terrified her parents at first. But she'd been determined to take what her father had done one step further. She'd longed to immerse herself in crime-solving. Stolen bicycles and an occasional domestic disturbance weren't enough to challenge her, she'd maintained.

As the years passed and she managed to stay out of harm's way while earning several promotions and commendations, her folks gradually had relaxed and accepted her choice.

Now she was the one questioning her career path. It wasn't the danger that got to her. Hell, as a missing persons investigator she rarely put herself at any significant risk. What was starting to bother her was the futility, the sameness, the feeling that no matter how many missing people she found, no matter how many criminals she helped bring in, there was a never-ending supply to take their place.

There was also that niggling certainty, growing stronger every day, that justice had little to do with who went to jail and for how long.

As she drove down Taryton's main street, past the Mayfair Beauty Shop, Arlene's Flowers and the All-Welcome Insurance Agency, Caro wondered why she didn't quit the Dallas Police Department and all that pressure. Surely, if she wanted, she could find a position keeping the peace in a little town like this, where it was big news when a couple of fourteen-year-olds stole a car and totalled it.

She had already questioned one of the boys who had crashed Amanda Arkin's car, a belligerent little snot with the unfortunate name of Dustin Upton. Obviously well coached by his attorney, his story had remained maddeningly static and unhelpful. He said his friend Chucky had picked him up in the red Cavalier, and Chucky hadn't said where the car had come from. Dustin hadn't suspected the car was stolen. He never actually drove the car himself, and he hadn't touched a drop of alcohol all night.

The kid obviously was lying through the teeth, but Caro had been unable to make any progress. The local investigating officer, a seemingly sharp guy named Tom Breedlove, had warned her that she would be up against a brick wall. He hadn't had any better luck with Dustin.

I've really sunk to the lowest depths when I can't crack a crummy juvenile car thief, she mused grimly.

She hoped the other boy, who had been shaken up pretty badly in the accident, would prove more fertile ground. Chucky Hoffman was still in the hospital with several broken bones and lacerations. He hadn't yet admitted to stealing any car, but his emergency room blood tests had revealed an astonishingly high alcohol content, so his legal footing was shakier than his friend's. Furthermore, he already had a juvenile record for breaking and entering.

He ought to be plenty scared.

As she pulled into a visitor's parking place beside the one-story hospital, she reviewed her strategy. She would go soft at first, sympathetic to Chucky's pain and to the dilemma he found himself in. She would emphasize that she wasn't interested in his guilt or innocence, only with information that would help locate Amanda Arkin. And she would explain how helpful he could be in finding the lost girl—who could just as easily be his sister or his girlfriend—before any harm came to her.

If Chucky was unmoved by the tender approach, she would threaten to stuff his IV bag down his throat.

As it turned out, none of her carefully orchestrated tactics was necessary. Two men, casually but neatly dressed, approached her the moment she asked at the front desk for Chucky Hoffman's room.

"Are you... are you Corporal Triece?" the taller of the two asked, his disbelief evident. He was slim and attractive in a *GQ* sort of way, with perfectly styled, short blond hair, wire-rimmed glasses, manicured fingernails and a Bermuda tan. If it had been any day but Christmas, she decided, he would have been wearing a double-breasted suit instead of razor-creased khaki trousers and a designer flannel shirt.

He had to be a lawyer.

She rolled her eyes and showed him her badge, primed for another battle. When would she get a few gray hairs and a wrinkle or two?

The man surprised her by flashing an oily smile. "I'm Barry Seddle, Chucky's attorney. And this is Assistant DA John Calvin. We understand you're interested in the car Chucky allegedly stole."

Allegedly, right. Caro nodded. "The car belongs to a Dallas teenager who's been missing for several days. Anything Chucky can tell me about how and when he came into possession of the car—"

"Alleged possession," Barry reminded her.

"—might help find the girl," she continued without missing a beat.

Barry adjusted his glasses. "Naturally, I would want Chuck to offer his full cooperation. However, the risk of his accidentally incriminating himself..."

It didn't take long for Caro to figure out the game here. She turned to the dapper, young ADA, who looked anything but happy to be hanging around the hospital when he could be home with his family. "Mr. Calvin, is it?"

He nodded. Although neat and conservative-looking, he didn't reek of wealth the way Barry Seddle did.

"Amanda Arkin has been missing for four days," she said, her tone deliberately grave. "Now that her car has turned up and she hasn't, I have to suspect foul play. If Chucky knows anything, or if he saw anything, it could be the break I'm looking for. And it might be the difference between life and death for Amanda." When she saw that her bit of melodrama had no effect on John Calvin, she added in a more matter-of-fact tone, "I really need for him to be honest with me—without watching every word he speaks."

"Well, there you go," Barry said to John. "See, Chucky's a witness in a possible murder case. Now, wouldn't you like to help out the Dallas Police Department by granting Chucky immunity?''

John's mouth hardened into a thin line as he pondered the situation. Finally he spoke. ''If Chucky offers Corporal Triece his full cooperation, and if he gives me what I want on that little bastard Dustin Upton, I'll reduce the charge to . . . unlawful possession of an alcoholic beverage.''

Barry smiled triumphantly. ''Let me talk to Chucky and his dad.'' He strolled off, leaving Caro to cool her heels in the waiting room with the ADA.

They found a couple of uncomfortable plastic chairs.

''You like working for the county?'' she asked, more to fill the awkward silence than out of any real desire to know.

He shrugged. ''I'd rather put little scumbags like Upton and Hoffman in jail than defend them, even if the pay's lousy. But I hate cutting deals.''

''Yeah, I know what you mean. We haul 'em in, and the defense lawyers get 'em out.''

There was another uncomfortable pause before John spoke again. ''So you think the girl was murdered?''

Caro shuddered as Russ Arkin's chilling prediction about finding Amanda in a ditch came back to haunt her. ''I'll know more when I get the evidence report back on the car,'' she replied as casually as she could manage. She wasn't supposed to get emotionally involved in her cases, but in the back of her mind she couldn't help dreading the possibility that Amanda would end up another Marcy Phelps. ''From what the investigating officer tells me, there was no obvious blood other than a little of Chucky's, no clothing, no purse. Just some empty beer cans.'' And no body in the trunk. She'd asked about that first thing.

''Who was the officer?'' Calvin asked.

''Breedlove.''

''Tom. He's a good man.''

''I'm hoping Amanda just decided to ditch the car because she knew the police would be looking for it by now.'' But in her gut, Caro knew that wasn't the case.

Barry returned a few minutes later, beaming. Chucky had agreed to the deal. He would be allowed to plead guilty to the lesser charge, provided he cooperated fully in all questioning. Caro wanted the first shot.

Considering that Chucky's partner in crime hadn't sustained even a scratch in the accident, Caro wasn't prepared for how bad a shape this kid was in. He had a full cast on one arm, a splint on one leg, and a face that looked like someone had stuffed his head into a food processor. Yesterday he'd probably been a good-looking boy—and would be again, once his plastic surgeon got done, she reminded herself. This was no time to get soft.

Officer Breedlove showed up in time to sit in on the questioning, and of course Barry Seddle was there, too. Chucky, nervous at first, calmed down after repeated reassurances from his lawyer. Then he spilled his guts.

"Me and Upton, we was just messin' around, you know, playing chicken on the railroad trestle."

"Chicken?" Caro repeated.

"Yeah. We'd stand in the middle of the bridge and wait for a train, then see who ran first. Ah, you won't tell my mom that part, will you?"

"No," she assured him. "And what time was this?"

"I dunno, before midnight, I think. We had some beer Upton stole from his icebox at home. His dad drinks tons."

Caro was uninterested in this part. "Go on."

"Anyway, we saw these car lights down on the riverbank, where there's not even a road. So we got closer, you know, thinking maybe some guy was parking there with his chick and we'd give 'em a scare. But then this guy got out and we didn't know him, so—"

"Are you sure you didn't know him?" Caro asked. "It must have been pretty dark."

"There was a moon. Anyway, we couldn't see him that good, but we sure didn't know the car, so we figured we didn't know the guy."

Caro accepted that explanation for now. "Okay, go on."

"Well, he got out of the car, and then he pulled a handkerchief or something out of his pocket and started polishing the car—like you do right after you wash it, to get all the water spots off. We laughed about that, 'cause it was so muddy down there the car was just gonna get dirty again."

Caro swallowed. The mysterious man had obviously been wiping the car clean of fingerprints. Hell.

"Then the guy opens the door again, and he reaches inside and puts the car in gear and starts to push it. And we realized he was trying to sink it in the river. But then it got stuck in the mud and it wouldn't go any farther. He pushed it and pulled it and even got in and tried to drive it, but it was stuck good. Then he took off running through the woods."

"What did you do then?" Caro asked.

"We figured the car had to be stolen or maybe used in a bank robbery or something, and we thought there might be a reward. So we found some old boards and got it unstuck from the mud. And since the keys were in it, we thought we'd just drive it back up to the highway.''

"Who was driving?" Tom Breedlove asked.

Caro shot him a warning look. What the hell did she care who was driving? But these people had their own agenda—nailing Dustin Upton, who did not seem to be a popular teenager among the legal and law enforcement communities of Taryton—so she bit her tongue.

"Oh, Upton drove," Chucky said without any further prompting.

Breedlove smiled. "Sorry, Corporal," he said to Caro.

Caro continued her questions. The kids had intended to turn the car in, but somehow they never did. The two six-packs of beer they'd consumed—the empties found in the car—might have impaired their judgment a wee bit.

"Now, this is really important, Chucky," she said when he'd ended his story with a graphic description of how the car had become wrapped around a telephone pole. "The guy who ditched the car—what did he look like? I know you said you couldn't see him real well, but anything you can remember would help."

Chucky thought for a moment. "He was big—real big."

"You mean, fat?"

"No, I mean big like a football player. And he had a kind of round face."

"Was he white? Black?"

"White. And his hair was medium-colored, you know, not black or blond. And it was sort of choppy, like he must have cut it himself or something."

Caro took furious notes. This was better than she'd expected. "And his clothes?"

"Baggy. Baggy jeans, or overalls, maybe, and a big jacket, like a ski jacket. Blue or brown, maybe."

Caro looked to see that Breedlove was taking notes, too. "You got that?"

"I'll put the description out right away," he said.

She smiled back at Chucky. "That's really good. You have a good memory. Is there anything else? Shoes? Gloves?"

Chucky closed his eyes, as if trying to visualize. "Gloves, I just remembered that. Work gloves, like my dad wears in his shop. I don't remember his shoes. He was standing behind the car most of the time, and they would have been muddy, anyway."

They went over everything again, but Chucky could add little to the details he'd already given. Caro promised she would tell the DA that Chucky had cooperated marvelously, and the boy almost smiled.

She and Tom Breedlove rode together in his car to the river bank where Chucky said the mysterious man had abandoned Amanda's car. Although it had rained the previous night, the deep tire tracks left by the Cavalier at the river's edge were still plain. Any footprints, however, had been obliterated. And there were no other obvious clues lying around. Still, Breedlove promised to get an evidence person over to comb the site. She suspected that in a department the size of Taryton's that person might be Breedlove himself.

It was almost dark. Caro sneezed as she climbed back into Breedlove's cruiser. Her last dose of cold medicine was wearing off. She fished in her purse for a tissue, and suddenly she realized she was bone-tired. She longed to be home in front of her TV, watching some inane Christmas special.

On the long drive home, it occurred to her that the sketchy description of the suspect Chucky had provided could fit a lot of people. And one of those people—six-foot-two, two hundred and twenty pounds, already a star on his college football team—was Scott Humphrey.

How could her father have done this to her? Amanda asked herself over and over as she lay on her cot, her stomach rumbling with hunger. She'd known he was opposed to abortion, but to resort to kidnapping and putting her into a virtual prison? That wasn't the Daddy she knew.

It was kind of ironic that if she'd had just a few more hours, she would have told her father about her decision to keep the baby, and this nightmare could have been prevented.

If he understood what a hellhole this place was, and how cruel Odell was, he wouldn't leave her here. It was Christmas Day, for God's sake, and she'd been allowed nothing but oatmeal since last night's green-bean uproar. Why hadn't her father at least called her?

The only thing that kept her sane was the tapping on her pipes. She and her mysterious tapper had kept it up for almost an hour, repeating patterns. It had been reassuring to connect with one of the other girls, but they'd been unable to truly communicate. Amanda had tried Morse code, which she'd learned so she could pass her ham radio operator's test, but the other girl hadn't caught on.

She heard the scrape of the deadbolt. Oh, joy, more leftovers. Or maybe she was being allowed another trip to the bathroom. But it was Henry who opened the door.

"Aunt Odell says you can come eat Christmas dinner if you promise to behave like a lady," he said in a deadpan voice.

So, Henry was Odell's nephew. She pondered his invitation for all of five seconds. "Okay, no problem." She would curtsy and apologize to Odell if it meant a chance at real food. Even green beans were starting to sound good.

As she walked out the door and past Henry, he stopped her with a hand to her arm, then softly touched her hair. "You have pretty hair," he said in a gentle voice.

"Uh, thanks," Amanda said nervously, then slipped out of his grasp. She skittered down the hall well ahead of him.

Amanda's outlook improved considerably when she sat down at the long plank table. The turkey dinner smelled heavenly. And Odell actually smiled at her.

They all bowed their heads as Odell said grace. During the interminable prayer, Amanda felt a sharp kick under the table. She managed not to yelp, but she did crack one eye open. The very pregnant girl across from her—Terri?—was staring straight at her, and she looked like she was holding back a grin.

What the—?

Then Amanda understood. Terri's foot found Amanda's again, gently this time, and she tapped out "shave and a haircut, two bits" with her toe.

So Terri was Amanda's restless upstairs neighbor.

When the prayer ended Amanda started to smile at Terri in earnest, but the other girl gave her a stern warning frown and an almost imperceptible shake of her head.

The girls weren't allowed to talk during mealtimes, but surely smiling wasn't taboo! Still, Amanda heeded the warning. Terri had obviously been here awhile, if the size of her pregnant stomach was any indication.

She would have enjoyed the turkey and dressing, mashed potatoes and corn a lot more if Terri had let her. But the girl was determined to communicate something. Each time she thought she could get away with it, she would form a letter with her fingers.

E-c-s-a . . . what the heck did that mean? Amanda wondered.

Terri had to stop when Odell asked her to help clear the table. But during dessert—a mouth-watering pecan pie—Terri resumed her gesticulating: P-e. Ecsape? Oh, escape! So, Terri was a bad speller.

It suddenly dawned on Amanda what Terri was trying to tell her. She thought they should try to escape. Ha, fat chance. Amanda had seen the chain-link fence topped with barbed wire that surrounded this place. She'd seen Odell's shotgun and her two guard dogs. What chance did any of them have against those odds? Sure, she'd like to get out of here, but she'd just as soon not get shot or maimed in the process.

Escape. She shook her head at Terri.

Terri became very agitated after that, so much so that Odell asked her if she needed to visit the ladies' room.

"No, ma'am," she replied distractedly. The moment Odell's attention was off her, Terri started with the letters again. O-r-w-e-d-i—

"Terri, what are you doing?" Odell demanded.

Amanda's heart jumped into her throat.

"My hands itch," Terri complained without missing a beat. "They always do in cold weather."

Odell sighed. "I'll give you some hand lotion before bedtime."

Terri didn't risk any further communications. Amanda tried to make sense of the aborted message. Orwedi. Or wedi. Or we di. Or we . . . *die? Escape or we die.*

A chill ran through Amanda, and the pipe tappings took on a new significance. They would have to do better than "shave and a haircut" if she wanted to learn more about Terri's mysterious warning. Morse code was the way to go, but how could she teach it to Terri?

Odell surprised everyone by passing out a small wrapped gift to each of the girls. Amanda was less pleased with the two pairs of pastel socks than she was with the wrapping paper. Surreptitiously she tore off a small piece, no bigger than a baseball card, and shoved it into her pocket.

She wondered where she would ever find a pen or pencil. Fortunately, Odell unwittingly provided that, too. After the meal was completed, the dishes cleared and the wrapping paper thrown out, Odell sent all of the girls to their rooms for the night. All but Amanda.

As soon as they were alone, Odell set a piece of paper and a pen on the table in front of Amanda. "Are you truly sorry for the way you behaved yesterday, Amanda?" she asked.

"Yes, ma'am."

Odell patted her on the shoulder. "Well, we'll consider it forgotten, if you'll just do one more thing for me. I want you to write a letter to your father. In it, you'll explain that you need some time alone, that you're safe, warm, dry and well fed, and he's not to worry about you."

"But—"

"I'll tell you exactly what to write, and you write it," Odell persisted, forcibly placing the pen in Amanda's hand.

Amanda's next words were barely above a whisper. "You told me my dad knew where I was. But he doesn't, does he?"

Odell didn't answer the question. "We'll sit here until that letter is written," she said instead. "All night, if we have to."

Amanda didn't doubt it. "Okay," she said, forcing herself to sound meek and beaten. "I'll write whatever you want me to. But...could I go to the bathroom first? All that wonderful food on such an empty stomach..." She let the sentence trail off meaningfully.

Odell pursed her lips together in displeasure. "All right. You can use the one right off the kitchen." She escorted Amanda all the way to the bathroom door—to be sure she didn't get into the kitchen knives, no doubt. But Odell didn't seem to notice that Amanda still held the pen clutched in her hand.

As soon as she had some privacy, Amanda made use of the facilities, in case Odell was listening. At the same time, she pulled the piece of wrapping paper out of her pocket and smoothed it out on the tank lid, then began writing on the back as fast as she could: *A,* dot dash. *B,* dash dot dot dot...

Technically Caro had until noon before she was obligated to turn the Arkin case over to CAPERS. But given what she'd learned in Taryton the day before, there was no question that foul play was involved in Amanda's disappearance. So first thing this morning, with the approval of Lieutenant Hall and Sergeant Quayar, she had walked the file downstairs.

To her dismay, Deputy Chief Deacon Raines, who'd been in charge of CAPERS for as long as Caro could remember, had immediately turned the case over to Austin Lomax. She would have much preferred that one of her buddies from the old days, a seasoned investigator she trusted, take over Amanda Arkin. But she knew better than to second-guess the intractable Chief Raines, who had once been her supervisor.

So she was stuck with Lomax—again.

He was talking on the phone when she approached his desk. He saw her, acknowledged her with a nod, then kept right on chatting, forcing her to stand there like a ninny waiting for him. It sounded as if he was talking to a mechanic. It was something about car parts, anyway.

Hoping to irritate him, she started casually inventorying his desk. She picked up a framed photo and examined it. The subject wasn't the wife or girlfriend she'd expected, but a huge Labrador retriever sitting in a vintage Jaguar. She noted three half-empty cups of coffee in various stages of calcification. Only carbon dating would reveal how long they'd been sitting there. A little orange pot contained an anemic-looking sprig of ivy, badly in need of watering. Scott Turow's latest legal thriller lay open on Lomax's blotter, no more than ten or fifteen pages read.

In contrast to the mess on the surface of his desk, his half-open file drawer looked neatly organized, each folder meticulously labeled. She was relieved to see that he was conscientious in that respect.

She idly picked up the novel and began reading the back cover, even though she'd already read the book. A strong hand snatched the paperback out of her grasp and slapped it back down on the desk.

"Do you mind?" Lomax said. "This desk isn't much, but it's all I've got and I don't like other people poking around on it."

"And I don't like cooling my heels while you schmooze with your mechanic about your precious Jaguar."

His eyes, which were a particularly electrifying shade of blue, opened wide with surprise. "Excuse me, but I don't trust my Jaguar to any mechanic. I work on it myself. That phone call was official business—and none of yours, I might add. Who put a burr under your saddle this morning, anyway?"

"You aren't exactly Mr. Sunshine yourself."

"Yeah, well, rough weekend."

"Me, too." That was as close to an apology as either one of them was going to issue, she figured. "I brought you the Amanda Arkin file."

"You mean I get your sloppy seconds again?"

She stiffened in momentary outrage. Her work was not sloppy. Then she realized he was grinning. Teasing her. Trying to lighten the mood. And she'd been about to take his careless comment too seriously. Lately she'd been much too sensitive.

"I guess I'm just not much good with pregnant teenagers," she replied flippantly.

He sobered. "Another pregnant girl? What's the story?"

She told him as much as she knew. He put on his glasses and scanned the various documents, asking occasional questions. He snorted when he saw the copy of the reward flier with which Russ

Arkin had blanketed the city. "Peachy," he muttered. "Have we gotten the evidence report back on the car yet?"

Caro shook her head. "Should be any time. Uh, Lomax, I'd really like to keep a hand in this case."

He looked up over the top of his glasses. "Oh? Why's that?"

"I'm more familiar with it than anyone. And it's . . ." She hesitated, unsure if she wanted to really say aloud what was on her mind.

"What?" Lomax prompted.

She sighed. "It's just that I feel like I failed Marcy Phelps. And now I almost feel personally responsible for Amanda Arkin—like I'm getting a chance to redeem myself. Plus, I think her father has come to trust me, and I don't want to seem like I'm betraying that trust by just shuffling this case off on someone else."

Lomax closed the folder sharply. "I appreciate the offer, Caro, but I work alone."

Oh, brother. Of all the arrogant, stupid . . . What overworked CAPERS detective turned down an offer of help, no strings attached? Plus, she'd heard his partner, Frank Feldman, was out with the flu. Maybe Lomax hadn't been working here long enough to feel overworked . . . yet.

Caro bit her lip until her temper was in check. "Look, Lomax, I don't have any intention of second-guessing your decisions or stealing your glory when the case is solved. But I know how busy y'all are, and I don't want this case to languish from a lack of manpower. So if you need someone to make phone calls or question a witness, or even keep the girl's father off your back, I can do it."

"I'll send up a distress signal if I get overwhelmed," he said with annoying smugness.

"Okay, fine. Then I won't tell you what I learned last night when I dropped by the impound lot to check on Amanda's car. It's unofficial, anyway." She turned and sauntered away from his desk.

Predictably, he followed her. "What? You talked to the Physical Evidence guys? What'd they say?"

"It'll all be in the official report, which you'll be getting any moment. You don't need my input."

"Hey, c'mon, Caro, no fair holding back. What did you find out?"

My, he was even more curious than she'd bargained for. Hungry, that's what he was. Eager to solve a challenging case and make a name for himself. He followed her out the door and up the short flight of stairs while she did her best to ignore him. Before she could enter the Youth Division, however, where Missing Persons was located, he grabbed her arm and halted her.

"I'll report you to your supervisor for impeding an investigation," he said. Although he was grinning, she was half afraid he'd do it.

"I'll report you to your supervisor for refusing an offer of perfectly good legwork."

He seemed to consider her threat. Then he released her arm. "Okay. Since you are familiar with the case, you can assist in a strictly secondary capacity. Just don't make a nuisance of yourself."

"A nuisance? Do you have any idea how many years I worked in CAPERS?"

"Four."

That took the starch right out of her. Austin Lomax had been checking up on her?

"And if you're so hot to work on murder cases," he continued, "what are you doing in Missing Persons?"

"That's immaterial," she said frostily. Her reasons for requesting a transfer four years ago were very personal, and not up for discussion. "Do you want to hear what I found out from PES or not?"

Chapter 5

Austin normally enjoyed driving. His official car was a '90 Ford Bronco, black, which his department had picked up at an auction of vehicles seized in a drug raid. It had plenty of get-up-and-go and was much more fun than the boring four-door sedan he'd had before.

But today driving was a chore. He was already a little nervous about the upcoming interviews. On top of that, the woman riding in his passenger seat was sorely distracting him. It wasn't that Caro Triece was saying or doing anything. But she didn't have to. Her light floral perfume filled the small, enclosed space, reminding him with every breath that she was here, and he wished she were anywhere else.

Austin was really ticked at himself for letting Caro manipulate him the way she had, dangling her little bits of information in front of his nose until he'd lunged for them like a dog after raw meat.

Her information hadn't even been that great. The Physical Evidence folks had found traces of blood and skin on the door of Amanda Arkin's Cavalier, as well as a torn fingernail—probably Amanda's, if the bright pink polish was anything to go by. The evidence indicated a possible struggle in the car. That was really no surprise at this point.

Also found in the car were three medium-length gray hairs, which might or might not have any bearing.

Regardless of what he'd agreed to, Austin hadn't actually intended to include Caro in the Arkin investigation, not in any meaningful way. Unfortunately, he'd made the mistake of mentioning Caro's offer of assistance to the unsmiling Chief Raines. If he'd known Raines was a card-carrying member of the Caro Triece Fan Club, Austin would've kept his mouth shut. But instead of the support he'd expected, Raines had ordered him—*ordered him*—to allow Caro to work on the Arkin case and any other case she took an interest in.

Raines had made no secret of the fact that he wanted Caro back in CAPERS. This was the first time in four years she had shown an interest in anything outside her own small realm of Missing Persons, and Raines intended to take advantage.

"You're damn lucky to have her on your side," Raines had said, tapping Austin on the chest with his finger.

Damn lucky, my ass, Austin thought now. Caro didn't intend to restrict her "helpfulness" to the Arkin case. On his way out of the Police and Courts Building this morning he had run square into her. She'd asked where he was off to in such a hurry, and he'd told her, and before he knew it she was tagging along, claiming a special interest in the Marcy Phelps case, too.

He slowed the car and scanned the house numbers on Amalfi Drive in the modest north Dallas neighborhood where the Phelpses lived.

"It's one more block," Caro said.

He floored it to the next block, found the house number, pulled up crookedly with one tire on the curb and cut the engine. But he didn't get out right away. He took a deep breath and consciously cleansed his mind of everything except the case at hand. The mystery surrounding Marcy Phelps's disappearance and death was his priority now.

He got out of the car, quickly taking note of the yellow ranch house with orange shutters, recently painted. He couldn't say he agreed with their sense of color, but the house was obviously well maintained. The winter-dead grass had been mown and edged in preparation for the colder months, and the shrubs were healthy and neatly trimmed.

"The Phelpses are pretty comfortable, huh?" he commented to Caro.

"They're not hurting." She turned away from him and sneezed twice, then fished around in her purse for a tissue.

"You ought to be home in bed with that cold, instead of running around in this weather," he said. *Instead of bothering me.*

"No time to be sick."

"But plenty of time to hang around where you're not needed." The ill-conceived words were out of his mouth before he could think better of them. He hadn't meant to let his irritation show so plainly.

Instead of jumping down his throat, as he expected, she merely looked him up and down with appraising eyes. "It's true what they say about you."

He wished he had enough self-discipline not to rise to her bait, but he flat out didn't. "Oh? What exactly do they say?" he asked, trying to sound utterly unconcerned.

"That you're a hot dog. You don't want to share the work because you don't want to share the credit when the case is solved. That attitude might have served you well in Auto Theft. In fact, I understand you built quite a reputation in your former position. But things work a little differently in CAPERS."

Austin was well aware of his image, and he liked it just fine. He made a mock bow in Caro's direction. "Thanks for the advice, Corporal, but I fail to see how you should be lecturing me about CAPERS when you haven't worked there for four years. Furthermore..."

He forgot whatever else he was about to say. His first barb had found its mark. The blaze of self-righteousness went out of Caro's eyes and she looked down at her shoes.

"You're right, of course," she mumbled as she headed for the Phelpses' front door. "Come on, let's get this over with. I'll try and stay out of your way."

Austin wished he could take his words back. He preferred a feisty Caro to this more subdued one. It was much harder to resent her presence when she was acting humble.

Mr. and Mrs. Phelps met Austin and Caro at the door before either of them could even ring the bell. "Come in, Corporal Lomax, Corporal Triece, you're right on time," Audrey Phelps said, as if they'd just arrived for a weekly bridge game. She smiled pleasantly, if a tad vacantly. Bob, her husband, also smiled, though not with his eyes.

They were still in denial, Austin thought. As Caro had predicted, they had been close to useless as witnesses when he had questioned them at the station last Friday. And now, with their home reeking from the scent of funeral flowers, they still were trying to act as if their family hadn't been irreparably ripped apart.

"May I take your jackets?" Audrey asked. "Would you care for some coffee? Tea?"

"No, thanks, we're fine," Austin answered for both of them. "I'm sorry to intrude at such a rough time, but I think we'll all sleep better at night when we find out what exactly happened to Marcy."

Audrey's smile faded, and a trace of determination flashed in her tired eyes. "I agree," she said, "but I fail to see how questioning Mindy and Debby will accomplish anything. Corporal Triece, you already talked to the girls at length. They don't know anything. How could they possibly know anything?" The question sounded slightly desperate.

"Anyone in the family might have seen something, heard something, that he or she doesn't realize is significant," Austin said, using his standard spiel. "And we have some new areas to focus on." Like the identity of the man who fathered Marcy's child. "If you'll get Debby and Mindy, we'll finish up as quickly as possible and then get out of your way."

The Phelpses acquiesced, but only reluctantly.

Sitting at the dining room table, with the parents hovering in the kitchen barely out of earshot, Austin questioned Mindy first while Caro sat back and observed. As Caro had indicated, the girl, now a college sophomore, had a superior, condescending attitude. She shared Marcy's fair coloring, but unlike Marcy, she was fashion-model thin and sported a haircut Austin found repulsive. The top part was long and pulled into a ponytail, but everything that grew below the tops of her ears was buzzed so short her scalp showed through.

"I knew the police weren't doing enough," she said before Austin could even fire off his first question. She cast accusing eyes toward Caro as she mouthed off. "All these months Marcy was wandering around, pregnant and probably scared to death, and y'all were hardly looking for her." Mindy pulled a pack of cigarettes from the pocket of her leather biker jacket and lit one, taking a long draw.

Trying to prove how adult she is, Austin mused. She didn't come close to convincing him.

He started to defend Caro's investigation, then stopped himself. Caro had done everything that could be done, so far as he could tell. It didn't matter whether this little snipe believed that or not.

"We have more to go on now," he said. "Our best lead will come if we can find the father of Marcy's baby. As her older sister, you were probably closer to her than anyone. Did she have any boyfriends?"

Mindy snorted. "No. She had a crush on that twerp who's on 'Beverly Hills 90210.' That's as close as she got."

"It may have seemed that way, but obviously that's not the case. She got a lot closer to some boy...or some man. What did she say about the boys she knew in school?"

Mindy studied her purple-polished fingernails. "She didn't talk about any boy in particular."

"How about in general?" Austin prompted.

When the girl didn't answer, Caro spoke up for the first time. "Mindy, you told me you knew your sister better than anyone."

"I did," Mindy said, sitting up straighter. "If she'd had a boyfriend, she would have told me."

"Even though you were away at school?"

"I told you, she called me all the time and wrote me letters."

"Letters." That piqued Austin's attention. "Did you keep any of them?"

Mindy shrugged, but when she answered, her words were uneasy. "Corporal Triece asked me the same thing. I didn't know where they were at the time, but I've found some of them since."

And you didn't see fit to bring that to Corporal Triece's attention? Austin bit the inside of his cheek to keep from snapping the comment at Mindy. By the look on her face, she knew she should have turned the letters over to the police long ago.

Caro said nothing, but the penetrating stare she focused on Mindy was enough to unnerve anyone.

"I can get the letters for you," Mindy offered, her arrogance momentarily subdued.

"I'd appreciate that," Austin replied. "It can wait till we're done here. Now, assuming Mindy didn't have a boyfriend, you do realize that leaves a rather unpleasant alternative."

Mindy nodded, refusing to meet Austin's gaze.

"Please, Mindy, think hard. Was there any male she came into regular contact with—a neighbor, relative, teacher, church youth leader? Whether you think it's possible she was raped or seduced by such a person or not, that doesn't matter. Understand, I'm not going to go charging in making unfounded accusations. But you might be able to give me a place to start."

She was shaking her head even before he finished talking. "No, there's no one."

She was lying, Austin was sure of it. And he was out of his depth. He'd always considered himself a good interrogator, knowing just when to put the pressure on. But his suspects had usually been car thieves, tough street kids with multipage rap sheets, or hardened criminals who would just as soon knife you as answer questions. Leaning on a teenage girl, no matter how tough she pretended to be, was foreign to him.

He had a sudden and very alien desire for help. He looked over at Caro. She'd worked in Sex Crimes for years. From what he'd heard, she knew how to handle suspects, victims and everyone in between with however much sensitivity was needed.

As quickly as the thought materialized, he banished it. Returning his attention to Mindy, who was looking more uncomfortable by the minute, he viewed this moment as just another career challenge. He was good at meeting challenges. This was also an excellent opportunity to prove to Caro Triece that he could handle whatever came along without her help.

"You know," he said, trying to sound casual, "kids are molested a lot more often than people generally think. I mean, my own sister was. By a camp counselor." Never mind that his only sibling was a brother. "The saddest thing is, the kids are afraid to talk about it, and the molester keeps getting away with it, hurting one child after another."

"What are you getting at?" Mindy asked suspiciously.

All right, so much for subtlety. "Look, if this person who raped Marcy is a family friend or relative, he could easily have . . . approached you at some point."

Mindy bristled and her mouth moved into a snarl, reminding him of a dog Austin had once seen facing a skunk. "I have never been molested," she said, hissing the words. "If there is any family friend capable of anything like that—and that's a big if—he's never approached me."

"And what about Debby? She could be next."

Mindy shook her head vehemently. "No way. Debby's smarter than that."

"And Marcy wasn't?"

"Stop putting words in my mouth, okay? This theory of yours is way off base. There's no 'family friend' who would do what you're talking about."

"Then who? Who could have fathered your sister's child?"

There was a pause. "It had to be a stranger. That's the only answer." She crossed her arms and stared at him, daring him to contradict her.

Mindy's parents must have picked up on the change of tone in their daughter's voice, because Bob Phelps put his head through the dining room door. "Is everything okay in here?"

"It's fine, Daddy," Mindy mumbled. She looked up at Austin, her expression almost pleading. "I'll get those letters now, okay?"

Austin nodded.

Audrey and Bob Phelps were even more reticent about allowing the detectives to question their baby. At first they insisted on staying in the room, until Austin assured them he was not in the habit of browbeating ten-year-olds.

"I'm eleven," Debby objected. With brown hair and hazel eyes, she didn't resemble her older sisters at all.

"Are you?" Caro said, smiling. "That's right, you had a birthday recently . . . Christmas Eve, right?"

"Yeah. Don't worry that you missed it, everyone else did, too," she said, issuing a fatalistic sigh.

"I'm afraid we did overlook it," Audrey said apologetically. "What with everything that was going on . . ."

Don't apologize to us, Austin wanted to say as he stared into Debby's sad eyes, seemingly wise beyond her years.

The Phelpses were finally convinced to let the detectives conduct their questioning in peace, and Austin was actually grateful for Caro's presence. It wouldn't have been proper for him to question the child alone.

He soon discovered that Debby was the brightest of the whole clan. Although he suspected no one had spelled out the hard facts of the case to her, she knew all about Marcy's pregnancy. She seemed so well versed that Austin wondered if she'd read the newspaper.

"I'm an aunt, you know," she said, fiddling with a lock of her hair. "If they find the baby, will we get to keep it?"

"I don't know," Austin replied. He sensed that Debby would be even more sensitive than Mindy to any hedging he might attempt.

He went through the same series of questions he'd asked Mindy, and Debby made a seemingly sincere effort to answer honestly. If there was any "favorite uncle" attached to the Phelps family, Debby could shed no light on him.

"Please, think hard, Debby," Austin said. "Has there been any other man present in the house? Even a repairman." He was grasping at straws.

"Well, there was Ray, but I don't think..." Her voice trailed off.

"Ray who?" Austin asked, trying not to sound too anxious. This was a new name.

"Seifert. Mindy's boyfriend." She made a face.

"You don't like him, I take it."

Debby shrugged. "He's gross. He called me 'kid' and 'shrimp' and 'sport,' and he smoked." She pantomimed gagging.

Debby went on to explain that Mindy had met Ray Seifert in college, that he was "old"—twenty-two or -three—that he'd stayed at the Phelps house for a couple of days over Christmas vacation and again at spring break.

"Your parents didn't object to Ray?" Austin asked.

"They liked him okay. Of course, he was completely different around them, real polite, 'yes, ma'am—yes, sir.' Made me want to puke."

"And how did Marcy feel about him?"

"She thought he was cool 'cause he rode a motorcycle. And he showed her a joint once. You know, marijuana. She went on about it for days."

So, Marcy'd had a crush on her older sister's boyfriend. That was something she probably wouldn't have confided in Mindy. And Ray Seifert had been hanging around during spring break. Mid-March. Right about the time Marcy's baby had been conceived.

Austin exchanged a knowing glance with Caro. He was sure she was thinking the same thing he was. A slight tickling at the back of his neck told him he was onto something.

"Were Ray and Marcy ever alone in the house?" he asked.

Debby darted a nervous glance toward the door to the kitchen.

"Debby, anything you tell me will be kept in confidence. We won't tell anyone unless and until it becomes important to the investigation. Nothing we can do at this point will bring your sister back, but you might be leading us one step closer toward finding Marcy's baby."

Debby took a deep breath. "There was one time," she said slowly, thinking it through. "Daddy was at work, Mom was shopping or something, and Mindy left to go get a pizza and a movie at the video place."

"And she left Ray here alone with Marcy?"

"I was here, too, but I was in my room. I didn't like being around Ray."

"So what happened?"

Debby shrugged helplessly. "I don't know. I really don't know. I can't remember."

"Did Marcy say anything about it, or act any differently afterward?"

"No, but she was sick the next day. I remember that because we all went to church, even Ray, except Marcy didn't because she said she didn't feel good. But I think she was fibbing."

"Why?"

"'Cause she was doing laundry! She washed a bunch of sheets and towels while we were at church. No one does laundry when they're sick, do they?"

Austin didn't comment. He busied himself flipping his cassette tape over to the other side, all the while watching Debby's face as she mulled over her memories of those long-ago events and wondered at their significance. Suddenly she grew still, and her eyes widened to the size of half-dollars.

"Corporal, when you have sex, does it mess up the sheets?"

Austin nearly fell out of his chair. He'd never had an eleven-year-old ask him questions about sex before. But what really astounded him was that this little girl had put the clues together almost as quickly as he had.

He sent a panicked look to Caro. She responded with a nod of understanding. "Yes, it does make a mess sometimes," she replied to Debby's question. "Do you think that's what happened? Do you think Marcy and Ray Seifert had sex?"

God, Austin thought, if Debby's parents had any idea of the conversation going on in here, they would chase both detectives out with a meat cleaver.

Debby shrugged. "I don't know. Nobody tells me anything."

"Are Ray and Mindy still dating?" Austin asked, though he was still recovering from the shock.

She shook her head. "They broke up last summer."

Right about when Marcy disappeared.

Austin let Debby go after cautioning her not to talk about their conversation to anyone else, not even her parents, but he didn't think he had to worry about that. Audrey and Bob Phelps didn't seem like the type of parents who were easy to confide in.

"We'd like to speak to Mindy again, if we may," Austin said to Bob Phelps after Audrey had hustled her youngest daughter away—to debrief her, no doubt.

"I'm sorry, but she left," Bob replied, sounding not at all sorry. "We thought you were through with her."

Well, fine. Mindy would just have to make a trip downtown. Maybe in a hot interrogation room, her memory about her former boyfriend would improve.

"Oh, but she did leave you these." Bob handed Austin a stack of letters. "You'll return them, won't you?"

"Yes, we'll return them." But only if they didn't prove useful in nailing Ray Seifert for sexually assaulting Marcy Phelps.

As soon as he and Caro were safely in the car away from prying eyes, Austin issued a gusty sigh. "Okay, what are you waiting for? Where's the 'I told you so'?"

"What do you mean?" Caro asked innocently.

"You know what I mean. I about lost it back there. If you hadn't stepped in, I don't know what I would have said to that little girl."

"Oh, I expect you'd have come up with something. In fact, I thought you handled things rather well. You managed to intimidate Mindy—no easy task—and earn Debby's trust in record time. You didn't need me after all."

Surprised, Austin looked over at Caro, searching her face for some sign of sarcasm. But there was none.

"Thanks," he murmured. Her praise meant more to him than it should have.

Henry liked the new girl, he decided, and that was something. He didn't often allow himself to like another person. Experience had taught him that emotional attachments only led to grief. Hadn't his own mother, whom he'd adored, dumped him on Aunt Odell's doorstep when he was only seven?

He'd always been a troublesome child. He'd been told that often enough. But that final incident, the one that had so upset his mother, hadn't been his fault. He hadn't meant to burn up that cat. It had been an accident. He'd only been trying to scare Whiskers. But his mother, tight-lipped and almost fearful, as he recalled, hadn't wanted to listen to any explanations. She'd simply packed up his clothes and carted him off to his aunt's, and he'd seen her only a handful of times since then.

He hadn't seen much of his father, either, but he didn't care so much about that.

He'd fared no better in school than at home. He'd tried to make friends, like Aunt Odell had told him to do, but none of the other kids wanted to sit with the "retard." Even when he tried to explain that he wasn't retarded, he just had "adjustment difficulties"—a wonderfully adult-sounding phrase he'd picked up from the school counselor—it hadn't mattered. No one wanted to be friends.

There'd been a girl, once. Jenny was a fat girl—really fat—so in a way she'd been as unpopular as Henry. But she was smart, something he admired because he was smart, too, although sometimes he had a hard time proving it. He'd liked Jenny, a little, especially after she started sharing her cookies with him at lunch. Henry loved cookies.

But everything had changed the day he'd tried to kiss Jenny behind the gym and touch her breasts. He thought that's what boys did when they liked girls. But Jenny had slapped him, hard, screaming something about how all boys wanted was sex. He'd tried to explain that he'd only been trying to do something she would like, something that was expected of him, but she hadn't listened. No one ever listened.

Jenny hadn't shared her cookies with him after that.

For years, now, the only person Henry had loved was his Aunt Odell. Not that Odell loved him back. She wasn't his mother, after all. But she'd always been there for him, praising him when he did something right, patient when he made mistakes. He lived for her praise. He knew that someday he would do something so right, so splendidly perfect, that Odell would finally love him.

So it really was strange that Henry found himself liking the new girl, when he knew she was a sinner. Aunt Odell would never approve. But Amanda was different from the rest. Her hair was the prettiest reddish color he'd ever seen, and soft like bunny fur. And her eyes looked like little bits of sky were trapped in there. But it went beyond her looks.

Sometimes she smiled at him. The other girls looked at him with contempt, as if he were dirt on their shoes. But not Amanda. She smiled, friendly-like. He was sure that, if she was allowed to talk to him, she would tell him she liked him, too. And maybe someday she would even let him kiss her and touch her breasts, and more. He'd never forgotten the mistake he made with Jenny, and he wasn't sure whether kissing and touching were sins, anyway.

The last day or two, he'd found himself doing things that he knew would make Odell angry if she knew. He'd stolen one of her pretty-smelling bars of soap and smuggled it to Amanda. And he'd cut Amanda an extra-big slice of the cheesecake they'd had for dinner that night. Somehow, earning Amanda's smile had become the most crucial thing in his life—even more crucial than Odell's mission.

The mission was supposed to be the holiest, most important thing in the world. And for all these long months, it had been. But suddenly, saving the lives of babies—and even punishing their evil mothers, the part Odell didn't know about—didn't seem as gratifying as it once had been. For the first time in his adult life, Henry contemplated a life away from Odell, a life where he could pursue other interests besides saving babies. A life with a girl who could love him.

A life with Amanda.

A little warning voice inside his head came to life. *Don't set yourself up for a fall,* it said. *Don't expect too much of people and you won't be disappointed.* All right, so maybe he was expecting too much. Putting the cart before the horse, as Aunt Odell was fond of saying. But Amanda's smile had to mean something. Before long, he would find out what.

Chapter 6

Chloe Krill sat on the leather sofa in her living room, her feet curled underneath her, waiting for Don to get home. They hadn't enjoyed much time alone since Justin's arrival. But this evening, Justin was staying at his grandmother's house four blocks away. Tonight, she and Don would talk.

Odd little thoughts kept popping up in Chloe's mind, events and circumstances she hadn't thought much about during the exciting months of preparation for Justin's arrival—or perhaps she had deliberately ignored them. But now she found that her memory was suddenly, frighteningly accurate, not to mention persistent.

Travis Beaman was a tax attorney. He did not normally practice family law. Why did he not refer the Krills to another attorney, someone more familiar with cases of this type, to handle the specifics of Justin's adoption?

Even more puzzling, Travis had asked them not to mention the purpose of their visits to any of the secretaries or clerks, except for his own secretary. "Adoption is such a private issue, and I think it's better that as few people as possible are involved," Travis had said, and the Krills had agreed. It had sounded sensible at the time.

But Travis employed some of the best clerical help in the business, and paid them well. Now Chloe wondered...couldn't his staff be trusted to keep matters confidential?

A peculiar instance at a Fourth of July picnic given by the Krills came to mind. Travis and Don had been off in a corner of the backyard, speaking about something in hushed voices. When Chloe approached, they had suddenly stopped talking, and her husband had looked at her with something akin to alarm and, well, guilt. Smiling, she had asked them what they were whispering about. She'd been ready to tease them about talking business at a party. But Don had scowled and told her it was nothing she needed to concern herself with.

Don had never kept secrets from her before—none that she'd found out about, anyway. But something about the way he'd looked at her had warned her off. She hadn't pressed. She had deliberately pushed the incident from her mind.

The two men, who had been friends since high school, had excluded her from talks about the adoption having to do with money, and that had been all right with her. She didn't really want to know. If she'd thought about the money aspect for too long, it would have seemed to her that they were buying a baby.

She wouldn't be thinking about it now if it weren't for Marcy Phelps. Chloe had followed the stories in the paper, greedily reading the columns of newsprint, shorter each day, devoted to the girl's mysterious disappearance and death. She couldn't stop imagining the fifteen-year-old's naked, ravaged body, floating in the freezing water.

Had Marcy held her baby before she died? Had anyone tried to save her life, or had she simply been allowed to bleed to death?

Chloe heard Don's key in the door. Her heart seemed to expand inside her chest, followed by a shortness of breath. This was her husband, for God's sake. They'd been married twelve years. Why did she feel so afraid?

He came in the front door. She heard the familiar sounds of his setting down his briefcase, opening the closet, hanging up his coat. Then he walked into the living room. He was not a large man, nor a classically handsome one, especially now that his hair was thinning. But Chloe had loved him almost from the day she'd met him at her church. Her family had thought she was marrying below her station, but she'd known he would make good with his printing business. And he had. He'd bought her this beautiful house. They had nice cars, clothes, vacations.

And a fifty-thousand-dollar baby.

He started to pass through the darkened room when he saw her sitting on the couch with just the one lamp on, and he froze. "Honey? What's going on? Where's the baby?"

"He's at my mother's. I thought we needed some time alone. We need to talk."

A slow smile spread across Don's face and his stance relaxed. "Just you and me? Alone?" He crossed the room and sat down next to her, touching her hair with one finger. "You look awfully serious."

"This is serious. It's about Justin's adoption."

Immediately he stiffened. "For chrissakes, Chloe, are you going to start that again?"

"Yes, and I'm not going to let it go until I get some answers. You keep brushing it off, like it's not important."

"It's not important. We have Justin. He's our child now, and that's all that matters."

"I don't agree. I want to know about his biological mother."

"She's entitled to her privacy."

"But you know who she is, don't you?"

Don looked away. "I . . ."

"Please, Don, don't lie to me. In all the years we've been married, we've always been honest with each other. It's the whole basis of our marriage. So tell me the truth."

She could see the inner struggle reflected in Don's face. *Please, please, don't lie,* she prayed.

"I know her name," he finally admitted with a sigh. "Travis slipped. He shouldn't have, but he did. Chloe, don't stir things up for her. She's starting her life over."

"Is she?" Chloe asked sharply.

"What do you mean?"

"I mean, judging from the medical fees we paid, the girl had some problems. Did she survive childbirth?"

"I don't know the details of—"

"Yes, you do. Damn it, Don! You do know. You've known Travis longer than you've known me. He told you, didn't he? He told you that Justin's mother is—was—Marcy Phelps."

Don grew very still, and a strange light came into his eyes, the glazed look she had seen in the eyes of an animal frozen by headlights. As quickly as it had come, the light was replaced with anger. Unreasonable anger.

He grasped Chloe's arms in a painfully tight grip, and his voice was almost a growl. "Now you listen to me. I will not sit here and let you interrogate me like some criminal. You will drop this subject. And you won't mention your paranoid suspicions to anyone else."

"Let go, you're hurting—"

He gave her a little shake. "Do you understand?"

"Completely." Dear God, she'd been right. Her suspicions had been a shot in the dark. She hadn't really believed that Marcy

Phelps was Justin's mother. All she'd wanted was for Don to deny it, to reassure her that the adoption had been legal and fair. He hadn't.

Now she would have to take matters into her own hands.

He released her, and his face relaxed into a more normal expression. "Would you like to go out to dinner?"

So, just like that, the subject was closed. How could he calmly sit there and talk about eating? "No. I think I'll go over to Mother's and see how she's getting along with the baby."

"What happened to our evening alone?"

"I'm not in the mood." The words were full of barely suppressed fury. She couldn't remember ever speaking to Don like that before.

He watched her with a troubled expression as she rose and crossed to the closet in the foyer to get her coat.

During the short drive to her mother's house, Chloe realized that any action she took might lead to her losing Justin. That was a possibility almost too horrible to contemplate. But she couldn't rest easy—wouldn't be able to look herself in the mirror—until she knew whether she had adopted Justin at the expense of a young girl's life.

Amanda had to admit one thing—Odell took care of her girls the best way she knew how. After those rocky first few days she had fed Amanda well, made sure she got plenty of exercise, saw to her "spiritual" needs by teaching lessons from the Bible and allowed her eight to ten hours of sleep each night. The only work Odell required of the girls was housekeeping, mending and some light yard work—raking and so on. They were given clothing when they needed it, and daily showers were required.

If not for the fact that they were prisoners, it really wasn't a bad life. And that's what Odell was counting on, Amanda was sure. Because the Good Shepherd Home was relatively comfortable, the girls became complacent, biding their time until they had their babies and would be released. Supposedly.

But Terri had other suspicions as to what fate actually awaited the girls. As soon as Amanda had slipped Terri the copy of Morse code written on wrapping paper, they had begun communicating in earnest—although Terri's spelling was appalling—staying up half the night tap-tapping on the pipes. Amanda had learned that four girls had already had their babies and left the home. But if they'd been released, why hadn't they brought the cops here? That was the first thing Amanda would do when she gained her freedom.

She had to agree with Terri. If those four girls were alive, Odell would have been caught by now. Which of course meant that she and/or Terri had to escape, no matter how acceptable conditions at the Home seemed to be.

So long as it wasn't raining, the girls spent at least an hour each day exercising outdoors. Usually they just walked briskly around the large, fenced yard behind the house, but on this mild and sunny day, Odell had organized a badminton game. This worked out well for Amanda and Terri, because they were able to exchange a few whispered words during the excitement and confusion.

"I think I've figured out the weak link in the chain," Terri whispered as their team rotated positions.

The two girls had already suggested and discarded various plans for escape that ranged from wresting Odell's shotgun away from her to poisoning and electrocution. But Odell's security was too tight, her precautions excessive. Amanda wouldn't have been surprised to learn that Odell was a former prison warden.

Amanda gave Terri a questioning look, waiting for her to elaborate on her new idea.

Terri surreptitiously nodded toward her left and behind her. Confused, Amanda's gaze followed in that direction until it rested on . . . Henry. He stood to the side, watching the game, scratching Phoebe the bloodhound on her wrinkled neck. Although he appeared relaxed, his gun was within reaching distance.

Henry, a weak link? Amanda didn't think so. He was strong as an ox and blindly loyal to his aunt. In Amanda's estimation, they had even less chance of overpowering Henry than they did Odell.

It was Amanda's turn to serve, and the team rotated once again. Terri tossed the shuttlecock to Amanda. "He's sweet on you," she whispered. "Think about it."

She did think about it, the rest of the afternoon and into the evening, and she decided that Terri might be onto something. Although he wasn't obvious about it, Henry did seem to show Amanda a little favoritism. He'd brought her extra soap and lotion, served her generous portions of food and definitely had smiled at her a couple of times.

They couldn't overpower Henry, but if he really did have a crush on her or something like that, perhaps she could use that to her advantage. Bringing her soap was a long way from helping her to escape, but she could subtly encourage him and see where it led. He was a grown man, and he hardly ever left the home, so he probably didn't have a woman. He might be really desperate for some female affection.

Yes, this plan, distasteful as it was, had possibilities. After all, wasn't the sexual urge the strongest of mankind's biological needs? Perhaps Henry's need for intimacy with a woman would be stronger than his desire to please Odell.

The plan wouldn't be without its dangers. Henry had keys to every lock, which meant he could enter her room at will. He could rape her if he wanted to. But she was counting on the fact that Odell was a pious woman and wouldn't condone sexual misconduct under her roof.

As soon as the girls were locked into their rooms for the evening and all was quiet, Amanda removed the metal shade from her lamp and peeled the insulation off the pipes in the corner of the room. It was going to be a long night.

Caro had barely been at her desk five minutes on Wednesday morning, contemplating the impossible list of things she had to do for her own cases as well as Lomax's, when a shadow fell over her. She looked up to see Russ Arkin standing there. If anything, he looked worse than he had on Christmas—more like a vagrant than a prosperous businessman.

She felt terrible for the insensitive way she'd treated him the first time he'd come in. If any man needed a little compassion and understanding, it was Russ.

She managed a smile. "Russ. What can I do for you?"

He dropped a small plastic bag on her desk. "I received this in the morning's mail. It's a letter from Amanda. I probably shouldn't have opened it. I should have brought it directly to the police. But I just . . . had to. . . ."

"I understand, Russ. A letter, huh? Written in her handwriting?"

He nodded.

"That's great! That means Amanda is alive." Or at least she was at some recent point.

"I only handled it by the edges, in case you could get fingerprints off it or something," Russ said.

Caro nodded. "That's good, you did right. You know I'm no longer the lead detective in Amanda's case."

"I know. I talked to that Lomax guy. But I trust you. And you're still helping with the investigation, right?"

"Yes, I . . . you trust me? But I was wrong. I thought Amanda had left of her own accord, and I was wrong."

"It was a fair assumption to make, based on your experience, I imagine. And I was being pretty obstinate. Anyway, you've worked hard on the case and you've been thorough. If they took it away from you, it wasn't because I complained."

"Is that what Lomax told you? That they took the case away from me because I wasn't doing a good job?" That son of a bitch.

"No, no, not in those words," Russ said hastily. "He just explained that since the case was no longer a simple Missing Persons complaint it had been handed over to Crimes Against Persons. That they were better equipped, you know."

Yeah, like they have bigger brains in CAPERS? Caro stifled the illogical negative thought. "About the letter." She opened the plastic bag and peered inside. It contained two loose-leaf pages, folded in half, and the envelope they'd come in. The envelope was postmarked just the day before, December 26, from Kips Point, Texas. "Does Kips Point mean anything to you? Do you know anyone there?"

"No. I never heard of it before today. But I checked a map. It's only about fifteen miles from Taryton."

Good, that would save her the trouble of looking it up. "You read the letter, of course. What does it say?" Caro's hands trembled as she gingerly pulled the pages from the bag by the edges so as not to disturb any latent prints that might still be identifiable.

"You're going to read it, anyway," Russ said as he pulled over a chair and sat down. "See for yourself."

Caro scanned the two pages, penned in a neat and very distinctive style. In it, Amanda said she had left home because she needed to do some thinking, and she had abandoned her car because the license tags were about to expire and she didn't want to be pulled over, and she didn't have money for gas, anyway. She told her father where to find the car, instructing him to pick it up and keep it safe for her. She said she was staying with a friend, that she was safe and warm and well fed, and she would contact her father when she was ready.

Caro read the few paragraphs again. On the surface, it seemed to explain away the circumstances of Amanda's disappearance. But the explanation about the car was pretty farfetched.

"Do you believe this is on the level?" Caro asked. "Is this something Amanda would do?"

"Absolutely not. She would never abandon her car. I mean, if she's staying with a friend, why didn't she just park it in her friend's driveway?"

"Because she knew the police would be looking for the car, and she didn't want them to find her?" Caro theorized, although the scenario seemed unlikely.

"She wouldn't need to go to such lengths. If she wants to stay with a friend, she can stay with a friend. I wouldn't object. But forget about motives and such, and look at the letter again. Don't you notice something peculiar about it?"

Caro did as Russ had asked. "I don't know what you mean."

"Okay, well, I'm no detective, but remember me telling you that Amanda was a state spelling bee champion? Look at the spelling in that letter! 'All right,' a-l-r-i-g-h-t. 'Decision,' d-i-c-i-s-i-o-n. 'Grateful,' g-r-e-a-t—"

"Yes, yes, I see!"

"I think Amanda wrote that letter under duress, and she was trying to signal me with those spelling errors."

"You're absolutely right. I'm ashamed I didn't catch it right away. You have a very clever daughter, Russ. I'll take this down and show it to Lomax, and then we'll take it over to Physical Evidence for tests. You'll have to come with me. They'll want to get a set of prints from you, to eliminate any of yours that might have gotten on the letter—even though I know you were careful."

"Sure, no problem."

"This is great," she said as she placed the letter and envelope in clear plastic document protectors. Unable to contain her enthusiasm, she said again, "This is absolutely great!"

"Do you have to act so damn happy about this?" Russ asked, looking rather disgusted. "My daughter has been kidnapped and is being held captive somewhere, suffering God knows what."

"But she's alive. Frankly, Russ, up until you showed me this, the chances of her being found alive were dropping with every day that passed."

"Oh."

"But now we have another piece of physical evidence. If we can't find fingerprints, the PES folks might be able to trace the paper, though it's a long shot. And we still might be able to track down the guy who abandoned Amanda's car. I'll keep you informed, I promise." She touched his arm, wanting to reassure him. "We'll find her. I swear to God, if she can be found, we'll do it." She stood decisively. "Come on, let's go. It's only a short drive to PES. And when we're done, I want you to go home and eat or sleep or something. Maybe shave, change your clothes? You look awful."

Lomax wasn't at his desk, so Caro took the letter and Russ to Physical Evidence. That chore taken care of, she dropped Russ off at his car, then parked her five-year-old Caprice in the lot by the municipal building. She noticed Austin's black Bronco, parked crookedly in a space that wasn't a real space. Didn't that guy ever park legally?

At least he was at the station somewhere. She couldn't wait to show him the photocopy of Amanda's letter. He would love it. He seemed to delight in finding little bits of evidence and offbeat clues that would shed light on an investigation—like those letters Marcy Phelps had written to her older sister. Caro had started reading them aloud in the car on the way back to the station, and Austin had nearly crowed every time Ray Seifert's name came up. The girl had obviously been smitten with Mindy's boyfriend, and he had become a main candidate for the father of Marcy's baby—and possibly her kidnapper as well.

Problem was, he couldn't be located.

Caro found Austin at his desk, having obviously just returned from somewhere. He still wore his brown leather bomber jacket over faded jeans that flouted the department's dress code. His aviator-style sunglasses were shoved on top of his head, his hair was tousled, and his face was slightly windburned.

He must think he looks pretty sharp driving around like that in his cool, shiny Bronco, she thought, not sure whether she wanted to smile or frown. Nah, on second thought, he didn't just *think* he looked good. He probably had a line of cars with women drivers trailing behind him everywhere he went. He would look even better on the weekends, driving his own car, the silver Jaguar she'd seen in the picture.

She was supremely annoyed to discover she found Austin Lomax attractive. Of course, any human with two X chromosomes would find him attractive. Unfortunately, he knew it.

"Hey, Caro, what's up?" he said as he dumped an armload of file folders and a large white bakery bag onto his desk.

Caro looked at her watch. "Sleep in this morning?"

"As a matter of fact, I was up in Denton," he said cheerfully, ignoring her attempted dig. He was almost as good at that as Tony. "Ray Seifert was seen at his old address less than a week ago. The Denton police have agreed to stake the place out. Oh, and get this. He has another sexual-assault charge pending against him. Sixteen-year-old."

"Hot damn. He's our man," Caro said, forgetting her earlier peevishness. She watched as Austin removed a huge cinnamon roll from the bag and took a bite out of it. "Do you have any idea how much butter is in one of those things?" she asked. "Your arteries aren't just going to harden, they're going to petrify."

"Yeah, yeah, I know. I brought an extra one for you."

"You did? Oh, good, hand it over." She was hungry, she realized.

"Any particular reason you're lurking around my desk this morning?"

"Mmm, yeah. Geez, this smells wonderful." She chewed and swallowed her first bite of cinnamon roll before continuing. "Russ Arkin received a letter from his daughter this morning."

Austin's eyebrows flew up. "No kidding? And you had to wait until my hands were good and sticky before you told me. Where is it? What's it say?"

Caro repeated the text of the letter from memory as best she could, then explained about the spelling errors and Russ's feelings about the matter.

Austin was duly impressed. "You already took it over to PES?"

"I didn't want to waste any time. I should have brought you a copy."

"That's okay, I trust you. I'll see a copy of it later."

That was the second time that morning someone had told Caro they trusted her. Illogically, it made her feel warm inside. Or maybe that was just the cinnamon roll.

She wiped her hands on a paper napkin. "Well, I guess I better get back to—" She halted as Austin's phone buzzed.

He picked up the receiver. "Corporal Lomax."

She started to walk away. She had a million things to do, and apparently so did he. But he snapped his fingers at her, and when she turned he gestured impatiently for her to come back. His expression was intense as he listened to his caller.

"Who is this?" he said, motioning Caro closer still. He angled the receiver away from his ear, silently inviting her to listen in.

Since he was perched on the edge of his desk, she had to lean in to bring her ear close to the receiver. She placed her hand on his shoulder to steady herself. And through the receiver she heard a woman's voice, muffled.

"You'll have to speak up. I can't hear you," Austin said. Caro could feel the warmth of his breath against her cheek.

"I can't tell you who I am," the woman said in a terrified voice. There were sounds of heavy traffic in the background. "I just wanted you to know that Marcy Phelps's baby is fine. He was adopted by a good family—"

"By you?" Austin demanded.

"Y-yes. But there was something illegal or wrong about the adoption."

"I think that's fairly obvious, given the circumstances surrounding Marcy's death."

Caro punched him on the arm. Now wasn't the time to play tough cop! The woman was frightened, ready to hang up at a moment's notice. In fact, she reminded Caro of some of the rape victims who would call the police, unsure of whether they should even report the offense.

"Look, this is all very interesting," Austin continued, oblivious to Caro's nonverbal criticism. "But if you're trying to help me find the person responsible, I'll need more information."

"Couldn't you just…you know, check up on people who do that kind of thing?"

"You mean, illegal adoptions? We don't exactly have a list of that type of offender. I'll need more information. A lawyer's name, something."

"I can't."

"Why not?"

"Because you'll take him. You'll take my baby away from me."

"Now, ma'am, no one's going to—"

The line went dead.

Caro realized then that she was plastered to Austin's body, clinging to his shoulder like a tenacious frond of ivy. The phone conversation had been stimulating for more reasons than one. She disentangled herself and took a couple of steps backward, trying her best to look disapproving.

"I suppose you could have handled that better?" Austin asked, lifting one eyebrow skeptically.

She shrugged. "Oh, probably not."

"You think it was on the level?" he asked, more seriously this time.

"Yeah, I do."

Suddenly he was all business. "Okay, our mystery lady told us more than she thinks she did. Given the sounds of traffic and sirens in the background, she was calling from a big city. We can hope that means the call was local. If the adoption took place in Dallas, there must be a record of it. Don't they file new birth certificates when a baby is adopted?"

"I think so," Caro said. "What about the court records for the adoption itself? I know the original birth certificate and the information about the birth parents would be sealed, but maybe not the adoptive parents."

"Great. Why don't you go to Vital Statistics and the courthouse, and wherever else you can think of. Start with December 13—that's the earliest Marcy could have died, according to the ME, and move forward. Male white babies."

"Okay, I'll..." She put her hands on her hips and cocked her head to one side. "Did I just hear you order me to go pawing through birth certificates and court documents?"

"Uh-huh. You wanted to help, remember?"

"Yeah, I remember. Just so *you* remember. Scott Humphrey is supposed to be back from his vacation today. I'd planned on bringing him in for questioning."

"You want to take his statement?"

She did and she didn't. It had been a long time since she'd grilled a suspect. Questioning witnesses, that was one thing, but if Scott was responsible for Amanda's disappearance... "You're the lead detective now. You do it."

"Okay."

She started to walk away, then paused. "Say, Lomax, a silly thought just occurred to me. If someone had Marcy stashed away some place, and then virtually sold the baby in a highly questionable private adoption..."

"Yeah?"

"Do you think that same person might have... Nah, it's too ridiculous."

"Go ahead, please. What are you thinking?"

"Well, do you think that same person could have Amanda stashed away, intending to sell her baby?" Caro's gaze caught and held with Austin's as he considered her theory.

After a moment he broke eye contact and walked over to the wall, where a large laminated map of Texas was hung. "Okay, here's Taryton, here's Kips Point, and over here is the dam where Marcy's body was found. They're about a hundred-and-fifty, two hundred miles apart."

"But both areas are east of Dallas—east, southeast, whatever—and both girls are from Dallas and ended up in the boonies...." Caro's voice trailed off. Okay, she was stretching it.

To her surprise, Austin took her seriously. "Can you think of any other similarities between the two cases? Aside from the fact that both girls were pregnant?"

"Well, they both disappeared without a trace. But Marcy was out riding her bike. The bike was never recovered. And Amanda, of course, was in a car, and the car was found. The two girls were in totally different parts of Dallas. And there was never a letter from Marcy or anything like that. So, no, I'll have to say the cases are more dissimilar than similar."

Their gazes locked again, and then she slowly shook her head. "Nah," they said together.

"See, I told you it was silly," she said before grabbing the rest of her cinnamon roll and walking off.

Chapter 7

Caro dialed the Humphreys' number from memory. They were supposed to have returned from their skiing vacation the day before, but she'd gotten no answers to the intermittent phone calls she'd made yesterday.

As she listened to the phone ringing on the other end, she mechanically popped two cold capsules and searched the top of her desk for her teacup. Failing to find it, she swallowed the pills dry. Her head cold was lingering, probably because she hadn't gotten a decent night's sleep in over a week.

Thoughts of Amanda and Marcy kept her awake or invaded her restless dreams. Sometimes it was Russ Arkin's pain-filled eyes or Audrey Phelps's vacant smile that haunted her. Last night, for some reason, she'd dreamed about Austin. She didn't remember the specifics of the dream, only that he had posed some kind of life-or-death threat to her.

So now she had another reason to dislike him. He was giving her nightmares.

Caro's box of Kleenex wasn't where it was supposed to be. She finally spotted it two desks away from hers. She was just about to hang up the phone in defeat and lunge for the tissue when someone answered.

The sleep-scratchy voice sounded as if it belonged to Dr. Humphrey.

She sniffled. "Is Scott there?"

"May I ask who's calling?"

"Yes, this is, um, Brandy, a friend of his from school."

"Scott's here, but he's asleep. Can I have him call you?"

"Yes, he has my number." Caro hung up quickly. So, the kid was finally home. She relished the idea of pouncing on Scott while he was drowsy and unsuspecting, so she could gauge his reaction.

And the parents' reaction. Would they be genuinely surprised to hear of Amanda's disappearance and their son's possible involvement? Or did they already know? Did they have his alibis all worked out?

She supposed she ought to check with Austin to see how he wanted things handled. That was annoying, and it shouldn't have been. He was the lead detective on the Arkin case, and he was doing a perfectly competent job. The fact that she was merely assisting shouldn't bother her, either. During her years in CAPERS she had often played a supporting role in her colleagues' cases. But for some reason Caro was itching to grab the bit in her teeth on this one and run with it.

Was Tony right? she wondered. Was she bored with Missing Persons and subconsciously yearning to be back in CAPERS?

The idea held a certain appeal—until she really thought hard about it. Working on felony cases like homicides and rapes, she would again be actively involved in interrogations, testifying in court. Sometimes she would make mistakes, and guilty men would go free. That was an unpleasant fact of police life, something she could live with. But what about the innocent ones who got caught up in the justice system and were hurt by it? That was the part she had trouble with. She couldn't stand the idea that her zeal for police work could hurt people . . . even kill them.

That's why she'd refused when Austin had asked if she wanted to interrogate Scott. She strongly suspected the kid was somehow involved in Amanda's disappearance, but she wasn't up to the task of extracting that information from him. She'd had a hard-enough time with those two joyriders in Taryton, who should have been a piece of cake.

She ought to be relieved that Austin Lomax was in charge. By merely assisting, she could exercise her rusty investigative skills without making those tough judgment calls.

Her phone buzzed. Before she answered it, she scooted over to retrieve her box of tissue.

"Corporal Triece."

"Caro, it's Austin. Whatcha got for me?"

Ah, she'd almost forgotten that she'd left a note on his desk earlier that morning. Pride washed through her as she recalled her previous day's success. "I think I have the identity of Marcy Phelps's baby."

"You're kidding."

"What, you didn't think I could do it?"

"Well, it seemed like a long shot, with as little as we had to go on."

"It really wasn't that hard." Just sweet-talking a judge into issuing an investigative subpoena, then hours and hours of tedious research, going over zillions of court cases and birth certificates, tracking down attorneys, narrowing down the field of candidates, until only one was left.

"So, who is it?" Austin asked impatiently.

"I'll come downstairs," she replied before hanging up. She knew Austin hated to be kept in suspense. By the time she reached his desk, he would be frothing at the mouth, making her moment of revelation all the more enjoyable. If she was right, they were on their way to finding the person who'd last seen Marcy alive.

She met Tony coming into Missing Persons as she was on her way out. "Hey, Tony, you still want to come with me to pick up Scott Humphrey?"

"Scott . . . oh, the Arkin girl's boyfriend." Tony smiled wickedly. "Sure, I'll tag along and scowl, if you think it'll help. You believe he did it?"

Caro shrugged. "Dunno. He loosely matches the description of the man who tried to sink Amanda's car in the river."

"And you're hoping."

She sighed. "It sure would be nice to find her. Alive."

"Do you think there's much chance of that?"

"Since her father got that letter, yeah. I mean, why would the perp go to all the trouble of having her write a letter if he was just going to kill her? He wants us to stop looking for her."

Tony cocked his head and blew a huge, purple bubble. "We might have stopped looking, if not for finding her car. But have you considered that the perp might be using the letter to mislead us as to the time of death?"

The possibility hit Caro like a bucket of cold water. "You mean, he coerced Amanda into writing a postdated letter, killed her, then mailed the letter days later?" Unfortunately, Tony's idea made sense. "But if that's the case, we're not dealing with any ordinary crime of opportunity or passion here. We're talking about a cold and calculating murderer who meticulously plans his every move."

"A guy without a conscience," Tony said morosely. "Makes me think of Ted Bundy, or someone like that."

Psychopath. That word, a barely whispered echo in Caro's mind, gave her a chill. "I think we're getting ahead of ourselves," she said with deliberate casualness. "Let's just see what our Scotty has to say. Can you leave in a few minutes, as soon as I give this stuff to Lomax?"

"Sure, whenever."

Caro's optimistic mood was completely shot. Why hadn't she considered the time-of-death angle? Was it because she wanted so badly to find Amanda alive? She was doing it again, becoming too passionate about a case. And she knew better! Letting herself get too close, emotionally, to an investigation would only impair her judgment.

She ought to wash her hands of it—both the Arkin and the Phelps cases, in fact, before she got herself in too deep and messed something up. Yes, that's what she would do. She would hand over the paperwork on Marcy Phelps's baby, pick up Scott Humphrey as she'd promised, then return to her comfortable world of runaway teenagers and deserting spouses. She couldn't deal with psychopaths or crazies of any variety, not anymore.

Once upon a time she'd relished the prospect of tearing into a rapist or child molester, ripping his story apart in the interview room until he was sobbing, begging her to leave him alone. No more. She'd lost that hard edge. And she'd decided long ago she didn't want it back.

"So, who and where is Marcy's baby?" were the first words out of Austin's mouth the moment he spotted Caro striding purposefully toward his desk. Today she was wearing baggy black trousers tucked into red cowboy boots, and a plaid flannel shirt big enough to cover three women. Rather than disguising her diminutive size, as she probably intended, the getup emphasized her fragility.

Caro laid a stack of photocopies on his desk. "He's in Highland Park."

Austin gave the photocopies hardly a glance. "How do you know?"

"I'm not a hundred-percent sure." She looked at Austin's steaming cup of coffee. "Let's go to the break room. I need some tea."

Austin nodded, gritting his teeth. The more anxious he appeared to hear Caro's story, the longer she would drag it out. She seemed to enjoy torturing him.

"I went through all the district court records for adoptions that took place after December 13," she explained as they walked down the hall and into a small kitchen that held a row of vending machines, a microwave, and a few tables and chairs. The room always smelled vaguely of popcorn.

She poked around in the sink until she found the mug of her choice, with a black-and-white cat on it, continuing her story while she washed the cup, filled it with water and stuck it in the microwave. "Given the ME's report, December 13 would have been the earliest possible date of birth."

Austin resisted the urge to remind Caro that he already knew that. In fact, he was the one who'd told her to use December 13 as the cutoff date. But if he started arguing with her, she would never finish her story.

"I threw out all the girls," she said, "then all the boys born before December 13, then all the nonwhites—that's another assumption, by the way. Who's to say the father of Marcy's baby wasn't black or Hispanic or green or purple with spots?"

"But he was probably white," Austin said. "Marcy simply didn't come in contact with many green-and-purple men—or any other color, for that matter."

"That's what I figured. I just wanted to point out that my methodology isn't foolproof."

"I understand. So you considered white babies only."

"Right. By then I was left with a group of twenty or so, and I went to the Records building and started looking up birth certificates on microfilm."

Austin winced. Just five minutes of watching microfilm speeding across a screen gave him a splitting headache. Suddenly he was immeasurably glad he'd drafted Caro for this chore, even if he did have to drag the details out of her. "And?" he prompted.

"I checked for the hospital and attending physician, figuring Marcy didn't have benefit of either. I mean, even if she wandered out of a hospital or was spirited out, it would have been reported."

"Right, I follow."

"So I came up with two nonhospital births, attended by midwives. I contacted one by phone. She assured me she remembered the birth in question, that there were no problems, and she had done a follow-up visit with her patient."

"And she could be lying."

"If she was, she was a good liar. But you're right, it's possible."

"Go on. What about the other one?"

"Her signature on the birth certificate was an illegible scrawl."

"And that's your prime candidate, right?"

"Right. Justin Krill."

"Krill?" Austin grew very still. "The adoptive father isn't by any chance Don Krill, is he?"

"Yeah, that's him."

Austin felt a headache coming on. He must have made a face, because Caro jumped to defend her conclusion.

"I don't blame you for being skeptical, but look at the place of birth. River Rock, Texas. I checked a map. It's a hundred and fifty miles from the Cedar Creek dam. In Texas, that's not all that far."

Austin nodded. "I've actually been through River Rock. It was on the way to my grandmother's."

The microwave buzzed, and Caro went about fixing tea.

Austin pulled a couple of quarters out of his pocket and got some Sno Balls—pink, coconut-covered cupcakes—from the vending machine. "River Rock is about a three-hour drive from the Cedar Creek dam. Actually, Cedar Creek is closer to Dallas than River Rock. And it seems to me the perp wouldn't have reported the real birthplace on the certificate, anyway."

"You think I'm reaching, don't you?" Caro asked.

"I hope you are."

She frowned. "Why do you say that?"

"Don Krill. You know who he is, don't you?"

"Yeah . . . city council, right?" She blew on her tea to cool it.

Austin was mesmerized for half a second, watching her puckered lips. He shook his head to clear it. "Krill is only about the third most politically powerful individual in all of Dallas, behind the mayor and city manager. To even suggest that his newly adopted child is part of some black-market baby scam—"

"Is that so bad? He could be useful if we decided to open the lid on this and get the media involved. We could get all the coverage we wanted."

"Jeez, Caro, what rock have you been living under? Krill hates the police. He and Chief Livingston can't say a civil word to each other. Krill actively lobbies against any city employee pay raises, including ours. If we come nosing around, insinuating that his kid was born to a runaway teenager who died in childbirth and whose body was dumped in a lake, he'll find a way to shackle us. He might even manage to get us fired, who knows?"

"Is he really that ruthless? I mean, you sound like you've tangled with him before."

"I have. Remember two years ago when we got our new contract with the city? I was one of the union representatives involved in the negotiations. Krill acted like a real bastard. It was in the paper."

"I guess I didn't pay much attention to that stuff," she said with a shrug.

"Anyway, to answer your question, he *is* that ruthless. And he's no dummy. If his wife knows where the baby came from, you can bet Krill knows. And he's not about to volunteer any information that will get him into trouble."

"All right, so we can't confront Don Krill till we have more conclusive evidence. Why don't we approach his wife? She's the one who's suffering pangs of conscience."

"And she'll do what she has to to keep her child. No, I'd say she'll be even more dangerous than her husband if she's cornered. Anyway, she'll call him at the first sign of trouble."

Caro nodded, then thought for a moment. "Okay, how about the lawyer who handled the adoption? He's probably closer to the source, anyway."

Austin thought about this approach. "Maybe. Do you have his name?"

"It's Beaman, I think. Travis Beaman. It's in the photocopies."

"You want to check him out?" Austin asked, wondering just how far he could stretch Caro's generosity.

"I would, but I have to go pick up Scott Humphrey. He's finally back from vacation. Unless you want to go."

Austin considered that option. "I've got a lot going on here. As long as you can scare Humphrey, I'd rather you go."

She stood up straighter. "I can scare him. Anyway, Villaverde's going with me. The way he stares with those black eyes, he'll scare the pants off the kid."

"Okay. Sure you don't want to question Scott once we get him here?"

"Positive." She answered too quickly, and her eyes widened for just an instant, almost like she was spooked by the idea of conducting an interrogation. She clasped her hands around her cup and headed for the door. "Oh, and I really won't be able to give you much more help on these cases. We're shorthanded in Missing Persons, and Sergeant Quayar says she's gonna bust me back to foot patrol in Deep Ellum if I don't quit foisting my work off on Villaverde."

As they walked back down the hallway, Austin didn't know whether to be relieved or disappointed. He hadn't wanted Caro's help in the first place, but she had proved useful. He never would have had time to dig through all that paperwork. "Well, if you're really that busy—"

"Don't pretend to be sorry, Lomax." There was a sharp edge to her voice. "Now you don't have to worry about me 'getting in your way.'"

Had he really said that? He touched her arm, halting her before they reentered CAPERS. "Look, I was way out of line when I said you'd be in the way, okay? I appreciate all the help. And if you change your mind . . ." He let the sentence trail off when Deputy Chief Raines sauntered out into the hall.

Raines stopped midstride when he saw Caro. "Well, hello, lady," he said, smoothing his thinning gray hair with the palm of his hand—primping, Austin thought, irritated. "It's a downright pleasure to see your face in these parts again."

"Hi, Chief." Caro smiled warmly. It occurred to Austin that she'd never smiled at him like that. "I'm only up one flight of stairs."

"Then you ought to visit more often," Raines said. "I've been meaning to thank you personally for stepping in and helping out. Poor Lomax here has been given quite a baptism of fire with two such high-profile, pain-in-the-butt cases when his partner is out with the flu. I know he appreciates help from a seasoned pro like you. Right, Lomax?"

"Yes, sir." Jeez, Louise! He hadn't been made to feel like such a bonehead since his rookie days. It wasn't as if Caro had any seniority over him. In fact, he'd entered the police academy a year ahead of her, and they'd both gone into investigative work at about the same time. He'd checked. It just so happened he'd spent eight years in Auto Theft, while she'd sharpened her detective's teeth in Sex Crimes.

"I'm glad I could be of assistance, sir," Caro said. "But I was just telling Corporal Lomax that I need to be focusing on my own job at the moment. Tony Villaverde has been taking on some of my load, and I really can't—"

"Nonsense. I'll fix it with Quayar and Hall. We need your help, Caro."

"I'm flattered, really," she said. "But I think Austin has things well in hand—"

"And far too much legwork to handle on his own. The media folks are watching us, and I want both of these cases given top priority. If that means extra personnel assigned to them, then so be it. I don't want any mistakes made." Raines was looking at Austin when he said this, but Caro was the one who winced and rubbed her stomach, like she was working on an ulcer.

"I understand," Austin said resignedly.

The Chief turned to Caro. "What about you? Can I count on you?"

"Yes, sir," she answered, looking just short of miserable.

Raines beamed. "Fine, fine. Keep me posted."

Caro shrugged after Raines went on down the hall. "I tried."

"I know. I thought you wanted to work on these cases."

"I did. I mean, I do." Her answer didn't hold a lot of conviction.

"Is there a problem?"

She shook her head, crossed her arms over her breasts and avoided his gaze. "No, no problem. I'll let you know when I get back with Scott Humphrey." With that she turned and practically fled down the hall and away from him.

Russ Arkin had prepared Caro for the reception she was likely to get from the Humphreys, who used their money to insulate them from all unpleasantness. But she was still surprised by the garish display of wealth.

Their house, which backed up to the Las Colinas Country Club golf course, was obscenely huge and grotesquely modern in blinding white stucco and smoked glass. Tony pulled his LTD into the driveway and parked behind Scott's black Porsche, which was next to a Rolls-Royce.

"You do the talking. I'll just scowl," Tony said.

"Sounds like a plan."

The doorbell played Westminster chimes. Caro half expected a butler to answer, but the distinguished, silver-haired gentleman dressed in a silk robe who opened the door was no doubt Dr. Humphrey himself. His face was noticeably red from windburn.

He frowned and looked down his nose at them. "Yes?"

Caro flashed her shield. "I'm Corporal Carolyn Triece with the Dallas Police Department, and this is Corporal Anthony Villaverde. Is your son Scott at home?"

Dr. Humphrey immediately puffed up his chest. "What's this about?" he demanded importantly.

"We're investigating the disappearance of Amanda Arkin, and we would like to question Scott."

"Amanda's missing?" The man exhibited surprise, but not concern. "Surely you don't think Scott knows anything. We've been on vacation for the past week."

"Could you go get Scott, please?" Tony put in, using his best Sergeant Friday deadpan voice. Caro silently thanked him for his perfect timing.

"He needs to come down to the station with us so we can take his statement," Caro added.

"This is preposterous!" Humphrey blustered. "You can't just come barging into a private home and make demands like—do you have a warrant or anything?"

Ah, he thought he was so clever. Dr. Humphrey apparently believed that his money and supposed intelligence placed him and his family above the law. Caro relished her next question. "Do we need a warrant? I assumed Scott would gladly cooperate in helping us find his girlfriend."

Humphrey wavered. A woman Caro assumed was Mrs. Humphrey appeared, also dressed in a silk robe but with her blond hair perfectly coiffed. It looked as if she, also, might be windburned under her makeup, but Caro couldn't be sure. "Roger, what's going on?"

"Go get Scott," the doctor barked. "We'll get this cleared up right now."

That's what you think. Caro exchanged a secret look with Tony and bit her lip to keep from smiling. "May we come inside?" she asked pleasantly.

"No, you may not. Scott will be with you in a minute." He closed the door in their faces.

"I hate this guy," Caro said. "I hope all the neighbors are watching out their windows when we take Scotty away. Let's try and look like cops so they'll all know."

Tony chuckled. "You have a mean streak, Caro."

Moments later the door reopened and Scott himself appeared, heavy-lidded and in need of a shave. Caro did a lightning-quick assessment of his appearance, comparing him to Chucky's description of the man who tried to sink Amanda's car in the river. He was a big, burly guy, with a roundish face and medium brown hair. Uncombed as it was, his hair could be described as "choppy," Chucky's word. Unfortunately, he also had chapped lips and cheeks and a red nose. Damn.

"Tell them, Scott," Dr. Humphrey said.

"Look, I don't know anything about Amanda's disappearance."

"You didn't know she was missing?"

"Well, yeah, I knew she'd split, but I mean, I don't know how or why or anything."

"And you were so concerned about her you went on a skiing vacation."

"There was nothing I could do."

Dr. Humphrey jumped in. "I don't like your tone, young lady."

She took a step forward until she was almost nose-to-chin with him. "You know what? I don't care what you like."

Tony placed a restraining hand on her arm. Nice touch, she thought. Tony was good.

"Lena, call Mark Glashier—now," Dr. Humphrey said. "Scott, don't you utter another word until our attorney gets here." He gave Caro a penetrating look. "I know he's allowed to have an attorney present. You didn't bother to inform us of that fact."

"I'm not arresting Scott . . . yet. I'm under no obligation to inform him of his rights. Do you think he needs an attorney?"

Dr. Humphrey didn't answer.

"Your attorney can meet us down at the station, second floor, the old Police and Courts Building on Commerce. We'd like you to come with us, Scott."

"Not unless you have a warrant," Dr. Humphrey said.

"You'd like us to arrest him?" Caro asked incredulously. "Is that what you're saying?"

"Dad," Scott broke in, "I'm going with them. If there's any way I can help them find Amanda, I will." He looked at Caro. "Can I get my jacket?"

He sounded so sad and resigned, Caro had a hard time maintaining her head of steam. "Sure."

He reached into a closet in the entry hall and came up with a blue ski jacket, which he donned as he headed out the door.

Caro opened the back door of the LTD so Scott could climb in. As he did, she noticed the handful of bits of colored paper hanging from the zipper of his jacket. "What are these?" she asked as she inspected them, although she already knew.

"Lift tickets. We just got back from Vail last night."

She looked at the tickets one at a time. December 24. December 25. December 26. Damn, damn, damn. Unless he was awfully damn clever, he was in Colorado the night Amanda's car was abandoned.

Chapter 8

It was Amanda's turn to do the dishes. When dinner was through she gathered a stack of plates from the table and went obediently into the kitchen. This might be her best chance—or her only chance—to talk to Henry, as he was in charge of kitchen cleanup. Odell had taken the other girls into the den to watch a video, their reward for good behavior during the day.

Amanda didn't really care about the movie. It was some religious film, anyway. She was just glad that Odell was safely occupied.

"The pecan pie was good," she said in a low voice when she was sure she and Henry were out of everyone's earshot. "Did you make it?"

Henry set a stack of dirty dishes on the counter next to the sink. "Yeah. Aunt Odell taught me to cook good. She said since I probably wouldn't ever be married, I should learn how to do for myself."

This was one of the longest speeches Henry had ever made in Amanda's presence. It was almost a relief to hear someone besides Odell talking. "Why does Odell think you won't get married?" she asked, although the answer was fairly obvious. Henry was weird. Creepy. He had odd facial tics, and sometimes he made faces and grimaces for no reason. Occasionally he muttered to himself, too.

"Because I'm different," he said, smiling self-consciously.

As she ran hot, soapy water into the sink, Amanda pretended to be confounded by his explanation. "Different, how?"

Now he actually blushed. "You know, I don't talk so good and I make faces. People don't like me."

"Just because you make faces? That's silly. It's what's on the inside that matters. Whether you're a good person."

"That's what Aunt Odell says. She says that because I'm helping her with her holy work, I'll go straight to heaven."

"What holy work is that?"

"You know, with you girls. She stops you girls from killing your babies." He said this in a soft, almost reverent voice. "Were you going to kill your baby, Amanda?"

She thought very carefully before answering, unsure how much he already knew about her. She didn't want to get caught in a lie at this point. "I thought about having an abortion. You know what that is, right?"

"It's when you kill the baby inside you."

"Yes, but some people don't believe a baby is a baby until it's born. So it's not really killing."

"They're wrong."

"Yes, I think maybe it is wrong. I had already decided I would let my baby be born. But of course, Odell didn't know that when she . . . when she took me."

Henry stopped scraping the plates into the garbage. He grew very still, and then a slow smile spread across his face. "I knew it. I knew you were different from the others. I tried to tell Aunt Odell that, but she said you were a sinner."

"Everyone is a sinner at one time or another," Amanda pointed out. For once, she was grateful for her strict Catholic upbringing. The nuns had instilled her with enough ammunition to hold her own in any discussion of this nature. "But Jesus taught forgiveness," she continued. "The important thing is whether we learn from our mistakes, and whether we're sorry or not. Isn't that right?"

Henry screwed up his face, as if he was thinking hard. Then he looked at Amanda and asked, very earnestly, "Are you sorry?"

She nodded and bit the inside of her lip as hard as she could until moisture formed in her eyes. "Yes, I am. I should never have had...relations with the boy who fathered my baby. He didn't love me, he just said he did. He's the one who made me go to that awful clinic where Odell found me. But I couldn't go through with it. And I don't ever want to see that boy again." She silently apologized to Scott.

"I'm glad," Henry said.

They worked in silence for a while, with Amanda washing and Henry drying. Phoebe, the bloodhound, lay on the floor and watched them solemnly. Henry's shotgun leaned against a corner of the room, reminding Amanda that this brief episode of camaraderie was only an illusion.

"Henry," she said, breaking the quiet, "what does Odell do with the babies?"

"She gives them to parents who will love them."

"Oh. Oh, dear." Amanda injected a note of alarm in her voice as she placed a protective hand over her abdomen.

"Don't you want that? Don't you want your baby to have a good home?"

"Yes, but . . . well, *I* want to give it a good home. I had decided to keep the baby, you see. My father was going to help me with the money and clothes and food, so the baby would have the best of everything. And then, someday, I would meet a nice man who would love me and my child, and we could get married and make a family. . . ." Her voice broke, and she sniffled loudly.

Henry said nothing, but his brow was pulled low as he stacked plates and put them in the cabinets.

"Do you think," Amanda ventured, "that Odell would let me keep my baby?"

Henry shook his head. "I don't think so. See, the babies bring in money to help run the home. We get . . . fees, you know, from the couples who get the babies."

Amanda was appalled, though she did her best to hide her reaction. Not only was Odell drugging and kidnapping teenage girls, she was profiting by selling their babies! The woman was a monster.

Now Amanda began crying in earnest, amazed to find out she could summon tears at will, even without biting her lip. "But I want to keep my baby." She paused dramatically. "Hey, I know. Maybe she could just let me go. Then she wouldn't have to feed me or buy clothes for me. I wouldn't tell anyone about her, I promise. Could you talk to her, Henry? Could you explain?"

Henry placed a tentative hand on Amanda's shoulder. "Don't cry, Amanda," he said, looking genuinely distressed. "It'll be okay. You can have other babies when you get married—lots of them."

"But I want this one. I already love it. It's part of me. Or maybe that's something men can't understand."

"I understand." He nodded energetically. "But I can't talk to Odell. She don't listen to me. And she won't let you leave. No girl has ever left the home, not till after they have their babies."

"And then what happens to them?" Amanda couldn't help but ask.

Henry withdrew his hand, much to her relief, and shrugged. His lack of response made her shiver.

Amanda dried her tears with her dishcloth. "Won't you help me, Henry? I think you're the only one around here who cares what happens to me, my only friend. Won't you help me keep my baby?"

Henry frowned. "I'll think on it. I'm pretty smart, you know."

"I know. And thank you." She stood on tiptoe and kissed his cheek, struggling to keep her revulsion under wraps.

Henry turned bright red. "I'll finish up in here. You can go watch the rest of the movie with the others."

As Austin drove the ten minutes or so to the law firm of Smith, Clovis and Beaman, he mentally reviewed his earlier phone conversation with his brother, Dean, who worked in the DA's office. Dean had told him that Travis Beaman, who had handled Justin Krill's adoption, was a senior partner in a high-profile tax law firm. The firm was well established, but due to the lousy economy, it didn't have the herd of wealthy clients it once did, and several associates had been let go in the past year.

Travis himself had an impeccable reputation. He was in his late forties, reputedly in good health, married with no children.

It was unusual that he was the attorney of record for an adoption, though not shockingly so. Most adoptions weren't terribly tricky from a legal standpoint, and Beaman had probably handled it personally at the request of the adoptive parents. Apparently he and Don Krill were good friends.

Austin had thought long and hard about how to approach Beaman. If Justin Krill was really Marcy Phelps's baby, Beaman wasn't about to let that fact slip out. The lawyer would have covered his tracks well. If, however, the whole adoption was legitimate, Beaman might be a good-enough guy to allow Austin a peek at the confidential adoption file—especially if he was worried about Austin's suspicions being made public. Austin would be able to eliminate Justin as a candidate and concentrate on the other adopted babies on Caro's list.

Smith, Clovis and Beaman occupied the entire eighteenth floor of the Southland Life Building. From the ankle-deep, sage-green carpet to the solid cherry paneling and antique brass accents, the firm's decor quietly screamed affluence—although there was an empty wall in the waiting area where a painting had once hung.

Austin felt sure the receptionist, a classy redhead with upswept hair and a demure blue dress, had been hired as much for her looks as anything. Or maybe it was her name. A discreet nameplate identified her as Ms. Dubois.

"May I help you?" she asked in a honey-smooth voice.

"I'm Corporal Austin Lomax with the Dallas Police Department," he said, trying to sound quietly ominous as he offered his badge. "I'd like to see Travis Beaman, please. Is he in?"

She checked a list on her desk. "He's in. I don't suppose you have an appointment?"

"No, but I won't take much of his time. And it's a matter of some urgency."

The redhead smiled knowingly, dimpling her cheek, then picked up the phone and talked with someone Austin presumed was Beaman's secretary. "You're in luck," she said when she'd concluded the conversation. "He's in conference, but he'll be done in about fifteen minutes if you'd care to wait."

"Thanks, I would."

Fifteen minutes turned into thirty and then forty-five, and Austin was tempted to blow the whole thing off. This might be nothing but a wild-goose chase, after all. But it occurred to him that Beaman might be deliberately testing his patience, hoping he would go away. So Austin held his ground.

At last the great attorney deigned to see the lowly detective. His secretary—another very attractive woman—led Austin through a maze of hallways, past offices and work stations that appeared oddly quiet and deserted. Man, Dean hadn't been kidding when he'd said the firm had laid some people off.

Beaman occupied a corner office, naturally. The secretary tapped discreetly on the door, opened it without waiting for a reply and ushered Austin inside.

The Cowboys could have held scrimmages inside the office. Austin had never seen anything so ostentatiously huge. He thought about his own little cubbyhole, with its cheap government-issue desk and bare tiled floor, and he wondered if he hadn't gone into the wrong line of work.

The man himself was unremarkable looking, with thinning, iron-gray hair and an expensive suit that did a good job of camouflaging his girth. He had wire-rimmed glasses and good teeth—or maybe they were capped.

"Good afternoon, Officer Lomax," Beaman said, standing behind his massive, carved mahogany desk and offering his hand. His smile was pleasant but distant as he indicated a delicate, antique-looking chair across from him. "Have a seat. What can I do for you?"

Austin almost pointed out that he was Corporal Lomax, not Officer. But he decided not to start out on the wrong foot by antagonizing Beaman. "Thanks for seeing me," he said instead, shaking the lawyer's hand. He sat down in the chair, which was much too delicate for even a man of his moderate size. He wondered if the chair had been chosen deliberately, to make clients feel uncomfortable and vulnerable so they would cough up more money.

"I know you're busy so I'll keep this brief. I'm investigating a case with a possible connection to one of your clients, and I believe you're in a position to clear it up quickly."

"I'll do what I can, of course," Beaman said, "but you realize I can't violate my clients' confidentiality."

Austin nodded. He'd figured as much. "The case I'm working on involves a teenage girl who died in childbirth and whose body was dumped in a lake. You're probably familiar with it." Austin watched Beaman closely.

"You're talking about that Phelps girl," Beaman said. His face and voice reflected nothing but calm assurance, but he fiddled with his coat button. "What possible connection does she have with this firm?"

"The police have reason to believe Marcy Phelps's baby was illegally adopted. It's possible the adoptive parents, and even their lawyer, didn't know the circumstances surrounding the child's birth."

"Their lawyer...meaning me? I'm primarily a tax attorney."

"But you've handled at least one adoption. Justin Krill."

Beaman abruptly dropped any semblance of civility he'd previously shown. "I handled that adoption as a favor for a friend. And you had better not go nosing around the Krills and upsetting them. God knows they've been through enough pain."

"That's why I came to you first. If you can prove, to my satisfaction, that the child wasn't born to Marcy Phelps—"

"For heaven's sake, Justin Krill's biological mother is personally known to me. She's the daughter of a friend of mine. I knew the Krills were trying to adopt, and I got the two parties together and handled the adoption as a favor. Now, is that all?" he said dismissively.

"What's her name? The biological mother, that is."

"I can't tell you that. I'm legally obligated to protect her privacy."

Austin sighed impatiently. "Mr. Beaman, I can get a subpoena that will allow me to search your records," he bluffed. "I have enough evidence. I was hoping you would make this easy."

"Look, I don't know where you ever got this crazy idea that Justin Krill is Marcy Phelps's baby, and I would like nothing better than to open the Krills' file and show you how wrong you are. But to do so would open me up to a lawsuit. So you just go and get your court order. Make a fool out of yourself. I really don't care. Now, if you'll excuse me, I have better things to do than discuss nonsense. Ms. Paladin will show you out."

The lovely Ms. Paladin opened the door at that precise moment, having been summoned by mental telepathy, it seemed. Her demeanor was noticeably cooler as she escorted Austin to the reception area.

Austin had thought he might hit up the secretaries for information. But neither Ms. Paladin nor Ms. Dubois appeared overly impressed with his status as a detective. Hell, a firm this prestigious probably paid the help well enough that they knew better than to divulge secrets, anyway, no matter how romantic the notion of assisting with a police investigation.

Austin left Smith, Clovis and Beaman with no more evidence than when he'd entered. In fact, from an intellectual standpoint, Beaman had been very convincing as the outraged attorney falsely connected to a crime.

As soon as he returned to the station, Austin sought out Caro. She was probably back with Scott Humphrey by now, and Austin was eager to see what he could get out of the kid. He was disappointed to find Caro's desk empty. The dry-erase board over Sergeant Nona Quayar's desk reported Caro as out to lunch.

"You looking for Corporal Triece?" Quayar asked. "If it's important, I'll beep her. She's probably across the street at Dave's Dive, although I don't see how she can stand that barbecue. Snout sandwiches—ugh." For a large woman, Quayar was able to shiver with amazing delicacy.

"She and Tony Villaverde were supposed to pick up a suspect for me," he said.

"Oh, right. He's come and gone."

"Who questioned him?" Austin asked, bewildered.

"Corporal Triece, I think. I'm sure if she'd learned anything mind-boggling, she'd have let you know right away."

Now, that was odd. Caro had been dead set against interrogating Scott. What had changed her mind?

"She's riding with Corporal Villaverde. If you can't reach her on the car phone, I'll beep her."

"It's not that important," Austin said with a dismissive shake of his head. "I'll catch her later." He was amazed at how eager he'd been just now to share a little bit of noninformation with Caro, to see her reaction, get her feedback. Less than a week ago he'd simply wanted her out of his face.

Raines was right about her. She had a quick mind, even if she was a little prickly, and she obviously hadn't forgotten the lessons she'd learned working in CAPERS. But she was also accustomed to running her own investigations. If Austin wasn't careful, she'd be trying to grab the reins away from him. He decided he needed to back off, or next thing he knew his co-workers would be thinking he couldn't solve a case without hanging on to Caro Triece's apron strings.

When Austin returned to his own desk, he found about a zillion messages to deal with. He flipped through them disinterestedly until he reached one that grabbed his full attention. It was from a Sergeant Norm Wiggs of the Denton Police Department.

Without even taking off his jacket, Austin picked up the phone, dialed the number and asked for Sergeant Wiggs. *Please, let this be good news,* he prayed. He wasn't disappointed.

"Corporal Lomax? Yeah, we got your man. Ray Seifert showed up at that house where he used to live. He's in custody and he'll be arraigned this afternoon. We don't have a prayer of getting bail denied on this type of sexual assault, so if you want a crack at him—"

"I'll be there in forty minutes." Yeah, he was definitely in the right line of work.

Odell ushered an obedient Amanda into her room and locked the deadbolt. There, that was the last one. All of the girls were snug in their rooms for their afternoon rest period, and Odell would have a few minutes of blessed peace.

Sometimes the stress of maintaining order and discipline among the ten teenagers gave her splitting headaches. Every night she would drop into bed exhausted, dreading the morning. Sometimes she even wished she didn't have to be so harsh with the girls. But then she would remind herself that they were sinners.

Amanda was coming along nicely, Odell thought with satisfaction as she made her way toward her small office, her daytime sanctuary. After those first couple of shaky days, during which Odell was convinced Amanda would be another troublemaker like Terri, the girl had settled down and was now one of the home's most pleasant, well-behaved residents. Odell wished all of them could be like Amanda.

When she reached the office, she unlocked the desk, pulled out her cellular phone and began checking in with her answering services. She had one in each of the major cities of Texas—Dallas, Fort Worth, Houston, Austin and San Antonio. Also in each of those cities she had a contact person who could provide her with names and addresses of young pregnant girls considering abortions. One was a school counselor, but the rest worked at abortion clinics, either as nurses or psychologists.

Odell was very selective about which girls she ultimately brought to the home, and she never took too many from any one area, so that no discernible pattern would develop. Currently she had two from each city.

The home was filled to capacity right now. Terri would be leaving soon, however. The girl claimed she'd conceived toward the end of May, but Odell suspected the baby was closer to term than that. She needed to start thinking about replacing Terri.

She was surprised when the Dallas answering service gave her a message from her brother. Now, what would he want? Since Travis never contacted her except in a dire emergency, she returned his call right away.

"Odell," he said. As always, there was never any affection or emotion in the greeting. He kept the conversation brief and to the point. "I don't know how it happened, but the police are onto us. Somehow they've connected me and the Krills to our little Marcy Phelps."

"Oh, God." Odell barely breathed the words.

"Why in the hell didn't you do a better job of disposing of that girl's body? You could have buried it in the woods, where it might never have been found."

"Please don't curse, Travis. You must understand that the girl needed a Christian burial," Odell said quietly, but with absolute conviction. "If the poor child has any hope of escaping the fires of hell—"

"I appreciate your compassion. But we can't take that kind of chance anymore, not with things heating up like they are."

"Yes, I agree."

"Look, it might not be as bad as we think. The cop who came here was just fishing. He didn't know anything for sure, and I certainly didn't give him anything to work with."

"But how do you suppose the police got your name in the first place?"

"I don't know. Even if they did manage to unseal the adoption records, Justin's biological mother is listed as 'Patricia Smith.' I guarantee you Marcy's name was never mentioned around this office."

"Who else knew?"

"Just Don Krill, and he knows better than to tell anyone. Even his wife doesn't know. I'll talk to him, though. Odell... maybe we should stop."

"No," she said flatly. She slipped off one of her orthopedic shoes and massaged her foot.

"But we've already found parents for four children, and there are at least six girls at the home who are too far along for abortions. That's ten in all."

"Thirty-four. We have to save thirty-four. Or don't you remember?"

"I don't remember the exact number, not the way you do. We were just children back then." She could hear the weariness in his voice. They'd had this argument before. Travis had never felt as guilty as Odell about their sins.

"Maybe you were a child, but I wasn't," she reminded him. "I was twenty-three when I assisted with the last one." Odell's stomach churned and her heart pounded every time she recalled that sweating, moaning teenage girl and the five-month fetus she had delivered. The baby, no bigger than a potato, had writhed briefly before dying. Odell's father had placed it in a paper sack.

She remembered each case just as vividly, in horrid technicolor. And every day of her life, she regretted that she hadn't put an end to the slaying. She could have. But she'd been frightened, so frightened, because she had helped. Travis had helped, too.

Odell had started assisting her father when she was sixteen and too ignorant to understand exactly what was going on. She wanted more than anything to be a nurse, and at first she was so excited that her father was letting her help that she didn't question why those ladies came to their house instead of her father's office.

Then one day she'd figured it out. And when she'd confronted her father, he'd told her they would all go to jail if she opened her mouth. She'd been so timid and gullible, so in awe of her father, that she'd continued to assist him with his devil's work, all the while dying inside.

The idea for the Good Shepherd Maternity Home had come to her several years ago—a way to atone for her sins. She had assisted in killing thirty-four babies. If she saved an equal number from the abortionist's knife, perhaps she could yet see the kingdom of heaven. And perhaps she would no longer be tormented by the nightmares.

The preparations had taken years. She'd had to develop contacts, renovate the old farmhouse, obtain a gun and learn how not to be afraid of it. And she'd had to depend on Travis for a lot of money. But her scheme was working, and it would continue to work, at least for a while. She wouldn't let it all go until she had no other choice.

"You never really believed you could save all thirty-four, did you?" Travis asked, jerking her back to the present. "We've known all along that sooner or later the police would catch on to you, no matter how many precautions we took."

"I was hoping it would be later rather than sooner."

"We're lucky to have gone this far. It's a miracle none of the three girls you've released so far have been able to lead the police straight to you."

"They can't lead the police to me when they have no idea where the Good Shepherd Home is. They're drugged when they come here, and drugged when they leave. Henry drives them hundreds of miles away before he puts them out of the car."

"But don't you think it's odd that we've never heard anything on the news, or read anything in the papers, about those girls being found?"

"There've probably been stories in their hometown papers," Odell reasoned. "None of them was from Dallas. Only Marcy, and we've heard plenty about her."

"I still think we should quit while we're ahead. We could let the girls go and leave the country. Lord knows there's not much left here to stay for. I don't know how much longer this firm will be able to hold off the creditors."

"I'm not ready to give up yet," Odell said. "Let's wait and see if there are any more problems. Maybe this will wash over. I can't help but believe the Lord is watching over us, protecting us."

"I don't know, sis. This is getting a lot more uncomfortable than I'd bargained for. I never dreamed the police would start to catch on from this end."

Odell didn't like this wavering in her brother's attitude. "Just make sure you have those new parents in line. Terri Zamasko could give birth at any time."

"Look, Odell, I'm getting pretty tired of you ordering me around—"

"Ah, here's Henry," Odell interrupted. There was a pause. "Would you like to speak to your son? Or perhaps you'd like me to bring him up for a visit. I know your dear wife would be thrilled.''

Silence greeted her taunting. Finally Travis spoke again. "You've made your point. All right, we'll continue a little longer. Like you said, maybe the trouble will wash over."

But just in case, Odell planned to save as many babies as she could in whatever time she had left. She would stop being so selective about the girls she brought to the home. She would put two to a room, if she had to. Whatever it took.

Chapter 9

After her hasty lunch of barbecued chicken and iced tea at Dave's, Caro threw on her quilted jacket and reluctantly headed back across the street. She was bummed out about Scott Humphrey. Since he'd demonstrated to her satisfaction that he was not a suspect in Amanda's case, and since Austin wasn't anywhere to be found, she and Tony had gone ahead and taken Scott's statement. He had confirmed everything Russ Arkin had said, and he had added absolutely nothing new. That meant the Arkin investigation had slowed to a crawl.

Preoccupied as she headed up the long flight of stairs into the Police and Courts Building, Caro wasn't prepared for an assault. But as she reached for the door handle, she found herself grasped by the shoulders and thrown up against the wall—not hard enough to injure her, but certainly with enough force to make her yelp in surprise.

"Why did you pick up Scott Humphrey and interrogate him like some common criminal?" Russ Arkin demanded, his face twisted with fury. "I told you he had nothing to do with Amanda's disappearance."

It was all Caro could do not to level the guy. Somehow she managed to respond calmly. "I did what any competent investigator would do under the circumstances. And you're right, he had nothing to do with Amanda's disappearance. I knew he was innocent five minutes after I started talking to him. But I had to find that out for myself. And if you don't take your hands off me, I'll have you brought up on assault charges."

Her threat garnered no response from Russ.

"Mr. Arkin, if you don't let go, I'll knee you in the groin so hard you'll be a candidate for the Vienna Boys Choir."

That seemed to shake him loose. He looked down in surprise, first at one hand, then the other, as if he couldn't believe what he was doing. Trembling, he gradually loosened his hold.

"That's better. I know you're distraught, Russ. I know you're going through hell. I think about it all the time. And we're doing our best."

He stared at her through bloodshot eyes. "It seems your best isn't good enough."

"Sometimes it isn't," she agreed with a sigh. Just then she spotted Austin standing a few feet away, watching them alertly, apparently ready to intervene at a moment's notice. She shook her head, indicating she didn't need any help.

He approached, anyway, an unwelcome distraction.

"Russ, you remember Corporal Lomax, don't you?" Caro asked, nodding toward Austin. The sudden burst of civility seemed out of place.

"Yeah, sure, how are you?" Russ said in a wooden voice, offering his hand in a perfunctory shake.

"Look, why don't we all go inside?" Caro suggested. "We can sit down, have some coffee and Austin and I will—"

"I was just on my way out," Austin interrupted, "and I'm kind of in a hurry. And Caro, I need you to come with me."

"Oh, but—" she started to object.

"It's okay," Russ said. "I shouldn't be here wasting your time like this, anyway. I didn't expect it to drag on like this...." His voice cracked and a sheen of moisture formed over his eyes.

He looked so pitiful that Caro couldn't help herself. She touched his arm, then squeezed it gently. "I won't give up on Amanda. Don't you give up, either. Call me tomorrow morning, and I'll bring you up to speed, okay?" It wasn't like her to offer hope and optimism in a case like this. It especially wasn't her style to intimately touch a man she wasn't close to. But Russ's utter dejection got to her. She'd never seen such pain in a man's eyes.

He pulled away awkwardly. "Thanks, Caro. Sorry for the...you know, for acting like an ass."

"It's okay."

As Russ turned to leave, Austin was already grabbing Caro's hand to drag her down the stairs toward his Bronco, which was parked illegally on the street. "You're a strange lady," he said with a laugh. "First you threaten to turn the guy into a soprano, then you get downright mushy with him. Sounds like love to me."

"Can it, Lomax," she said in disgust, then reconsidered. "So you saw the whole thing?"

"Pretty much."

"And you didn't feel compelled to 'save' me?" His self-control surprised her. Most men, even her colleagues, refused to believe she could take care of herself. What she lacked in brute strength, she made up for in quickness.

"I figured you could have turned the guy into mincemeat if you'd wanted to. Jeez, I can't believe he was stupid enough to assault a cop in front of a police station. He could have gotten himself shot." Austin opened the passenger door for her—not out of any sense of chivalry, but for expediency, Caro figured.

She unlocked his door from the inside as he walked around. "He's not thinking too clearly, poor guy," she said as Austin climbed in. "He really loves his daughter. It's kind of refreshing, in a way." She automatically fastened her seat belt. "Am I entitled to know where we're going? Or is this some clever ploy so you can drag me to your den of iniquity and have your way with me?"

The silence stretched uncomfortably as he started the engine. Finally he turned, giving her what could only be described as a leer. "Nice thought, but when I said I needed you, that's not what I meant. We're going to Denton. The police there picked up Ray Seifert this morning."

"All right! That's the best news I've had in days." Her enthusiasm quickly gave way to wariness. "What do you need me for?"

"They won't be able to hold him for long after his arraignment. I tried to get an arrest warrant for the sexual assault on Marcy, but the judge wouldn't go for it, not based on the admittedly iffy testimony of an eleven-year-old. Without the victim's testimony, there's no hope of making the charge stick. But we can still take a crack at him."

Not on a bet. "You can crack all you want. Leave me out of it, please."

He gave her a sideways look. "Were you, or were you not, once known as the Terror of the Sex Crimes Unit?"

She forced a laugh. "That was a long time ago."

He was silent for a few moments as he negotiated downtown lunchtime traffic. As soon as he was headed up the I-35 on-ramp, he continued. "You can't have forgotten everything. Anyway, I've never in my life questioned a sexual offender. I don't want this messed up."

She stared at him, her mouth hanging open. "Wait a minute. Did aliens invade your body and replace your brain?"

"Huh?"

"You're actually asking for my help? A week ago you didn't want me within a hundred feet of you or your cases."

"Yeah, well, a week ago I thought I was going to solve both these cases in record time and get a medal or something." He shook his head and gave a short, self-deprecating laugh. "Now I'm starting to look downright incompetent. I'd be crazy not to take advantage of your expertise in this type of situation."

"So I'm supposed to make you look good?"

"Yeah," he answered without hesitation.

The man constantly amazed her. At least he was honest. "Well, sorry to disappoint you, but I have no intention of interrogating Ray Seifert. You might as well take me back to the station."

"I can't. Don't have time."

"Hell," Caro muttered. "Give me the phone. Sergeant Quayar is going to have a fit."

He pulled his portable cellular phone from his pocket and handed it to her. "Don't worry. Chief Raines talked to Quayar and Hall. You're cleared to work with me whenever I need you."

Just what I always wanted, she thought as she dialed the number. "Sergeant Quayar? This is Corporal Triece. I'm being kidnapped by Austin Lomax—"

Austin took the phone out of her hand and put it to his own ear. "This is Corporal Lomax. Triece and I are on our way to Denton to interrogate a suspect in the Marcy Phelps case. That's not a problem, is it?" He listened a moment, then nodded. "Good, good. I really appreciate your loaning her to me. She's been a big help. Thanks." Then he laughed. "You got it, Nona," he said before disconnecting.

"You call my sergeant 'Nona'?"

"We worked the same beat over in Southeast for a while before she transferred to Youth Division. She's a crack-up."

"Quayar, a crack-up? I always thought her face was made of stone."

Austin grinned. "She smiles for me."

Yeah, and so does most of the world's female population. Austin probably had conquests all over the department.

"So, you want to tell me about it?" he asked casually.

"About what?" Caro didn't think he was talking about Sergeant Quayar.

"Why you refuse to question Seifert."

She squirmed a little in her seat. "Interrogations aren't my cup of tea, that's all."

"You questioned those kids in Taryton. And Scott Humphrey."

"The kids were witnesses, not suspects."

"And Scott?"

She filled him in on what she'd discovered about their previously prime suspect. "Anyway, you weren't there. I didn't handle any of the interviews very well."

"You found out what we needed to know."

She shrugged. How could she explain that a rape suspect was a whole different thing? Yeah, she'd once been the Terror, all right. And she'd terrorized one poor man right into his grave.

"Fine," Austin said, the single word clipped.

They rode in silence for thirty minutes or so, with Caro growing more uncomfortable with each mile they traveled. She'd seldom seen Austin truly angry with anyone. She was the one with the hot temper. Normally she didn't back off an argument this easily. But, oddly, she found herself wanting to appease him. She actually felt guilty for making the affable Austin mad.

"There's a part of me that comes to the surface when I'm dealing with a rapist or a murderer," she began cautiously, "and it's a part I don't like."

"Look, you don't owe me any explanations—"

"Apparently I do."

He flexed his arms and squeezed the steering wheel until his knuckles turned white, then relaxed. "Only if you want to."

Hell, maybe she *should* talk about it. It amazed her that no one in the department had connected Charlie Northcutt's death with her transfer to Missing Persons. But they all had their own problems, she supposed.

The only person she'd ever told was the staff shrink, and somehow his attempts to absolve her of guilt had been less than effective.

"Have you ever been afraid of something inside you?" she asked Austin.

He thought for a moment. "You mean, like when I'm at the firing range, blasting away at a target, and I'm fantasizing about taking down some poor sucker, and I realize that not only am I capable of killing, but that I might even enjoy it a little? Is that what you're talking about?"

She studied him, gauging his sincerity. Maybe he would understand. "Yeah, something like that."

"They say all humans have a killing instinct, and it just takes the right conditions to bring it out. It's a part of being human. But it does scare me sometimes. Did you...I mean, you never killed anyone, did you?"

"Yes. Oh, not with a gun or a knife. It wasn't that swift or sure." She stopped, uncertain whether she could continue.

"Tell me about it," Austin said. It was not a demand, but a gentle invitation, one Caro felt compelled to accept.

She took a deep, steadying breath and plunged in. "You might remember the case. Charlie Northcutt. He was in his twenties, borderline mentally retarded, lived with his mother. He was convicted of raping and impregnating a thirteen-year-old neighbor girl. The girl picked him out of a lineup, and subsequently he gave a full confession. Within six months of going to jail he killed himself—"

"Oh, yeah, I remember now," Austin said. "After he died, the supposed victim recanted her accusation. Said she never even had intercourse with the man, that it was her boyfriend who got her pregnant and she made up the rape so she wouldn't get in trouble. Sad case." Austin shook his head, then glanced over at Caro. "I take it you were involved somehow."

Even four years later, the memory filled her with self-loathing. But she forced herself to admit what she'd done. "I interrogated Charlie Northcutt for six hours. I didn't let up on him for one minute. I didn't let him see his mother, which was all in the world he wanted. He was scared to death, and I loved it."

Austin took the Oak Street exit and waited patiently for her to continue.

"I browbeat the man until he was in tears, begging me to leave him alone. And then you know what I did? I told him that if he wanted to see his mother, all he had to do was confess and I'd let him go. Then I led him step-by-step through the confession. By then he would have admitted to anything if he thought it was what I wanted to hear."

Austin said nothing, but he reached under the seat and retrieved a box of tissue, which he laid on the seat beside her. It was only then she realized her cheeks were wet with tears.

"Damn," she muttered as she grabbed a handful of tissues and mopped her face, then blew her nose. She had never, in eleven years on the force, cried in front of a fellow officer. At home, in bed, in the dark, yeah, but not on the job. "You mention this to anyone, Lomax, and I'll...I'll..." Hell, she couldn't even think of a decent threat.

He smiled as he pulled up in front of the Denton police head-quarters. "My lips are sealed." He cut the engine, and then he did something that totally flummoxed Caro. He reached over and smoothed a lock of her hair behind her ear in a gesture that could only be described as a caress. "So, you helped send an innocent man to jail. It happens. We're trained to go into every interrogation assuming the suspect is guilty. And ninety-nine percent of them are. It sounds to me like you were just doing your job—and doing it well."

Caro blew her nose again, acutely aware of Austin's hand resting lightly on her shoulder. "Yeah, I was good at my job," she said, her voice muffled by the tissue. "But I enjoyed it just a little too much. It's like what you were talking about. All cops believe they can kill, if they have to. But what if we find out we enjoy it? I had not one ounce of compassion for that poor man. I was no better than a...a Neanderthal, feeling that surge of triumph as he kills a wild animal with a rock. If doing my job well means losing my humanity, I don't want any part of it."

"And I still maintain that the killing instinct is part of our humanity. As long as we control that instinct, and channel it into socially acceptable avenues, we're okay."

"What I did to Charlie Northcutt was not socially acceptable by anyone's definition."

"I think you could be wrong about that. You know how faulty human memory is. Just try questioning three different people who all witnessed the same accident. You've probably built that scene up in your mind until you think you behaved like some kind of monster. It couldn't be as bad as all that, or Northcutt's attorney would have made a stink about it."

"Yeah, maybe," she replied, unconvinced.

"C'mon, we've got work to do."

"Go ahead. I'm staying here."

He didn't argue with her. Instead he climbed out of the car, calmly walked to the passenger door and jerked it open, then reached across her and unfastened her seat belt. "Stop whining and get out of the damn car. If you don't want to interrogate Seifert, then at least be there to coach me. Or don't you want to find out who kidnapped Marcy Phelps?"

"You know, Lomax, you can be a real ass at times." But she was smiling as she said it. And she got out of the car.

Ray Seifert gave new meaning to the term "hostile witness." He was obviously well acquainted with the procedure of being interrogated. With his lawyer a comfortable two feet away, Seifert wasn't about to admit anything. His expression was smug, his answers glib, and he made Austin all too aware of the killing instinct. He wanted nothing more than to fit his hands around Seifert's scrawny neck and throttle the truth out of him.

But Austin conducted his questioning by the book. "How did you feel when Marcy's body was found?"

The smug smile abruptly fled Seifert's face, and his complexion paled noticeably. "She's dead?"

"Do you mean to tell me you didn't know her body had been recovered?"

"No! I told you, man, I've been up in Oklahoma for the past month, working my ass off twelve hours a day on a construction job. I don't read the papers, and if it was on TV I missed it. What happened to her?"

"I thought you could tell me."

"Whoa, wait a minute. If you're trying to pin her murder on me you can just forget it. I've been up in Oklahoma for weeks, and I got a lot of people who'll swear I never left until last night."

"That's interesting. You're providing an alibi for her murder when I haven't even told you when she died."

"When did she die?"

Either Seifert was genuinely upset, Austin thought, or he was good at faking it. "Around the middle of December, give or take a few days."

"I was on the job twelve hours a day, seven days a week. I didn't even have a car, man. I'm telling you, I haven't seen the girl for months."

"When was the last time you saw her?"

"I already told you, it was some time before Mindy and me broke up. April or May. It was way before Marcy disappeared."

Austin stood up and began to pace. "I suppose you don't know anything about Marcy's baby, either." He watched Seifert's face closely. He noticed that Caro, too, had stopped filing her nails and had grown very still.

Seifert's eyes widened in surprise. "Marcy was pregnant?"

Suddenly Caro was out of her chair, slapping the palms of her hands on the tabletop and leaning menacingly toward the suspect, reminding Austin of a cobra. "Of course she was pregnant, because you got her that way."

"Whoa, whoa, wait a minute," Seifert said. "I didn't have nothing to do with that."

"Oh, yeah?" Caro said, almost nose to nose with Seifert. Even the attorney was unconsciously backing away from her. "That's not what Debby Phelps says. She was listening at the bedroom door that day you raped Marcy. You remember, don't you? That day during spring break when Mindy went to the video store and you decided to get yourself a little from her baby sister?''

"Hey, that girl was no baby," Seifert objected.

Austin sent up a silent prayer of thanks. Seifert had just as good as confessed. Caro sat back down, and the lawyer whispered a few frantic words into Seifert's ear.

"She was no baby," Seifert repeated. "But I didn't rape her."

"Debby Phelps says you did," Austin said, continuing the interrogation. He chanced a look at Caro, but she was back to filing her nails, glancing up every few seconds.

"Debby Phelps is a little girl with a big imagination," Seifert said. "I can't believe you'd even listen to her."

"Fortunately, we don't have to rely on her testimony," Caro interrupted again. "When Marcy found out she was pregnant, she promised you she wouldn't tell anyone. But she didn't keep that promise."

Damn, but Caro could bluff, Austin thought. He would remember never to play poker with her.

"She confided in her teacher, Melanie Blaylock," Caro continued, idly tapping her nail file against the tabletop. The lawyer whispered something else to Seifert—probably reminding him that Melanie Blaylock's testimony would be hearsay evidence and not admissible in court.

Caro went for the kill. "And then there's the baby. When we catch up with him—and rest assured, we will—a DNA test will prove you're the father. It seems to me, Ray, that you had a very good motive for kidnapping little Marcy and stashing her away someplace where she couldn't slap a paternity suit on you. It's the only motive we've got. So you better tell us the truth now. Getting caught in a string of lies won't look good to a jury."

Seifert conferred briefly with his lawyer before responding. "Okay, look, I had sex with Marcy, okay? Consensual sex."

"Ray," the lawyer interrupted, "I don't think you should—"

Seifert became very agitated. "They're trying to pin a murder on me, you idiot, don't you see? If they catch me lying about this, they'll think I'm lying about everything." He turned back to Austin. "Marcy invited me into her bedroom and started taking off her clothes. What was I supposed to do?"

"Just say no," Caro murmured, quietly enough that only Austin heard her.

"And then later she told me she was pregnant, but I don't know that I was the father. That girl was hot to trot, I'm telling you. She could have been doing it with her whole high school football team for all I know."

"Marcy Phelps, hot to trot?" Austin said, skeptically shaking his head. "I don't think so. In fact, I think she was a virgin. A scared little virgin."

Seifert began picking at a splinter in his hand. "She said she wasn't. And she didn't act scared. But she wasn't very experienced."

The lawyer said nothing. He just looked on with his arms folded, wearing an expression of extreme annoyance.

Austin sat back down, rubbing his hand over his face. Abruptly he changed tack. "Look, Ray, there's been no murder committed. Marcy died of natural causes. If she ran away and met you someplace, if you lived with her in Oklahoma or wherever, there's not much we can charge you with. The worst I can imagine is, um, improper disposal of human remains."

He shook his head. "No way, man."

"Now, come on, Ray. It's easy to imagine what happened. She had the baby, you couldn't get her to a hospital in time, she died, you panicked. It's natural. You drove her to—"

"I'm telling you, I ain't seen that girl since last spring."

"Then how did you find out she was pregnant?"

"We talked on the phone." His eyes darted back and forth nervously. "She was gonna take care of it, you know? I even gave her the money. But then she split. I figured she used the money to buy a bus ticket or something."

"And you never saw her or heard from her again?"

"I never saw her or heard from her again, and that's the God's honest truth."

Austin went at Ray Seifert from several different directions, but his story didn't change. After another hour, during which Caro had nothing to add, he called it quits.

"You think he's telling the truth?" Austin asked Caro as soon as they were out of Seifert's hearing.

Caro chewed her lower lip. "Unfortunately, yeah. I don't think he knows what happened to her. We can check with his employer in Oklahoma, take a look at the place where he was living, but..." She spread her hands in a gesture of helplessness.

"And if he's guilty of anything more than sexual assault, he'll be long gone before we can arrest him again. Too bad we don't have anything to charge him with that'll stick." But Austin didn't really care about Ray Seifert now. If Caro was right—and Austin tended to believe she was—he would be no more use in the Phelps investigation.

Austin waited until someone came to take Seifert back to his holding cell, but Caro disappeared. He found her a few minutes later in a break room, making tea from the tea bags she kept in her purse. She looked kind of pale. And pensive.

"That was damn good work you did," he offered as he perused the vending machines. No Twinkies or Ding Dongs. A generic cinnamon roll would have to do. He shoved quarters into the machine and pushed the appropriate button.

She shrugged. "He was easy."

"Not to me, he wasn't. I'm curious. What made you jump in when you did?"

She stirred her tea with a plastic spoon. "When he acted like he was surprised to hear Marcy'd been pregnant, I knew he was lying. It was the first show of weakness I saw, and I . . . just couldn't let it pass."

"How did you know he was lying?" Austin had interrogated plenty of car thieves, fences and chop shop owners. Sometimes it was easy to spot a lie. But with Seifert, Austin never would have been able to pick that exact moment as the one when truth was suspended and lying began.

She shrugged again.

He pulled a chair up next to hers and straddled it, then busied his hands by unwrapping the cinnamon roll. "Did you enjoy it?" he asked, dipping his head and peering into her face.

She suppressed a smile. "If you have to ask, you're doing something wrong."

The sexual innuendo produced a tiny frisson of pleasure along his spine, but he pushed it away—for the moment. She wasn't going to evade his question that neatly. "Did you enjoy making Ray Seifert talk?" he clarified.

She set her cup down with a thunk and looked him in the eye. "Yeah. Yeah, I did, smart ass. I wasn't sure I could ever do that again. But I guess it's like riding a bicycle."

"And you don't feel guilty?"

"For making him talk, or for enjoying myself?"

"Enjoying yourself."

She took a deep breath, apparently taking his question very seriously. "I felt a little sick to my stomach. Scared, maybe, to know it's still there inside me."

Austin didn't have to ask what *it* was.

"But I guess if I didn't enjoy making slime squirm, I wouldn't be able to do it so zealously. And someone has to do it, or guys like Seifert go free."

"Then are you glad I made you come in that room with me?"

She bristled. "You didn't make me do any..." Then she stopped and stared at him through narrowed eyes. "You want my gratitude, is that it? You want me to admit that you were right and I was wrong, to fall on my knees and thank you for forcing me to face my fears—"

"A simple 'thank-you' would do." He grinned. With her prickly self-righteousness, Caro made herself such an easy target. And he loved yanking her chain. When she didn't respond, he reached over and touched her chin with his finger, nudging it until she was facing him. "Come on, Caro, you can say the magic word."

At that moment, Austin noticed two things. One was that Caro hadn't batted away his hand when he had touched her. He had invaded her personal space—something he bet she didn't normally allow, even from her close friends like Villaverde—and she'd let Austin touch her face. The second thing was that she was looking at his mouth.

He lost all interest in teasing her. Without thinking much about it, he leaned closer and captured her full lips with his.

He could almost taste her surprise. He definitely felt her brief acceptance, the instantaneous exchange of passion contained in one shared breath, the barely audible sound in the back of her throat, the hand that fluttered on his shoulder. Then all at once she was pulling away, jumping out of her chair, her hand over her mouth as if she'd done something unspeakable.

"Are you nuts?" she said, her words no more than a frantic whisper. "Anyone could walk in here."

He should have said something clever, like, Is that your only objection? A lack of privacy? I can fix that. But he was more than a little shaken up himself. He certainly hadn't planned to kiss her. He'd thought about it before, but he'd never dreamed he would actually be dumb enough to do it. So rather than being witty or urbane, he blurted out, "I'm sorry, Caro. I didn't mean to. It just happened."

His totally graceless reply seemed to take the starch out of her. Maybe she recognized that his distress was at least equal to hers. "Well..." She reclaimed her chair, although she scooted it a few inches farther from his, and she sipped at her tea, clutching the cup as if it might spring twenty leaks at any moment.

He sat up straighter and rubbed the back of his neck. Slowly he felt his cocksureness returning. "Surely you've thought about it."

He expected total denial. Ridicule, even. So she surprised him when she said, "Yeah, I've thought about it." At least she'd admitted there was tension between them.

"I didn't think I'd imagined..." His voice trailed off.

"Nevertheless, that was total insanity."

"Total," he agreed, even as his body clamored for more of her. He wondered, not for the first time, what she would look like out of those oversized, shapeless, sex-disguising clothes she wore.

"We have to work together. We can't even be thinking about—"

"Absolutely."

Suspicion returned to her eyes. "Are you making fun of me?"

"No, no." He shook his head vehemently. "I agree with you one hundred percent. We'll forget it ever happened." *Fat chance.* He knew he would relive that minuscule taste of ecstasy a thousand times over the next twenty-four hours.

"All right, then."

"I'll go thank Sergeant Wiggs for helping us out. I'll meet you at the car."

She nodded. "Oh, Austin? Thank you."

It took a moment for Austin to realize she wasn't thanking him for the kiss.

Sergeant Wiggs had left the station, so Austin scribbled a note telling Wiggs that if he ever needed a favor from the DPD, all he had to do was ask. On his way out of the station, as luck would have it, he ran square into Ray Seifert, who apparently had just made bail.

Austin tried to ignore him. He had about reached his slime tolerance for the day, and it wouldn't take much to provoke him. But Seifert flagged him down.

"Hey, you believe me, don't you?" he asked Austin.

Austin continued on his path toward the exit. "I don't know, should I?"

"You seem like a reasonable guy. Now, that gal who's with you, she's another story."

Sensing some sort of imminent male bonding, Austin slowed his pace and managed a weak laugh. "She's tough, all right."

"It's hard to talk about, well, you know, in front of her."

Seifert was getting downright chatty, and his lawyer was nowhere around. Austin decided to take advantage of the situation. "Women can be a pain," he agreed, thinking again of how Caro's mouth felt against his own, wondering what it would feel like on other parts of his body.

"Like, I didn't just get the girl pregnant and drop her. I mean, it takes two, you know? And I tried to do the right thing. I told her not to tell anyone because I thought it would be better for her if no one ever found out. Her parents would have stroked out."

They just about did, Austin wanted to say, when they identified her body. But he bit his tongue.

"And I paid for her to get rid of it. I even found the clinic and made the appointment for her. I did the best I could."

Something clicked in Austin's mind. He thought about another young girl who had missed her appointment at an abortion clinic. "What was the name of the clinic?"

Caught off guard by the sharpness of the questions, Seifert stopped in his tracks. "Uh, I dunno. Does it matter?"

Austin stopped, too. "Yes, it matters. Think. What was it called?"

Seifert screwed up his face in a sincere-appearing attempt to remember. "I think it was the Woman's Blah-Blah Clinic, something like that. Over on Harry Hines."

"Women's Services Clinic?" Austin corrected him. His skin tingled with anticipation.

Seifert showed instant recognition. "Yeah, that's it."

Oh, God. That was the same clinic Amanda Arkin had gone to.

Chapter 10

"We can't just charge in there and round everybody up for questioning," Caro said. She and Austin were back at the station, discussing how to proceed now that they had this new, interesting piece of evidence provided by Ray Seifert. Austin was seated, his feet propped on the edge of his desk. Eating again. At least it was a granola bar this time.

Caro, too edgy to sit, was pacing the small area in front of his desk, her hands shoved into the pockets of her oversize green cardigan. "It might be pure coincidence that both Marcy and Amanda visited the same clinic. And if it isn't, a showy display of police authority might drive our suspect underground, or prompt him to cover his tracks. We don't even know what we're looking for."

"So what do you suggest?" Austin asked, arms crossed, challenging. He was once again cocky and superior, proud of the fact that he had "ferreted out" this piece of information from Seifert.

Caro suspected Seifert had simply volunteered his juicy tidbit, but she didn't say so. Let Austin bask in his own glow. He seemed to enjoy it so thoroughly. At least they now had something to occupy their minds besides that stupid, stupid kiss.

"I think we should approach the owner of the clinic," she said, "this Dr. Wayrick, gain his cooperation and ask to see personnel records. We can find out which current employees were also on the payroll back when Marcy disappeared—and if they were actually at work that day. If we can discover any mysterious absences that coincide with the dates Marcy and Amanda vanished, we might have a suspect.''

Austin popped the last bite of his granola bar into his mouth and made a production out of chewing it thoroughly. ''Okay. Let's show up without warning, though. I'll get a subpoena tonight and we'll hit the clinic at the crack of dawn tomorrow, so we can catch Wayrick on his way in. I don't want to take the chance of his being 'in surgery' all day. How about if I pick you up at your house about six tomorrow? We can stop and have breakfast.''

''Six in the morning?'' she squeaked. She had visions of herself dragging herself out of bed to answer the door in her bathrobe, complete with morning breath, puffy eyes and Medusa's hair. And Austin would be standing on her front porch, perfect as usual.

''What's wrong, you don't like getting up early?''

''Do you?''

''I get up at four-thirty every morning, run three miles—''

''Then you stuff your face with sugar doughnuts, I'll bet.'' Three miles? She hadn't done that since the police academy, and then she'd thought she was going to die. No wonder he looked so good.

''If I didn't eat high-calorie foods, I'd waste away to nothing. Fast metabolism.''

She put her hands over her ears. ''I don't want to hear it. People with fast metabolisms should be shot. I'll be ready at six.'' She gave him directions to her apartment, which was actually half of a seventy-year-old duplex in East Dallas.

''The M streets,'' Austin commented. ''Nice neighborhood.''

''It's okay—convenient, relatively safe and kinda pretty.''

''And let's not forget, it's close to Lower Greenville. You do much partying over there?''

His question caused a flurry of butterflies to attack her stomach. Was he just making idle chitchat, or gearing up to ask her out? ''No, I don't go out much. Look, I gotta go. There are a couple of things I need to check into before I go home tonight. I'll see you tomorrow morning.''

She made a hasty escape, but the slightly bewildered expression on Austin's face stayed with her for a few minutes. As she made a stop at the ladies' room, she allowed herself the luxury of imagining—just for the heck of it—going out on a date with Austin. Maybe they would go to a movie, some silly action-adventure flick, and they would share popcorn and squeeze hands during the scary parts....

She must be out of her mind. So the guy was slightly attracted to her. That didn't mean anything. And even if it did, she'd made it a hard-and-fast rule never to date a fellow cop—especially one she worked with. Cops were notoriously unlucky in the relationship department. Two of them together were usually disastrous. Besides, she definitely didn't want to be just one on his list of conquests. She'd be right up there with Sergeant Quayar, swooning to accommodate his every request.

"Nice of you to grace us with your presence," Tony said from his desk as she entered Missing Persons. A few snickers from around the room followed his greeting.

She walked over to his desk, placed her hands on the top, and leaned over, unsmiling. "You know damn well this schedule is not my choice."

As usual, her acidity had no effect on Tony. He merely smiled and said, "You could try being a little nicer to me, since I'm carrying half your caseload."

"Which I appreciate. But I could do without the snide comments. Sorry I barked." She sat down and began shuffling papers. She shouldn't be so grumpy. After all, she and Austin had gotten some decent breaks today. Then again, it wasn't work that was getting to her. It was the way she was starting to feel around Austin Lomax.

He irritated the hell out of her. Sometimes she wanted just to smack him. And yet she'd trusted him enough to tell him about Charlie Northcutt. And she'd let him kiss her. No, worse, she'd kissed him back. Much as she wanted to forget it had ever happened, she couldn't push it out of her head for long.

Tony was in her face again, having rolled his chair over to her desk. "Caro, you really okay?" he asked, no longer teasing.

"Yeah." She flipped through phone messages, hardly registering what they said. "Hey, Tony, how long you been married?"

"Nine years. Why?"

"You happy?"

"What kind of question is that? Of course I'm happy. I've got the greatest wife in the world. You ever seen me even look at another woman? You ever seen me hang around here when I don't have to?"

She pointed an accusing finger at him. "What about Christmas?"

He rolled his eyes. "My in-laws were at my house. That's different. Why are you asking me this?"

She shrugged. "No reason." She forced her mind back to work matters. "I'm on to something hot, Tony. Or it could be, anyway. Austin and I may have found a connection between the Phelps and Arkin cases."

"No kidding?" Reflexively he reached into his breast pocket for a cigarette, which he hadn't carried around for ten months. "Damn. You got any gum?"

As she rifled through her desk drawer looking for an errant stick of Juicy Fruit, she explained what Ray Seifert had revealed. "Ah, how about a cherry cough drop?"

Tony pulled a face. "Never mind. So, what's your next move?"

"We're going in tomorrow to ask the doctor at the clinic some questions. Meanwhile, I have a hunch about something. Want to help me follow it up?"

Tony immediately started rolling his chair backward. "This sounds like more work."

"Just a few phone calls. To every police department in the Metroplex."

He groaned. "You gotta be kidding."

"Look. I'm thinking that if these two girls are connected to that clinic, maybe there are others. Two could be a coincidence. If I could find even one more, we'd know for sure we were barking up the right tree."

"This is a shot in the dark, and you know it."

"But shots in the dark sometimes pay off. Think about it, Tony. We might be on the verge of breaking up a . . . a serial kidnapping and baby-thief ring or something."

Tony sighed in defeat. "I'll give you exactly one hour on this wild-goose chase. Then I'm going home."

"An hour, that's great. Now, we're looking for missing teenage girls, presumed runaways, possibly pregnant. Any names we come up with I'll take with me tomorrow and try to compare them to a patient list at the clinic."

"Okay," he said dubiously. "You take the Dallas area, I'll take Fort Worth, and we'll, uh, meet in Arlington, I guess."

"Thanks, Tony. You're a good friend, you know that?"

He actually blushed as he turned back to his own desk and began flipping through his Rolodex.

By the end of their shift at three o'clock, they had barely scratched the surface. There were dozens of little municipalities surrounding Dallas and Fort Worth, and each had its own police department with its own missing persons files, and there was seldom any coordination among them. Still, Caro had come up with one case that fit the profile she was looking for—a college freshman from Texas Christian University in Fort Worth, pregnant, mixed-up and missing. Like with Amanda Arkin's case, authorities had assumed Julie Yates needed some time to herself.

"And listen to this, Tony," Caro said excitedly after begging for every detail of the case over the phone. "After she'd been gone a week, her parents received a letter from her saying that she was okay, and that she was staying with friends in Dallas for a while. They thought it was on the level, and the police took her off the critical list. It seems she's always been kind of unstable. But now that she's been gone three months and no word, they're starting to get worried again."

Tony's level gaze met hers. "Just like Amanda Arkin."

"Exactly! And—get this—Julie's roommate said she was talking about getting an abortion."

"But why would she come all the way to Dallas? Surely they have similar clinics in Fort Worth."

"Maybe she knew someone else who'd gone to that clinic. Or maybe she just wanted to get as far away from friends and family as she could, who knows? Anyway, I'm gonna get a look at those patient files if I have to break in and steal them."

Tony gave her a thumbs-up. "Awright, Caro! Sounds like the Terror is back!"

Her face froze midsmile. "Don't call me that. I'll never be like that again."

"Like what, an aggressive, no-holds-barred detective?"

"This work on CAPERS cases is strictly temporary."

"For now," he said with a knowing smile.

"What's that supposed to mean?"

"Just that I heard Captain Raines is holding his breath, hoping this little taste of CAPERS will lure you back into his fold. Four years is a long time to punish yourself for something that wasn't your fault."

She grew very still. "You know? You know why I transferred to Missing Persons?"

He shrugged. "Well, yeah."

"Damn that Austin Lomax," she said, struggling not to shout the words. "How dare he betray a confidence. What'd he do, tell you in the men's room? Couldn't he keep it to himself for even a day? That son of a—"

"Whoa, whoa, Caro. What does Austin have to do with this?"

"Didn't he tell you about Charlie Northcutt?"

"Hell, no. I've known about you and Charlie Northcutt since it happened."

She felt the breath being sucked out of her lungs. "You've known all this time, and you never said anything?"

Tony looked confused. "I figured if you wanted to talk about it, you would."

"Does everyone know?"

"A few people put it together. It didn't make its way around the police grapevine, if that's what you're worried about."

Caro couldn't believe it. All this time her friends had known about Charlie Northcutt, and they'd all been tiptoeing around her, waiting for her to snap out of it. Well, she wasn't going to return to CAPERS. Just because she was taking this temporary assignment very seriously didn't mean she wanted to do it on a permanent basis.

"You wouldn't want me to leave Missing Persons, would you?" she asked, trying to make the question sound light. But suddenly his answer was important to her. Tony was just about her best friend. "I mean, how would you survive here without me?"

"I might get some of my own work done," he quipped. But then his grin faded away, and he chewed on a ragged cuticle a few moments before continuing. "No, seriously, Caro. I've been meaning to tell you this for a while, but...well, I've put in for a transfer to CAPERS myself."

"You're kidding." It was all she could think of to say. She'd had her quota of surprises for the day, and she just couldn't cope with this one.

"It looks like I might get it, too."

"That's...that's great, Tony."

"You're not mad? I know I should have told you sooner, but I guess I didn't want to think too hard about transferring away from you. We've worked together a long time."

"Of course I'm not mad. It'll be awful here without you, but that shouldn't hold you back from something you really want to do."

"Thanks. You know, Raines would take you over me in a second."

"You don't have to worry on that account." She smiled, even though the thought of coming to work every day without Tony sitting at that desk right in front of hers made her chest ache. For four years he'd been her anchor, her reality check, and he always gave her a smile when she needed it most. "You'll be good in CAPERS, Tony. I hope you get it."

He shrugged off her good wishes. "Hey, you coming to my New Year's Eve party?"

"Oh, I don't know. I can't seem to enjoy New Year's Eve. All I can think about is drunk drivers, and there's always two or three homicides—"

"And you want to sit home brooding about it, right? C'mon, Caro, lighten up. We'll expect you at eight. Fran's counting on your stuffed mushrooms. And she might even have a man for you to meet."

Caro groaned. "Look, I'll come, but no fix-ups. How many times do I have to tell you guys I'm perfectly happy without a man in my life?" An image of Austin flashed briefly in her mind.

"Until you can say it and sound convincing," Tony said with a wink.

It was still dark when Austin pulled up in front of Caro's duplex the next morning, but a corner street lamp illuminated the area like daylight. Her place looked almost exactly as he'd pictured—a small, undistinguished house with a wide front porch and faded green shutters, a postage-stamp yard that looked as if no one had raked it all year. Not as attractive as its neighbors, the house nonetheless appeared sturdy, practical.

He opened the door of his Bronco, hoping Caro wasn't ready yet, that she would come to the door flustered and not quite dressed, so she would be forced to ask him inside while she finished up. He was dying to see what the inside of her house looked like. But before he could even get out of the car, the front door opened and she emerged.

If the house didn't surprise him, Caro herself did. She was dressed up, wearing a pencil-thin skirt and a clingy sweater under a wool blazer. Her hair, which she almost always wore in a single braid, was swept into an elegant twist at the crown of her head, with several curly tendrils framing her heart-shaped face. And she was wearing makeup.

"You look nice," he couldn't help saying the moment she was inside the car.

"Yeah, well, don't expect to see me in heels too often. I just thought maybe a thin sheen of sophistication might impress the doc. If he thinks we're on his level, maybe he'll be more inclined to confide in us." She shrugged. "It's probably dumb, but any little edge we can get . . ."

"It can't hurt." Hell, if this Dr. Wayrick had a hormone anywhere in his body, he would be falling out of his chair to please Caro. Any man would. Austin had always thought she was pretty, but today she was a knockout. And for a few, giddy moments, he'd thought she'd dressed like that for him.

"Did you get in your three miles this morning?" she asked, tilting her head coquettishly.

"No. Really, I only run two. And I don't do it every day. And I don't always get up at four-thirty."

"My, my. Confessions so early in the morning?"

"My conscience was bothering me. I lied to impress you—very juvenile of me."

She didn't ask why he'd wanted to impress her. If she had, he might have patiently explained that a man always feels the urge to impress the woman he's interested in. But it was probably just as well. She might laugh in his face. He wouldn't put it past her.

"Did you check out those other adopted babies?" he asked.

"Oh, yeah. Nothing promising. Justin Krill is still the best bet. Any more thoughts on that?"

"I can't get a search warrant for Beaman's records. There's no concrete evidence that Justin is Marcy's baby. I mean, not that you didn't do some good work, but you arrived at his name by process of elimination after an anonymous phone call."

"I know. But I still think there's something to it. I wish that woman would call back."

"Yeah, me too."

They stopped at a diner on Knox Street for breakfast. Predictably, Caro ordered a bran muffin, fresh fruit and hot tea. She didn't even butter the muffin. Austin had a Denver omelet. Maybe he should think about eating more healthy foods, he mused as he took a bite of hash browns slathered with catsup. He was thirty-five, and that wasn't all that far from forty. He glanced at Caro's dry-looking muffin, then shook his head. What was the fun in living to a ripe old age if you had to eat that stuff?

Caro insisted on paying for her meal, even though this whole breakfast thing had been Austin's idea. Although he was annoyed, he couldn't help but admire her independence. He couldn't stand a clingy woman.

They'd talked little over breakfast, and they were quiet now as Austin negotiated his way onto Central Expressway. Bumper to bumper at 7:00 a.m. At this rate, Wayrick might beat them to his office.

"Oh, Austin, I almost forgot," Caro said suddenly. "Yesterday afternoon I made a few phone calls to other police departments—just following up a hunch, really—and I discovered something kind of intriguing."

"Yeah?" He felt a vague sense of unease, and he didn't know why.

"There's another missing pregnant girl, from Fort Worth."

"Yeah, so?"

"Her case sounds very familiar. She was considering an abortion, she disappeared without a word—and her parents received a letter in her own handwriting assuring them she was fine, just like the letter Russ Arkin received."

"Mmm-hmm."

"Is that all you're going to say? Don't you think it's odd?"

He shrugged one shoulder. "You think this girl ties in? All the way from Fort Worth? C'mon, Caro. I know you're anxious to get this thing solved, and so am I, but you're taking shots—"

"—in the dark. So I've been told. It's worth checking out."

"Sure, I guess," he said noncommittally. "The subpoena only mentions records related to Marcy and Amanda, though, so we can't legitimately demand any information about this other girl." He was deliberately giving her lead short shrift, and it took him a few moments to figure out why. It was because he didn't like her taking initiative on this case. He was the lead detective. She was supposed to be following his orders. Someone had to be in charge or the investigation would bounce all over the place. And yet, did it matter whose idea it was if results were produced? He had to admit, the possibility of tying a third girl into the investigative soup was intriguing.

He deliberately changed the subject. "A reporter from the 'Morning News' caught me walking to my car yesterday. I told him we'd found the father of Marcy's baby, but I didn't tell him who it was. But was he satisfied? No way. He had the gall to call me incompetent."

"He was just trying to bait you, hoping you'd reveal something really juicy to salve your wounded pride."

"It almost worked, too. I've never had to deal with the media before."

"I did only once, after I'd finished an undercover assignment trying to catch a serial rapist who was stalking women at this apartment complex. We caught the guy when he went for another woman instead of me. It was embarrassing."

Austin paused before speaking again. "You think we'll catch the guy this time?" He immediately wished he'd kept quiet. He was letting his insecurity show, and to the one person he most wanted to think he was competent.

"As long as we're making progress, there's a good chance. I tell myself that, anyway."

Austin tried to let her words reassure him, but he knew he wouldn't take another easy breath until they had a real suspect in both cases.

The sun was just breaking over the horizon as they arrived at the Women's Services Clinic, an unprepossessing beige cinderblock structure slightly set back from the road. It was the kind of building Austin normally wouldn't even notice. He pulled into the bumpy parking lot and wedged the Bronco between the only other two cars in evidence, an old Ford Fiesta and an even older Toyota. Austin guessed that neither belong to the doctor.

He and Caro walked up to the front door, which was locked. The office hours were listed as eight until five, and it was only seven-forty-five. But by relentlessly banging on the glass, he produced a middle-aged woman—possibly a nurse, possibly an office worker dressed in white to appear reassuringly medical. She was scowling and pointing to her watch, mouthing something. Austin opened his shield and held it against the glass, whereupon the woman's face immediately went blank. She scurried to the door and opened it.

"I'm sorry, I didn't know you were police," she said breathlessly, ushering them inside. "Is there something I can help you with?"

Austin scrutinized the woman, whose name tag identified her as Nancy Frieze. She was nervous, as most ordinary citizens were in the presence of police. Too nervous? "We'd like to see Dr. Wayrick," Austin said. "We were hoping to catch him early, so we wouldn't have to interrupt his workday." His busy, important work.

Austin felt slightly sick at the thought of what went on under this roof, day in and day out. He looked at the depressing waiting room, the dingy furniture, the peeling linoleum floor, the brightly colored paintings on the wall that tried to make the place more cheerful—and failed miserably. He would have to be dead and buried before he would let any woman carrying his child set foot in a place like this.

"Dr. Wayrick hasn't arrived just yet," Nancy Frieze said, scurrying into her little cubicle of a reception area. She ran her index finger over a page in an appointment book. "His first appointment is at nine, but he usually gets here well before that. Could I ask what this is about?"

"It's a confidential matter," Austin replied, though he tried to keep his tone friendly. He might need the woman's cooperation later.

The phone rang and she answered it, immediately launching into what was obviously a well-rehearsed spiel about exactly what services the Women's Services Clinic offered. Austin tried not to listen.

"What a depressing place," Caro said softly as they found two chairs in the waiting room. "I can't believe poor little Marcy came here. She must have been terrified."

"I imagine she was terrified even before she came here. It doesn't sound like her parents did a very good job of preparing her for real life."

At eight o'clock Nancy Frieze unlocked the front door. Immediately two black women entered, one in her teens, the other probably her mother. They signed in at the desk, then settled as far from Austin and Caro as possible, whispering to each other.

They probably believed Caro was a patient, Austin thought, and that he was her boyfriend, ready to fork over hundreds of dollars rather than take on the responsibility of a child. He felt an immediate and illogical protective instinct surging through his body. He wanted to announce to everyone who entered the clinic—and several more women did—that Caro wasn't pregnant.

He was about to demand that Ms. Frieze let them wait in the doctor's office when she called them. Dr. Wayrick had arrived, presumably via some back door, and was ready to see them.

Dr. Thurman Wayrick wasn't at all what Austin had expected. He was tall, distinguished, with just a touch of gray at his temples. Then again, what was an abortionist supposed to look like, Boris Karloff?

The doctor smiled as he held out his hand and introduced himself. "And you are . . . ?"

"Detective Corporal Austin Lomax."

"Detective Corporal Carolyn Triece," Caro said, shaking his hand. "We don't want to waste any more of your time than necessary, so we'll get right to the point. We have two teenage girls—one missing and presumed kidnapped, possibly dead by now, and one who was already found dead, her baby missing. They've both been connected to this clinic. First we want to verify that they were patients here. And then we want to find out if the connection means anything." Austin pulled the subpoena from his jacket pocket and laid it on the doctor's desk.

Dr. Wayrick's eyes widened. "You think someone here is involved in something criminal? Kidnapping? Murder?"

"Perhaps unknowingly," Austin clarified, not wanting to alarm the doctor excessively. He wanted Wayrick to be cooperative, not panicked. "Someone who works here could be unwittingly providing the perpetrator with information—names of patients, that sort of thing."

"Everyone who works here understands that our patient files are confidential," Wayrick said, obviously outraged. "If any sort of information is leaving this office, it's either being stolen . . . or one of my employees is in serious violation of medical ethics, not to mention inviting a mammoth lawsuit. I take it you're referring to the Arkin girl. Amanda Arkin—that's it, isn't it?''

Austin was surprised Wayrick had volunteered that information. "Then you can verify that she was a patient here?''

Wayrick looked over the subpoena before answering. "Certainly. When her disappearance made the headlines, everyone here was talking about it. We all remembered her—although I didn't actually perform any procedure on her, you understand. She came primarily for counseling, as many of our patients do. Despite what you might think, we do more than just pregnancy terminations here.''

"What about Marcy Phelps?" Caro asked. "Was she a patient also?''

Wayrick seemed to consider the question carefully. "I can't recall the name, but I'll have my office manager look in the files.'' He started to pick up the phone, but Austin stopped him.

"We'd prefer it if you didn't talk to anyone else on your staff about this matter, at least for the moment.'' He pulled Marcy's yearbook photo out of his pocket and showed it to Wayrick. "That's Marcy. She would have been here last June.''

While he waited for a response, Austin held his breath. What if Seifert had gotten the name of the clinic wrong? Austin had had to prompt Ray's memory, he recalled.

Wayrick studied the photo, then sucked in his cheeks and looked up. "Yes. Yes, I remember this girl. I believe I gave her an initial exam, verifying her pregnancy. I remember her because she wasn't taking the news well. I had to give her a sedative.''

"Okay, now we're getting somewhere," Caro said. "Can you give us a list of current employees who also worked here during the time of Marcy's visit?''

"That's not a problem. We're a small staff here. And three were hired recently, so..." He quickly wrote down the names Caro had requested. They included another doctor, two nurses, Nancy Frieze and the staff psychologist, Virginia Dreyfus.

"They're all good people, I assure you," Wayrick said. "I can't imagine any of them being involved in anything even remotely underhanded.''

Austin ignored the testimonial. "Do you keep employment records here? Specifically, records of sick days and vacation days?''

"Yes, of course. Unfortunately, that's one of the unpleasant little tasks I do myself—writing the paychecks. I have personnel files right here," he said, rising and walking to a small filing cabinet in the corner of the office.

"Can you check and see who was here on June 6?" Austin asked.

Although it took a few minutes, Wayrick patiently went over paycheck stubs for that period and all the accompanying paperwork. And his conclusion was that no one had missed work that day, the day Marcy Phelps had disappeared. And everyone was present and accounted for on the day of Amanda's disappearance, too.

Of course, Wayrick could be lying. Austin didn't discount that possibility. The doctor seemed awfully eager to please. Maybe too eager.

Austin looked at Caro, hoping for a clue as to whether she thought he was coming clean with them. He remembered how astute she'd been in catching Seifert's lies. But she merely looked bored. Deceptively bored, Austin was sure.

He decided they should leave for now, regroup and discuss how to proceed. They advised Wayrick to keep their conversation confidential. "If anyone asks, tell them your wife's car was broken into last night, and we're following up on it."

"Yes, yes, I'll do that," he said with a conspiratorial smile. He seemed to be enjoying the cloak-and-dagger stuff.

"Oh, just one other thing," Caro said when they were almost out the door. She pulled a piece of paper out of her purse. "I have one additional name—Julie Yates. And this is her picture. Ring any bells?"

Austin looked on impatiently as Wayrick examined the picture, which had obviously been faxed to Caro yesterday.

Wayrick was no longer enjoying himself. In fact, his face had gone rather pale. "Yes, this girl was also a patient. Again, I examined her and verified her pregnancy, and as I recall we scheduled the procedure, but she didn't show up. That's not uncommon. Don't tell me something happened to her, too."

"Bingo," Caro said softly.

Chapter 11

Caro and Austin spent another couple of hours questioning the clinic's employees. None of them were able to recollect anything of value. The only person who might have been able to shed some light on things—Virginia Dreyfus, the psychologist—had the day off. They would have to catch up with her the following day. Wayrick assured them that, despite the fact that tomorrow was New Year's Eve, the clinic would be open and Dr. Dreyfus would be there.

"What are you waiting for?" Austin asked the moment they were alone in the car. He jerked the Bronco into reverse, nearly stripping the gears in the process, and roared out of the parking place while Caro was still struggling with her seat belt. "Aren't you going to say 'I told you so'?"

Caro's first instinct was to soothe the beast. But on second thought, she had done absolutely nothing deserving of anyone's anger, especially Austin's. "Aren't you going to say 'thank-you'? 'Good work, Caro'? Or are you so wrapped up in your ego that you can't acknowledge the fact that my shot in the dark paid off?"

He took a deep breath. "Just clear it with me next time you want to take a stab at something on your own. I want to know everything you're doing on this case at all times."

"Oh, yes, sir."

"Sarcasm doesn't become you."

"Machismo doesn't become you. Lighten up, Lomax. I informed you first thing this morning. If I'd asked you yesterday, you probably would have said not to bother, and I never would have stumbled onto Julie Yates."

He said nothing—probably because she was right and he was wrong and he knew it, she thought uncharitably. This was one of those times she wanted to shake him.

A call on the cellular phone saved them from continuing the argument, much to Caro's relief. Austin wasn't the only one with a temper.

"Corporal Lomax," Austin said after clicking the phone open. His face immediately relaxed into an easy smile. "Hey, Dean." He looked at Caro and added, "It's my brother."

His brother? Austin had never mentioned his brother.

"Holy . . . any details?" Austin asked, instantly alert. Then, after a pause, he said, "Thanks, Dean, I appreciate it," and clicked the phone shut. Then he hit the steering wheel with the heel of his hand. "Damn!"

"Who's your brother?" Caro asked. "What did he say?"

"He works in the DA's office," Austin answered distractedly. "He said Smith, Clovis and Beaman has filed Chapter 11, and Travis Beaman reportedly has left with his wife on an extended vacation to the Orient."

Caro's curse was a whole lot more colorful than Austin's. "Do you think Beaman flew the coop because of anything we did, or just to escape creditors?" she asked.

"Could be either, or both. But why don't we pay a little visit to Smith, Clovis et cetera and see if we can't shake something loose."

"Without a search warrant?"

"Maybe we can bluff or sweet-talk our way into those records. Their offices aren't far from the station. It's worth a try."

"I'm game." Privately, Caro thought Austin would have more luck with sweet-talk than with intimidation—especially if it involved convincing female secretaries to let him have his way. That's how it worked with her, anyway. She found herself wanting to please him whenever he turned on the charm. But the moment he got bossy, her back went up and she would purposely try to thwart him.

When they arrived at the law firm, everyone there seemed to be in a state of shock. The receptionist looked like a ghost who'd lost its way back to the graveyard. She offered no argument when Austin demanded to see Beaman's secretary. There was obviously little work going on. Every office they passed was either empty or contained little clusters of people talking in hushed voices.

Beaman's secretary, an attractive older woman, appeared close to tears. She was in the process of boxing up the contents of her desk. Apparently Caro and Austin had arrived just in time.

"Where's your boss?" Austin asked.

"Oh, it's you again," said the secretary, whose nameplate identified her as Ms. Paladin. "To tell you the truth, I don't know where Mr. Beaman is. He didn't show up for work this morning."

"We heard he left the country."

"And us holding the bag. It wouldn't surprise me," she said wearily. Abruptly she plopped into her desk chair and put her face in her hands. "What do you want?"

"I want to see a file. Just one file. A quick peek, and we'll be out of your hair."

She looked up, her mouth firming in resolve. "You must know, Detective, that I can't let you look at confidential—"

"I can get a search warrant," Austin interrupted. "Have you ever seen what happens when the police are given free rein to search for something as small as a file folder? They turn drawers upside down. And they aren't obligated to straighten things up when they're done, either."

"That may be, but—"

"Corporal Triece, you stay here and make sure those files don't go anywhere. I'm going to get a warrant. And, Ms. Paladin, you might consider what it would mean to your career to be named as an accessory—"

"Oh, all right," the secretary said, clearly having reached the end of her rope. She actually sniffed back a few tears. "I'll get you the damn file, but not because of your silly threats. I'm cooperating because I'd like to see Travis Beaman nailed. What file are you looking for?"

"Krill," Austin answered. "Don and Chloe Krill. An adoption."

Ms. Paladin appeared confused. "What does that case have to do with embezzlement?"

Oh, boy, Caro thought. It looked as if Travis Beaman had his fingers in more than one sour pie.

"Could you just get it, please?"

Ms. Paladin shrugged, then led them into a huge file room. She went right to the *K*'s, and in moments produced a slim manila folder, which she handed to Austin.

He laid it on a small table in the corner of the room, shoved his glasses onto his face and scanned the contents greedily, with Caro peering around his shoulder.

"Here it is," he said matter-of-factly, though Caro knew he was anything but. "The biological mother's name is Patricia Smith, 4662 Fairfax. Would you copy this page for us?" he asked the secretary.

"No, I can't," she said, standing up straighter. "I could get in serious trouble for even letting you into this room. If you return with a search warrant, I'll be glad to hand over the file. But the movers are scheduled to come tomorrow and box up this whole room."

Caro was already writing down the name and address in a pad she kept in her purse.

"I understand. Thanks," Austin said to the secretary. He gave her a sympathetic smile, as if apologizing for his earlier, antagonistic behavior. "No one will ever know we were here."

Caro felt glum as they left the law firm. "So I was wrong?" she asked when they were on the elevator.

"Maybe, maybe not. Let's make one more stop before we go back to the station."

"Let me guess, 4662 Fairfax?"

"You got it."

The 4600 block of Fairfax was in one of the more modest Highland Park neighborhoods, but Caro guessed that, despite the unassuming little houses and small front yards, some of these properties were valued at more than a quarter million dollars.

"What are you going to say to these people?" Caro asked. "You can't just bang on the door and ask if their daughter had a baby out of wedlock."

"Sure I can. You're too polite, Caro. But, actually, I don't think I'll have to say anything." He slowed the car down. "There's 4652, 4658 . . . Ha! And 4664. There is no 4662."

Adrenaline surged through Caro's body. "Hot damn! I'll bet there's no Patricia Smith, either."

They parked the car and knocked on a couple of doors and asked the people who answered if they knew of any Smiths who lived in the immediate neighborhood, just to be sure. But no one had heard of Patricia Smith.

"Now what?" Caro asked, although she knew what she wanted to do.

Austin smiled wickedly. "Let's pay a call on Chloe Krill."

"I was hoping you'd say that." They were closing in for the kill, and it felt good.

Although the Krills' neighborhood was less than a five-minute drive away, it was much more grand. The houses here could rightfully be called "estates." The Krill house in particular was one of

the most opulent, a huge but stylish English Tudor with mul-
lioned windows and beautifully aged red brick. No one answered
the door.

An old man was raking leaves from the lawn next door. While
Austin walked around to the back of the house to see if there were
any signs of life, Caro approached the neighbor. "Excuse me, but
do you know where the Krills might be?"

The old man eyed her suspiciously, then shook his head. "No,
I'm sorry."

She took her badge out of her jacket pocket and held it out for
his inspection. "It's very important that we get in contact with
them," she said. "Would you have any idea where they might be?"

"Oh, police, huh? Well, uh, I haven't seen 'em around in a day
or two. Since Don has family up north some place, they might be
visiting for the New Year's holiday. That'd be my guess, yes,
ma'am."

Caro handed him her business card. "Would you call me when
they come back? I mean, if you see their cars, or you see anyone
moving around at the house."

"Yes, ma'am, certainly. What's this all about?"

"It's a private matter," she replied.

Austin returned, shaking his head to indicate he hadn't found
anything useful. Caro thanked the neighbor for his help, and she
and Austin climbed back into the car.

Caro let out a great sigh. "The next-door neighbor says they're
out of town. Maybe I shouldn't have flashed my badge at him.
He'll probably run right to the Krills the moment they come
home."

"*If* they come home. For all we know, they left the country with
their buddy Travis Beaman. If they're afraid someone might challenge their right to keep the baby..."

"I sure as hell hope they didn't skip town." Her mood was fluc-
tuating from adrenaline-charged elation to despair from minute to
minute.

"We'll put the house under surveillance," Austin said.

"Can we do that?"

"I think Raines'll go for it. Something big is going on. All the
evidence points to it. We don't have it strung together yet, but any
fool could look at all the little trees we've collected and see a for-
est. Three girls, all patients at the same clinic, all missing, one
found dead, her baby gone..."

"A crooked lawyer who's falsifying legal documents, an anonymous phone call..." Caro added. "Is it enough? If we could
definitely tie Beaman or the Krills to Marcy Phelps..."

"It's enough."

"In that case . . ." Caro drew a deep breath. "Is it time to bring in SIU?" The Special Investigations Unit was a group of detectives within CAPERS that specialized in handling high-profile cases—serial killings, police shootings, or any investigation that required lots of manpower and money.

Austin made a face. "Surely you jest."

"I'm not wild about the idea, but multiple kidnappings and stolen babies and black-market adoptions are right up SIU's alley."

"Kidnappings? Maybe those girls disappeared voluntarily. We don't have any ransom notes, no hard evidence of foul play—"

"What about Amanda's car?"

"In the letter she explained that she'd abandoned it."

"Wiped clean of fingerprints? What about the fingernail and the blood?"

"Women break fingernails all the time. And the blood was microscopic. As for the fingerprints, that guy the joyriders saw was probably a car thief who lost his nerve, unconnected to Amanda. The way I see it, someone at the clinic could be influencing these girls, convincing them to go off someplace and have their babies in peace. Nothing illegal about that."

Caro was disturbed by his attitude. "Austin, you don't really believe that, do you?"

"No. I'm just trying to show you that we have some leeway as far as handing this over to SIU. We're making good progress on our own. Why spoil it?"

"We let Travis Beaman get away from us."

"Then we'll just have to catch up with the Krills. They know as much as their lawyer."

"Maybe."

"Do you want to call in Special Investigations?"

"I don't know. I just don't want to screw something up and get Amanda Arkin or Julie Yates killed."

"Like the SIU has never screwed anything up."

True enough, Caro conceded silently.

"Let's see what we can accomplish over the weekend," Austin said. "Monday we can call a meeting with Chief Raines and let him make the decision."

"All right," Caro agreed. If the truth be known, she wasn't quite ready to let go of this case. And that worried her.

Since Amanda wasn't as far along in her pregnancy as most of the girls at the Good Shepherd Home, she'd been drafted along with a couple of others to rake leaves in the front yard. She would have enjoyed the exercise, except for the bitter north wind that had started to blow. The thin jacket Odell had given her offered little protection. She wondered what had happened to the nice winter coat she'd been wearing when she'd been kidnapped.

Henry was watching from the front porch with Phoebe the bloodhound at his side. Amanda could feel his eyes on her. She could sense their predatory gleam; she had deliberately interested him in her as a woman, and he was responding. The prospect of taking her flirtation any further filled her with revulsion, and yet she knew Henry might be her only salvation.

And she didn't have much time to lose. She was worried about Terri, who had spent the last couple of days in her room in bed. Amanda had seen her only once, when their paths had crossed in the bathroom, and Terri had looked pale and drawn.

Via the water pipe and Morse code, Terri had assured Amanda that she still had more than a month before her baby was due. But as big as Terri was, it wouldn't be surprising if she went into labor any minute. They had to get help before that baby was born... before Odell sold the baby and something awful happened to the mother.

When Amanda had accumulated a huge pile of leaves, Henry appeared with a bushel basket. "Here, put them in here," he said. "Then take them around to the back and dump them in the compost cage." In a lower voice, he added, "Odell says you have to stay."

"You talked to her?" Amanda was surprised Henry had found the courage to confront his aunt. He was obviously devoted to her, but he was also a bit afraid of her—understandably.

Henry nodded. "She says it's too late for you to repent."

"The Bible says it's never too late. God will always forgive those who are truly sorry for their sins. Remember the story of the Prodigal Son?"

Henry nodded uncertainly. "Yeah, I remember. C'mon, Amanda, keep working. Heather and Mary are way ahead of you. And, anyway, Aunt Odell says I shouldn't listen to you just because you're different from the other girls."

Amanda made a show of piling leaves into her basket and stomping them down. "I understand why Odell feels the way she does," she said. "She has to be firm. She can't bend the rules for me or the other girls might give her trouble."

"That's right," Henry said.

"But that doesn't mean you couldn't help me." She picked up her basket and followed the other girls around the side of the house, where a locked gate prevented them from continuing.

Henry unlocked the gate and ushered them through—all but Amanda. He held her back. "How could I help?"

"You could let me out. You can unlock anything around here," she said, pointing to the wad of keys hanging from his belt. "The next time Odell leaves, you could unlock the front gate. And then . . . and then I could meet you somewhere," she continued hurriedly. "If you helped me, Henry, you'd be my friend for life. Maybe even more than a friend." Careful that the other girls didn't observe her, she squeezed his hand. Then she grabbed the basket and headed for the compost cage. Let him chew on that awhile.

She made two more trips to the compost heap, her bushel basket piled high with crispy brown leaves. Henry helped the other two girls, so it wouldn't appear that he was playing favorites, but he continued to watch Amanda at every opportunity.

When the chore was done to Henry's satisfaction, he ordered them all to return the rakes and baskets to the toolshed, then to go inside and wash up for supper. Amanda lingered behind, hoping for a response from Henry, but all he said to her was, "Hurry up, you don't want to be late for supper. Roast beef and mashed potatoes—and no green beans."

Amanda smiled and headed for the bathroom. She supposed everyone here would remember her for the fit she threw over eating green beans.

She was beginning to think Henry was going to ignore her outrageous request. He studiously avoided her gaze during dinner, and when it came to passing around pumpkin pie for dessert, the slice he gave her was the same size as everyone else's.

It was only later, when all the girls had been locked into their rooms for the night and the old house was settling down with its customary creaks and groans, that Amanda heard a soft knock.

She climbed out of bed and tiptoed to the door. "Who's there?"

"It's Henry. Can I come in?"

It seemed ludicrous that he would ask permission. After all, he was the one with the key, and no one's privacy had ever been respected in this house that she was aware of. "Yes, of course," she responded. She glanced at the exposed pipes in the corner, hoping Terri didn't pick now to start clanging out a message.

The deadbolt scraped and the door opened. And then he was standing in the darkened room. She couldn't see him, but she could sense his presence looming above her. And she could smell him. He always smelled faintly of something that reminded Amanda of a petting zoo. She quickly turned on the light.

He closed the door quietly behind him. "I've thought about it, and I can't do what you want me to, Amanda," he said. "I can't go against Aunt Odell like that. And even if I could, she would know what I'd done. And she'd be mad, real mad. She would hate me."

"Oh, no," Amanda said, as if this would be a real tragedy. For Henry, she supposed it would be. Odell seemed to be the only person in his life. Not that she showed him any love that Amanda could discern. But she did give him approval, and that was very important to Henry.

"Aunt Odell raised me," he said. "My . . . my mother and father didn't want me."

"I'm so sorry," Amanda said. "Of course. I wouldn't want you to make Odell mad. She's been good to you, hasn't she?"

Henry nodded.

"All right, then, what if you could help me without Odell ever finding out? Would you do it?"

"I don't know," he said sullenly. "Would I have to lie?"

"No," she assured him. "All you have to do is loosen the bars on my window, and then dig a little hole under the fence—behind the toolshed, where nobody can see. No one will ever know you helped me escape. And after I'm out, I'll get a little apartment somewhere not too far. And you can come see me."

He remained silent, but his face worked furiously as he considered her suggestion. Suddenly he smiled. "I could bring you a cherry pie," he said, buying into the fantasy. "You could eat the whole thing yourself, and not have to share it with nobody."

"Mmm, that would be wonderful. And you would have a friend, someone besides Odell. I know she's a good lady, but don't you sometimes wish you had someone closer to your age? I'll still need you, Henry. If I'm going to start a new life, I'll need a friend." She touched him then, letting her hand glide up his arm to his shoulder.

He stood very still, neither responding to her touch nor moving away from it. She stood on her toes and moved her hand to his neck, gently guiding his head down toward her upturned face. She closed her eyes and called up a vivid image of Scott. If she could just pretend it was Scott she was kissing, maybe she wouldn't give herself away by retching.

Their lips met clumsily, and at first nothing happened. Henry stood so still, Amanda might have been kissing a statue, and she wondered if he didn't know how to respond. Maybe Odell had so sheltered him that he didn't understand about man-woman things, except in the abstract. Then all at once he came to life, like an unconscious man who'd been doused with water. He threw his arms around her and pressed his mouth against hers, the kiss hard and wet and utterly repulsive.

She didn't know how long she would be able to stand it. She had to fight every instinct to keep from pushing him away and crying out in disgust. But she managed to give some semblance of enthusiasm—until he grabbed her breast.

Instantly she pulled away. "No, no, we can't do that, Henry," she said, calling upon every ounce of her acting ability so that she sounded excited and regretful that they couldn't go further.

"Why not?" Henry asked, breathing heavily. But he had stopped pawing her.

"It's wrong."

"You let your boyfriend touch you," he said almost spitefully.

"But I was a sinner then," she said, hanging her head. "I know better than that now. I've changed."

"You're a Jezebel," Henry said, apparently having his own cache of Bible stories to draw from. With Odell having raised him, he would almost have to know the Bible.

"I'm not," Amanda insisted. "I've changed."

He touched the side of her face. "Come on, Amanda. Let me touch you. Isn't that what you want?"

"I do want it," she agreed, nearly choking on the words. "But it's wrong."

"I'll help you escape. If you take off your clothes and let me touch you, I'll help you get out of here. You'll be able to keep your baby."

She was almost tempted. She would do just about anything to get out of this place. But she decided right then and there that she would rather die than submit herself to sex with Henry.

She didn't have to work very hard to summon tears. "I want to keep my baby more than anything in the world. But I won't sin with you. And I'm very disappointed that you would ask that of me. I thought you were my friend."

"I'm sorry, Amanda," he said, immediately contrite. "But I had to know. I had to be sure you'd really changed, that you'd really repented." He touched her hair with infinite tenderness, and for a split second Amanda actually felt guilty for manipulating him. "I knew you were different," he said. "I just knew it. Aunt Odell is right about almost everything, but she's wrong about you. I'll help you leave here."

Amanda's heart hammered relentlessly inside her chest. He'd been trying to trick her, and she'd almost fallen for it! Thank God he was so repugnant, or she might have taken him up on his offer. "Thank you, Henry," she said.

"It's no good about those bars, though. They can't be taken off—they're too strong. I'll have to think of something else." He kissed her cheek before leaving.

Amanda lay on her cot, but she couldn't sleep. If she depended on Henry to come up with an escape plan, she might be waiting a long time. She would have to devise another plan herself.

Chapter 12

It was bad enough to have to work on New Year's Eve, Virginia Dreyfus thought, trying to quell the panic building up inside her. But it was much worse to get to work and find two police detectives waiting for her.

The moment Virginia had walked through the front door, Nancy Frieze had informed her that corporals Lomax and Triece were in her office. "They talked with the rest of us yesterday," Nancy said self-importantly. "I would have warned you about this, but they asked us not to talk about it, so . . ."

Yeah, right, Virginia thought. That would be the day when Nancy Frieze called her at home to do her a favor.

"They're really very nice," Nancy said. "You don't have to be afraid."

"What about the patients' confidentiality?" Virginia asked.

"Oh, the detectives have a subpoena, all nice and legal. Dr. Wayrick said we could tell them anything they wanted to know about . . . well, you'll find out."

As she headed for her office, Virginia wondered if the detectives would want to look at her notes, or if they would take her word for what went on during counseling sessions. At least her notes were in her own brand of shorthand. No outsider would be able to decipher them easily.

What did they already know? she asked herself. She was tempted to spill everything. The stress of the last few days, wondering, waiting for someone to make accusations, had taken its toll. She wished to God she'd never heard of Odell and her nasty little maternity home. She would give back all the money Odell had paid her—with interest—if only she could forget this whole thing.

Before rounding the corner and entering her office, she took several deep breaths and tried to imagine how she would act if she had nothing to hide. She would feel inconvenienced, perhaps, but she would want to do her civic duty. Yes, she would have to be cooperative, but not too friendly.

She wiped her palms on her wool skirt and walked crisply toward whatever fate awaited her. "Good morning, I'm Virginia Dreyfus," she said, quickly taking in her two visitors. "I understand you want to speak with me?"

The man stood and introduced himself and his lady colleague, shaking Virginia's hand. He smiled, which reassured her somewhat. "We'll try not to take up too much of your time."

She nodded as she sized up her opponents. She remembered the woman from her previous visit, when Amanda Arkin had first disappeared. Virginia would have thought the corporal too young to be anyone official, except for those eyes. There was a certain toughness reflected in their hazel depths; those eyes had seen a lot.

Virginia recalled how short-tempered she'd been with Carolyn Triece during their first interview. She wished now she had been more generous with her information. As it was, she could expect no sympathy from Corporal Triece's corner. Those hard eyes showed no signs of softening.

The man was young, too, but he seemed more affable than his partner. Yeah, she figured she could handle these two. After all, she knew a thing or two about the interviewing process. She did it every day for a living—reading between the lines, watching body language and listening to voice intonation.

For once she was glad of how shabby her office was. Maybe it would engender sympathy. Rather than moving behind her desk, she chose a chair near the small sofa where the detectives had settled. It seemed less adversarial that way.

"I suppose you know what we want to talk to you about," Corporal Lomax said as he set a small tape recorder on the table a few feet from her. He pulled a pair of glasses from his jacket pocket and put them on.

"Well, I assume this is about Amanda Arkin."

Lomax nodded and pulled out a notebook from his breast pocket. He appeared relaxed, but Virginia wasn't fooled. It was all an act. "Amanda Arkin was at or near the Women's Services Clinic at the time of her abduction."

"Oh, then she really was kidnapped?"

"We have reason to believe she didn't disappear of her own accord. We found her car. Inside it were signs of a struggle."

Virginia didn't have to fake her horror. Lately she had avoided reading the papers or watching the news, perhaps subconsciously unwilling to know any more about Amanda Arkin's disappearance. "I'm truly sorry. She seemed like a nice girl. But I don't know how I can help. I told Corporal, uh . . ." She looked helplessly at the other woman.

"Triece."

"Yes, of course. I told her everything of relevance. I even went over my notes afterward just to be sure, but . . ." She shrugged.

Lomax referred to his own notes. "You told Corporal Triece that Amanda was 'far from calm and rational.' What led you to believe that?"

"Years of experience counseling disturbed young women. She was close to tears much of the time we talked, and she did a lot of fidgeting. I'm sure in your line of work you recognize the signs of distress as easily as I do." She could only hope they weren't as adept at spotting lies, because she'd just told one. Amanda had conducted herself in a calm, deliberate manner during their counseling session.

"She was distressed about the pregnancy?"

"Why, yes, what else?"

"You didn't get the idea she might be upset about something else? Afraid of someone?"

"No, not at all. Lots of young women who find themselves unexpectedly pregnant are afraid of how their boyfriends will react, but Amanda had already told the father of her baby, and she gave me the impression that he was being very supportive."

Lomax nodded. "So there was nothing at all unusual in her demeanor the last time you saw her?"

"I saw her only the one time, so I have nothing with which to compare her behavior, but she seemed to me to be just like the dozens of other young women who get themselves into trouble." Virginia sighed hopelessly.

"Okay. I want you to go back to Wednesday, December 21. Amanda had made an appointment with you for additional counseling, correct?"

"Yes, but she didn't show."

"Did you think that unusual?"

"Not at all. It happens all the time. I had our receptionist phone Amanda's home, but she didn't get an answer. Then I put it out of my mind."

"Were you in the office all day that day?"

"I believe so. I usually eat lunch at my desk, and I don't recall having left for any reason, so, yes, I'm sure I was here all day." She nodded for emphasis, thanking her stars that at least she had an alibi for the time Amanda disappeared.

"I see that your office has a window facing out to the parking lot. What can you recall seeing out your window that day?"

"Nothing," she answered with certainty. "My view isn't what you would call picturesque. I leave the drapes drawn all the time, especially in the morning when the east sun shines in that window. I don't pay any attention to the goings-on in the parking lot."

"Could you have heard anything unusual that day? Loud voices, car horns, anything like that?"

She shook her head helplessly. "No, I'm sorry."

"All right."

Virginia allowed herself a quiet sigh of relief. Perhaps this ordeal was almost over. And she'd done splendidly, even if she did say so herself—just the right amount of concern, mixed with consternation and a tiny bit of impatience.

"Let's forget Amanda Arkin for the moment. I want to show you another girl's picture." From the back of his notebook he pulled a color photo and laid it on the table. Virginia had to lean over to look at it, but it took her only a moment to realize the picture was of Marcy Phelps.

Dear God, they'd connected Marcy to the clinic. Her mental pat on the back had been premature, Virginia realized. Whatever composure she'd been maintaining abruptly fled.

"She looks familiar to me," Virginia said with a barely discernible tremble to her voice, "but I'm not sure."

"Her name's Marcy Phelps."

Virginia put a hand to her breast. "Oh, the little girl who was found dead in that lake? I remember reading about it in the paper, but . . . did she . . . was she a patient at the clinic?"

"You tell me."

"Honestly, I don't know. She looks familiar, but that might be because I saw her picture in the paper or on TV. I see up to eight patients a day, and I don't always remember them." Oh, God, oh, God, she thought in despair. He knows I'm lying. She could feel dampness forming under her arms and at the back of her neck. She only hoped the detectives wouldn't notice if beads of sweat started popping up on her forehead.

"Marcy would have been to the clinic in June. I know that's a long time ago, but please try to remember—"

"I'm sorry, I really can't tell you for sure."

"Do you see all of the clinic's patients?"

"Most of them. The doctors strongly encourage counseling before a pregnancy termination, and most of the young women take that advice."

"Then you probably would have seen Marcy."

"If she was a patient at the clinic."

"She was impregnated by her older sister's boyfriend. Does that story ring a bell?"

Virginia shook her head apologetically.

"Are you sure?"

"In my line of work nothing shocks me. No one story is more memorable than the next. I don't dwell on them, or my own mental health might be at risk."

"All right. I have just one more picture to show you...." He produced another photograph. Virginia immediately recognized the girl. Although the name escaped her, the girl was another of Odell's recruits. In a split second, Virginia decided not to lie again. Telling as much of the truth as she could would be easier.

"Yes, I remember this girl, although not her name. Don't tell me she's missing, too."

"For more than three months."

Virginia could feel the blood draining from her face as she accepted the realization that all three girls she had referred to Odell were missing or dead. Odell wasn't merely luring girls to her home with propaganda. She was taking them by force.

"Marcy Phelps was missing since June?" Virginia had to ask, for her own peace of mind. She remembered the story Odell had told about Marcy running away from the home and how Odell had worked with Marcy's parents to locate the girl, to no avail.

Lomax raised one eyebrow, the only indication that Virginia's abrupt question surprised him. "The last anyone saw of her was June 6."

Odell had lied. And if she'd lied about Marcy running away, she could be lying about everything. She could be the one who threw Marcy's body off the dam, trying to make it look like suicide. And she could, right now, have Marcy's missing baby.

Virginia tried to school the horror out of her expression as she asked one last question. "I thought she was in a maternity home."

The corporal's attention was now riveted totally on Virginia. Any semblance of casualness was gone. "Why did you think that?"

"Oh, I just thought I read it in the paper. But I must have it mixed up with some other story."

Lomax took off his glasses and stared at her. And stared some more.

Virginia cleared her throat. "Is that all?"

"No, that's not all, Dr. Dreyfus." He turned to Corporal Triece. "Maybe we should take her down to the station."

Virginia was near panic. Should she play innocent and demand to know what he was talking about? Ask to call her lawyer? Or simply refuse to cooperate? She knew they couldn't arrest her without a warrant. But could they get a warrant if they wanted to? "I don't understand," she said. "Have I said something wrong?"

His silent stare scared her more than any accusation could have. He knew she wasn't telling the truth. There was no doubt in her mind. Perhaps even now he thought she was guilty of hurting those girls.

Maybe she was; if not directly guilty, then she'd certainly been an unwitting accomplice.

Suddenly the enormity of what she'd done hit her square in the chest. She'd as good as sent Marcy Phelps to her grave. And who knew what horrible things those two other girls were enduring—if they were even alive? No, they had to be alive, Virginia thought, consoling herself. Odell wanted their babies.

"Why don't you tell us exactly what you remember about a maternity home?"

Virginia knew that the next few words she spoke would determine whether they would detain her or let her go. And abruptly the decision as to what to say came easily. She'd done nothing criminal. Unethical, yes, but she hadn't yet crossed that line that would send her to prison. And she didn't intend to start now.

"There's a woman named Odell," she began. And the words spilled out of her. She told them everything—about the referrals and the money she'd received, the details of how she contacted Odell and vice versa, Odell's repeated assurances that she took good care of "her girls" and how she carefully screened all prospective adoptive parents.

"I didn't see the harm in exposing those young women to some pro-life literature," she said. "I'm not necessarily pro-choice myself. I work at the clinic because that's where I could find work. If I'd had any idea what was really happening..." She had to swallow hard to dislodge the lump in her throat.

"What did you think when you heard about Marcy Phelps disappearing?" Lomax asked.

"The first I read anything about Marcy Phelps was when her body was identified. I don't remember when she disappeared. I don't always read the paper, and I almost never watch television."

"And what about when you heard of Amanda's disappearance?"

"I thought it an odd coincidence that two of the girls I'd referred to Odell had come back to haunt me in the same week. I even called Odell and asked her about Amanda, but she claimed that Amanda wasn't receptive to her attempts to get her to come to the maternity home, and I believed her. She's very persuasive."

"But you don't know this mysterious woman's last name, or where she lives, or where the home is," Lomax asked, one eyebrow lifted skeptically.

"No. She struck me as slightly paranoid about remaining anonymous, and now I can understand why. But I didn't push her, especially when she proved to be reliable about paying me just as she said she would."

"How did the payments come?" Corporal Triece asked, looking suddenly alert. It was the first she'd participated in the questioning.

"Cash, through the mail."

"Postmark? Return address?"

"No return address. I was curious, though, and I did check the postmarks. They were all from Dallas except one, which was from . . . Tyler, I think it was."

The two detectives exchanged a glance. Did Tyler mean something, she wondered?

They kept after her for what seemed like hours, going over and over the same questions. Virginia answered each query patiently and thoroughly, and as the interview wore on she sensed the two detectives growing less antagonistic toward her. She hoped that meant they believed her.

At some point it occurred to her that she should have called her lawyer, but she supposed by then it didn't matter. If she was going to incriminate herself, she'd probably already done it. The important thing now was to cooperate in finding those missing girls. That was the only way she could possibly avoid being dragged down with Odell.

"Not in? When will he be back?" Odell asked the unidentified woman who had answered the phone. Even on Saturday—even on New Year's Eve—there were always workaholics on hand at the law firm, and Travis was usually one of them.

"That's hard to say. He's out of the country."

"Out of the . . . Don't be ridiculous," Odell snapped. "This is his sister. If he'd left the country, don't you think I'd know it?"

"Apparently not."

"Look, I'm not one of his creditors. I'm his sister, Odell, and I demand that you put him on the phone."

"He's not in," the woman repeated without an ounce of civility in her voice. "You might try Tokyo." With that she hung up.

Odell couldn't believe this was happening. She tried calling Travis at home, but she got no answer there. She knew his financial situation was pretty grim, but could it possibly be so bad that he'd skipped the country? Without talking to her about it? Or—and this possibility filled her with dread—had the authorities found more concrete evidence regarding the illegal adoptions? Surely, if that were the case, Travis would have warned her.

Then again, her brother wasn't in the habit of consulting her about his activities. He usually didn't think any further than looking after his own precious skin. In fact, although he professed to want to atone for the sins of their childhood, Odell suspected his main motivation for becoming involved in her plans was money.

She sat down at her desk and put her head in her hands. Things were falling apart. One of the girls, Heather, had miscarried last night. That meant Odell would soon have another vacancy. Then, this morning, Odell had read in the paper that the police had located the father of Marcy Phelps's baby. That meant they were one step closer to connecting Marcy with the Women's Services Clinic.

Odell had made a drastic mistake in taking Amanda Arkin from the clinic parking lot. She had focused police attention on the clinic, and that might yet prove to be her undoing. She'd always known that someday she would overlook some detail and the authorities would catch up with her. But she hadn't thought it would be so soon.

Still, she wasn't undone yet, she thought as a sudden burst of resilience surged through her. She was doing God's work, and He would protect her. Without Travis and the money his adoptions brought in, she would have a hard time of it, but she still had some financial reserves. If she had to, she could abandon the babies on doorsteps, like they used to in the olden days. With the huge demand for healthy white babies, she knew the infants would be well provided for.

She decided it was time to step up her activities. She would bring as many girls into the home as she safely could. Even if she couldn't deliver all of the babies before everything came crashing down, at least the Good Shepherd Maternity Home would be filled with girls too far along to have abortions. Her goal of saving thirty-four babies—the exact number she had helped kill—seemed far away.

She would have to take some extra precautions regarding her contact with Virginia and the Women's Services Clinic, she decided. She wouldn't make any more calls from her cellular phone. Although it would be an inconvenience, she would have to use pay phones from now on.

She considered dropping Virginia altogether. The woman had been a nuisance lately, asking nosy questions. But Virginia had been Odell's best source. The psychologist had a knack for picking out the girls who would make the best residents for the home—like Amanda and Marcy, God rest her soul. No, there was no sense in giving up on Virginia, not yet. Odell would just have to be on her guard.

She smelled the unmistakably delectable odor of pot roast coming from the kitchen and realized that she'd been moping here in her office for a long time. Henry probably could use some help with dinner, although apparently he had things well in hand. Sometimes it amazed her that he could cope so well with his diminished mental capacity. He had proved himself invaluable lately, finally settling into his role guarding the girls. She'd been afraid he would take his authority too much to heart, but he seemed to be just stern enough to intimidate, yet never cruel for cruelty's sake. She was lucky to have him, for she could never have managed this place alone. Henry was a good boy, for all his peculiarities.

Caro was exhausted, mentally, physically, and emotionally. She couldn't remember ever working on any case that had wrung her out the way this one did. She'd been elated by the information Virginia Dreyfus had revealed, but disappointed that the psychologist couldn't lead them immediately to this Odell character. Still, it had seemed a simple-enough task to track Odell down through the answering service—then not so simple after all.

"Any luck?" Austin asked hopefully, looking up as Caro approached his desk. He'd sent her to check out Wanda's Answering Service, the outfit through which Virginia and Odell kept in touch.

"You won't believe this," Caro said wearily as she snagged a nearby chair and plopped down in it. "Odell is anything but stupid. She deliberately chose a real rinky-dink operation for an answering service. Wanda runs the business out of her spare bedroom. Odell pays her in cash, in advance, by mail. She didn't fill out any forms, so there's no address or phone number on record. She calls in every few days for messages. That's the only contact Wanda has with her."

"But the phone company has put a trace on the line, right?"

"Oh, yes. Wanda was most anxious to help, and she says she'll let us know the minute Odell calls in."

"Then we've got her."

"But how long will that take?" An uncharacteristic frustration welled up inside Caro. "Damn it, I was set to move in. Every day the case drags on is another day those girls are held against their will."

"But they're alive. Until we talked to Virginia, I wasn't holding out much hope. But if Odell is really a rabid pro-lifer, she'll keep those girls alive at least until the babies are born. That gives us plenty of time."

"Unless Virginia warns Odell and she slips away."

"Virginia's too afraid of us. She knows damn well we could arrest her at any time for obstruction of justice. She even signed a statement attesting to the fact that she'd deliberately misled the police to cover up her unethical conduct."

"And you still think it's best not to get a warrant right now?"

"If we'd arrested her, her lawyer would have had her out in a matter of hours, anyway. We might need her cooperation."

"Yeah, I guess you're right." Caro sat up straighter and tunneled her fingers through her wind-tangled hair, pushing it off her face. "We've made remarkable progress today. I should be pleased, I suppose. What's that you're doing?" Austin had a Texas map spread out on his desk.

"See for yourself. Remember the first time we talked about a possible connection between the Arkin and Phelps cases?"

"And we dismissed it then as too farfetched."

"But remember how we plotted points on the map? Marcy's body was found at the Cedar Creek spillway." He pointed to a red dot he'd made on the map. "Amanda's car was found in Taryton. Amanda's letter was postmarked from Kips Point." More red dots. "One of Virginia's payments was postmarked from Tyler. I also just received word this afternoon that the Taryton police located a trucker who remembers picking up a hitchhiker close to Taryton the night Amanda's car was abandoned. His description matches the one Chucky gave you for the car thief. The hitchhiker asked to be let off here, near a town called Caney—which, incidentally, isn't all that far from River Rock." He made two more red dots.

"River Rock—where Justin Krill was born." Caro studied the pattern—and there definitely was one. The dots were grouped in an area south and east of Dallas. Unfortunately, the pattern was far from tight. "That's about a four-hundred square-mile area. I don't think we're ready to search with dogs and helicopters just yet."

"Pessimist." Austin reached out and flipped a strand of hair off her face. "It's a start."

Her whole body tensed at the brief contact as a pleasurable chill wiggled up her spine. Her already-fuzzy mind locked up, utterly useless, as Austin looked at her and smiled that annoyingly charming crooked smile of his.

She mentally shook herself, forcing her thoughts back to business. "Any word about the Krills?" Chief Raines had nixed the idea of twenty-four-hour surveillance of the Krill home. Too expensive. But Caro had been hoping that the neighbor would come through.

Austin shook his head, still smiling. "We won't need them," he said confidently.

"In that case, is there anything else you want me to do right now?"

"How about making some more phone calls? Maybe you can locate another girl the way you did Julie Yates. Virginia said those three girls were the only ones she'd been paid for, but who's to say Odell is honest?"

"Okay," she said without much enthusiasm. What she really wanted was to go home and crawl into bed with a good book. She stood up and was just about to leave when she spotted Tony Villaverde heading their way, grinning ear to ear. "What are you doing down here, Villaverde?"

"Looking for you. Fran told me to track you down before I went home today and make sure you were coming tonight."

"I'm coming," Caro said, trying to inject some enthusiasm into her voice. "I'm going to drink myself into oblivion and sleep on your living room floor."

"Yeah, right." Tony turned to Austin. "You ever seen this lightweight drink more than half a glass of wine?"

"I've never even seen that," Austin said, his tone indicating that he'd like to.

"Well, you got plans for the evening?" Tony asked. "You're welcome to come to my party. In fact, we'll be celebrating more than just New Year's Eve." He looked at Caro. "My transfer came through."

"Oh, Tony, that's..." She felt like her mouth and throat were full of cotton. "That's really terrific," she managed to say as she gave him a hug. "Tony's transferring to CAPERS," she told Austin.

"Great, congratulations!" He shook Tony's hand. "Now you can look forward to being the new kid on the block, a title I'll gladly relinquish."

"Hey, thanks, man. Seriously, my wife and I would love to have you over tonight."

Caro realized she was holding her breath, waiting for Austin's answer.

"Thanks, but I already have plans."

She couldn't deny the disappointment she felt. Why, when she spent so many waking hours with Austin, would she want to see him during one of her brief periods of leisure time?

The answer to that was painfully apparent, even to a woman in denial. She was so attracted to the man she sometimes couldn't think straight around him. That, more than anything, was why she couldn't wait for this investigation to be over.

Chapter 13

Caro was glad she'd come to the Villaverdes' crowded, noisy party, she decided as she nursed her second plastic cup full of white wine. It felt good to relax and forget about work for a while. Now that the phone company had installed tracers on the lines at both Wanda's Answering Service and the Women's Services Clinic, there was nothing to do but wait until Odell tipped her hand.

It was both exhilarating and tense to be so close but feel so helpless at the same time. Caro hadn't truly relaxed in so long she wasn't sure she remembered how to do it. But the wine was definitely helping.

"And you had to bottle-feed all twelve puppies?" Caro asked the woman she'd been half listening to for the last few minutes, the Villaverdes' neighbor, who'd been waxing eloquent on her Doberman pinscher's whelping experience.

The woman started to answer when Fran Villaverde bustled between them with a squeal of delight, throwing her arms around Caro. "Oh, honey, it's so good to see you," she said, her black curls bouncing with every word. She was one of those round, bubbly cheerleader types who always had a smile, and it was impossible to remain in a bad mood around her. "I saw the stuffed mushrooms in the dining room," she continued, "and I knew you were here somewhere in this mad crush. I'm so glad you could make it."

"Did I have a choice?" Caro said, grinning. "I got the impression I would be drawn and quartered if I didn't show up."

"Well, I wasn't going to let you squirrel your way out of this party like you did the last one."

The neighbor wandered away to find another audience for her Doberman puppy story. Fran bit her lip guiltily. "She is a dear—the twins just love her. Then again, what kid wouldn't love someone with twelve puppies? Come on, let's sit down for a minute and catch up." She dragged Caro to a love seat in the corner of the living room and almost pushed her into it. "What do you think about Tony's transfer?"

"I'm devastated, what else?" Caro answered honestly. "There's no one else in our department I can rely on like I do Tony. But I think he'll do great in CAPERS. Homicide section, no less."

"Why don't you go with him?" Fran asked innocently.

"I was already there once, remember?" Caro said with a dismissive wave of her hand. "Four years in CAPERS is enough. Too much pressure. If I needed any reminders, the last couple of weeks I've been working on these two cases—"

"Oh, Tony told me. That Lomax guy's been driving you crazy, huh?"

"It's the work that's been driving me crazy. I'm not used to it. And I don't think I want to get used to it."

"But what about Lomax?" Fran persisted, making Caro wonder what Tony had told her. Fran was an incurable matchmaker, always on the lookout to hook up her single friends with suitable partners. She and Tony were so happily married, she wanted everyone else to be, too.

"He's okay," Caro said with a shrug.

"Tony says you kind of sparkle whenever you're around him."

"Oh, Tony's full of it!" Caro scoffed, though inwardly she was mortified. Was her response to Austin that plain for anyone to see? "Austin Lomax is an egotistical jerk. I don't 'sparkle' when I'm around him, I fume," she added for good measure.

Fran leveled her gaze at Caro. "Whatever you say."

"No, really, Fran I—"

"Well, if you're not interested in Austin, then you have to meet Glen. Remember I told you about him?"

"The aerobics instructor," Caro said with mounting trepidation. "He's not here, is he?" She mentally crossed her fingers.

"Yeah, he's right over there. Red sweater, black jeans? I know you two would hit it off. Glen!" she called, motioning with her hand while Caro tried to sink deeper into the sofa cushions. "Come over here, I'd like you to meet a friend of mine. Glen, this is Caro

Triece. She works with my husband." Fran turned to Caro. "Glen teaches aerobics at my health club and he's writing a fitness book. Oh, look, you both need refills on your drinks. Let me take care of that for you."

Fran snatched their glasses out of their hands and disappeared.

"Subtle, isn't she?" Caro said as Glen, a mountain of muscle with flowing blond hair, sat gingerly on the love seat next to her.

"Huh?" he said. Not a promising beginning.

"So, you're writing a book," she began, and that was all it took. For the next fifteen minutes he told her all about his idea for a book on how to be your own personal fitness trainer. He'd already written three pages, he related proudly. Caro entertained herself by thinking of all the ways she would get back at Fran. And when she'd run out of methods for torture, she tried to think of a clever way to extricate herself, although she could probably tell Glen his feet were on fire and he would dutifully whisk himself out of her presence in search of a hose.

In the end she didn't need to come up with anything brilliant. A strong hand grabbed her by the arm and practically lifted her off the love seat. "Excuse us for a minute," the man said. It took Caro several confused moments to reconcile the fact that the man was Austin Lomax.

"What are you doing here?" she asked as he dragged her into a private corner behind the Christmas tree.

"Rescuing you from Conan the Barbarian?"

"Glen and I were having a very interesting conversation," she said, unsure why she was bothering to fabricate such an outrageous lie. She should be grateful to Lomax for what he'd done, and she was, but she was also irritated by his high-handedness.

"Is that why you were studying the chandelier like it held the secret of life?"

"Never mind Glen. What are you doing here? I thought you had 'plans.'" She was alarmed at the shrewishness she heard in her own voice. What did she care about his plans? But she had to admit that, more than once, she had pictured Austin at some other party with a date, and the image had bothered her.

"I'm here on business," he said. "Odell called her answering service to check for messages."

Caro was instantly alert. "And?"

"The phone company couldn't trace the call."

"Why not?"

"They think Odell has a cellular phone."

"But they can at least trace cellular calls to the general area where the repeater is located, right?"

"Ordinarily. But if she puts her phone on call forwarding and then uses another phone and calls the cellular phone, she would reach the answering service without leaving any kind of clue. That type of call is virtually untraceable."

"I'll be damned," Caro said. Frustration welled up inside her, tightening her gut. She wanted to hit something, although for a change it wasn't Austin. "You came all the way over here to tell me that?"

"I had to tell somebody. I didn't want to be the only one whose New Year's Eve was ruined."

"Thanks a heap." She looked at him more closely then, noticing the fact that he hadn't shaved recently, and he was still wearing the same clothes he'd had on earlier. Not that this lapse made him any less sexy, but it did make her curious. "What happened to your date?"

"What date?"

"Didn't you say you had a date?"

"I said I had plans. There's a difference."

Caro felt a ridiculous surge of relief, which she promptly stifled. She might be a little fuzzy from the wine, but she should still be able to keep her mind on business. "What do we do next?"

He shrugged. "I don't know about you, but I'd like a beer."

"I mean about the case."

"I know what you mean. I still want a beer." Scowling fiercely, he brushed past her and plunged into the throng of party-goers, leaving Caro alone behind the Christmas tree.

With her back to the wall, she slowly bent her knees and slid to a sitting position on the floor, hoping no one would see her or bother her. After hearing Austin's news, she didn't want to be here anymore. The last thing she felt like doing was celebrating. All she could think about was those poor girls. How were they marking the holiday? Were they even aware of it? According to Virginia, Odell had said she treated the girls well, but that didn't mean anything. It was already firmly established that Odell lied.

Caro was trying to figure out how she could discreetly escape the party when a cold glass of wine—in a real wineglass—appeared before her face as if by magic. She looked up to find that Austin was attached to the offering. He had a bottle of beer for himself.

"I remember Tony said something about you drinking wine," he said as she accepted his gift. "Is white okay, or would you like red better?"

"This is fine, thanks," she said, amazed that he'd thought of her at all, much less remembered what she liked to drink. She took an appreciative sip.

He sat on the floor beside her, and they were quiet for several minutes. Finally he spoke. "Are you as bummed out about this as I am?"

"At least."

"You asked what we're supposed to do next, and to tell you the truth, I don't know." Austin began ticking off the frustrations on his fingers. "Amanda's letter had at least two sets of prints on it that weren't Russ Arkin's, but they didn't match up to any prints we have on file in the computer. The only physical evidence in Amanda's car that might be helpful were two gray hairs attached to the broken fingernail. But they're useless until we catch a suspect. Travis Beaman is still out of the country. The Krills haven't shown up yet, either. And now our prime suspect has outsmarted us." When he ran out of fingers on one hand he stopped and took a long pull on the beer bottle.

"I even checked with the FBI to see if they had any similar cases," he went on, "like a rash of disappearing pregnant girls, or missing girls connected to an abortion clinic. Nothing."

"When did you do that?"

"A little while ago."

"You've been working this whole evening?"

"I told you I had plans. Those were my plans, to keep working." When she looked at him questioningly, he added, "I didn't want to admit that I didn't have anything to do tonight, okay? Don't give me the third degree about it."

"Okay." She settled back against the wall and smiled. For some reason it tickled her that she and Austin both had to practically be dragged to a New Year's Eve party.

"I only came here to talk about the case," he said defensively. "I'm not much in the mood for parties."

"Then let's talk. Any other ideas?"

"I haven't come up with much, but . . . we could set up recorders at the clinic and the answering service, and tape any incoming calls from Odell. Maybe she'll give something away, or her voice or some background noise will give us a clue."

Well, it was something, anyway. Better than doing nothing. Caro had an idea of her own. "How many 'Odells' do you suppose there are in Texas? It's not a very common name."

"Are you suggesting we ask the Department of Motor Vehicles to check and see?" he asked, gazing at her skeptically. "Odell might be an alias."

"Hey, I didn't pooh-pooh your idea."

He actually cracked a smile. "Sorry. Okay, it's worth a shot. Your wild shots seem to pay off. Maybe we could also—what is that woman doing?'' He was staring at Fran, who had climbed up onto a chair and was tapping a glass with a knife to get everyone's attention.

"Quiet, everyone, quiet," she yelled above the party noise. "It's about thirty seconds to midnight, so everybody put on your Chap Stick—"

She was interrupted as a ten-second countdown chorus began. Tony, impatient for those last few seconds, pulled Fran off the chair and into his arms in a showy kiss.

All at once it hit Caro what was about to happen. In five more seconds everybody in the room would be kissing someone. She stared resolutely at a little drum hanging from the Christmas tree, acutely aware of the warmth of Austin's body next to hers, then the brush of his breath on her cheek. Somewhere a champagne cork popped, and midnight arrived.

"Well?" Austin said softly in her ear.

"Well what?" Her voice was breathless and girlish-sounding as panic rose in her chest.

"Happy New Year, Caro." He pressed a warm kiss on her ear, then her neck.

She turned toward him, helpless to stop herself. There was something so compelling about the huskiness in his voice, the smoky smell of his after-shave, and the sudden ache of loneliness that needed to be filled. She let him kiss her...no, she kissed him, hard and deep as the need expanded and encompassed both of them. His hands were in her hair and his tongue was in her mouth, and she suddenly felt connected to Austin Lomax in a way she'd never experienced with anyone. Maybe it was the shared frustration of the case, or the fact that they were working toward a common goal, or maybe it was simply a case of hormones running amok. But she didn't want to stop kissing him. She didn't want to break the fine thread of understanding that had finally been spun between them.

Austin pulled away first. It was only then Caro realized their embrace was being serenaded by a chorus of whistles and catcalls. She'd been so caught up she'd forgotten they were in Tony's living room with dozens of people—many of them her colleagues—all around them.

Her face burned with embarrassment. "I don't know about you, but I'm getting out of here," she said, struggling to her feet.

"I'm right behind you. Where's your coat and purse?"

"Hall closet. I didn't bring a purse."

"I'll meet you outside. You'll see my car."

It didn't even occur to her to argue. All she could think about was escaping. She would worry about the rest later.

Fran managed to waylay her at the front door. "Austin's an egotistical jerk, huh?" she teased. "He must have other attributes."

"Fran, please . . ."

Apparently sensing Caro's distress, Fran was immediately contrite. "Oh, honey, I'm sorry. Did we embarrass you?"

"I embarrassed myself." Caro reached for the doorknob.

"Wait a minute. Where's your coat?"

"Austin's getting it. There's been a new development in the case we're working on, and we need to go take care of some things," Caro fudged.

Fran wasn't fooled for a minute. She gave Caro a sly smile, and then a hug. "Don't work too hard. Happy New Year."

Caro hugged her back, then slipped out the front door into the crisp, clear night. Austin wasn't kidding when he said she'd see his car. The conspicuous silver Jag was wedged between two other cars, hanging half in the street. Apparently he hadn't been patient enough to find a proper parking space.

Austin appeared moments later. Silently he held her jacket out for her. She slid her arms into the sleeves, and he held her briefly, then let her go. "That was some kiss," he said as easily as if he were talking about the hors d'oeuvres.

She couldn't disagree with him; he would know she was lying. "Do you think we could just forget about it?" she ventured.

He gave a low, wicked laugh. "Not on your life." He took her hand and led her toward his car.

"No, Austin, really, I ought to be getting home. . . ."

He ignored her ineffectual protest, and part of her—the crazy part, she supposed—was glad. She didn't want to say good-night to him just yet.

The Jag was a sexy car, she had to admit. The engine roared powerfully beneath the hood, and she could feel the road under her. By watching Austin steer, she could tell that the Jag handled the curves beautifully. The heater, however, left something to be desired. It continued to blast cold air at her even after a couple of minutes, and she folded her arms tightly across her breasts.

"Where are we going?" she finally asked, fearful of his answer.

"My house."

She stifled a groan. Oh, Lord, what was she doing? If she had even an ounce of willpower, she would order him to turn around right now and take her back to the party, where she could get her own car and hightail it home.

"You don't like that idea?"

"Uh, well . . ."

"I thought I might rustle up some breakfast, and we could do some more brainstorming."

"Oh." She wasn't sure she believed him.

"We can do it another time if you're too tired—"

"No, I'm fine." And she'd be damned if she would fizzle out before him. If this was some kind of endurance showdown, she didn't intend to be outshone. She knew it was juvenile to feel so competitive toward Austin, but she supposed if a spirit of competition spurred them both to go the extra mile on this case, that made it acceptable.

Austin lived in east Dallas, not all that far from Caro's neighborhood, in a compact white frame house that stuck out among its brick neighbors.

"It used to be a farmhouse, and the city grew up around it," he explained as he unlocked the front door. The moment the door was open, a mammoth black dog was all over Austin, its front paws braced against his chest as he tried to dodge its wide pink tongue. "Hello, Shadow, yes, hello." As soon as Austin greeted the dog properly, it calmed down.

"You're a big guy, aren't you?" Caro said as she gingerly patted the beast's head. His sheer size was daunting, but he appeared harmless enough.

"That's Shadow," Austin said. "C'mon, boy, let's go outside."

Those were the magic words. The dog bounded after its master as Austin led the way presumably to a back door.

Caro peeked into the living and dining rooms, then wandered into the kitchen. The whole house had a sparse country look—not some decorator's idea of country, but the real thing. It was obvious Austin didn't rank housework among his top priorities, but then, neither did she.

"What kind of omelet do you like?" he asked as he strode into the kitchen. "Your choices are cheese, cheese and—" he rummaged through the refrigerator "—cheese."

He was really going to cook for her? She found the idea disturbingly intimate—almost as bad as dragging her straight to the bedroom. "I'll have cheese, thank you." One omelet wouldn't kill her.

"You want to make some orange juice?"

"Sure." She felt better keeping busy in the old-fashioned kitchen while Austin cooked—mixing the juice, setting the table, brewing coffee for him and tea for herself. With her hands safely occupied, she could resist touching him as he moved easily between the stove and refrigerator. She could only hope he really didn't have seduction on the agenda. Her body was vibrating in so many different places, she wouldn't stand a chance against him.

And going to bed with Austin would be madness.

Within a few short minutes they were sitting down at the kitchen table to a modest feast. Caro hadn't realized how hungry she was. She devoured her omelet and two pieces of toast. Austin matched her bite for bite.

When they were finished he set the dishes in the sink and refilled his coffee cup. Caro, too lazy to brew more tea, opted for coffee instead. She didn't really like the taste, but she figured the caffeine wouldn't hurt.

"You really want to work?" he asked, and she thought she detected a note of wistfulness in his voice.

Actually, she could think of several attractive alternatives, all of them involving the removal of key items of clothing and contact between various body parts. She forced a bright smile. "Sure, let's get after it."

He led her into a small den that he'd set up as an office, with an old rolltop desk—just as messy as his desk at work, with two aging cups of cold coffee. There was a short sofa pushed into one corner, a curtainless window, and a whole wall of bookshelves. Caro plopped down on the sofa, pulled off her boots and tucked her feet under her.

Austin handed her a legal pad and pen. He sat down at the old-fashioned rolling desk chair with his own pad, his ankle crossed over the other knee, glasses on. Caro had noticed that Austin wore his glasses only when he had to—due to vanity, perhaps?—so he was probably serious about this working thing.

"Brainstorm," he said. "Write down every idea, no matter how ridiculous or stupid you think it is. Turn off your inner critic."

"Okay." She'd been to a seminar once—probably Austin had, too—where this method was suggested, but she'd never actually used it to try and solve a case. It took a few moments to get started, but once she heard Austin's pen scratching frantically against his paper, her competitive instincts took over and her list of ideas began to take shape.

Some of the ideas were realistic. Caro suggested they save the next envelope Odell sent to either Virginia or Wanda and have it analyzed at the lab for paper content as well as fingerprints. Perhaps, if it wasn't a common brand, they could track down where Odell bought it. Austin thought of consulting with a mental health professional to get a psychological profile of Odell.

But as the night wore on, the ideas got sillier. It became impossible not to laugh at some of Austin's suggestions.

"Let's just set bear traps all over Texas for her," Caro said with a giggle, feeling punchy. It was close to three in the morning.

Austin didn't laugh. In fact, he wasn't smiling at all. "A trap, huh?"

"I'm just kidding."

He didn't respond. His expression was pensive, and it was almost as if Caro was no longer in the room.

Not wanting to disturb his thinking process—if indeed that was what was going on—she made herself more comfortable on the couch, stretching her legs out and leaning her head against the armrest. Within thirty seconds she was asleep.

Austin went to let Shadow in for the night. A trap. Set a trap. The words echoed over and over in his head. But what kind of trap?

When he returned to the office, an idea was beginning to germinate in his imagination. He started to tell Caro about it, but he realized she'd fallen asleep. Transfixed, he simply stared at her for uncounted minutes, moved by the quiet beauty reflected in her face.

He'd never seen her so relaxed, without that constant wariness she carried around with her. With her brown hair gilded by the lamplight and the serenity lent by sleep, she reminded him of a painting he'd once seen of the Madonna—young, innocent.

Young. Without that tough maturity reflected in her eyes, she really did look amazingly youthful for a woman well past thirty. And that's when it hit him. The elusive idea he'd been searching for all night suddenly clicked into place.

Chapter 14

Caro awoke to the questionable benefit of having a wide, pink tongue washing her face. "Oh—Oh! Get away. Yuck." She wiped her face with the back of her hand.

"Shadow! Come here!" Austin skidded into the den, and Caro immediately forgot the dog. Her host had obviously just gotten out of the shower, and he wore only a snug pair of jeans—not quite fastened all the way—and no shirt. "Sorry, he got away from me."

She quietly groaned as he left the room, dog in tow. If she didn't know better, she would think he'd flaunted himself in front of her that way on purpose, just to torture her. She had another reason for groaning. It was daylight outside. She'd spent the night at Austin's house, and Tony would know it because her car was still in front of the Villaverdes' house. No matter how she tried to explain, he wouldn't believe her. And he'd never let her hear the end of it.

She'd like nothing better than to blame this on Austin, but it was her own fault. She'd left the party with him, and she'd allowed herself to fall asleep. But it could be worse. At least she hadn't awakened in Austin's bed.

As Caro was finger-combing her hair and trying to get her bearings, Austin reappeared—slightly more dressed. He had on a half-buttoned shirt. But he was carrying two steaming mugs, so she would probably forgive him anything.

He handed her one of the mugs. "Tea." And he sat on the couch next to her, much too close. She felt stale and grungy next to his abounding cleanness.

"Th-thank you. What time is it?"

"Almost ten."

"Ten! I have to get home!" She started to rise, but he grabbed the back of her sweater and held her in place.

"Stop panicking. If I were going to pounce on you, I'd have done it last night. And the Villaverdes have already seen your car, so there's no reason to hurry on that account."

"They have?"

Austin grinned. "Tony called me this morning, doing the protective-older-brother routine."

Now Caro did groan. "What did you tell him?"

"What do you think I told him? That we were working and you fell asleep on my couch." He flashed that lazy, crooked grin, the one that did funny things to her insides. "I was tempted to make up something better, but I sort of like my face the way it is."

So did she. "I'll have to thank Tony for defending my virtue."

"Yeah, but tell him it's not necessary. You do a pretty good job defending your own virtue." As he spoke, he buried his hand beneath the mass of her hair, found the sensitive nape of her neck, and began a slow massage.

She let him.

"Do you know how bad I wanted to make love to you last night?"

"Austin, don't even—"

"I know what you're going to say, so don't bother. I agree completely. As long as we're working on this case, we'd be nuts to get involved."

She jumped off the couch like she'd been spring-loaded. "Not just while we're on this case," she argued, pacing the small room, clutching her mug close to her body as if it could defend her against Austin's charm, his appeal, his touch. "I can't get involved with you, period."

"Why not?" he asked, all innocence. He had no idea how close he was to making her abandon her good sense.

"Because we work together—even though normally we won't see each other on a day-to-day basis," she added quickly, forestalling his argument. "If we were to...you know, it would be difficult to keep it confidential, and it wouldn't look good, professionally speaking. It might even damage our careers. Besides, you know as well as I do that cops don't have the best track record when it comes to relationships, and two cops in the same relationship . . . I think we'd just be asking for trouble."

"Are you about finished?"

She racked her brain for more convincing arguments. Admittedly, what she'd said so far sounded disjointed and superficial. But it was more than just a vague worry about professionalism. Deep inside—for reasons unknown—she believed that to open up her heart to Austin Lomax would be dangerous. She simply couldn't risk it. But neither could she put that fear into words. The words didn't exist to describe it.

"I guess I'm done," she said forlornly. "Will you take me back to my car now?"

"Not yet." He appeared thoughtful for a moment, then abruptly shook his head, as if to clear it of cobwebs. "We still have business to take care of. I came up with a great idea last night after you fell asleep, but it's kind of wild, and I'll need your cooperation and support before I bring it up to Chief Raines."

Oh, we're back to talking about work. He'd certainly dismissed her rejection with no trouble. No moaning or teeth-gnashing. Ridiculously, she felt a little disappointed that he hadn't tried harder. "Okay, what's the idea?"

Obviously agitated, he stood up and moved around the room distractedly. Since there wasn't room for both of them to pace, she sat back down.

"Have you ever worked undercover?" he asked.

"Once," she answered warily, unsure she liked the direction this conversation was taking. "No, a couple of times. Remember I told you about posing as bait for the serial rapist? And once I played the part of a hooker. We were trying to catch this guy who was beating up prostitutes down on Cedar Springs."

"Great. Okay, this is the idea. You said we needed to set a bear trap for Odell, and that's exactly what we'll do. We'll get Virginia Dreyfus's cooperation—I don't think we'll have any trouble there. She's feeling pretty guilty about the whole thing. We'll have Virginia leave a message for Odell at the answering service. And when Odell calls back—assuming we still can't trace the call—Virginia will tell her about a new patient at the clinic whom she feels is a perfect candidate for Odell's maternity home."

"Meaning me?" Dear God, he'd gone off the deep end this time. "Austin, in case you haven't noticed, I'm thirty-three years old."

"Yeah, but you don't look it." She started to object, but he cut her off. "C'mon, Caro, admit it. You could pass for twenty. Besides, by the time Odell gets close enough to question your age, we'll have her."

Caro accepted that logic for the moment. "Okay, go on."

"When Virginia talks to Odell, she really lays it on thick—how this poor little girl is in such a quandary about her pregnancy, how shy and retiring she is. Remember, Virginia said Odell had specifically requested girls with a certain temperament—malleable, suggestible, nonaggressive types."

"But Odell doesn't take all the girls whose names Virginia has given her. For whatever reason, she ignores some of them. How do we know she'll want this girl?"

"Maybe Odell checks out all the names, only kidnapping the ones she can get to easily, without witnesses. We'll just make certain that the girl Virginia describes is perfect. We'll also make sure Virginia mentions the fact that the girl's parents are out of town, so Odell will know she's vulnerable. The temptation will be irresistible."

"So you want me to make myself available for kidnapping?"

"My brother has an empty rental house you can use," he said, ignoring her trepidation. "It's perfect. We'll have two detectives in the house with you at all times. And my dad has an old panel van you can drive. Your escorts can go with you anywhere undetected. Of course, you'll be wearing a body mike. You'll be safe as a babe in arms."

Caro took a few moments to mull over the scenario. It really wasn't so bad, she had to admit. "Have you pondered how much this operation will cost?"

"That's the big drawback. But the house and the van are free, so the only thing we'll have to pay for is some overtime. As paranoid as Chief Raines is about this case, I think he just might go for it. It's a mystery to me why the media haven't latched on to Amanda Arkin's kidnapping and run with it. Eventually they will, and then it might just blow up in our faces. I think Raines would like to get it solved before that happens."

Caro said nothing as she tried to find holes in the plan. But she couldn't. It was simple and straightforward. Either Odell would take the bait and they'd have her, or she wouldn't and they'd have wasted a lot of time and money. But what other options did they have?

"Can I count on you to back me up?" Austin asked.

After a slight hesitation, she nodded. "Yeah, I'll do it."

"Great. I'm going to call a meeting for tomorrow afternoon with Chief Raines, your superiors and my superiors. The sooner we get this thing underway, the sooner we'll find those girls." He held out his hand. "Come on, I'll take you back to your car. I have a lot of details to work out between now and tomorrow."

She placed her hand in his and let him pull her to her feet, but he didn't release her. Instead he pulled her right up against his chest, and before she could even think of objecting he kissed her, fast and hard.

"There's such a thing as taking a calculated risk, you know."

Caro wondered if he was talking about the undercover operation, their nonexistent relationship, or both.

Amanda was finishing the last of her orange juice after breakfast when Henry sidled up behind her, ostensibly to clear the table. "I need to talk to you," he whispered.

She glanced worriedly in Odell's direction, but Odell was busy reprimanding poor Terri for her table manners. Terri habitually drew the old woman's wrath like sugar drew ants, but at least Amanda's friend was looking better today. She had some color in her cheeks.

It wasn't Amanda's turn for kitchen duty, it was Terri's. But Amanda stood, anyway, and began stacking dishes. If Odell questioned her, she would simply claim that she'd gotten mixed up about the schedule.

The moment she and Henry were alone in the kitchen, she turned to him. "What is it?"

"The bars on one of the basement windows are loose," he said, his gaze darting frequently to the door. "I think I can get them off. And I can dig the hole under the fence behind the toolshed, like you said."

"That's wonderful, Henry!" she said, hardly able to believe that she'd actually convinced him to conspire against Odell. She wondered briefly if he were setting some other kind of trap for her. "Oh, but how will I get into the basement?"

"That's the hard part. You have to do something really bad. The basement is where Aunt Odell puts bad girls."

Amanda remembered that Terri had mentioned something about the "Dungeon," misspelled, of course, during one of their dialogues on the pipes. The message had been a bit garbled, but doubtless she'd been talking about the basement. No one had been sent there since Amanda's arrival, making her wonder just how bad she had to be to earn that punishment.

"What can I do that's really bad?" she asked as she began running sudsy water in the sink.

"Well, last time, Terri threw a pork chop at Odell. That made her pretty mad. And Jenny—she's not with us anymore—she started punching this other girl."

Amanda resisted the urge to ask just exactly where Jenny was.

"But what are you gonna do about the dogs?" Henry asked. "Phoebe probably wouldn't hurt you, but that Bella is mean."

Amanda already knew that. Apparently the German shepherd had attacked Terri during one of her many foiled escape attempts. "Could you bring the dogs inside?" Amanda asked hopefully.

He shook his head. "Bella won't obey me, only Aunt Odell. And I don't aim to get my arm bit off, no thanks."

"Well, I'll think of something. You just work on those bars...please?" she added quickly, so that Henry wouldn't think she was bossing him around.

"I'll try," he said.

Austin was feeling pretty pleased with himself. Chief Raines had jumped at the chance to take some sort of positive, dramatic action toward catching a serial kidnapper. He was pleased that Austin had found ways to implement the plan for less money, and he'd okayed the overtime with hardly a blink. After the meeting, it had taken less than two days to get everything in place. Virginia had left the message, and Odell had returned her call right on schedule, less than an hour ago. The psychologist had informed Odell of a patient named Marie Plummer, using all of the details Austin had supplied. Austin had listened to the taped conversation, and Virginia had done a damn good acting job.

Now all that remained was to wait for Odell to take the bait—admittedly the iffiest part of the operation. Despite Chief Raines's enthusiasm, he would give this operation no more than a few days to produce results. The budget simply couldn't bear more than that.

Austin watched as Caro took a tour of her new digs.

"Not bad, not bad," she said, raking her finger over a countertop and inspecting it for dust. Her cat, which she'd insisted on bringing with her to the rental house, jumped onto the counter and butted his head against her arm. She petted him absently. "All in all, this isn't bad for an undercover assignment. But I have to tell you, I feel ridiculous in these clothes."

"You look terrific." He had taken her to Northpark Mall and dragged her into a store that specialized in teen fashions, then picked out several outfits for her to try on. She'd bucked and hollered the whole time, but in the end she let him buy her a few things that would supplement her own wardrobe, to make her look a little more youthful. He'd purposely chosen some items that showed off her figure—more so than those oversized sacks she was so fond of. It was that, more than anything, that she was uncomfortable with.

Austin couldn't imagine why. She had a lean, supple-looking body a lot of women would kill for. But given the way she underplayed her natural beauty, he suspected she had problems dealing with her more feminine side, especially working in such a male-dominated field. She probably spent a lot of time defending her abilities to the various rednecks and chauvinists she encountered.

"Yeah, I'd say it's a pretty cushy assignment," he said. "You get to watch TV all day, eat food provided by the police department...."

Caro wasn't listening. She was busy inspecting the kitchen. "Okay, who bought this food?"

"I did."

"I should have figured. Frozen pizzas, frozen burritos, microwave popcorn, three flavors of Doritos, and enough Hostess snacks to give the entire Dallas Cowboys a sugar high. Do you ever eat anything green, Lomax?"

"I like guacamole."

She made a sound of definite disgust. "Never mind. You said I would have two detectives guarding me at all times. Who's the other one?"

"He's on his way. We'll both work a twelve-hour shift. At night you'll have Penny Hart with you. Raines didn't think it was necessary to have two people at night."

Caro smiled in obvious pleasure. "Oh, good, I like Penny. I was afraid you would stick me with some old fogy who wouldn't be any fun. Sometimes the most dangerous aspect of an undercover assignment is the possibility of dying of boredom."

"Not while I'm around," he assured her. He opened the case he'd brought with him from home. "Videotapes, everything from *Casablanca* to *Bill and Ted's Excellent Adventure*. I also have Nintendo, Game Boy and, if you're not into electronics, a couple of decks of cards. It'll be like a regular vacation."

"Yeah, except you don't have to wear this body mike with all this itchy tape. Where did you get this historical artifact, anyway?" she asked, gingerly touching the microphone beneath her shirt. "Why couldn't I get one of those new mikes, the all-in-one jobs that look like beepers?"

"Blame it on Narcotics. They get all the good, new techno-stuff, and we have to beg for their cast-offs." Actually, he didn't mind that they were using the old-style microphone, especially since he'd helped to install it on Caro's body. How else would he ever get a glimpse of her bare midriff, or any excuse to touch her there, even if it was only to wrap tape around her? There was little chance they would need the mike, anyway. He didn't intend to let Caro far out of his sight during the day, and it was doubtful Odell would actually attempt to break into the house at night.

The doorbell rang, and Caro went to answer it, with Austin just out of sight, listening intently. It was extremely unlikely that Odell would strike this soon, but he wasn't taking any chances.

"Tony!" Caro exclaimed, opening the door wider. "Don't tell me you're my other watchdog."

"You were expecting maybe Chief Raines himself?" Tony sauntered in, grinning, as Austin relaxed and stepped around the corner. "My first day on the job in CAPERS and what plum assignment do I get?" He let the question go unanswered.

"It's about time you got here," Austin said, letting his irritation show. Despite his teasing Caro, he was nervous as hell about the outcome of this plan. If it succeeded, he would have firmly established his reputation. If it flopped, he might spend months, years, redeeming himself.

"Hey, I wouldn't have missed this for the world," Tony said. "I wasn't about to leave you two alone in an empty house for long. You might get distracted and forget all about catching a kidnapper."

Caro hit him on the arm—and it wasn't just a friendly little punch, either. "Cut it out, Villaverde," she said, her face turning pink. "I've had enough, okay?"

Tony winced and rubbed his arm. "Okay, I get the message. What's the game plan?"

Austin was quick to take charge. "One of us will be stationed in a back bedroom, keeping an eye out the window at the street and monitoring the microphone, if necessary. If anyone approaches the house, I want to know about it in plenty of time. The other will keep Caro company."

"I think I can manage to keep myself entertained, thanks," she said, looking down her nose at them.

"All right, then, the other will patrol the house, checking all of the windows regularly and keeping the undercover officer in visual contact at all times," he said, falling back on impersonal jargon. No matter how pleasant a diversion this operation might be, it was still dangerous, especially for Caro, and he didn't intend to take his responsibilities lightly. "We know that at least one of the girls, Julie Yates, disappeared from her home, so it's not unreasonable to expect Odell to show up here. Two of the girls, however, were apprehended when they were away from home. So if nothing has happened by tomorrow, we'll venture out in the van."

"To the grocery store," Caro added. "That is, if we're not all dead from junk-food poisoning by then."

Tony, who seemed a little wary of Caro's less-than-cheerful mood, not to mention her punches, volunteered for the first shift in the back bedroom, leaving Austin alone with her. Although Austin had been hoping for an opportunity to spend some time with her and explore the real reasons she wanted to keep him at arm's length, he wasn't sure this was the best time. Caro seemed antsy, unable to focus on anything for very long.

He tried to teach her how to play a Mario Bros. video game, but she gave up in frustration after only a few attempts. Then they tried poker—which he'd sworn he would never play with her because she was so good at hiding her feelings—but she lost almost every hand and gave up on that, too. Television proved to hold just as little interest. Her attention span didn't stretch even to a half-hour game show, and before long she was pacing the house like a caged cat.

"Anything wrong?" Austin asked.

"I guess I'm not very good at sitting around and waiting," she said. "Even when I was an undercover prostitute, I was doing something."

"Yeah?"

She flopped down in an old recliner. "You know, walking around, talking to people, fending off johns and trying to make it look believable that I didn't want a new customer. I told them I was already booked and I was waiting for my next appointment."

Austin smiled. He would've liked to see Caro dressed up like a hooker, just for the novelty. "Well, I can't provide any activity quite that interesting, but if there's something else you'd rather be doing…" He knew what he'd rather be doing. He'd like to give that body mike she was wearing a real good test. When she didn't reply, he turned off the TV and added, "We could just talk."

She surprised him by agreeing. "Okay. You want something to drink?"

"Yeah, I'll make some coffee. And I bought you some of that herbal tea you like."

She actually smiled at him. "Thanks."

As they puttered around in the kitchen, Caro's nervous chatter was incredibly revealing. Austin learned about her small-town upbringing, her law-enforcement parents, the tough time she'd had in the police academy, always trying to look harder and meaner than anyone else to make up for her small size.

Noticeably absent in her dialogue was any mention of romantic liaisons. Austin decided he couldn't let that go unchallenged. "You ever been married?" he asked.

"No, have you?"

"Who'd have me?" he quipped.

"Oh, I expect if you really had your mind set on hearth and home, you could trick some poor, unsuspecting female into marriage. After all, you're over thirty, gainfully employed and not painful to look at. Any single woman of a certain age will tell you, those credentials are pretty impressive."

He took inordinate pleasure in the compliment, though it had been delivered with tongue firmly in cheek. "Okay, so maybe I don't really want to be married. What about you?"

She shrugged. "I came close once. And I'm not even sure why I chickened out, except it just didn't feel right. The idea of spending fifty or sixty years with the same person is a little daunting. Of course, the older I get, the shorter that future gets. Maybe by the time I'm eighty, marriage won't seem so scary."

"I hear you." He toasted her with his coffee. "Do you still see the guy?"

"Oh, God, no. He was pretty ticked off about the whole thing."

"Are you seeing anybody?" he couldn't help asking.

Wariness immediately showed in her eyes. "No." She quickly changed the subject. "I'm going to take Tony a cup of coffee. While I'm gone, you might be thinking about your life story, because I intend to give you the same type of grilling you just gave me."

He watched her sashay out of the kitchen. Grilling? He'd thought he was just making conversation. Well, okay, so he was asking most of the questions and she'd been providing the answers. Maybe if he reciprocated, giving her the scant details of his mostly routine and unglamorous past, she wouldn't be so afraid of letting him into her life.

Amanda's stomach was so tied up in knots she could hardly eat her roast beef and mashed potatoes. But that was all right. She had other plans for the meat. While Odell was occupied cutting her own slice of beef, Amanda rolled hers up and stuck it up the sleeve of her sweatshirt. The ham from her lunch sandwich was in the front pocket of her jeans.

All the planning she and Terri had done during those late-night Morse code sessions, all the brainstorming, all the preparations, boiled down to this evening. What she accomplished during the next few minutes might well determine whether she and the other girls lived or died.

Henry had informed her this morning during exercise that everything was ready. The basement window security bars were loose, the hole under the fence had been dug. He'd told her that if she headed due east she would arrive at a town called River Rock, although it would be a good ten-mile hike. He had agreed to meet her at the Dairy Queen the following day, give her a little money and help her find a place to stay. Not that she intended to get anywhere near Henry once she was free of this place!

Now all that remained was to set her escape in motion. And that meant relying on her limited acting abilities.

At least one thing was working in her favor. Odell was already in a foul mood. She'd been gone most of the day, leaving Henry in charge, and when she returned she'd been wearing a black scowl. Amanda wondered if she'd been on a kidnapping mission that had gone awry. Ever since the day Heather had miscarried and subsequently disappeared, Odell had been more on edge than normal.

But she wasn't so preoccupied that she couldn't deliver her nightly sermon. Tonight's lesson was Brotherly Love. How ironic.

Amanda knew that if she put it off much longer she would lose her nerve. After taking a deep breath, she pushed herself away from the table and lurched to her feet. "Stop kicking me!" she screamed at Terri, who sat across the table.

Odell stopped talking midsentence, and everyone stared in astonishment. After her first couple of days at the home, Amanda had been notoriously mild-mannered.

"Amanda, sit down," Odell ordered.

"Not until you make her sit somewhere else," Amanda said, pointing at Terri. "Every meal she kicks me, and I'm sick of it."

"Sit down!" Odell repeated, more forcefully this time. "I don't want to hear another word from you."

"Oh, yeah? Well, too bad. I'm sick of being quiet, and I'm sick of your Bible lessons and I'm sick of this whole place!" With every word Amanda shrieked a little more loudly, as if she were losing control. She flipped over her dinner plate, spilling gravy and peas everywhere. When Odell tried to grab her by the arm, Amanda eluded capture just long enough to pitch her glass of milk into Odell's face.

Odell was so shocked that for a moment all she could do was stare in open-mouthed horror. Amanda took the opportunity to strike again, leaping on Odell and wrapping her hands around the old woman's throat. She felt a surge of power flow through her. She was no longer acting. Her hatred toward Odell flared all around her, a palpable force, and if Henry hadn't pulled her off she could have done some real damage.

She fought against Henry, too, until she realized that if she made Henry mad he might foil her plans. So rather than punching or kicking, she resorted to verbal abuse. "Let go of me, you big ox!" she screamed.

He held her arms fast, and Odell delivered a stinging slap to Amanda's face. "What's gotten into you, child?" Odell demanded.

"The devil," Amanda replied, her eyes watering from the slap. "You're the one who called me a sinner."

"But I'm giving you the opportunity to atone for your sins," Odell said, sounding more bewildered than angry now.

That wasn't what Amanda was after. Grappling with her courage, she spit on Odell. "There's your atonement."

Odell closed her eyes, her hands bunched into fists, as if she had to control the urge to beat some sense into her wayward sheep. "Henry, take her to her room."

"No! I won't go to my room." Amanda renewed her struggle, although she was careful not to do anything that would actually hurt Henry.

Henry spoke up for the first time. "Aunt Odell, do you want I should put her in the basement?"

Amanda held her breath. Henry couldn't have delivered a better line if it had been scripted and rehearsed. At that moment she could have kissed him.

After a tense moment, Odell nodded. "Yes, that's an excellent idea." She looked squarely at Amanda. "I think you'll benefit from some quiet time to contemplate your sins."

"Why the basement?" Amanda asked, feigning alarm.

"Oh, you'll like the basement," Henry said as he started to drag her away, one of her arms doubled behind her back. His grip was painful, and she wondered if he wasn't enjoying his part in this drama a bit too much, but she couldn't really complain. He'd done his job well.

The basement stairs were off the kitchen, within hearing distance of the dining room, so Amanda put up a believable fight. "Wait a minute. Why do I have to go in the basement? Hey, it's dark down there. Can't you turn on a light?"

Henry very nearly pushed her down the stairs and then slammed the door, leaving her in absolute darkness.

Chapter 15

Amanda's heart felt like a jackhammer inside her chest. She'd done it! Stage one of her plan had proceeded without a hitch. She hadn't counted on the total darkness, however. She groped along the wall for a light switch. Finding none, she felt her way gingerly down the unstable wooden steps. Basements weren't common in Texas, so she'd never been in one before and, in fact, hadn't ever seen one except in movies and on TV. She could easily give herself a first-class case of the willies.

No, that was ridiculous. She'd come this far. She could handle a little darkness and a musty smell.

Her next step was to locate the window. Was there more than one? She hadn't thought to ask Henry that. She might have to try several before she found the one with the loose bars. And it was so damn dark she didn't know where to start. Now that her eyes had adjusted to the blackness, she should have been able to discern faint exterior light through the windows—moonlight, starlight, something. But she might as well have been submerged in a bucket of tar for all she could see.

She knew the wall to her left faced the dining room; obviously it wouldn't have a window. So she groped along it until she came to a corner, then began exploring the new wall with her hands, running them along the grainy concretelike surface from chest level to as high as she could reach.

A faint squeaking noise startled her. Oh, God, rats, she thought as panic welled up inside her. No, no, maybe they weren't rats, but little field mice. She could handle that. And as long as she didn't see them, she would never know how big they were. Still, she stepped carefully as she made her way around piles of boxes and lumber. If she stepped on one she would scream.

Finally she found a window. It was above her head, wide but not very tall. She wouldn't have any problem getting through it if she could boost herself up that far. Getting it open was the biggest challenge, she soon discovered. It wouldn't budge.

She needed something to stand on, but if she walked away from the window to search, would she find it again? Well, she'd have to, she reasoned. With her hands extended in front of her, she groped through the darkness, running into various unidentifiable objects. At last she stumbled into something she was able to recognize as a metal folding chair. Perfect.

Before she could drag it to the window, she heard a commotion at the top of the steps. What now? Surely Odell wouldn't change her mind and bring Amanda upstairs. It was Odell's voice, all right.

"We'll see if you're laughing tomorrow morning," she said, sounding very angry. A sliver of light spilled down the stairs as the door opened and someone was thrust into the basement.

"You can't do this to me." It was Terri! "That bitch is crazy! She'll beat me up."

It took Amanda a moment to realize Terri was talking about her. But Odell didn't respond except to slam the basement door.

"Hey, Amanda," Terri called out. "I'm coming down there. You wouldn't beat up a poor, defenseless, fat, pregnant girl, would you?"

Amanda wanted to laugh. She moved toward the stairs. "Just stay away from me," she called back, in case Odell was listening.

Terri's tennis shoes made slow, quiet thuds as she worked her way cautiously down the stairs. When she reached the bottom Amanda was there. They found each other in the darkness and hugged so hard it hurt.

"What are you doing down here?" Amanda whispered.

"I couldn't let you do this alone," Terri whispered back. "So I started laughing when Henry hauled you off, saying it served you right. Odell didn't like that, and as mad as she was, it didn't take much to provoke her. Now I can help you escape. Maybe I can boost you out the window, or distract the dogs while you run. I have a whole pocketful of meat."

"Oh, but Terri, when Odell finds out I'm gone, she'll blame you for helping me! I hate to think what she might do to you."

"Please, I can handle Odell. As long as I know help is coming, I can take anything she dishes out. Are you okay? Man, does that old broad know how to slap, or what?"

Amanda rubbed her face, which still smarted. "I'm okay. How about you?"

"I'm great. God, it's so neat actually to be able to talk to you!"

"I know. But let's not get too carried away. We've got work to do. How many windows are there down here?" she asked.

"Uh, one, two, three . . . four, I think. They're painted over so no light gets through."

Ah, no wonder it was so dark. "There's a slight problem," Amanda said. "Henry didn't tell me which window has the loose bars. We'll just have to try them all. Let's start with this one over here—if I can find it again."

Amanda found the window, and between her and Terri they managed to pry it open by sticking a board under the handle. Unfortunately, the burglar bars were as secure as Fort Knox.

"There's another window on this wall, further down here," Terri said, undaunted. "Let's try it next. Don't worry, we've got all night."

"We do?" Amanda was under the impression that her sentence to the dungeon would be a mere hour or two. "Odell actually leaves people in this disgusting place overnight? She would make a good character in a Dickens novel."

"A what novel?"

"Never mind."

"I've spent the night here a couple of times. Didn't you hear her? She said she'd see if I was laughing in the morning."

"Oh, that's right. Well, for once, I'm glad Odell is a sadist. Surely we can get the right window open and the bars off before morning."

And they did. The third window, which was almost behind the furnace, proved to be the one. Once they got it open, the bars pushed easily away. "Give me that meat you've been saving," Amanda said.

"Gladly. But don't you think we should wait until later when everyone's asleep? What if Odell steps outside and sees you?"

"I'm afraid to wait. Besides, last I saw, Phoebe was still inside. I don't know where Bella is, but the fewer dogs I have to deal with, the better."

"Okay, if you say so. Uck, this meat loaf is disgusting."

"My God, how long have you been saving this junk?"

"Couple of days." Terri transferred the cold, slimy bundle of meat into Amanda's hand.

Amanda cringed as she slid it up her sleeve. "The damn dog will probably take my arm off," she muttered. "Okay, I'm set. Wish me luck and I'm outta here. Can you boost me up?"

"Amanda, wait."

"What?"

"I want to go with you."

Amanda actually laughed. "You've got to be kidding. You're almost nine months' pregnant. A ten-mile hike will send you into labor at the very least, and kill you at the worst. That's assuming you can fit through the window and under the fence."

"I don't have to go the whole way with you. Just get me on the other side of the fence, and I'll wait in the woods until you bring help."

"But why don't you just wait here? Once I'm free, it won't take long—a few hours at the most."

"I might not have a few hours," Terri said, her voice suddenly thick with tears. "The baby has dropped, my back's been hurting all day... I'm afraid I'll go into labor before you can bring help, and then what'll happen to me? The old witch will kill me, that's what."

"But, Terri—"

"And I'm in good shape, thanks to all that exercise Odell makes us do. I probably could hike ten miles. Please, Amanda, don't leave me here. I'd rather have my baby in the woods than here."

Amanda saw her carefully constructed plan crumbling. It would be difficult for her to escape alone, much less with Terri in tow.

"Besides," Terri added, "when we get free, we can separate. Then if Odell and her dogs come after us, there's more chance that at least one of us can make it all the way to safety. It'll confuse Phoebe. She'll have a harder time tracking two people. And if it comes down to one of us distracting the dogs while the other one gets away..."

"Oh, sure, and the one left behind gets eaten. No, Terri, this isn't going to work. Let's just stick to the plan. I'll bring help back before anything can happen to you or the baby, I promise."

Terri snuffled. "Okay," she said meekly.

Amanda had heard her use that same tone of voice with Odell, when she was feigning cooperation. It made Amanda uneasy. "Come on, move that chair closer," she said gruffly, afraid that if she showed any softening, Terri would get her way.

Taking a deep breath, Amanda pushed the bars aside and crawled through the window. The yard was almost as dark as the basement. She could see only a few faint stars peeking through the clouds and the vague outlines of trees and buildings. Thank God Bella was nowhere in sight.

Well, there was no going back now. She turned to replace the security bars in front of the window, so nothing would readily appear out of place in the morning.

"Ouch! Hold it a second, I'm right behind you."

"Terri! Get back inside."

"I think I'm stuck."

Exasperated, Amanda grabbed Terri by the shoulders and started to push. "Get back inside."

"No. I'm coming with you and that's that. Ow! Quit pushing. I can't go backward, I can only go forward."

"Oh, for God's sake." Defeated, Amanda began pulling instead of pushing. If she didn't help Terri get unstuck, she might remain there all night.

"There, see? I'm already out," Terri said triumphantly as she laboriously maneuvered herself to her knees, then her feet. "We're as good as free."

"We're going to be dog food if you don't lower your voice," Amanda whispered as she put the bars back where they belonged. "I don't want to hear a single complaint from you about being cold or hungry or tired—"

"I won't! Let's go see what kind of hole Henry dug for you."

They strolled brazenly across the yard toward the storage shed. Amanda's senses were alert for any sign of man or beast, but all was quiet. Once they were behind the shed and out of sight from the house, she breathed a little easier. She felt along the bottom of the chain-link fence with her foot until she found a small depression.

Small was the operative word.

Amanda dropped to her knees and explored the hole with her hands. "Oh, for God's sake, this hole isn't big enough for me, much less you. How did Henry even imagine I could fit through there?"

"Now what are we going to do?" Terri asked.

"We're going to dig a bigger hole, that's what. Look around and see if you can find a sharp rock or a stick or something." Amanda began to scoop dirt out of the hole, digging into the firm red earth with her fingernails.

"Ha, found something better than a rock," Terri said. "Henry left his shovel out here."

"Great, give it here. I'll have this hole so big we can sail the *Queen Mary* through it." Amanda tried to sound confident, despite the fact that she'd never used a shovel in her life.

"The *Queen Mary?* How about the *Goodyear* blimp?" Terri hunkered down beside the hole, raking dirt away with her hands as Amanda loosened it with the shovel. It was slow-going, though, and Amanda grew more nervous with each passing minute. Odell didn't carry that shotgun around for decorative purposes.

"Uh-oh," Terri said. "I think we got company."

Amanda froze. Sure enough, she could hear a dog's tags tinkling in the still of the night. That noise was followed by a low, menacing growl.

"Bella?" Amanda ventured, turning to face the dog. She could just make out those shiny, white teeth in the darkness, only a few feet away.

Terri took the shovel and continued working while Amanda pulled a piece of meat from her sleeve.

"Look, Bella, see the pretty meat? Mmm, yummy, yummy."

The growling stopped, replaced by a confused whine, then a sharp bark.

"Shhh! Quiet, Bella," Amanda said in a soothing voice, holding out the meat. She felt the German shepherd's warm breath on her hand a split second before its powerful jaws snapped closed around the tidbit. "How's it coming?" she asked Terri.

"Just a little more."

"Hurry. I don't know how long the meat will last." The meat loaf was little more than crumbles, which Bella eagerly snuffled out of Amanda's hand. Next came another piece of roast beef, and then a slice of ham. "Good dog, good dog," she crooned the whole time.

"Okay, I think I can get through now," Terri said just as the front door of the house opened and a shaft of light from inside pierced through the darkness. The light didn't reach far enough behind the shed to reveal their hiding place, but both girls stopped cold.

"Bella?" Odell called questioningly from the direction of the front porch.

"Go on, Bella," Amanda urged in a voice that was barely a whisper. She pointed urgently toward the house. "Go to your mistress."

The dog looked over its shoulder toward the house when Odell called again, then dismissed the summons in favor of the possibility of more treats from Amanda.

"Terri, go now," Amanda ordered. She had only one piece of meat left, and she was breaking it up into small bites to make it last longer. She could hear Terri scuffling and grunting with the effort of squeezing under the fence. Odell called the dog halfheartedly once more, and then the door closed and it was dark once again.

"Okay, I'm through," Terri said, her breathing labored. "It'll be a cinch for you."

Amanda threw the last bit of meat a few feet away, forcing Bella to hunt for it, then turned and dived through the hole. She managed to wiggle through just as the dog came looking for more, whining and jumping at Amanda's retreating legs.

"Here," Terri said, "we can block the hole with this log so she won't follow us."

"Good thinking." Amanda hadn't even considered that possibility. With a few tugs and pushes, they wedged the rotting tree trunk into the hole as a confused Bella continued to whine. After one final shove, Amanda grabbed Terri's sleeve so they wouldn't lose each other in the darkness, and they set off into the woods. Bella's whines turned back into growls.

"We did it," Amanda said when the blackness of the thick trees had swallowed them up. She could scarcely believe they were free of The Good Shepherd Maternity Home. "We did it," she repeated, her elation growing. "But I'll feel better once we put some distance between us and that hellhole."

Terri said nothing.

"Terri?"

"My water just broke."

Austin hunched lower into his bomber jacket to ward off the cold as he and Tony walked up the alley toward the rental house. Part of him looked forward to another twelve-hour shift with Caro. He felt energized when he was around her—more alive and alert, constantly challenged, not to mention perennially turned on. On the other hand, it was pure torture being so close to her and not being able to touch her. By the end of his shift yesterday they'd both been a little cranky. He worried that by the end of this assignment, Caro would be thoroughly sick of him, and any chance they had of connecting would be dead.

Maybe that was just as well, he told himself. It probably wouldn't work out, for the reasons she'd brought up on New Year's Day. He would rather count Caro among his friends than end up with bitterness between them.

"Are we taking the van out today?" Tony asked.

"Yeah."

"Good. I'm sick of sitting around, waiting for something to happen."

"You and me both," Austin said. They slipped through the back gate and onto the patio, where Austin tapped on the glass door.

Corporal Penny Hart, one of the best-liked detectives working in CAPERS, answered. "Hi, guys," she said cheerfully. She was big and loud and redheaded, and she could be counted on to come up with a tension-breaking wisecrack. Austin had felt perfectly at ease leaving Caro in Penny's competent hands overnight.

"All's quiet, I trust."

"Boringly so, I'm afraid," Penny said. "There's doughnuts in the kitchen. Where's the car? I want to get home in time to see my urchins before they're off to daycare."

"Parked on the street at the east end of the alley." Austin handed her the key. They tried to make the shift change as unobtrusively as possible, but he could only hope Odell wasn't watching the back door. Seeing two men arrive and a woman leave at seven in the morning would completely blow their cover. "Where's Caro?"

"In the shower," Penny said. "She'll be along in a minute. I'm outta here. And I hope I won't have to see you tonight."

Austin couldn't agree more.

When Caro appeared a half hour later, Austin and Tony were seated at the kitchen table cleaning up the last of the doughnuts. She was wearing a long pink sweater Austin had seen on her before, but instead of her usual black trousers or full skirt, she had on a pair of wildly patterned tights that showed off her slender legs to perfection. Her hair was pulled into a ponytail with a bright pink ribbon. She made Austin think of a fancy confection behind the window at a candy shop—and he was the little boy pressing his nose against the glass.

"Is this teenagerish enough?" she asked, holding her arms out and twirling around.

"You look great," Tony said in a tone of voice out-of-kilter with his customary big-brother attitude. Austin stared into his coffee, not trusting himself to speak.

"In that case," Caro said, oblivious to the effect she was having on her male colleagues, "will someone wire me up?" She held out the body mike and a roll of tape.

Tony and Austin exchanged a look of purely male understanding. "I'll do it," Tony said, much to Austin's relief. He didn't completely trust himself to lift Caro's sweater and touch her warm skin just now, not even in the line of duty. He didn't particularly want to watch Tony touching her, either, so instead, he busied himself pouring more coffee, adding cream and sugar, and stirring until he thought the spoon might dissolve.

"There, I think that'll do it," Tony said.

"Great. Hey, did you pigs eat all the doughnuts?" Caro asked, wiggling her shoulders as she accustomed herself to her new hard wiring.

The evidence didn't lie. An empty bakery box sat on the table, with only a few powdered-sugar flecks in the bottom.

"Er, uh," Tony said.

"We thought you'd already eaten," Austin said, quickly searching through the cabinets for a likely substitute. "Here, how about some Twinkies?"

She wrinkled her nose. "Gross. What I'd really like is some shredded wheat and skim milk. Any chance?"

After pocketing one of the packages of Twinkies, Austin opened another cabinet. "Just Cocoa Puffs. And no milk. I sorta forgot that."

"Okay, I'm making a grocery list. That's the plan, right? Drive to the grocery store and hope Odell tries to nab me? Might as well make the trip count for something—in case it doesn't work, that is."

"Your faith in my plan is underwhelming," Austin said.

Caro stole the pen from Tony's shirt pocket and began scribbling on a paper towel. "Milk. Cereal—something non-chocolate. Veggies for salad. Salad dressing. Cheese. Chicken—"

"Hey, let's not get carried away," Austin objected. "I have to justify the costs of this operation, you know."

"I'll spring for the chicken," Caro said. "I'll make a stir-fry for dinner. How does that sound?"

"You cook?" Austin asked, surprised. Somehow he didn't think of Caro as the domestic type.

"Damn right I cook." She added rice and soy sauce to the list. "How soon can we leave?"

Austin looked at his watch. "All of the girls were taken between eight-thirty and eleven in the morning, so I guess we can leave in an hour or so. We'll need to transfer some equipment into the van."

"Okay," Caro said. "Anybody want tea?" She stood and went to the cabinet where she kept the herbal tea. When she reached up to open the door, she froze. "Uh-oh. I think the antenna wire came loose."

Austin was the closest to her. He couldn't avoid touching her this time, not unless he wanted to make an issue of it. He went to her and gingerly lifted the sweater, revealing her slender torso. She was wearing a modest sports bra, the kind some women wore in public during the summer, but he still felt like he was invading Caro's privacy. "Yeah, the wire came loose, all right. Hold up the sweater up for a minute," he instructed her. "Tony, could you hand me that tape? I think if we give the wire a little more slack, you won't have any problem. Just be careful how you move." In a couple of minutes he had the problem corrected. He could only hope Caro hadn't felt his hands shaking.

By eight-thirty they had the van outfitted for surveillance. Behind the front seat, the wildly painted vehicle had only one window on each side, heavily tinted, through which they could watch their surroundings. They wouldn't use a radio, in case Odell had a police scanner. Instead they would rely on Austin's portable phone if they needed to call in for backup. They had a camera with a telephoto lens for photographing any suspicious persons, and of course the receiver that would pick up signals from Caro's body mike.

With Tony and Austin secreted in the back where no one could see them, Caro pushed the button on the automatic garage door opener and backed out of the driveway.

Kroger's Food Store was less than a mile from the house, and the parking lot was packed.

"Wait until you can find a space close to the door," Austin said. "I don't want to have to sprint across a quarter-mile of parking lot if you get into trouble."

"I know, I know," Caro said irritably. She drove around in circles until she found someone pulling out of a desirable space.

"Remember, take your time," Austin coached her. "You don't want to look like you're in any particular hurry. Try to linger in the most deserted aisles, and especially in the parking lot when you have your groceries. And for heaven's sake, don't let a bag boy carry your sacks. And if you get into trouble, remember the phrase—"

"I know, Austin," she said. "I'm supposed to say 'Please don't hurt me.' We've been over this. I'm not a complete idiot."

"I didn't say you were. I just don't want to leave anything to chance."

"Well, give me a little credit. You act like this is the first time I've ever worked undercover."

"Oh, excuse me. I forgot. You have all this tons of experience, and I'm just this green yahoo from Auto Theft—"

"Hey, guys," Tony interrupted. "I don't think we're accomplishing much with this discussion. Can you save it till later?"

Caro sighed deeply. "You're right. Let's get this show on the road. Unless you have any more last-minute instructions?" She looked over her shoulder at Austin, her hazel eyes challenging him.

He refused to take the bait. "No, I think everything's under control."

"Good luck, sweetheart." Tony reached up and squeezed her shoulder.

She smiled for him. "Thanks." Without even a glance in Austin's direction, she got out of the van and slammed the door.

Austin expelled a long breath as he and Tony took up their positions in front of the window that faced the store's entrance. They were both silent as they watched Caro, walking with a jaunty hip-swinging gait, cross through the traffic and disappear inside.

"Don't take it so hard," Tony said. "She gets ornery when she's nervous, that's all. She didn't mean anything by it."

Austin didn't reply.

"You can't take her seriously when she lights into you like that," Tony continued. "If you just ignore her, in five minutes her mood will change."

"I don't need lessons on how to get along with Caro, thanks."

"Then I guess she's the one who needs lessons," Tony quipped.

Austin was suddenly ashamed of himself. "Hey, man, I'm sorry. I'm just stressed out about this whole thing, you know?"

"Yeah, I know," Tony said affably. "Don't sweat it."

Sounds from the grocery store, picked up by Caro's body mike, came in over the receiver. Austin fiddled with the dials, fine-tuning the signal, until he could even hear announcements made over the loudspeaker: "Price check on aisle nine." "Check approval on aisle five." And periodically Caro would talk to herself, as they planned: "Ooh, the new *Seventeen,* yippee," she said, having obviously stopped by the magazine rack.

She kept a running commentary on every purchase—lettuce, mushrooms, bell peppers in the produce section, yogurt, milk and cheese. Then she reached the cereal aisle. "Now where in the hell is the shredded wheat?" she asked herself.

"Yeah, by all means," Tony added. "Maybe that's why she's in such a bad mood. She needs her fiber."

Austin chuckled.

"Ah, there it is," Caro said. "Wouldn't you know it, top shelf. Why don't they design grocery stores for short peo—" The receiver abruptly went silent.

Both Tony and Austin turned to stare at the ominously quiet receiver. "What the—" Tony said, banging on the case with his fist.

"Aw, hell, you know what happened?" Austin said. "She reached up and pulled that antenna wire out again. Damn piece-of-crap body mike. If Narcotics wasn't so greedy...okay, what do you think? Should we blow our cover and go in after her?"

"It's my second day on the job and you're asking me?" Tony objected.

Tony was right. This was Austin's operation, and it was his decision to make. "Okay, it's awkward being out of voice contact with Caro. But chances are nothing's going to happen to her inside the store, right? And we're watching the front door of the store, the only way in or out. She can't leave the store under any circumstances without us seeing her."

"Right," Tony said.

"So we just won't take our eyes off the store entrance."

"Sounds reasonable."

"Okay."

They spent the next ten minutes staring intently out the small window. Tony was nervously chewing on a piece of grape bubblegum.

"Do you have to chew that stuff?" Austin asked irritably. "Christ, I could smell it a mile away."

"Would you rather I smoke? Those are the alternatives."

"Never mind. Hey, what's that?"

"It looks like a Diet Coke truck to me," Tony said.

"Yeah, but what's it doing stopping right in front of the damn store? C'mon, move it, you lard-ass truck."

The truck driver opened his door and climbed out, apparently intent on unloading some soft drinks, oblivious to the fact that his vehicle completely blocked the detectives' view of the front door.

"Ah, hell, that's it," Austin said, banging his fist against the side of the van. "Let's move. We can't see her, we can't hear her. Anything could happen. We can't worry about blowing our cover now."

Tony was in complete agreement. They climbed out of the back of the van and strode purposefully around the truck. Austin's stomach was tied up in knots, and the feeling wouldn't ease until he got Caro in his sights again. Just as he stepped on the mat activating the automatic door, Tony called out to him, his voice filled with alarm.

"Hey, Lomax, look here."

Austin turned. Tony was pointing to a plastic grocery sack lying on the ground, some of its contents spilled onto the sidewalk. Austin took two giant steps and reached the bag, grabbing it up in his hands. On top was a *Seventeen* magazine and a box of shredded wheat.

"Oh, God. Oh, God." He'd just fallen into the worst nightmare of his life.

Chapter 16

"Please don't hurt me," Caro said. The muzzle of the woman's .38 jabbed her in the side. She repeated the phrase, more insistently, as the woman—Odell, no doubt—calmly walked her down the sidewalk and around the corner of the building. Caro panicked for a moment. Wasn't that the code? Austin's plan had been to move in the instant he heard Caro say those four words.

Where is he?

"Please don't hurt me," she said one more time.

"I won't hurt you if you'll just be quiet," Odell said soothingly. "I'm doing you a favor, you'll see. Now, be a good girl, Marie, and get in the truck."

They had arrived at a white Suburban parked around the corner from the store's main entrance. There were a few other cars parked around them, but no people. No one could see them.

Caro's every instinct told her to use her training and defend herself; blithely climbing into a strange car with a crazed woman toting a gun was suicidal. But struggling might put her in more danger, Caro reasoned. And surely Austin would be here any moment. He was probably just waiting until Odell moved away from her, so as not to risk having the woman panic and pull the trigger.

Caro took her time climbing into the back seat of the truck. Reflexively she craned her neck around, hoping vainly to see some sign of a rescue. That's when Odell shoved a cloth over Caro's face.

Now she did fight, screaming and shoving an elbow into Odell's well-padded middle. But the older woman was built like a tank, and Caro was no match for her, especially as her strength waned under the onslaught of the noxious vapors she was forced to inhale. By the time she felt the prick of a needle in her arm, she was too weak to fight. Darkness quickly engulfed her.

Odell was trembling as she put her truck into gear. That was the closest she'd come yet to losing control during one of her rescue missions. She'd thought Marie Plummer would be an easy target. The girl was not only small, but also quiet and timid, according to Virginia. And she was staying alone in her house, so no one would miss her for a while. The maneuver should have been a cinch.

Odell had considered just walking right up to the house and ringing the doorbell, as she'd done with Julie Yates. But she hadn't liked the setup of the neighborhood. The houses were too close together, and they all had garages in front and roomy driveways, so a car parked at the curb might have stood out. Anyway, not every young girl was as gullible as Julie, who hadn't hesitated to open the door to a stranger.

So, starting early that morning, Odell had parked around the corner in a church parking lot that was dotted with other cars. The spot had afforded her an unobstructed view of the Plummer house, and she'd used binoculars to keep an eye on it. Fortunately, she hadn't needed to wait long. When the van had pulled out of the garage at a little after nine o'clock, Odell followed it.

The grocery store parking lot wasn't an ideal location, however. There was too much activity, too many people around. But Odell didn't have time to wait for another opportunity. She didn't like staying away from the home for any longer than necessary. Henry could only be trusted so far.

Because the parking lot was so visible, she'd decided not to pull the same scam she'd used with Amanda Arkin. It was too likely someone would see them struggling in the front seat of Marie's van. Instead she had approached Marie as she'd exited the grocery store, her arms full, preoccupied as she searched her purse for her car keys. A gun shoved into the girl's ribs, coupled with a terse command that she not say a word, had done the trick nicely.

But she hadn't counted on the deceptively small young woman's uncommon strength. Once Marie had finally found her courage, she'd fought like a pit bull, screaming and kicking and jabbing with elbows sharp as pikes. Thank goodness they'd been well away from any potential witnesses. A rag containing a bit of ether, held over Marie's face, had muffled the girl's screams and then put her out just long enough that Odell could give her an injection of a strong tranquilizer. Neither drug was likely to harm the unborn baby.

Once Marie was unconscious, Odell had breathed a sigh of relief. She'd quickly tied the girl's wrists together behind her back with a nylon stocking, then arranged her on the floor of the back seat and covered her with a blanket.

The worst was over now, she thought as she exited the parking lot via the alley behind the grocery store. No one was following her. An added benefit was that she wouldn't have to dispose of Marie's vehicle. Once again, the Good Lord had protected Odell's mission. She was cheered by that thought.

She didn't stop looking in the rearview mirror until she was well away from Dallas. Only then did her muscles gradually relax, her jaw unclench. As she passed through the town of River Rock, ten minutes away from home, her thoughts turned to her other problem. That unpleasant business with Amanda the night before had upset Odell terribly. During the last week or so, the girl had been a model of obedience. Why had she suddenly turned crazy like that?

Odell didn't like putting any of the girls in the basement. But there was nothing like a night of sleeping on the cold, hard floor in pitch-black darkness to give a young girl plenty of time to ponder her sins. Such harsh punishment wasn't called for often, but whenever Odell resorted to it, it worked like a charm. She was confident Amanda would emerge from the basement penitent.

As for Terri, there wasn't much hope for that little tramp. Odell probably shouldn't have put her down there with Amanda, but she'd let her temper get the best of her. Ordinarily she didn't allow the girls to spend time together like that. Not that she worried about them confiding in each other, or hatching any kind of plan. First they would have to get over their anger at each other, and that would take longer than a night. No, she was more worried that they would hurt each other, and with Terri so near term, too.

Well, what was done was done. Odell had left before dawn this morning, but last night she'd instructed Henry to bring Terri and Amanda upstairs first thing when he got up, and to make sure they ate some breakfast. By now both girls were probably resting in their rooms, reflecting on the simple comforts they'd done without last night. Hopefully it would be a long time before either girl defied her again.

Odell pulled up to the front gates and got out of the car to unlock them. She was glad to be back at the Good Shepherd Home, as always. She felt completely safe here in this secluded spot of woods. She had chosen this place as much for its out-of-the-way location as for the size and layout of the house itself. Her property was at the end of a long, twisting, narrow lane that was clearly marked Private, No Trespassing. There was almost no chance anyone would stumble onto the home by accident, which was exactly how she liked it.

She drove the truck through the gates, honked the horn to summon Henry, then got out to padlock the gate again. By the time she'd driven all the way up to the house, Henry still hadn't appeared. Bella greeted her enthusiastically, but Phoebe was noticeably absent.

"Henry!" she hollered through the open car window, honking once more. Still no response. "Oh, for heaven's sake, that boy will be the death of me," she muttered as she climbed out of the car. "Probably watching TV, and has it turned up so loud he can't hear me."

Her apprehension grew as she entered the house, still calling for Henry, and got no answer. It was quiet as a graveyard. Something felt terribly wrong.

Odell checked Amanda's room first. It was empty.

A girl named Kendra occupied the room next to Amanda's. Odell unlocked the door and entered, startling the girl, who had been lying on her bed reading. "What's going on?" Odell demanded.

Kendra, a blonde so fair and pale she almost wasn't there, looked bewildered. "I don't know. What time is it? I need to go to the bathroom."

"Use the bedpan," Odell said tersely. "I don't have time to take anyone to the bathroom right now." She slammed and locked the door. Apparently Henry hadn't even let the girls out to use the facilities.

Next, Odell checked the basement. Empty. She was about to head back up the stairs when she noticed the window behind the furnace. The screen was missing, and a metal folding chair had been pulled up to the wall under the window. Even as she gave it a closer inspection, she already knew what had happened.

This can't be true, she thought. Those two little hellions couldn't have figured a way out of this place. How would they have gotten over the fence?

But apparently they had. That explained why Odell had heard Bella barking last night. That explained why Henry had dropped everything and left with Phoebe in tow. She hoped that for once that worthless bloodhound would earn her keep.

There was no note from Henry, which didn't surprise her. He could barely write, anyway. Then she remembered Wanda. Odell had hammered it into her nephew's head that if there was any kind of serious trouble and he needed to reach her, he should leave a message with the answering service in Dallas.

She fished the pocket-sized cellular phone out of her purse and called Wanda. The woman seemed unusually flustered, and it took her an uncommonly long time to search for Odell's messages, but in the end there weren't any.

Odell could think of only one course of action. She would get her shotgun and her dog and set out in search of the runaways. There was still a chance she could find them before they summoned the authorities. Two young girls wouldn't make much progress in these vast woods at night, especially with Terri so close to her due date. And Bella, a former search-and-rescue dog, was a good tracker.

It was only when Odell was outside again that she remembered Marie Plummer. She couldn't leave the girl unconscious in her back seat. She could awaken at any time.

In the name of speed, Odell grabbed the unconscious girl under the arms and dragged her out of the truck. Marie murmured something incoherent. Oh, Lord, she would wake up soon, Odell thought, and she didn't have another syringe prepared.

There was a utility closet just off Odell's office, with a latch on the outside. That would have to do. She dragged Marie up the porch steps and inside, huffing and puffing all the way. Then it was just a few more feet to the closet. Odell maneuvered her inside the small space, propped her up against the wall, then closed and locked the door.

That matter taken care of, she took the pillow from Amanda's room, gave Bella a good sniff of it, then set out on foot. At least it wasn't terribly cold or wet, she thought as Bella roamed well ahead of her, zigzagging through the trees as she'd been trained.

Less than half an hour later, Odell heard the familiar baying that indicated Bella had found something. Odell quickened her pace, praying the shepherd hadn't simply treed a possum. Soon she came upon a small house—no more than a shack, really—with boarded up windows. There was no clear path leading to it, indicating it hadn't been lived in for many years. Bella stood outside the door, which was hanging by only one hinge, and barked sharply.

"Good girl, Bella," Odell said. If the girls had taken shelter here, this would be an easier job than she thought. She opened the door and peered into the dim interior. It took a moment for eyes to adjust to the darkness. Then she saw a huddled form, wrapped in a blanket, in the corner of the room.

It was Terri, and her eyes were wide with sheer terror.

"Well, what do we have here?" Odell asked smugly.

Terri clutched the blanket more closely around her. "What does it look like? I'm having a baby," she replied with false bravado. "You just keep away from me, you old witch. You aren't gonna hurt me or my—oh!" Her face contorted with pain.

"Good Lord, you're in labor," Odell said. The realization jolted her.

"No kidding," Terri said when she could talk again.

"Where's Amanda?"

"She went to get help. You'll be in jail by tonight."

"That may well be," Odell agreed pragmatically. "But first things first. We have to get you out of this filthy place. You can't have a baby here." No telling what ungodly germs were lurking in this place, ready to infect a defenseless newborn.

"Try telling the baby th—" Terri was cut off again by another contraction.

The pains had been only seconds apart, Odell realized. There was no way she could get Terri back to the home and the sanitary delivery room there. The idea of delivering a baby under these conditions appalled Odell, but she didn't want to frighten Terri more than was necessary.

"Let's at least go outside where I can see what I'm doing," she said, reaching a hand toward Terri. "Come on, you'll have to stand. I can't carry you."

Terri cringed. "Get away from me! I don't want you delivering my baby. I can do it myself."

"Oh, Terri, now, don't be silly. I've delivered hundreds of babies. I've been a midwife for almost thirty years."

"You mean you've been selling babies and killing the mothers for thirty years."

"Killing—what in heaven's name are you talking about?"

"I figured it out—ohhhh, dammit, this hurts."

Odell ignored the cursing, still reeling from what Terri had said. Did she actually believe Odell would devote herself to saving babies' lives only to kill the mothers?

"You take the babies away," Terri said when the contraction had passed, "and then the mothers disappear. If you let them go free, they'd have turned you in. So you have to kill them. Besides, I saw Henry putting Jennifer into your truck, and she looked like she was dead. He drove her away and we never saw her again."

"My, don't you have an active imagination. No wonder you've tried so many times to leave the home. Terri, I can assure you I haven't killed anyone. After each girl gives birth, she's given a sedative. Then Henry drives them far away from here and leaves them some place where they'll be found and returned to their families. And the only reason—don't fight the pain. Breathe. That's a girl. The only reason I haven't been caught is because none of you girls know where the home is located. Think about it. Do you know where we are?''

"Near some place called River Rock."

The correct answer surprised Odell. "And how did you find that out?''

"Henry told Amanda."

"Henry." Odell shook her head. She'd known that Henry had a soft spot for Amanda, but she had firmly believed that Amanda was too afraid of him to cozy up to him. Who in their right mind wouldn't be a little afraid of Henry? "Come on, Terri, come with me out of this dirty place. I'll put my jacket on the ground for you to lie on. We've got work to do."

"Why are you being so nice to me all a sudden?" Terri asked, her eyes filled with mistrust.

"Am I so awful to you at other times?"

"Yeah," she answered without hesitation.

Odell couldn't help smiling. "I guess you would see me as an old witch. But there is something about the birth of a child that brings out the softie in me. When I'm delivering a child, I really feel that I'm traveling the path God has set for me."

"Well, you better start traveling, then, 'cause this kid is here!"

Austin went through the appropriate motions. He'd questioned every employee and customer at the grocery store, none of whom had seen anything of consequence; he'd called for backup to help him comb the neighborhood. Outwardly he was the picture of calm efficiency. But he was running on automatic. Inside he was numb and cold.

He wished like hell he'd never suggested that Caro go undercover. He wished he hadn't been so worried about blowing their cover and had gone looking for her the moment the microphone had failed. He even wished he'd never been given this case. Better still, he should be back in Auto Theft. Here he'd been trying to make a big splash, and instead he'd botched everything up and put a colleague in mortal danger.

Worry for Caro's welfare consumed him. Was she hurt? What if Odell discovered the body mike? As long as Odell believed Caro to be a pregnant teenager, no harm would come to her. Austin had to believe that. But if Caro's cover was blown, what then? If Odell had so little regard for life that she dumped a young girl's body in a lake, could murder be that big of a jump for her?

If anything happened to Caro... God, he hadn't realized how much he'd come to care for her until this moment. He wished they hadn't parted company this morning on such a sour note. The minute he found her, he would make amends for everything—and he would tell her just how he felt. The fact that he might not get that chance pressed at him from all directions.

No one else seemed to be condemning Austin for the blunder. Even Tony, who was closer to Caro than anyone Austin knew, hadn't tried to point a finger of blame. Although Tony was obviously troubled by Caro's disappearance, he was applying himself to the job at hand. In fact, everyone around here was ready to jump in at the slightest provocation. That's what police officers did when one of their own was in trouble.

Unfortunately, there wasn't much to do beyond canvassing the neighborhood around the house to see if anyone had noticed anything out of the ordinary. Caro, like the rest, had vanished into thin air.

Austin's phone buzzed. He was on it in an instant.

"Corporal Lomax, there's a woman here to see you. Actually, she asked for Caro first, then you. She won't give her name, but she says it's important."

"I'm coming."

He made his way to the public entrance to CAPERS, hoping against hope he was about to get a break. As soon as he opened the metal security door leading into the vestibule he saw her, a petite, attractive blond woman somewhere in her thirties. She had her arms folded and her head bowed, looking very unsure of herself.

"Hi, I'm Corporal Lomax," he said, trying to sound relaxed and friendly when he was feeling just the opposite. "How can I help you?"

The woman offered her perfectly manicured hand, which shook badly. "I'm Chloe Krill. My neighbor told me you and another officer stopped by the house while my husband and I were out of town. Is... is there a problem?"

By the looks of her, the woman was terrified. Austin took a chance. "I think you know what the problem is." When she didn't reply, he added, "The baby?"

At that, Chloe burst into noisy tears.

Ah, hell, this was all he needed. The receptionist wordlessly handed Austin a wad of tissue, which he passed to Chloe. "Come on, now, Mrs. Krill, there's no need for all this. Everything's going to work out okay." He put a comforting arm around her frail shoulders.

"D-Don's gonna k-kill me," she said.

"He'll understand," Austin soothed, though from what he knew of Don, he doubted the man understood anything but his own needs. "He'll realize you're just following your conscience. Right?" He led her back through the maze of desks and cubbyholes into his own space, sat her down in his chair and fetched her a cup of water.

"Don told me the whole story last night," she said when she'd composed herself. "The adoption wasn't legal. We bought our baby. Justin's natural mother was Marcy Phelps, that girl they pulled out of the lake. She died in childbirth."

Austin could take little enjoyment in having his and Caro's theory confirmed. "I know this is very difficult for you," he said. "I appreciate your coming forward, and I assure you I'll do everything I can to protect you from criminal charges—"

"I don't care about criminal charges!" she said passionately. "I just want to keep my baby. What if Marcy's family tries to take Justin away from us?"

"I doubt it will come to that," Austin said, more because he needed to calm Chloe down than anything. "No matter what the consequences are, the fact that you came forward will weigh in your favor. But right now I need more information from you. I don't have time to explain the whole situation, but there are lives hanging in the balance. Who sold the baby to you?"

"Our lawyer, Travis Beaman, handled it for us," she said. "When Don found out Travis had declared bankruptcy and then fled the country, he got really nervous. That's when I insisted he tell me everything. He had no idea I planned to go straight to the police."

"Mrs. Krill . . ."

"The woman who sold us the baby is Travis's sister, Odell Beaman. She lives in east Texas somewhere, I think. She runs a home for unwed mothers."

Finally! A first and last name. Austin wrote down the name, already mentally making a list of the next few steps he could now take. "Do you know anything else about her? Her age, what kind of car she drives? Do you have a phone number, anything?"

Chloe shook her head helplessly. "We never actually met her."

Austin smiled, anyway. He asked a few more routine questions, but it seemed that Mrs. Krill had related everything she knew. "That's okay, this will help tremendously. I can't thank you enough, Mrs. Krill," he said as he escorted her to the exit.

"You're not going to arrest me?"

Even if he'd had time, he didn't have the heart. "I don't think that's necessary. Go home, now, and try not to worry. Someone will be getting in touch with you."

She gave him a watery smile, then turned and walked away.

Austin literally sprinted back to his desk and got on the phone with the Department of Motor Vehicles. Unfortunately there was no driver's license on file, but Odell Beaman did have a vehicle registered. Within minutes he had her license plate number and a description of her car—a white Suburban. Unfortunately, the address on file was that of her brother. Travis Beaman's house had already been checked out. It was empty.

He immediately put out an APB. He was just hanging up when Tony approached his desk, looking very agitated.

"Phone company security just called," he said, slapping a piece of paper onto the desktop. "Our friend Odell blew it. She made a phone call to the answering service without doing whatever it is she normally does to cover her tracks. She was using a cellular phone, but they've narrowed it down to a half-mile radius. The repeater that transmitted the call is located near River Rock."

River Rock—of course. Justin Krill's place of birth, as indicated on his birth certificate. "Great," Austin said. "Get on the phone and see if you can rouse some law enforcement authorities there." He related the information he'd just gotten from Chloe Krill. "See if you can pinpoint an address. Go through the utility companies. She has to use electricity." As he issued orders, he fished through his desk for a road atlas.

"I'll get right on it," Tony said. "Where are you going?"

"I'm heading east. Tell the locals I'm coming, and update me the minute you find out anything. I'll probably need backup. Hell, call in the FBI and let them take over. I just want to make sure this thing's done right from now on."

Chapter 17

Caro awoke slowly, disoriented. Her stomach clenched with nausea, and she was glad she hadn't eaten breakfast. Breakfast...shredded wheat. She'd gone to the grocery store.... It came back to her all at once, and she tasted fear sharp and bitter on her tongue. Something had gone terribly wrong, and Odell had taken her hostage.

Stay calm, she told herself, tamping down the urge to scream. Okay, so she'd been drugged and stashed someplace small and dark with her hands tied behind her back. At least she wasn't dead, or seriously injured. And her wits were slowly returning as the fear receded. Apparently the cavalry wasn't coming to the rescue. It was up to Caro to escape.

"Safe as a babe in arms, my Aunt Fanny," she grumbled, recalling Austin's assurances. When she saw him she would punch his lights out. Holding that pleasant thought in her mind, she focused her attention on getting herself free.

With a little effort she managed to maneuver to her feet, although she was still dizzy from whatever drug Odell had given her. She leaned against the wall as another wave of nausea washed over her. When it passed, she began inching her way to the left. Two baby-steps later she encountered a row of shelves. A few steps to the right were more shelves. There was a door in front of her, which appeared to be the only exit. She could see a thin line of light beneath it.

She turned her back to it and explored with her bound hands, but she couldn't find a knob or latch of any kind. *Okay, I'll try something else.* She stepped back, took a deep breath, then threw her weight against the door, shoulder first. Pain shot all the way down her arm, but the door didn't budge.

"Hmm, not like in the movies," she murmured. She would break bones long before the door gave way.

If she could just get her hands untied! But her bonds were tight, and she couldn't reach the knots. Maybe there was something in this closet she could use to cut the cords. With her back to the shelves she felt around, locating a ball of twine, masking tape, a hammer, an open package of ball-point pens—but no scissors or hacksaw or utility knife.

She fumbled around some more, chancing on a box of some sort. Curious, she pushed and pulled at it until she got it open. Matches! Maybe she could burn through the cord around her wrists. Then again, maybe she could burn down the whole building. But she had to risk it. What other choice did she have?

In such an awkward position, she had a hard time just figuring out how to strike one of the matches. That accomplished, it took several tries to turn the match so that the flame even came near the cords.

"Come on, come on." The heat grew too intense and she let go of the match. Then she smelled an odd acrid stench and realized her sweater was on fire. "Ouch! Dammit, dammit, dammit!" She dropped the box and backed up against the wall, smothering the flames—but not before she burned her hands and her back.

For a few moments, the pain blocked out all other conscious thought. Then she felt a kind of numbness taking over—probably her endorphins kicking in. She wondered how badly she'd injured herself.

There was nothing to do but try again. She squatted down and retrieved the matches, gritted her teeth against the pain, and struck another one. Finally, when she was about to run out of matches, not to mention choke from all the smoke she'd generated, the ties gave way and her hands were abruptly freed.

She felt around on her body, frantically searching for any burning embers she might have missed. When she'd assured herself that nothing else was on fire, she automatically checked the antenna wire on the body mike. It was disconnected, and it might have been that way since the grocery store. No wonder Austin hadn't rushed to the rescue—he'd never heard her give the signal. All right, so she wouldn't punch him when she saw him. Suddenly she wanted to see him, to touch him, to let him comfort her—

There was no time to feel sorry for herself. She had to get this closet door open before Odell returned.

With her increased mobility she was able to explore the higher shelves. Miracle of miracles, she found a flashlight that worked. She waved the beam frantically around the closet, trying to banish the darkness. And there, right in front of her face, was a pair of scissors. She wished she'd found them before she'd roasted herself.

The door indeed had no knob or handle on the inside. But by peering through the cracks at the light from outside, she could see where the outside latch was located. It should be simple, she told herself. Most likely a junk closet wouldn't have a sophisticated lock.

She didn't have a credit card, but perhaps the stiff plastic from the package of pens would do the trick. She worked the plastic free of the cardboard, dumping the pens on the floor. With the scissors she cut out a flat piece, the task made more difficult by the fact that her left hand didn't seem to work very efficiently. She knew then that her burns were more severe than she'd thought.

When she had a nice, flat piece of plastic, she jammed it into the space between the door and the facing, just beneath the latch, and worked it upward. She was rewarded with a rasp of metal against metal as the latch lifted and the door fell open.

The sense of accomplishment was almost overwhelming. Her eyes filled with tears, whether from relief or the pain of her hands or the smoke, she didn't know. But she didn't allow her elation to rule her for long. She was far from home free.

She was in a little office of some sort, and although the light was on, there was no one around. No phone, either. She searched through the desk, finding a key ring with about a dozen keys, each one numbered. Figuring this might be useful, she took it. Then she pulled a small automatic gun—a Walther PPK/S .380— from a leg holster concealed inside her boot. She was glad now she'd decided to carry the slim, stainless-steel weapon, although Austin probably would have had a fit if he'd known about it. With gun in hand, she began searching the rest of the premises.

She was in a house, she decided, but a damn big one. The front rooms—kitchen, living room, dining room—were deserted. In another section of the house she found what looked like a doctor's examination room. Was this, then, The Good Shepherd Home? Whatever it was, it appeared to be deserted.

Peering around each corner, she made her way to the back of the house. She found a long, dimly lit hallway lined with six doors. The first one was open, and the small bedroom, hardly big enough to turn around in, was empty. The next door was locked from the outside.

"It's about time," an impatient female voice called from inside the room. "Hurry up, I have got to go pee."

"Hello? Who's there?" Caro called, surprised to have found a live person.

There was a long pause. "Kendra. Who are you?"

"I'm a police officer." Making an educated guess, Caro tried the key marked number two. The deadbolt slid free and the door opened.

A pretty, pale blond girl stared incredulously at Caro, then at the gun. "You aren't going to shoot me, are you?"

"No, I'm the police. Are you being held here against your will?" Caro asked what seemed an obvious question, but she had to be sure.

"Me and a bunch of other girls." All at once hope suffused Kendra's face. "You're gonna get us out of here?"

"That's the idea. How many girls are there?"

"Uh, nine, I think."

Nine? Oh, Lord. Caro feared she was about to become a one-woman SWAT team.

Kendra peered nervously around Caro. "Where's Odell and Henry?"

"I don't know. Which means we'd better hurry."

The next ten minutes were sheer bedlam as Caro unlocked first one door, then another, freeing three additional girls in various stages of pregnancy. Despite her attempts to keep them together, they ignored her and headed for the bathroom. She let them, because she figured they wouldn't listen to her, anyway, so long as their bladders were calling.

Caro was relieved to discover Julie Yates in one of the rooms, but Amanda was still to be found.

Upstairs was a similar hallway with five more rooms. Two were empty, but the others held more captives. Caro opened the last locked door, disappointed that the girl inside was not Amanda. She herded all the girls downstairs, rounded up the strays and quickly counted heads. "That's only seven," she said. "Where are the other two?"

There was a moment of contemplative silence until one of them asked, "Where's Amanda?"

"And Terri. I don't see Terri."

"They slept in the basement last night, remember?"

Caro quickly checked the basement and, finding it empty, she gathered her little flock together and ordered them not to move until she returned. When it was time to run, she didn't want to have to track down any stragglers.

With her gun drawn, she eased out the front door. The huge farmhouse was surrounded by an eight-foot fence topped with barbed wire, and the front gate—the only entrance to the property, she soon discovered—was securely padlocked. She knew without even trying that none of the little keys on the pilfered key ring would fit the huge Master lock. "Now what?"

She heard a noise behind her and whirled around, but it was only Kendra, brazenly defying Caro's order. "See?" she said. "You're a prisoner just like the rest of us. That's probably not even a real gun. You're just another pregnant girl."

The other girls had followed Kendra outside and were now standing mutely in a tight knot on the front porch. Caro saw no point in trying to convince them she was a detective.

Odell's white Suburban was parked in the driveway. The doors were unlocked and the keys were in the ignition. "Just stand back," Caro said as she opened the driver's door and climbed in. She would show these girls who was a prisoner and who wasn't. She cranked up the engine, turned the truck around, pointed it toward the gate, fastened her seat belt . . . and floored it.

The violent jolt from the impact jerked Caro against the shoulder harness and snapped her head forward, but the chain that held the gates didn't break. She backed up the truck and tried again. Finally, on her third attempt, the chain gave way. Her head was spinning. The truck's hood was crunched in and the engine didn't sound so good, but who cared? The girls cheered and whistled. Caro leaned out the window and motioned for them to join her. It was a tight fit, but all seven and their protruding stomachs managed to wedge themselves into the vehicle.

"Fasten your seat belts," she dutifully ordered as she put the truck in gear and headed down the narrow, twisting dirt road that led away from the Good Shepherd Home.

"You gotta be kidding," someone groused.

"I'm about to pee in my pants," another complained.

"Why didn't you go back at the house?" Caro asked.

"There wasn't time for everybody to go."

"Well, there are worse things than peeing in your pants," Caro said. Like burning your hands. Every movement she made sent searing rockets of pain all the way up her arms. Still, she'd do it again. Her escape and rescue might not have been textbook pretty, but it had worked. "Anybody know how to get to the nearest town?"

No one did. They had never left the home before. So when she reached a two-lane blacktop, Caro arbitrarily turned right. The road had to lead somewhere.

Over the next ten minutes the girls overcame their reticence, and soon they were all talking at once. Caro got a jumbled version of what had been going on. Odell had singlehandedly kidnapped more than a dozen pregnant girls from cities all over Texas. After the girls had their babies, they disappeared. No one knew what had happened to Amanda and Terri, who apparently was close to term, only that they had been alive and well the night before.

That, at least, was encouraging.

She was not going to cry, Amanda told herself. If she was smart enough to escape The Good Shepherd Home, she was smart enough to get herself out of these damned woods. But it seemed like she'd been walking for days, and she'd encountered nothing but trees, trees and more trees.

She'd hated leaving Terri behind. But it seemed the only sensible solution. After her water had broken and the contractions begun, Terri had valiantly tried to continue. But she hadn't lasted long. When they'd stumbled onto an abandoned house, which would at least provide some shelter if it started raining, Terri had declared that she wasn't moving another inch.

"It takes a long time to have a baby, right?" Amanda had asked. "Hours and hours, sometimes days?"

Terri groaned. "What a cheerful thought."

"I mean, surely I'll be able to bring help before the baby actually gets here. I just don't want you to worry."

"I won't," Terri said in a small voice. "Just go. The sooner you leave, the sooner you'll be back, right?"

"I'll be back by daylight," Amanda had promised.

As it turned out, her promise had been rash. Going had been slow in the pitch black. Branches seemed to reach out with wills of their own to scratch her face and catch her hair. She'd walked through spiderwebs and tripped over roots, all the while not even sure she was still headed in the right direction. Ten miles over rough terrain was a helluva long way, she realized.

Then the crowning glory of bad luck: she'd fallen into a hole and twisted her knee, like one of those stupid heroines in an old B movie. At that point she'd dragged herself to the base of a large tree, intending to rest awhile and wait for daylight. She'd dozed fitfully, fearful of every slight noise she heard.

When morning finally dawned, the sky was overcast, and Amanda wasn't able to use the sun to navigate. Hobbling along as best she could, she continued in what she thought was a straight line. But several hours later, she saw a fallen tree covered with fungus that looked awfully familiar. She was afraid she'd been walking in circles.

Poor Terri, she thought, plodding along, refusing to give up. Had she had the baby by now? Could she do it without anyone to help her? Well, of course she could, Amanda scolded herself. Women had been delivering babies for centuries, and she didn't imagine the baby would wait just because there wasn't a doctor around. But what if Terri had trouble? If this harebrained escape plan resulted in anything happening to her friend . . .

It didn't bear thinking about.

She walked on, mechanically putting one step in front of another, concentrating on staying upright. She heard a noise in the distance and stopped to listen. There it was again, a dog baying. And it sounded like Phoebe.

Oh, dear God, she prayed, don't let Odell find me. Not after all this. Amanda would rather wander the woods forever than put herself under that witch's control again. But the dog was getting closer. She could hear it running through the brush now, howling spasmodically. Moments later Phoebe crashed into view, tongue lolling as she leaped over a log.

Amanda froze. She didn't think the dog would attack her, but she wasn't sure.

Phoebe skidded to a halt a few feet away, much to Amanda's relief, and continued to bay loudly. At that point she knew there was no escape for her. Any moment now Odell would appear with her shotgun, and Amanda would be dragged in disgrace back to the Good Shepherd Home. The only decision she needed to make was whether to tell Odell where to find Terri.

Was it better to leave her friend to her own devices, or send Odell to help deliver the baby? She knew what Terri would want. Even if she were dying, she would want Odell to stay as far away as possible. That was the answer, then. Odell could torture Amanda, and she would never tell her where to find Terri.

Phoebe abruptly stopped howling and turned to retrace her path. That's when Amanda saw a shadow moving through the woods toward her, leaves crunching under heavy boots.

It was Henry! Thank you, God, thank you, thank you. Henry would help her. He would show her the way out of the woods and into town. She waved and smiled happily as he drew closer. "I thought I'd be lost in these stupid woods forever!" She wondered if she should hug him.

Henry stopped a few feet from her. He wasn't smiling. "Why didn't you meet me at the Dairy Queen?" he demanded. "I waited and waited."

She thought the answer to that question was obvious. Then again, Henry wasn't the brightest person she'd ever encountered. "I've been lost," she said. "I didn't realize how far it was into town, and also I tripped and twisted my knee. Look, look how swollen my knee is."

Henry appeared unconvinced. "Why did you take Terri with you?" His voice was low, full of suspicion.

She'd never seen him in quite this mood before. "I had no choice," she explained patiently. "How was I to know Odell would put Terri in the basement, too? She followed me. I tried to stop her." That, at least, was true.

"Is that why you dug such a big hole under the fence?" he asked, smug now, as if he knew he'd caught her. His facial tics seemed more pronounced than usual.

She wondered if he'd actually witnessed the escape, or if he only examined the hole under the fence this morning and figured out that she'd enlarged it. "I couldn't get through the hole myself. I had to make it bigger," she reasoned. "Anyway, Terri was the one with the shovel. I was busy distracting Bella."

It was like talking to a brick wall. He didn't appear to be listening or trying to understand. Suddenly his eyes filled with tears. "You called me a big, dumb ox," he said. "Why did you say that?"

"I was acting!" This was incredible. "I was pretending to be a very bad girl, remember? I was trying to convince Odell that I was out of control. Henry, you know I didn't mean it. It was all an act. Henry?"

She reached out to stroke his sleeve. His face softened, and he almost let her touch him. Then he jerked away. "Where's Terri?"

"We split up," Amanda said carelessly. "You know I can't stand her."

"I thought the fight was all an act," he said, obviously confused.

"Well, it was, my part was. But not hers. Did you hear what she called me? She called me a bitch. I hope she wanders around in these woods until she's eighty!"

Apparently she'd said the wrong thing. Henry's face hardened. "That's not a very Christian attitude."

Amanda tried to appear contrite. "I'm sorry. But she made me mad. Can we forget about Terri? I'm tired and hungry and my knee hurts."

"I can't forget about Terri," he said, clearly disturbed. His mood seemed to be flickering back and forth among anger, anxiety, and hopefulness. "Now that she's free, she'll bring the cops. They'll put Aunt Odell in jail. And she'll know that it was all my fault. She'll never forgive me."

"Okay, we'll find Terri," Amanda said, thinking quickly. "She can't move very fast, not when she's almost nine months along. She's probably lost, just like me. But she headed south and I went east. She's probably miles away from here. What would she find if she went south?"

"I don't know," Henry said, his brow creased in deep thought. "I'd need a map."

"Where's your truck? I bet you keep a map in your truck."

"That's right, I do," he said, brightening. "The highway's about two miles that way. Can you walk that far?"

Amanda breathed a surreptitious sigh of relief. She'd almost lost his trust, but now he appeared to be falling in with her plans again. "I can walk," she said, "but not very fast." To think, she'd been only two miles from the highway, from salvation. She would still make it. But now she would have to get away from Henry. It shouldn't be that difficult.

Hang on, Terri.

After an arduous forty-five minutes or so, Amanda could see that the trees were thinning out. Soon Henry's old green pickup truck came into view, parked on the side of a dirt road. The sight made her heart leap. She was close to dropping from exhaustion and her knee was throbbing. She thought about home, her father, Scott. Perhaps she was just a few hours away from seeing them again.

Henry hoisted Phoebe into the back, started to open the passenger door for Amanda, then paused, his brow creased in concentration the way it did when he was thinking something through.

Amanda was filled with apprehension. Henry was no Rhodes scholar, yet he did possess some logic. Was he thinking about what she'd told him? Was he about to catch her in a lie?

"What's wrong, Henry?" she asked.

"I was just thinking . . . if I find Terri and bring her back to the home, Aunt Odell will be real proud of me."

"That's right, she will."

"And then Terri will open her big mouth, and that'll be the end of it."

"What do you mean?"

"She knows I helped you escape. You told her, didn't you?" It was an accusation.

Amanda's heart fluttered erratically. "Well, I didn't come right out and tell her, no. I wasn't talking to her hardly at all."

"But she saw that the bars on the window were loosened. And she saw the hole dug under the fence. So she knows you had help, and she'll tell Aunt Odell."

"I don't think you need to worry about that," Amanda reasoned. "Even if she does know, why would she tell Odell anything? She has nothing to gain."

"Because she's a sinner, that's why." Abruptly he jerked the door open. "Get in."

Amanda climbed into the truck, feeling like she was walking through a mine field. She had to find some way to reassure Henry that everything would work out okay. But he had a point about Terri. If he let her get away, she would bring the cops to the home. And if he caught her and brought her back to the home, she would almost certainly tell Odell of Henry's part in the escape. Of course, Amanda was going to bring the house down before either of those two possibilities could happen. But Henry didn't know that.

Henry slid behind the wheel and reached into the glove compartment. He pulled out a stack of maps, found the one he wanted and began to study it. When Amanda leaned over to have a look—it would be nice to know where she was—he pulled away from her so she couldn't see.

"You say she headed south?" he asked Amanda.

"Yes, that's right."

"South is down," he murmured to himself, frowning as he concentrated on the map. Then he smiled, and it wasn't a pleasant smile. "I know where to find her. And I know just how to deal with her, too."

"What are you going to do?" Amanda asked, trying to sound merely curious.

"I'll make sure Terri never tells anyone anything, ever again." He cranked up the truck and threw it into gear.

Amanda went cold as a block of ice inside. Surely he didn't mean... "Henry," she said cautiously, "you can't hurt Terri."

"Oh, it won't hurt much," he said, as if this was supposed to reassure Amanda. "My hands are real strong. I just squeeze, kind of like squeezing the juice out of an orange, no harder than that. Then after a minute, two minutes, it's over. She'll be gone, gone to her eternal punishment." He spoke as casually as if he were explaining how to check the oil in a car.

Amanda tried not to let the horror show on her face. Henry planned to kill Terri, murder her. All this time, Amanda had thought Henry was basically good, a slow-witted, obedient nephew eager to please. But if he could kill another human being with not even a twinge of conscience . . .

"Henry, that doesn't seem a very Christian thing to do," she said, using one of his own favorite arguments.

"Oh, but it is," he argued. "Terri is a sinner, just like the others. I'm meting out God's justice."

The others? " 'Vengeance is mine,' sayeth the Lord," she tried again.

"Yes, and I am his tool of vengeance," Henry said. "The first time, I wasn't sure. I mean, it was really an accident. I was supposed to drop off the sinner in Corsicana, but she woke up before we got there, and she started fighting me. I broke her neck. At first I thought I'd done something bad, but then I felt this . . . this goodness filling me up, like her life was coming into my body. And I felt strong and good, and I knew I'd done the right thing."

Amanda wanted to throw up. She grabbed on to the door handle to steady herself. Henry was a murderer, and she was completely under his control. If she didn't say and do exactly the right thing, he could easily consider her among the sinners and justify her death. She looked at his hands, gripping the steering wheel, and she swallowed hard.

"How many s-sinners have you punished?" she felt compelled to ask. "All of the girls?"

"All except Marcy. She died from hmm . . . —uh, I can't remember the word, but she bled too much. We dropped her off the dam, Aunt Odell and me did. That was right before you came to the home."

Amanda remembered. A young girl's body had been found at the Cedar Creek spillway the day before Odell had kidnapped Amanda.

"Odell said she ought to have a decent Christian burial. I didn't think so. She was a sinner, too."

"Where do you put the bodies?" Amanda asked, masking the horror from her voice.

He flashed a self-satisfied smile. "In an old well in the woods. It's wide and deep. Plenty of room in there. Room for ten, maybe twenty sinners. They'll never be found."

Now Amanda was sick. Her stomach rolled and she coughed, grateful that she hadn't eaten in a long time. No matter how she tried to block it, she saw a vision of Terri being dumped down a well. And the baby? If Henry found Terri, what would he do about the baby?

That was it! "Henry, you can't kill Terri," she said suddenly. "If you kill her, you'll be killing the baby, too. And while she might be a sinner, the baby is innocent."

Her logic had an immediate and profound effect on Henry. He slammed on the brakes so suddenly that Amanda had to put her hand on the dash to keep from being pitched onto the floor. Then he just sat there, hands flexing on the steering wheel as his mouth worked silently. His face was a picture of torture.

"I can't kill a baby," he finally said.

Amanda relaxed a bit.

"That would go against everything Odell has done. She would never, ever forgive me. But if she finds out that I helped you escape..." Suddenly he turned on Amanda, an unreasoning rage pouring out of him. "It's your fault! You're the one who tempted me with your harlot's ways. You made me wander from the righteous path."

Amanda shook her head mutely. Her mind, frozen with fear, refused to give her the words she needed to defend herself.

He reached out and stroked her hair, almost reverently, then grabbed a handful and yanked.

She yelped in surprise and pain. "Henry, you're hurting me."

Seeming not to hear her, he pulled until she was sprawled across the front seat, then fitted his other hand around her neck. "Whore of Babylon!" he shouted, bending her head back so she was forced to look at his twisted face.

"I'm not a whore," she objected as tears of pain clouded her vision. "I've repented. Henry, you mustn't—"

His hand tightened on her neck, cutting off her words. "God is your judge, and He says you're guilty." Then, for just a moment, his expression softened, suffused with regret. "It won't hurt for long, Amanda. Trust me, it's better this way."

Chapter 18

Austin was fifteen miles outside the town of River Rock, driving his Bronco over eighty, when his cellular phone rang. He snapped the device open with a frenetic flick of his wrist. "Corporal Lomax. Who's this? What do you have?"

"Got a pencil?"

"Oh, Tony." Austin realized he had long since lost his professional objectivity. He was barely rational. But he kept visualizing Caro in various situations, none of them pleasant, and the tormenting thoughts made him wild with the need to do something, hear something. He pulled a pen from his jacket pocket and found an old gas receipt to write on. "What's going on?"

"I have an address for Odell Beaman. And I just talked to the sheriff down there, Don Fowles. He knows the place, and he'll meet you there with all the backup he can muster. The closest FBI field office—"

"What the hell?" Austin interrupted, slamming on the brakes to avoid rear-ending a white truck stalled in his lane. A gaggle of women swarmed around the disabled vehicle. They all looked up and began waving and shouting frantically.

"What's going on?" Tony asked.

"Ladies with car trouble. Hell, I don't have time to play Sir Galahad now," he muttered. He was starting to pull past them when a familiar pair of neon leggings caught his eye. The woman wearing them, who had her head stuck in the truck's engine, looked up, and Austin slammed on the brakes again.

She stared at him in disbelief.

He dropped the phone and was out of the car and to her in a split second. "Caro, thank God." Relief coursed through him like a raging river. Without a second thought he pulled her to him and held her, reassuring himself that she wasn't a figment of his imagination. Her body was soft and warm against his. He pressed his face into her hair. She smelled like . . . smoke?

"Ouch! Let go, let go!"

He released her immediately. "Are you hurt?" he asked, scanning up and down her body.

"I'm fine," she said through gritted teeth. "Your concern is touching, but right now there are more pressing matters than my health. We have to get these girls to a safe haven, and then we have to find Odell and someone named Henry and two missing girls, one of them Amanda. Where's your phone?"

"In the car. But if you're calling for backup . . ." He cocked his head, listening. "Hear those sirens?" Moments later two county sheriff's cars crested the hill, sirens wailing and lights flashing. Overkill, in Austin's opinion.

One of the girls burst into tears. Another whined that she had to go to the bathroom. The new arrivals screeched to a halt and jumped out of their vehicles, reminding Austin of an outtake from *Smokey and the Bandit.* One of the men swaggered over importantly.

"What's going on here?"

Caro, heedless of her rather bedraggled appearance, stepped right up to the man. "I'm Corporal Carolyn Triece with the Dallas Police Department," she said smoothly, though she declined to offer her hand. "These girls have been held captive, some of them for months, by a woman name Odell Beaman—"

"Yes, we've been apprised of the situation," the sheriff's deputy said, eyeing Caro speculatively. "We were just over at the Beaman place. Quite a setup." He looked at the white Suburban, then back at Caro. "You're the one who was snatched this morning? And you escaped? And you took all these girls with you?" Skepticism quickly turned to admiration.

Caro wasn't about to bask in any praise. "Look, we don't have time to chitchat. Odell and her nephew Henry are still at large and two girls are missing."

With a minimum of fuss she took control of everything and everybody. Her first order of business was to transport the girls to safety, dividing them up and directing them into the squad cars. A local police car from River Rock arrived, along with an unmarked car driven by an off-duty sheriff's deputy. Caro gave orders like a pint-sized General Patton. The others jumped when she spoke. In other circumstances, Austin would have found it amusing. Now he was just grateful for her competence.

"You say the Suburban was the only car parked at the Beaman place?" the local cop asked.

"That's right," Caro said.

"That means Henry's old green truck is out and about somewhere," Austin pointed out.

"Damn, I thought they were all on foot," she said. "Get the license number from DMV, if possible, and put out an APB. These people are armed and dangerous as hell. What are the chances of getting a helicopter?"

"I'll call in one from Dallas," Austin said. Aside from that small contribution, he just stood back and watched as Caro took firm control of what used to be his investigation. A couple of weeks ago that would have bothered him, but somewhere between losing Caro and finding her again, he had also lost all desire to be a hero. He just wanted this thing over.

And then he wanted to take Caro Triece to a Caribbean island, preferably one with no phones, and stay there with her for a month or two. He would never let the woman out of his sight again. That's something, he thought, suppressing a grin. A couple of weeks ago he'd wanted her as far away from him as possible.

"Get the lead out, Lomax, we're rolling," Caro said, abruptly obliterating his brief moment of fantasy as she climbed into the passenger seat of his car.

He shook his head to clear it and slid behind the wheel, appalled at his own stupidity. He wasn't exactly on Caro's A list, and not likely to share an island with her any time soon. He'd let her down. He'd almost gotten her killed, and she would probably never forgive him.

He wasn't sure he could ever forgive himself.

"River Rock's straight ahead, ten miles," she said, sounding suddenly weary. "Did you get the directions to the police station?"

"Yeah. Right at the third street past the flashing yellow light." The local cop shop was to serve as Command Central, from which Caro would direct the search for Odell, Henry and the two girls.

As soon as he was cruising at seventy, he looked over at Caro. Her eyes were closed, her face tense with obvious pain. Then he saw the problem.

"Caro, your hands..." They were red and blistered, and in places completely raw. He remembered the smokey smell of her hair. "There was a fire?"

"A small one. It's no big deal."

"Like hell. You've got third-degree burns, and that's nothing to mess around with. I'm taking you to the nearest hospital."

"No, you're not," she said firmly. "I'll go later. Dammit, Lomax, I'm not missing the end of this."

There was an almost pleading note in her voice, and Austin knew he had her. She recognized that her injuries were serious enough to warrant concern, and if he pressed he could get her to a doctor. But he understood her need to see the operation through. After all she'd suffered, to miss finding Amanda and arresting Odell would be like reading a book with the last page torn out.

"Okay," he said.

There was a long, uncomfortable pause.

"How did you know where I was?" she asked. "For that matter, where did all those other guys come from?"

He explained about Odell's careless phone call and Chloe Krill's confession. "That narrowed it down to a general area, but the rest was pure luck. Tony had just tracked down an address when—"

The phone rang again as if on cue.

"Go ahead, answer it," Austin said. "It'll be Tony, wondering what the hell I'm doing."

With a shrug, she picked it up from between the seats. "Corporal Triece." Whatever Tony said in response brought a smile to Caro's lips. "Yeah, it's me. I'm okay, no thanks to you bums." Her smile faded. "I know, Tony.... No, I don't have time to explain it all now. We still have a few loose ends here. We'll get back to you." After a few more assurances that she was fine—which was a blatant lie—she hung up. Then she looked at Austin reproachfully. "I shouldn't have said that—about you being a bum. I know it was an honest mistake—"

"It was a first-class screw-up."

"It was that damn body mike, wasn't it? The wire came loose."

"Yeah." He appreciated her attempt to pin the foul-up on something other than his miserable hide. "The body mike, a Coke truck and total ineptness on my part. I'm sorry, Caro. I don't know what else to say, except that it'll be a cold day in hell before I ever run another undercover operation."

"Cold days come along in hell every once in a while," she murmured.

He started to ask her what she was talking about, but before he could even take a breath she cursed.

"Lomax, you just missed the turn."

He put on the brakes. "What turn?"

"That fork back there. The highway into town went left and we went right."

"Nobody told me about any damn fork," he grumbled, throwing the car into reverse. Then he stopped and stared into the distance.

"What's wrong?" Caro asked, immediately sensing his alertness.

"That speck of green up ahead. Looks like a green car...or truck."

"Yeah..." Suddenly she was all business. "I'm glad we're in an unmarked."

"I'll just drive by casually...."

It turned out to be an old truck, suspiciously similar to the description of Henry's. A big dog was the vehicle's only occupant, but both doors were open like the driver and passenger had vacated in a helluva hurry. The gun rack held a shotgun.

Austin stopped the Bronco, and he and Caro both got out to check over the abandoned vehicle. But the dog, a bloodhound, had other ideas. It growled menacingly, protecting its territory.

"Now, come on, fella, we won't hurt you," Caro said.

"Uh, Caro, it's a girl dog."

"Whatever. Austin, you know dogs. You make friends with her."

"Not likely. I'm as fond of my appendages as the next—hey, did you hear that?"

"Yeah." A high-pitched scream had erupted from the woods. Austin reflexively drew his gun from his shoulder holster. Caro had a gun, too, a tiny stainless-steel revolver. He didn't even want to know where she'd been stowing it, or why.

They exchanged a look. No words were necessary. They split up, heading into the woods a hundred feet apart so they could confront their adversary from opposite directions.

Austin heard another scream. Within seconds he'd found the source, a young woman who was struggling to remove a large man's hands from around her throat.

"Freeze, Police!" Austin bellowed.

The man—Henry?—did in fact freeze, raising his head like a wild animal caught in a hunter's gun sight. He stared at Austin with burning, malevolent eyes that weren't entirely human.

"Let her go," Austin said.

He realized with a start that the bedraggled girl was Amanda Arkin, though she didn't quite match the pretty, perky Amanda in the photograph Austin had memorized. She stopped struggling and stared at Austin with pleading eyes. Austin was both relieved to find her alive and terrified she wouldn't remain that way for long unless he handled this just right.

"Let her go," he repeated. "It's all over now, Henry." From the corner of his eye he saw a movement. Caro was approaching from behind Henry, quiet as a cat. Austin had to struggle not to look at her or show by his expression that they had company.

With practiced precision she struck, giving the back of Henry's knees a karate kick. The attack surprised him enough that he loosened his hold on Amanda. That was all the girl needed; she managed to pull away from him. Henry turned in confusion to see what had assaulted him. Austin was on him like a cannonball, knocking him to the ground.

The man was huge, but he was panicked, thrashing around with little coordination. Austin put a knee to Henry's back and with two lightning-swift moves he had the man's arms immobilized. "I've got him," Austin said, now with one knee pressing down on Henry's neck. The prisoner kicked wildly, but he wasn't going anywhere. "In my glove box I have some handcuffs."

Without a word Caro went to fetch them.

Amanda stood a few feet away, breathing heavily and rubbing her throat.

"Are you okay?" Austin asked.

"Yeah, I think so," she replied in a trembling voice.

"She has the devil in her," Henry said, his words muffled because his face was pressed into the spongy ground.

"Don't we all?" Austin countered, shaking his head. It was apparent the guy was pretty disturbed, but at least he had stopped struggling. "You're under arrest, bud, and that means you have the right to remain silent. You understand?"

"Like on TV?" Henry ventured, sounding now more like a scared little boy than an attempted murderer.

"Exactly." Austin rattled off the rest of the Miranda warning.

"You're going to put him in jail, aren't you?" Amanda asked, growing agitated. She stood several feet away, her gaze riveted on Henry. "He's a murderer, you know."

"Almost," Austin said, conjuring up a smile for her. "Are you sure you're okay?"

"No, not me," she answered impatiently. "He killed four girls and stuffed their bodies down a well."

Austin's smile froze on his face.

Caro returned just in time to hear Amanda's revelation. Her eyes grew as big as poker chips. "Did you do that, Henry?"

"They had the devil in them," Henry offered, as if this were a perfectly acceptable defense for murder.

"Holy God," Caro said. Something had finally shocked the unflappable Carolyn Triece.

She pulled a thin plastic strip—Flex-cuffs—from a cellophane package and handed it to Austin, who then busied himself securing Henry's hands. Meanwhile Caro talked softly with Amanda, trying to reassure her, explaining that her friends from the Good Shepherd Home were safe.

"Except for Terri. We have to go back and get her," Amanda insisted, close to tears. "She's having a baby all by herself in this terrible shack...."

"We'll find her," Caro soothed.

"But I don't even know if I can show you where it is. It's about a zillion miles into the woods, and I'm not even sure what direction. I've been walking all night and I twisted my knee...." She began crying in earnest.

Caro held the girl while she sobbed, but the storm of tears didn't last long. She quickly pulled herself together. "Maybe...maybe if we go back to the home and start from there, I can find the shack again."

Terrific, Austin thought. Now they were probably going to have to deliver a baby. He hauled a surprisingly meek Henry to his feet. "You're not going anywhere except a hospital," Austin said to Amanda. And maybe, once he got there, he could convince Caro to accept treatment. "Don't worry, we'll take care of Terri."

"But I'm the only one who can find her," Amanda pointed out. "These woods are huge. You could walk in circles for days."

"She has a point," Caro said.

"Okay, okay." He wasn't going to argue with these two. Together they had more grit than a barracks full of marines. They'd reached the road. Austin opened the Bronco's back door and deposited Henry inside. "You're gonna behave, right?"

Henry nodded, completely subdued. The bloodhound, watching from its vantage point in the truck, whined in confusion but didn't move.

Without being asked, Caro climbed in beside the prisoner. He wouldn't dare misbehave within her reach.

Austin started to shut the door, then thought of something. "Hey, Henry, do you know where this shack is?"

"Yeah," he said sullenly.

"Can you take us there?"

"Why should I?"

Amanda, who'd been keeping a safe distance between herself and the prisoner, moved closer. "For the baby, Henry. It could die if we don't get it to a hospital."

He was immediately contrite. "All right, for the baby."

The pain was more manageable now. Caro had found her purse in the back of Odell's Suburban. In the absence of large quantities of morphine, which was what she really wanted, she'd made do with aspirin. But that and all the adrenaline flowing through her system had at least dulled the agony of her burned hands to something she could function around, although an occasional wave sometimes hit her.

Sitting in the back seat of Austin's Bronco, she kept a wary eye on Henry, who blubbered occasionally and talked strings of nonsense to himself but otherwise appeared to be little threat. His grip on reality was tenuous at best. If he really did murder someone, he probably would never be convicted. She listened as Austin updated the sheriff via radio and called for backup and an ambulance to converge at the Beaman home.

"What about Phoebe?" Henry suddenly asked.

"Phoebe?" Was there another player in this drama that they didn't know about?

"His dog," Amanda supplied.

"Oh, the one guarding your truck," said Caro. "She'll be okay. We'll send someone to pick up the dog and the truck." Taking advantage of his momentary lucidity, she added, "You don't by chance know where your aunt is, do you?"

He shook his head. "She left this morning. Haven't seen her." He paused, his face screwed up in concentration. "She's gonna be mad at me."

Not half as mad as I am, Caro thought. After seeing the hulk nearly squeeze the life out of Amanda, she was fighting mad. It had felt good to kick him in the knees. She enjoyed seeing him handcuffed, defeated. And yet... she felt sorry for him, too. Yes, an unmistakable grain of compassion clouded her thinking. Her first instinct was to push that softness aside. Cops didn't feel sorry for criminals. Or did they? Was compassion a weakness, or was it something she'd been missing, an essential part of her humanness that gave her some much-needed balance?

If she were called on to interrogate Henry, could she do it? Could she wrench a confession out of him? A few weeks ago, her answer would have been a resounding no. He reminded her too much of

Charlie Northcutt. But she hadn't felt sorry for Charlie, not until he was dead.

They had arrived back at the Good Shepherd Home, which was now crawling with uniforms and swathed with yellow crime-scene tape. The ambulance had not yet arrived. A young-looking deputy, full of officiousness, directed Austin to park outside the gate along the narrow dirt drive. This was probably the biggest thing ever to happen to these small-town cops, and they were reveling in it. Caro could only hope they weren't destroying evidence with all their tromping around.

The eager-beaver deputy rushed up to the Bronco as soon as he realized who was inside. He opened Caro's and Amanda's doors. "You want I should take Henry here down to the judge and magistrate him?" he asked.

This case was going to be a jurisdictional nightmare, Caro thought. "Not just yet," she replied. "We still need him for something. Has there been any sign of Odell?"

"Nothing. Sheriff Fowles thinks she might have hitched a ride out of the area."

Caro hoped not. Finding Amanda alive and well was sweet success. Breaking up Odell's operation was an added bonus. But Caro would feel cheated if she didn't bring Odell to justice.

Austin opened Henry's door. "Okay, big guy, lead the way," he said.

Henry appeared confused.

"You were going to help us find the shack where the baby is, remember?" Amanda added. She got out of the truck and walked around to where Austin was assisting Henry to his feet. "Terri and I went under the fence behind that building over there, and we headed straight that way." She pointed due east. "Then Terri went into labor. We didn't go very far before we found the shack. It can't be more than a mile or two."

"Half a mile," Henry corrected her, finally comprehending. "Straight that way. Can I get something to eat?" He nodded toward the house. "It's past lunchtime, and I didn't even eat breakfast."

"This nice deputy will get you something, right, uh . . ." Caro looked at his name tag. "Right, Eddie?"

"Sure thing. Hey, you should see a doctor about those burns. How'd that happen, anyway?"

She self-consciously put her hands behind her. "Later. Take good care of our prisoner, please," she said crisply. "I want everything done by the book. You understand what I'm saying?"

"Yes, ma'am. Sheriff Fowles wouldn't stand for anything less."

She nodded, somewhat reassured.

"Can we go now, please?" Amanda implored.

"We should wait for the paramedics," Caro argued sensibly.

"To hell with that," Austin said. "I can carry the girl back here. I just want to find her."

"Okay," Caro agreed. "Let's go."

Amanda walked ahead of them, limping slightly on her injured knee. The woods were thicker here, the underbrush knee-high. Caro wondered how those two girls had made any progress in the dark last night.

"Look," Amanda said excitedly, "you can see where we walked last night, where the plants are beaten down. There's sort of a trail."

"Great, that should take us right to her," Austin said, leading the way.

Caro brought up the rear of the little procession, wondering what they would find. She hoped for Amanda's sake that Terri and the baby were all right. Caro could tell that Amanda felt responsible for Terri's predicament, and the girl would take it hard if any harm had befallen her friend.

They'd been trudging for about fifteen minutes when Austin stopped abruptly. "There, is that it?" he asked Amanda in a hushed voice, pointing ahead.

Caro squinted in the direction he pointed. Sure enough, there was a structure of some sort in the distance.

"I never saw it in daylight," Amanda said, "but that must be it." She quickened her pace. A few moments later she stopped cold. "Oh, my God."

Austin and Caro stopped, too. "What?" they asked in unison.

"The dog."

Caro squinted again, wondering if she needed glasses. Sure enough there was a big German shepherd sitting in front of the broken-down shack.

"What about it?" Austin asked.

"That's Bella. Odell's dog. Either Bella followed us here last night or... Odell is in there with Terri."

Chapter 19

This was one complication Austin hadn't counted on. People with guns and ill intent he could handle. A snarling animal that couldn't be reasoned with was something else again.

"You," he said to Amanda, "go back and get us some help. Talk to Sheriff Fowles directly," he added, fearing what some of those yo-yo's posing as deputies would do without supervision. "And bring the paramedics and a stretcher. The ambulance is probably there by now."

Amanda's chin jutted out. "Terri's in there, and I'm not leaving until she's safe. I can help you—"

"That is not an option."

"What are you going to do about Bella?" Amanda asked, obviously trying to distract him.

Good question. The minute the dog had caught their scent it pricked up its ears and bared its teeth. "I'll shoot the damn dog," he said rashly.

"No," both women objected.

"Shh! Keep it down."

"If you discharge your gun, you'll warn Odell we're here," Caro pointed out. "We want to take her by surprise."

True enough, he conceded with a nod.

"It's too bad we don't have any food," Amanda whispered. "Bella can be bribed."

"Who says we don't have food?" Austin rummaged around in his jacket and came up with the Twinkie he'd pocketed that morning, a lifetime ago. "Will this work?"

Caro stared in blatant amazement, murmuring, "I'll never criticize your eating habits again."

Amanda nodded enthusiastically. "Yeah, Bella will eat anything. Hand it over."

"Uh-uh." Austin pointed in the direction they'd just come. "Go."

"Bella knows me," Amanda reasoned. "I can distract her while—"

"Absolutely not. Caro, take Amanda back to the house."

Amanda looked at Caro and, seeing no support from that quarter, slumped in defeat. "All right, I'm going," Amanda said. "And I don't need an escort. Just be careful. Please don't let anything happen to Terri."

That's all Austin needed, an eighteen-year-old telling him how to do his job. He forced himself to be patient with her and try to allay her fears. She'd been through a lot. "We'll do our very best."

When she'd gone, he turned to Caro. "Do we go, or wait for backup?"

"I say we go. If fifteen people try to take this place with a siege, we lose the element of surprise. You bribe the dog. I'll sneak up and take Odell. Shouldn't be too difficult. If she's busy delivering a baby, she won't be toting around her gun."

"You're gonna take her with that peashooter?" He nodded derisively toward the little stainless-steel gun she'd pulled from her boot.

"Okay, then *I'll* distract the dog—"

"Nah, I'll do it." Austin figured Caro didn't need dog bites on top of her other injuries, and she'd already proved to his satisfaction that she knew how to sneak up on someone. Her performance with Henry had been stellar.

The shepherd had drawn closer. Thankfully it wasn't barking. Austin quickly unwrapped the Twinkie and held it toward the animal. "Nice Bella. Good dog. Pretty dog." He'd always had a way with dogs. He hoped this one wouldn't prove to be the exception. He didn't really want to harm the animal.

Bella immediately stopped growling and came closer still, sniffing furiously. Austin broke off a piece of the cake and offered it to her, watching from the corner of his eye as Caro slipped toward the shack, slinking low up to the boarded-up window and peeking in between the planks. She looked back at him, signaled him that she was okay, then moved toward the doorway.

It didn't take long for Bella to demolish the Twinkie. Austin managed to scratch her behind the ears as he crooned reassuringly to her. By the time the dog had licked Austin's fingers, she was wagging her tail.

"Some watchdog you are," he murmured. "Want to go for a walk? You do?" He had no intention of letting Caro handle Odell by herself. He walked slowly toward the house, the dog at his heels, then cut around to the opposite side. Capable as Caro was, he wouldn't leave anything to chance.

As she cuddled the squalling infant, Odell felt a glow of accomplishment, almost as if she'd given birth to the child herself. She had saved the life of this baby girl, saved her from the abortionist's knife. She was large and healthy, and Odell could only hope the deplorable conditions of her birth wouldn't leave any lasting effects. There had been no time to take Terri outside for the birth. The baby made its appearance within seconds of Odell's arrival, and Odell's part in the delivery had been reduced to catching the infant as it came out, then tying and cutting the cord with an unsterilized pocket knife. It would be a miracle if the child escaped without an infection, but at least there had been no serious complications so far.

Odell had wrapped the baby in Terri's sweatshirt. Terri, who had managed to wiggle back into her clothes, wrapped her wretched blanket around her shoulders and watched Odell anxiously.

"Can I hold her now?" she asked Odell.

Odell looked up. "That's not a good idea, dear. You don't want to get too attached to her."

"Why in the hell not?"

Odell cast her eyes heavenward. "Please, your language. It will be that much harder when you have to give her over to her new parents. The couple I've selected are so excited—"

"I'm not giving her up," Terri said. "I'm keeping her."

"Now, Terri, you know that would be foolish. You can't even provide for yourself, much less a helpless baby. If you really care for the child, you'll want what's best for her. Anyway, you don't have a choice in the matter."

"Like hell! You might have taken the other girls' babies away from them, but not mine. It's over, Odell, can't you see that?"

"It's not over yet," Odell said harshly.

"Amanda will bring the cops—"

"Then why hasn't she? Why hasn't anyone come to rescue you, hmm? I still have hope. If Henry stopped her before she could tell anyone, we're still in business."

"Henry's the one who helped us escape," Terri said defiantly.

Odell shook her head. "That might have been his original intention, but I think he changed his mind. He wasn't at the home when I got there, and he took Phoebe with him—and his gun."

That silenced the chit.

Lord, she hoped she was right about Henry. That was another problem. She'd given him far too much trust, and he'd betrayed her—after all she'd done for him. She'd taken him in when his own parents had become afraid of him; she'd counseled him and tutored him, took him to church, taught him how to cook and wash so he could take care of himself when he no longer had her. He worshipped her, and it seemed inconceivable that he would defy or deceive her. But apparently he had.

What a burden her life had become. But this—this new life in her arms—made everything worthwhile.

"What are you going to do with me, now that I've had the baby?" Terri asked. "Are you going to drug me and dump me—" The words caught in her throat. She looked past Odell toward a boarded-up window.

Odell turned to look, too. One of the boards hung loose, letting in a stream of light. But she saw nothing there out of the ordinary. She returned her attention to Terri. "I'm not sure what I'll do with you," Odell said earnestly. "You and Amanda know the name of the town we're near, thanks to Henry's big mouth. I can't just release you."

"I won't tell," Terri said. Her eyes darted to the window again.

Odell laughed without humor. "You would go right to the police and you know it."

"She won't have to." A stranger burst into the shack, gun drawn and pointing straight at Odell—and straight at the baby.

Terri screamed.

Odell stared in disbelief as she backed up against a wall, holding the baby closer against her chest with hands still bloodied from the delivery. Staring at the intruder, Odell realized she wasn't a stranger after all. "Marie?" Odell asked in a shaky voice.

"Detective Corporal Carolyn Triece, Dallas Police Department. You're under arrest."

Odell looked quickly from side to side.

"Don't even think about it," the woman said. "My partner is at the window behind you. There's no escape. I want you to slowly give the baby to Terri over there, then put your hands in the air."

Odell felt a rush of desperation welling up inside her. Now she knew what an animal felt like when it had been cornered by a hunter. Her whole world was crumbling. "No, I won't do it," she said, scarcely breathing the words.

"You have no choice," a man's voice chimed in. He'd entered from the other side of the shack, gun drawn. Bella had followed him.

My God, even her dog had betrayed her, Odell thought. But she wasn't finished. No, not by a long shot. She held the trump card. She held the baby. No cop would shoot a woman holding an infant.

"Of course I have a choice," Odell said, growing more sure of herself. "As long as I'm holding the baby, you can't do anything."

"Oh, yeah?" the man said. He stuck his gun in a holster under his arm and took two threatening steps toward Odell.

The moment he moved, she shifted the baby into the crook of her left arm, revealing the .38 she'd slipped out of her jacket pocket. "Stop right there. I'll kill you."

The man froze.

"Or her." Odell nodded toward Terri. "Or the baby," she added recklessly. She had the power. God would protect her, as He always had. "I'm walking away from all of you right now, and you can't stop me. You can't!"

"There's nothing for you to go back to," the lady cop said confidently. "Your home is crawling with police officers. Your nephew is in custody, soon to be charged with murder."

That little bombshell threw Odell. "Murder? If this is about Marcy Phelps—"

"Not Marcy. We know she died of natural causes. I'm talking about the other four. Henry says he killed four women and stuffed the bodies down a well. He was trying to strangle Amanda Arkin when we caught up with him."

Odell felt the blood drain from her face. Dizzy, she staggered before regaining her balance.

The man moved forward again. Odell tightened the grip on her revolver and pointed it at him. "No closer." She could see the indecision playing on his face; he thought she was bluffing. Aiming just past his shoulder, she squeezed off a shot. The gun's report was deafening. The bullet lodged in a wall, sending bits of wood and plaster flying through the room. Then all was silent. Even the baby stopped crying.

Now they knew who was in charge here, Odell thought smugly as she viewed the three pairs of wide, startled eyes. "Move away from the door," she said to Marie—or whatever her name was.

The lady cop held her ground. "No," she said. "If you know your way around guns, you know either Austin or I could shoot you without injuring the baby."

"You wouldn't risk it," Odell said, although the gritty determination in the woman's eyes worried her. Good Lord, how in the world had she ever assumed this cop was a young girl?

"Try firing that gun again and you'll find out," the man called Austin said, his voice grim.

"You would shoot me in cold blood for trying to save the lives of unborn children?" Odell said, shaking her head in disbelief. "What kind of people are you?"

Odell watched the lady cop closely. An understanding seemed to come over her face. After a tense silence, during which the players in this deadly game watched one another, sizing one another up, the lady cop spoke again. "If this is about saving lives, you wouldn't shoot anyone," she said. "You could kill all of us and escape with the baby, but escape to what? You can't return to your home. Your girls are gone. Your nephew is in jail. Your brother has fled the country. You have nothing to gain by running and everything to gain by cooperating. As a fugitive, you can't save any more babies."

Odell weighed the cop's words. If she ran, what would she be running to? She couldn't start up her operation again, not without money, a home, or Travis's help.

The baby began crying again, as if on cue.

"You've saved this one," the woman said. "And Marcy's baby. Doesn't that count for something? Isn't it enough?"

"I've saved three others, too," Odell said, raising her chin in defiance. "But it's not enough. Thirty-four. I must save . . . thirty-four. . . ." The enormity of her task hit her then. She would never reach her goal now. It truly was over. And trading on this baby's innocence by using it as a pawn wasn't going to make her path to heaven any smoother—or slow her descent to hell. Before she even realized she'd given up, the gun slipped from her limp fingers.

The two cops rushed forward at once. The baby squalled, and Terri screamed again.

In seconds it was over. The baby was stripped from her grasp and given to its mother. Odell abruptly found herself facedown on the floor with a knee pressed into her back. Her wrists were cuffed behind her back with a strip of plastic.

Adding insult to injury, Bella trotted over and sniffed at Odell's prone form, whined in confusion, then looked back to the man. The man absently scratched the dog behind her ears and, apparently reassured, she licked his hand. Damn dog. Loyal as a whore, Odell thought irreverently.

They were a strange little procession hiking through the woods. Odell was in front, silent and stoic. Caro walked slightly behind and to the side, holding Odell by the arm both to support her and prevent her from making any sudden moves. Austin followed, carrying Terri and the baby. Bella the German shepherd brought up the rear.

A legion of lawmen and two paramedics with a stretcher met them about halfway, much to Caro's relief. She was more than happy to turn mother and newborn over to the medical experts. But she kept a firm grip on her prisoner, never mind what that did to her hands. Odell was her responsibility, and she wouldn't let up until the woman was safely behind bars.

Austin fell in step beside her. "You've read Odell the Miranda, right?"

"Yes." Ordinarily Caro would have taken offense at what would appear an obvious lack of confidence in her abilities. But in this instance she knew better. Having come this far, Austin was entitled to double- and triple-check every detail.

Besides, he was the lead detective in this case, a fact she'd rather conveniently forgotten when the tension was high. Letting her instincts rule, she'd run roughshod over everyone in sight, Austin included. But it certainly wasn't because she didn't believe he was capable.

She hoped he understood that.

When their procession emerged from the cover of the woods, cheers and whistles rang out. Amanda, who probably would have returned to the shack if the sheriff had allowed her to, now ran up to the stretcher and awkwardly embraced Terri and the baby. But the hug lasted only moments as the paramedics shooed Amanda away and headed for the ambulance.

Sheriff Fowles, easily identified by his shiny gold badge and a certain seasoned look, approached Caro. "Good work," he said tersely.

"Thanks." Caro wondered if perhaps they'd stolen his glory by capturing Odell and Henry without his aid.

"We'll take her now," he said, reaching toward Odell.

"No! I mean, I'd like to be in on the—"

"She's all yours," Austin interrupted, relinquishing his hold on Odell.

Caro turned to object, but the adamant look in Austin's eyes silenced her. She watched as the sheriff escorted the prisoner to a squad car and assisted her into the back seat. A sinking feeling settled in her stomach—the comedown from her adrenaline high, no doubt.

"Our job's done for now," Austin said.

"Who's going to interrogate them?" she asked.

"I will. Later. We'll let the locals book them here for whatever, and then we'll get Odell extradited to Dallas for the kidnapping charge."

"I'm sure a few other police departments across the state will want to take a crack at her, too," Caro said. "She's kidnapped girls from all over Texas."

"Don't worry, we'll get her first. But meanwhile . . ." He nodded toward the ambulance, where the paramedics were closing the rear doors on Terri's stretcher. "You have an appointment with the hospital, I believe."

"Hey, I'm okay—"

"Don't even think about arguing. Unless you'd rather retire from the force with a disability. It's kind of hard to be a detective when your hands have rotted off from gangrene—"

"Okay, okay."

Austin waved down the paramedics. They took one look at Caro's hands and stridently insisted she come with them to the emergency room.

A smug smile flashed briefly across Austin's face but was immediately replaced with a look of concern. "I'll clean up here and then I'll join you, okay?"

"Don't bother yourself," she said, just to irritate him. "Do what you need to do."

He refused to be irritated. "I'll be there inside an hour. Don't go anywhere. I don't plan to chase you all over Texas a second time." Then he leaned over and brushed her lips with his.

The kiss was unexpected, not to mention unprofessional. She was about to berate him for it, but somehow she couldn't find the words. A few minutes later, as she rode in the back of the ambulance with a talkative Terri and her bawling infant, Caro realized she felt too relieved and happy to be mad at anybody.

The next few hours went by in a blur, thanks to painkilling wonder drugs. Caro vaguely remembered doctors and nurses working on her hands and her back, cleaning, medicating, bandaging her up like a mummy. She remembered dozing for a while in a waiting room. When she'd awakened, feeling a bit more lucid, she'd decided to visit Terri and the baby.

That was where Austin finally found her. He'd been gone much longer than the hour he'd promised, but Caro didn't begrudge him the time. Given the pandemonium that was reigning as she'd been carted off in the ambulance, she was surprised he'd broken away before midnight.

Austin took a brief statement from Terri, but her answers were less than complete. Clearly she wanted to put the ordeal behind her and focus on the future—her baby.

"Her name's Sally," Terri offered proudly. "Do you want to hold her?"

"Uh . . ."

"Oh, go on, Austin," Caro said, hiding her smile.

Unable to weasel out of it, Austin cradled the infant clumsily against his chest, a dopey grin on his face, and Caro thought he'd never looked more appealing.

Promising to check on Terri soon, Austin and Caro left the room and headed down the long corridor toward the hospital's front entrance. Now that they were alone, Austin had fallen oddly silent. It almost seemed that, without a life-and-death situation between them, he was ill at ease.

As they exited the hospital, two people waved at them from the parking lot. It was Amanda on crutches . . . and Russ, Caro realized with a start. She almost hadn't recognized him with that big smile on his face.

"Daddy, that's them, the ones who saved me," Amanda said excitedly as she hobbled closer. She was smiling, too. In fresh clothes and wearing makeup, she looked much more like her picture. Other than a sprained knee and some bruises on her neck, she didn't appear to be badly traumatized by her experience. "I'd introduce you," she said, "but I don't even remember your names."

"We've met," Russ said. He shook hands with Austin. "Thank you, Corporal Lomax. I understand you did a helluva job with this thing."

Austin actually scuffed his feet. "Hey, no charge."

For a moment Russ just stared at Caro. Then he opened his arms and enveloped her in a bear hug. "Thanks for bringing my girl home safe," he whispered in her ear.

Caro awkwardly hugged him back.

"How's Terri?" Amanda asked.

"She's fine," Caro replied. "I've never seen such a doting mother. She won't let go of that baby for a minute."

"She's going to come live with us until she gets her life straightened out," Amanda announced proudly. "Daddy said it was okay."

"Sweetheart, she might not even want to come to Dallas," Russ pointed out.

"Well, she's not going back to live with her father, that's for sure," Amanda huffed. "He beats her."

"No, we won't let that happen," Russ agreed in a soothing voice.

They all exchanged a bit more small talk before going their separate ways. Caro started to open the passenger door of Austin's Bronco, then drew back in alarm. There were two huge dogs in the back. "Oh, Austin, you didn't . . ."

Austin shrugged apologetically. "The sheriff was going to have them destroyed. They're not bad dogs, once you get to know them. And I think Shadow might like having a couple of girlfriends." He opened his door, reassured the dogs, then indicated that it was safe for Caro to get in.

She did. Oddly, she wasn't the least bit afraid. If Austin said they were okay, she believed him.

They remained silent for the next several minutes. Caro's hands were starting to sting again, and she took that as a sign that she was coming out of her painkiller fog. She had a bottle of prescription pills in her purse, but she decided not to take any. Better to put up with some discomfort than to feel like she had cotton batting wrapped around her head.

"I didn't even ask you how everything came out," she said, breaking the silence. "I felt kind of bad, cutting out like I did and dumping the cleanup detail in your lap. Then again, it is your case."

"Is it? Could have fooled me earlier today when you were shouting out orders like a marine drill sergeant."

Caro bit her lip. He was right. Without even thinking about it, she'd blithely taken over the situation, making decisions without even consulting Austin. And damn if he hadn't let her, now that she thought about it. "Er, sorry about that. I guess I was going on instinct."

He surprised her by laughing. "Caro, believe it or not, I didn't care who was running things so long as the job got done—which it did. Being in charge ain't all it's cracked up to be. And if there's any glory to be had, you can have it. I'm just glad it's over."

Caro could hardly believe her ears. Was this the same hot dog who'd resented her offer of help less than two weeks ago?

"I talked to Chief Raines," Austin said, grinning. "He was pleased to hear you'd jumped in with both feet. He thinks he's going to lure you back to CAPERS—maybe Homicide Section this time."

She snorted. "Yeah, right."

"So you're just going to go back to your nice safe little Missing Persons work?"

Now that he mentioned it, the prospect was not all that appealing. After the mental and physical challenges she'd met since working on this case, the idea of sitting at a desk with a phone in her ear all day was less than alluring.

"You didn't answer right away."

"Yes, I'm going back to Missing Persons," she replied testily. And she would think about putting in an application for transfer to CAPERS. But she wouldn't tell anyone—not Austin or Tony or Chief Raines. This was a decision she had to make on her own.

Chapter 20

Phoebe the bloodhound nuzzled Caro's ear from the back seat. Irritated, she elbowed the dog away. But she found it endearing that Austin had discovered a soft place in his heart for a couple of mutts who earlier today had threatened to eat him.

"Did you get Odell and Henry magistrated?" she asked, now that her mind was functioning again.

"Yeah. The judge charged them with kidnapping and false imprisonment, then gave me authority to transport them back to Dallas for questioning."

Caro shook her head, confused. "Then why aren't you there, questioning them?"

"Odell won't say a word until she has a lawyer, and that will take a while. Henry . . . well, he's not exactly in touch with reality. We sent him to the psych ward at Parkland for evaluation. Besides, I told you I would come to the hospital, and I wanted to do that."

"I would have waited," she said offhandedly. But it touched her that he'd thought it important to keep his word. "Any idea who has jurisdiction over this thing?"

"I imagine Clemson County will get the trial for false imprisonment. As for the kidnappings, all of the various DAs involved are going to get together and decide where the best place would be to try the case."

"I hope they opt for one big trial rather than multiple trials all over the state. Otherwise we'll spend the rest of our natural lives testifying."

Austin nodded. "I think that's the plan—one big trial."

"What about the murder charges against Henry?"

He hesitated before answering. "Unless we can come up with some bodies, he probably won't be charged. When I brought up the subject again, he acted like he didn't know what I was talking about. He might have made the whole thing up. Like I said, he and reality are only passing acquaintances."

"If he didn't kill those girls, where are they?"

"Tony's checking into it. Unfortunately, we don't have their full names—Odell's not talking."

Caro mulled this over. Her gut told her there was something to Henry's impromptu confession. If she could just talk to Henry for ten minutes, she would know. Maybe they would put him on medication at Parkland that would make him lucid again. Then she'd like a crack at him. She'd find out where those bodies were if she had to—

My God, what was she thinking? Images of Charlie Northcutt assaulted her. She could still hear the echo of her own voice... "Let me take a crack at him. I know he's guilty as hell, I don't care what his mother says. I'll get a confession out of him if I have to pull it out his nose."

"You okay?" Austin asked. "We can stop some place and get something to drink if you need to take some of that Darvon."

"No, I'm fine."

"No thanks to me, right?" He gave a halfhearted laugh.

Caro's heart constricted at the thought of Austin blaming himself for her injuries, the kidnapping, the whole foul-up this morning. Although during her captivity she herself had harbored fond plans to punch Austin's lights out, her anger had been fleeting—probably manufactured so she could focus on something other than her fear. Since she had learned what happened in the grocery store parking lot, she knew Austin wasn't at fault.

She peered at him surreptitiously through her lashes, and what she saw on his face made her whole body ache, obliterating even the pain of her burns. He didn't just feel guilty; he was consumed with self-blame.

At that moment she felt a connection with him so strong it took her breath away. As if she'd crawled right into his head, she knew exactly what he was feeling. She'd felt the same crippling emotions when she'd learned of Charlie Northcutt's death. For four years she'd let the guilt rule her life, paralyze her, separate her from the work she loved. She couldn't stand it if Austin allowed that to happen to him.

"I know it wasn't your fault," she said softly.

He looked like he'd just tasted something sour. "It was my operation. I was responsible for your safety. If not mine, whose fault could it possibly be?"

"No one's. It's just one of those things. What could you have done differently?"

"I could have gone after you the moment I lost voice contact with you," he said harshly. "But no, I was so damn concerned about blowing our cover and ruining my brilliant plan that I let that crazy woman snatch you off the street right under my nose."

"What did Tony want to do?"

"That doesn't matter. The decision was my responsibility." He took a deep breath and continued. "When I realized you were gone this morning, you can't imagine what that did to me. I was really scared that something awful would happen to you, that I would never see you again, never get a chance to tell you—"

"Austin please, don't." She wanted to know how he felt about her—but not here, not like this, not when the burden of his guilt clouded his emotions. He might be grateful she was alive, relieved that she wasn't seriously injured. Guilt could easily magnify those feelings into something more. She didn't want to hear him say something he might have to take back later, when he was thinking more clearly.

Maybe she was even more fearful of having to reciprocate, to tell him how she felt. She wasn't ready. She might never be ready.

"It wasn't your fault," she said again.

He stared straight ahead, hands gripping the steering wheel, a muscle in his jaw working furiously.

Caro could see that arguing was useless. She could forgive Austin from now till the cows came home and it wouldn't make a dent in his misery. He needed to forgive himself, first, and that was something no person could do for another.

She understood that concept better than anyone would ever know.

Catching a serial kidnapper was a cinch compared to the aftermath, Austin thought irritably as he withstood another round of questioning, this time by Deputy Chief Raines, and the Chief was not nearly as enamored with Austin as the reporters had been. The two of them went over every nuance of the events that had occurred the morning of Caro's kidnapping not once, not twice, but three times.

Each time Austin calmly answered the Chief's questions. It was on the tip of his tongue to apologize for the foul-up, to admit that he'd been too green to run a covert operation of that magnitude, to beg for another chance. But he did none of those things. Sometime during the night, he had come to the conclusion that, were he faced with the same situation again, he would probably do exactly as he'd done. If that made him a bad cop... well, he was about to find out just exactly how faulty his judgment had been.

"How long was it between the time you lost voice contact and the time you left the van?" Raines asked.

"I'm not sure. About five minutes, I think. Long enough for Caro to get through the checkout line."

"And when did the truck pull in front of the store?"

"After the truck pulled up, it was no more than a few seconds before Villaverde and I left the van."

"A few seconds?"

"Twenty-two seconds, okay?" Austin snapped, losing his patience. He had a sudden sympathy for all the witnesses he'd ever interviewed who couldn't remember exactly what they'd seen or done, the exact time frame. He removed his glasses and wiped his hand over his face. "I wasn't looking at a watch, okay?"

"Yeah, okay." Raines jotted a few notes down. "If I'm being overly thorough, it's because my butt could be on the line over this thing. I was in on the planning stages of the operation, remember. I okayed it down to the last detail. And I have to answer to the Big Guy for any, er, irregularities."

"I understand."

There was a tap at the door. Chief Raines, suddenly all smiles, motioned for someone to enter. Austin didn't have to turn around to know who it was. He felt her, smelled her, sensed her on some psychic level.

"Caro, my God, you look like the Mummy's Wife," Raines said, staring at her bandaged hands. "What are you doing here? I understood you were under strict orders to stay home and rest."

"Orders from whom?" she said, her eyebrows arched almost to her hairline. She gave Austin an accusing glance, as if perhaps he'd had the temerity to give her an order. He shrugged, as if to say "It wasn't me."

She busied herself digging into her purse, coming up moments later with the decimated body mike with bits of tape hanging off it. She dropped it onto Raines's desk. "I think you need to send this back to the Cracker Jack company," she said, straight-faced.

"Maybe next time we can spring for a piece of equipment from a bubble-gum machine."

Austin smiled inwardly. He should have known Caro wouldn't stand idly by if she suspected he was getting a grilling. She probably thought that if she made it clear she didn't blame Austin for the kidnapping, no one else would, either. It was a noble gesture, barging in here full of disdain for the faulty body mike, but unnecessary. Austin and Tony had both explained numerous times about the equipment failure. Still, he was touched that Caro thought she had to "save" him.

Raines cleared his throat. "I've been apprised of the problem with the mike," he said. Then he added, almost as an afterthought, "The press is going to have a field day with that angle. I can see the headline now—Budget Cuts Leave Police with Second-Rate Equipment, something like that."

"Maybe it'll work in our favor," Austin felt obliged to point out. There was little enough to be optimistic about. "Maybe next time we'll get the use of some better equipment."

Raines shrugged. "Maybe. Caro, how did you burn yourself? That seems to be the one answer no one has."

She shuddered delicately. "All right, I guess I'll have to reveal my idiocy sooner or later. My hands were tied behind my back, and I wanted to free them, so I found some matches and burned the cord, along with several layers of skin."

Austin swallowed hard, imagining the courage it must have taken to hold a burning match while it seared flesh.

Chief Raines paled. "Damn, Caro."

"When you think about it, it was all for nothing. Minutes after I escaped, the entire Clemson County Sheriff's Department descended on the Good Shepherd Home. If I'd just sat in that closet for a few more minutes, I'd have been rescued." She gave Austin a meaningful look.

"Somehow," Austin said, "I can't picture you sitting around waiting to be rescued."

She narrowed her eyes. "Was that a compliment or an insult?"

"Oh, definitely a compliment."

Raines cleared his throat again, as if to say he didn't want any teasing banter in his office, not when he was trying to unravel the messiest day in recent Dallas Police Department history. "Seriously, Caro," he said, "I understand you did a helluva job yesterday. This Sheriff Fowles thinks you're the best thing to come along since chunky peanut butter, and the girl's father, What's-His-Name Arkin, thinks you should be given a medal or something. Why don't you put in an application—"

Caro's expression immediately shuttered. "Could we talk about this later?"

Raines nodded, looking decidedly disappointed. "Yeah, sure. Run along, both of you. Caro, go home if you're not feeling up to par. Don't let Sergeant Quayar give you any flack about it, either. And Lomax—"

"Yes, sir?"

"I don't think you have anything to worry about. In your position, I'd have done the same thing. For what it's worth, I don't believe you and Villaverde were in any way remiss in your duty."

"It's worth a lot," Austin said. "Thanks." As soon as they were out of the Chief's earshot, he added in an undertone, "No matter what he says, I think Raines is sizing you up to fill a vacancy in Homicide—mine."

"Oh, Lomax, they wouldn't fire you over this. If they do, I'll . . . I'll resign, too, as a protest."

He grinned at her passionate offer. "I don't think that'll be necessary. You know how it is," he said as they walked back through the maze of desks to his cubbyhole. "Any time an undercover operation goes wrong, the brass has to scrutinize it ten ways to Sunday, just to make sure it doesn't happen again. I don't really think my fat's in the fire."

"Please, don't mention fire."

"Sorry. How bad is it? I mean, does it hurt? Now?"

Caro grimaced. "Not really," she said, though he suspected she was underplaying her discomfort. He'd burned his hand on a stove once, and he could still vividly remember the mind-numbing pain. That was only a minor injury compared to Caro's. He still didn't understand how she'd managed to get far enough past the pain to do everything she'd done that day.

"The burns really aren't that serious," she said. "But I'll always have scars on my hands and back."

"Your back?" He hadn't realized.

"My sweater caught fire. I told you it was dumb."

"I think it was incredibly brave." Since she looked uncomfortable with his praise, he quickly changed the subject. "Did you hear the latest?" he asked, flipping absently through his phone messages. "I interrogated Odell this morning and she decided to cooperate. Spilled her guts. It's a sad story, really. It seems her father, a doctor, forced her to help him perform abortions back when she was a teenager. For years she was convinced she was doomed to hell. And then she came up with this scheme to save the same number of babies as she'd helped to abort."

"Is that what she meant when she kept saying 'thirty-four'?" Caro asked.

Austin nodded. "Seems kind of crazy to think she could earn points with God by kidnapping teenagers."

"Kind of?" Caro sat on the edge of Austin's desk. "Why couldn't she join a protest at an abortion clinic like all the other pro-lifers?"

"You have to admit, she was one clever lady to pull it off for as long as she did."

"What about Henry? Did you ask her about the murders?"

"Odell admitted that Henry was 'odd,' but that's all she'd give him. She didn't believe he was capable of killing, although she didn't rule it out completely. And the girls who had their babies at the Home—" He picked up a list from his desk. "Odell gave their names as Jennifer Brown from San Antonio, and Tanya Liese and Jillian Wysocki from Houston. There was another one, Heather Collins from Austin, who miscarried. Odell says she gave them a tranquilizer, and then Henry drove them away and abandoned them in places where they'd be found and returned to their homes."

"And?"

"All four are still missing."

Caro winced. "How about that? This case might turn out to be a homicide, after all."

"I'm willing to bet on it. Incidentally, I spoke with Henry's doctor a few minutes ago. He's responding well to medication, and we can question him now. I was on my way to Parkland when His Highness summoned me." Austin shrugged into his leather jacket. "Mind if I tag along?"

That surprised him. He'd thought Caro would stay as far away as possible from Henry's interrogation. "Sure, if you're up to it."

They took the elevator down to the basement garage—the only place he could park where the reporters couldn't follow. On the short drive up I-35 to Parkland Hospital, he paid close attention to Caro. Her face was a tight mask of tension—whether from apprehension or the discomfort of her burned hands, he could only guess.

A receptionist directed them up to the psych unit on the eighth floor. There, a psychiatrist by the name of Dr. Wayne Lassiter met them. He expounded at length on Henry's condition—officially diagnosed as schizophrenia.

"I've seldom seen such an elaborate delusional framework as Henry has constructed," the doctor enthused. "He apparently has numerous voices who have been speaking with him since childhood—God's messengers, angels, whatever. The delusion itself isn't so uncommon. But the fact that he's been able to hide it from others all these years, to pass himself off as merely 'odd'—that's the fascinating thing. It's a shame he didn't get psychiatric intervention before now.''

A shame? Austin thought it was more like a tragedy of disastrous proportions, and the parents of those missing girls—undoubtedly dead—would likely agree with him.

"Will he be competent to stand trial?" Austin asked.

"I expect so. However, I'd be surprised if you get a conviction."

"Not guilty by reason of insanity," Austin murmured. "Helluva break for him, if he did what I think he did."

Austin and Caro were taken to an observation room, where from the outside they could look through a two-way mirror and see Henry within, chatting casually with a suited man who was no doubt his attorney. His grimaces and facial tics, so evident the day before, were almost unnoticeable today.

"You can go on in," the doctor said. "I'll be observing, but only to monitor Henry's mental state. I understand that you need to do your jobs, but if I feel the questioning is doing him harm, I have the right to call a halt."

Austin didn't care who listened, so long as they didn't blab to the press. He reached for the doorknob, but before he could twist it, Caro laid a hand on his. "Wait."

He looked at her expectantly. He'd known that sooner or later she would get cold feet.

"I want to do it."

"You're kidding," Austin blurted out.

"I want to interrogate Henry. I think I can get him to tell me where those bodies are."

Austin could think of nothing he'd like better than to see Caro rip Henry a new one. Mentally ill or not, the guy had squeezed the life out of four innocent young girls. He didn't deserve to be handled with kid gloves. And maybe she could exorcise a few ghosts of her own.

Austin opened the door and gestured for her to enter. "Be my guest," he said, making sure she knew how pleased he was. "I'll be right outside. Yell if you want some support."

She flashed a nervous smile and entered the room, closing the door behind her. Austin watched through the mirror as she greeted Henry affably.

Henry stood and extended his hand. "Hello, ma'am," he said.

"Do you remember me?" she asked.

"Not very well."

Austin couldn't help but admire Caro's skillful questioning of the suspect. She handled Henry very differently from the way she'd treated Ray Seifert. She never lost her temper, or even raised her voice, perhaps sensing that to scare Henry would be counterproductive.

With questions that grew increasingly provocative, Caro led Henry up to the night Odell had delivered the first baby and drugged the young mother, Tanya Liese. Henry maintained that he had driven several hours away to the outskirts of Houston, where he'd deposited Tanya in a convenience store parking lot.

"Can you tell if he's lying?" Austin asked the doctor.

"It's hard to say. If this story is part of his delusion, he'll stick to it like glue. He might have convinced himself that the lie is true."

Inquiries about the other two missing girls brought similar responses. Then Caro changed tack. She began what sounded like an innocent discussion of the land surrounding the Good Shepherd Maternity Home, of Henry's hunting adventures with Phoebe the bloodhound, his fondness for hiking and nature. He revealed that while his father had not actually taught him to shoot a gun, he had given him permission to use a large hunting lease that a client had given him in lieu of a legal fee.

"There's an old hunting lodge there and everything, with animal heads on the walls. Aunt Odell let me stay there overnight once."

"Sounds like a wonderful place," Caro said wryly.

Austin squirmed at the thought of sleeping in a room with dead animals peering down at him from the walls.

"Does anyone else use the lease?" Caro asked.

Henry shrugged. "I don't think so. I've never seen anyone there, and there's plenty of game."

Caro cocked her head to one side and placed one finger on her chin. "Is there by any chance . . . a well on this property?"

Henry's gaze shifted from side to side, his mouth working furiously while no words came out.

Clever girl, Caro, Austin silently cheered. He'd never have thought to go this roundabout path toward the truth. Get off the subject of the missing girls altogether, and the delusional framework doesn't get in the way.

"It...a well?" Henry stammered, turning pale. "I don't know. I never . . . noticed, I don't think."

"Yes, you do know, Henry. You remember. It's the well that's full of dead bodies—the girls you killed because they had the devil in them."

Henry shook his head vehemently. "I never killed no girls."

"Are you sure, Henry?" Caro asked. "You told Amanda you killed them."

"Amanda lies. She has the devil in her."

"Is that why you tried to kill her?" When he remained sullenly silent, Caro continued. "I saw you with your hands around her neck, Henry. Would you have put her in the well with the others to rot?"

"I wouldn't have killed her," he said. "She has a baby inside her, so I couldn't. I just wanted to teach her a lesson. She ruined everything. She pretended she wanted to be my girlfriend, and she made me lie to Aunt Odell. Because of her I almost..."

Austin could see the doctor growing more agitated. He would have called a halt to the questioning, but Austin laid a hand on his arm. "Wait, just one more minute."

"Almost what, Henry?" Caro said.

"I almost hurt a baby, an innocent."

"And that would have been much different than killing, say, a girl who'd just had a baby."

Henry nodded enthusiastically, as if relieved that someone finally understood his dilemma.

Caro stood. "Okay, Henry, that's enough for now. You've been a big help. Would it be okay if I came and talked to you again?"

"Sure."

She said goodbye to the lawyer, who understandably looked a bit green. But there'd been little he could do. Caro hadn't even come close to infringing upon Henry's rights.

She came out of the observation room, allowing the doctor to go inside and soothe his patient. As soon as the door closed, she slumped against it, nearly gasping for air. She'd been more nervous than she'd let on.

Austin grinned. "That was a thing of beauty."

"Then why am I sick to my stomach?"

"You probably just need some lunch."

"No, what I need is a hug."

He tensed, remembering the last time he'd hugged her. Ignorant of her injuries, he'd hurt her and she'd pushed him away.

"I'm serious, Austin. My knees are like a couple of wet noodles."

He could hardly say no. Mindful of the bandage beneath her sweater at the small of her back, he embraced her gingerly.

"Harder," she said.

He obliged, although it was sweet torture holding her warmth against him, smelling the delicate scent of her hair, feeling her breathe. He stroked her hair and didn't even try to suppress the passionate thoughts that assailed him. Such thoughts had predictable biological results, and he hoped she noticed. He wanted her to know exactly what she did to him. She could stop him from telling her how he felt, but there were some things Caro and a whole SWAT team couldn't stop.

"Better?" he asked after a minute or two.

"Yes, much. I think I can walk now." She took a deep breath and let it out in a loud puff. "Let's see if we can track down Travis Beaman's hunting lease. I'll bet Sheriff Fowles can find it. And then I'll take you up on lunch. My treat, though. I owe you one."

When they got outside, Austin noticed for the first time that day how gorgeous the weather was—not too cold or windy, with the sky an unimpeachable blue. A billboard over the highway admonished drive-by football fans to cheer for the Cowboys, and he realized that he had no idea whether America's team had made it to the playoffs.

He opened the Bronco's passenger door and handed Caro inside. She didn't seem to mind his occasional show of gallantry, and he liked that about her. He'd once thought she might be a tad defensive about her femininity because of the way she dressed and her tough facade, but he'd come to realize that that was just Caro. She dressed for comfort, she wore makeup if she felt like it and she didn't take crap from anyone, man or woman.

Now, if he could just get her femininity to respond to him. . . .

He climbed in and stuck his key in the ignition.

"Hey, Austin, before we go back to work . . ."

"Yeah?"

"I never even thanked you for coming to rescue me."

"I lost you. It was my duty to find you," he said simply. "Anyway, it wasn't much of a rescue."

"It was more than duty. You tried to tell me, and I cut you off at the knees. All I offered you were smart-ass quips. I'm sorry."

He shook his head. "No apology necessary. We were both under a lot of strain." He reached for the ignition again, but she laid her bandaged hand over his and stopped him.

"I'm trying to get something going here," she said. "A little heart-to-heart discussion, you know?"

Austin pulled his hand away. He couldn't think clearly with her touching him. "Will you hear me out this time?"

"Yes."

And was he really ready to risk getting blown out of the water again? He'd already reconciled himself to the fact that Caro wasn't ready for a relationship . . . not with him, anyway. Now she was getting his hopes up again. To stall, he asked, "What made you change your mind?"

"Oh, I'm feeling different about a lot of things," she said breezily, although he sensed an underlying tension. "Maybe I'm simply in the mood to take a chance."

"But maybe I'm not in the mood," he ventured, perversely intending for his words to sting a bit. But then he softened and added, "You can't just expect me to blurt out something that personal on the spur of the moment."

"Okay, then I'll do the blurting. You were right when you said there's such a thing as a calculated risk. You're starting to grow on me, Lomax. The more time I spend with you, the stronger my attraction gets. And even though the odds are against us, I think we'd be crazy to ignore this . . . thing that's sprung up between us."

Austin was speechless. All right, so it wasn't the prettiest declaration of feelings he'd ever heard, but it was a damn sight more than he ever expected to hear from Caro Triece's lips.

She stared at him defiantly, arms crossed. "Okay, it's your turn."

"Right." He tugged at the neck of his shirt, which suddenly felt too tight. This might be the only chance he had to make her understand, and he'd better get it right. "Bottom line? When I thought I might never see you alive again, my guts were twisted inside out. I knew then that I was starting to care for you way too much. But there's not a damn thing I can do about it."

He'd intended to be a little more poetic when he told her how he felt. But apparently whatever he'd said had worked. She went all misty-eyed on him. Before he could do the same, he slipped his hand under her hair to the nape of her neck and pulled her to him.

The kiss was long and hard and, for once, not tinged with guilt or hesitation or regret. When they came up for air, he pressed his cheek against her hair and inhaled deeply. The fragrance of her hair would forever be burned into his memory.

"When you move back over to CAPERS, what would you think about me as a partner?" Austin said. God, was he crazy? Talking about work at a time like this? "Frank Feldman is retiring, you know."

"Who said anything about CAPERS?"

"You didn't have to. You're in that risk-taking mode. Besides, you didn't tell Chief Raines no."

She pulled back and looked at him, indecision playing around her face. "Okay, you caught me. I'm thinking about it. But you'd actually want to partner with me? And also spend time with me when we're off duty? Don't you think we might get sick of each other?''

"Not in a million years.'' He kissed her again, and she surrendered to it. He knew he had a long, hard battle ahead of him. But this first step had been the hardest. Now that she'd forgiven herself for Charlie Northcutt's death, it was like watching a dormant flower suddenly turn toward the sun and bloom. She was reaching out for what she wanted in life, what she deserved—including love. And he was just the one to give it to her. He would spend the rest of his life convincing her that some risks were worth taking.

Epilogue

The mild March day was perfect for a wedding. The bride, flouting public knowledge, wore a dress of frothy white lace that did a good job of hiding the slight outward curve of her tummy. The groom, looking flushed and eager, tugged at the collar of his starched shirt with one hand while holding the bride's hand in a death grip with the other. The maid of honor stood stiffly next to the bride in a pink taffeta dress, her hair tortured into unaccustomed curls.

The father of the bride grinned like a chimpanzee. Having just walked his daughter down the aisle, his biggest part in the show was over. He sat in the first pew of the chapel, as relaxed and happy as anyone had seen him in a long time.

Caro sat toward the back, willing herself not to cry and make a fool of herself. She wasn't normally a sentimental soul. She'd never been one to watch a sad movie more than once or get misty-eyed over Kodak commercials. But lately it took almost nothing to set her off.

She supposed she had Austin to thank for that. Over the last couple of months he had courted her relentlessly. And, unlike most men she'd dated, he wouldn't be satisfied with dinners and movies and great sex, either. He always wanted to talk. He'd forced her to discuss her feelings, to reveal parts of her psyche that had been hidden even from herself. She'd uncovered raw emotions she'd never known existed. She'd covered the full spectrum of human feeling. Stripped of the protective shell she'd worn most of her life, she felt everything more deeply.

She supposed she was in love.

Sometimes her new outlook on life felt wonderful, and sometimes it was a damned nuisance. Like now, she thought as she sniffed into a tissue. Why couldn't she just enjoy the exchange of vows between Amanda Arkin and Scott Humphrey, instead of sniveling like a ninny?

Oh, but the wedding was sweet! They were just a couple of kids, totally unprepared for married life. They both were in school and neither had any visible means of support other than their parents. But their love for each other and for their unborn child demanded nothing less than this public, legal declaration.

A couple of months ago, Caro would have said the marriage didn't have a chance in hell. But maybe it did. Amanda and Scott were two strong, good people who were willing to take a calculated risk. And, as Caro had recently learned, sometimes calculated risks paid off.

Austin's arm stole around her shoulders, and she placed one gloved hand on his knee. This was the first time she and Austin had appeared together in public as a couple, although they'd been seeing each other for almost two months. For a while she'd wanted to hold their relationship to herself and savor it, fearful that under public scrutiny it might tarnish. And Austin had indulged her. Neither of them was particularly anxious to become fodder for the police department grapevine, anyway.

But she'd just discovered that she was inordinately proud to be seen with Austin, to acknowledge him as her man. For him she'd worn a feminine, silky dress she wouldn't be caught dead in at work, and he was in a suit with a tie and everything. They made a damn fine-looking couple, even if she did say so herself.

The Beamans' false imprisonment trial was scheduled for the following month in Clemson County. Odell would be tried separately—in Dallas, thank goodness—for the kidnappings, because apparently Henry had never taken part in that activity. But he would have his own day in court, and it wouldn't be pretty. Sheriff Fowles and his men had found four decaying bodies in an abandoned well on Travis Beaman's hunting lease. Everyone was confident about convictions.

Terri Zamasko had taken refuge with the Arkins as soon as she and her baby were released from the hospital. Her father had made no attempt to get her to come home, which was fine with everyone. She'd found a job at a day-care center, where she could keep

Sally with her, and she was planning to move into her own apartment in a few days. At night she was studying for her GED.

Probably one of the saddest consequences of the whole Beaman affair was the fate of Chloe Krill. It had taken tremendous courage for her to come forward, knowing she was risking the loss of her adopted son, and what she had feared most had come to pass. Marcy Phelps's parents had decided they wanted to raise Justin themselves. The baby was their last physical tie to their beloved daughter. And though they felt sorry for the Krills, they had sued for custody. Two of the other three babies Odell had sold were involved in similar situations.

As if that weren't enough for poor Chloe, the State had filed criminal charges against her and Don for purchasing a child. Chloe had also initiated divorce proceedings.

That thought made Caro sob into her tissue, and Austin squeezed her shoulder. He leaned over and whispered, "You marshmallow, you."

She didn't even argue with him. Maybe she was getting soft in her old age. But she'd come to the conclusion that "soft" wasn't such a bad state to be in. She could still interrogate a suspect, as she'd proved several times over the past couple of weeks since her transfer to CAPERS—Robbery Division, this time around. But she found a measure of understanding for the men from whom she'd wrenched confessions. She'd fine-tuned her ability to put herself in another person's place, to walk in his shoes. If anything, this made her more skilled in her dealing with the seamy underworld she regularly encountered.

She left the homicides to Austin, figuring it was best if she didn't tread on his territory. He'd certainly become more humble after the kidnapping ordeal, but he still had a male ego. If they were going to make a go of this relationship thing, she instinctively knew it was best if they didn't compete at work.

The organist started up the recessional hymn, and Scott and Amanda marched triumphantly down the aisle, all smiles. Terri followed, teetering precariously in her unfamiliar high heels, but the groomsman walking next to her steadied her just when she would have pitched head over heels, and she gave him an embarrassed smile.

As soon as the wedding party had passed, the guests began filing out of the pews. Caro started to make her move, but Austin held her back. He sat back down and patted the spot next to him.

"No hurry," he said. "They'll probably be taking pictures for the next half hour, anyway. So, what do you think about this church? Kinda nice and old-fashioned, isn't it?"

"Yeah," she agreed cautiously.

"I don't know, but there's something about a wedding that makes me want to run out and buy a ring. You really like this church?"

Caro's heart banged around in her chest like a ricocheting bullet. "It's nice," she said, her voice shaking. "But I think they only let Catholics get married in a Catholic church."

"Oh. Well, so much for that idea. Come on, let's go get drunk on free champagne."

Caro already felt drunk. Austin was actually thinking about marriage! Oh, he wasn't really ready to jump in with both feet. He was just testing the waters with one tentative toe, and he'd found them to be pretty chilly. But Caro hadn't said, "No way, you're out of your gourd." And judging from the mischievous smile on Austin's face, that fact hadn't escaped him.

* * * * *

Get Ready to be Swept Away by
Silhouette's Spring Collection

Abduction
&
Seduction

These passion-filled stories explore both the dangerous
desires of men and the seductive powers of women.
Written by three of our most celebrated authors, they are
sure to capture your hearts.

Diana Palmer
Brings us a spin-off of her Long, Tall Texans series

Joan Johnston
Crafts a beguiling Western romance

Rebecca Brandewyne
New York Times bestselling author
makes a smashing contemporary debut

Available in March at your favorite retail outlet.

MILLION DOLLAR SWEEPSTAKES (III)

No purchase necessary. To enter, follow the directions published. Method of entry may vary. For eligibility, entries must be received no later than March 31, 1996. No liability is assumed for printing errors, lost, late or misdirected entries. Odds of winning are determined by the number of eligible entries distributed and received. Prizewinners will be determined no later than June 30, 1996.

Sweepstakes open to residents of the U.S. (except Puerto Rico), Canada, Europe and Taiwan who are 18 years of age or older. All applicable laws and regulations apply. Sweepstakes offer void wherever prohibited by law. Values of all prizes are in U.S. currency. This sweepstakes is presented by Torstar Corp., its subsidiaries and affiliates, in conjunction with book, merchandise and/or product offerings. For a copy of the Official Rules send a self-addressed, stamped envelope (WA residents need not affix return postage) to: MILLION DOLLAR SWEEPSTAKES (III) Rules, P.O. Box 4573, Blair, NE 68009, USA.

EXTRA BONUS PRIZE DRAWING

No purchase necessary. The Extra Bonus Prize will be awarded in a random drawing to be conducted no later than 5/30/96 from among all entries received. To qualify, entries must be received by 3/31/96 and comply with published directions. Drawing open to residents of the U.S. (except Puerto Rico), Canada, Europe and Taiwan who are 18 years of age or older. All applicable laws and regulations apply; offer void wherever prohibited by law. Odds of winning are dependent upon number of eligibile entries received. Prize is valued in U.S. currency. The offer is presented by Torstar Corp., its subsidiaries and affiliates in conjunction with book, merchandise and/or product offering. For a copy of the Official Rules governing this sweepstakes, send a self-addressed, stamped envelope (WA residents need not affix return postage) to: Extra Bonus Prize Drawing Rules, P.O. Box 4590, Blair, NE 68009, USA.

SWP-S295

Southern Knights

Join Marilyn Pappano in March 1995 as her **Southern Knights** series draws to a dramatic close with *A Man Like Smith*, IM #626.

Federal prosecutor Smith Kendricks was on a manhunt. His prey: crime boss Jimmy Falcone. But when his quest for justice led to ace reporter Jolie Wade, he found himself desiring both her privileged information—and the woman herself....

Don't miss the explosive conclusion to the **Southern Knights** miniseries, only in—

INTIMATE MOMENTS® Silhouette

THE
MEN OF
MIDNIGHT

RITA award-winning author Emilie Richards launches her new miniseries, **The Men of Midnight,** in March 1995 with *Duncan's Lady,* IM #625.

Single father Duncan Sinclair believed in hard facts and cold reality, not mist and magic. But sprightly Mara MacTavish challenged his staid beliefs—and hardened heart—with her spellbinding allure, charming both Duncan and his young daughter.

Don't miss **The Men of Midnight,** tracing the friendship of Duncan, Iain and Andrew—*three men born at the stroke of twelve and destined for love beyond their wildest dreams,* only in—

INTIMATE MOMENTS®
Silhouette

MENM1